Catherine Cookson was born in Tyne Dock and the place of her birth provides the background she so vividly creates in many of her novels. Although acclaimed as a regional writer – her novel THE ROUND TOWER won the Winifred Holtby Award for the best regional novel of 1968 – her readership spreads throughout the world. Her work has been translated into twelve languages and Corgi alone has 40,000,000 copies of her novels in print, including those written under the name of Catherine Marchant.

Mrs Cookson was born the illegitimate daughter of a poverty-stricken woman, Kate, whom she believed to be her older sister. Catherine began work in service but eventually moved south to Hastings where she met and married a local grammar school master. At the age of forty she began writing with great success about the lives of the working class people of the North-East with whom she had grown up, including her intriguing autobiography, OUR KATE. Her many bestselling novels have established her as one of the most popular of contemporary women novelists.

Mrs Cookson now lives in Northumberland.

Other books by Catherine Cookson

KATE HANNIGAN
THE FIFTEEN STREETS
COLOUR BLIND
MAGGIE ROWAN
ROONEY
THE MENAGERIE
FANNY MCBRIDE
THE BLIND MILLER
THE LONG CORRIDOR
THE UNBAITED TRAP
KATIE MULHOLLAND
THE ROUND TOWER
THE NICE BLOKE
THE GLASS VIRGIN
THE INVITATION
THE DWELLING PLACE
FEATHERS IN THE FIRE
PURE AS THE LILY
THE INVISIBLE CORD
THE GAMBLING MAN
THE TIDE OF LIFE
THE GIRL
THE MAN WHO CRIED
THE CINDER PATH
THE WHIP
HAMILTON
THE BLACK VELVET GOWN
GOODBYE HAMILTON
A DINNER OF HERBS
HAROLD
THE MOTH
BILL BAILEY
THE PARSON'S DAUGHTER
BILL BAILEY'S LOT

The 'Tilly Trotter' Trilogy
TILLY TROTTER
TILLY TROTTER WED
TILLY TROTTER WIDOWED

The 'Mallen' Trilogy
THE MALLEN STREAK
THE MALLEN GIRL
THE MALLEN LITTER

The 'Mary Ann' Novels
A GRAND MAN
THE LORD AND MARY ANN
THE DEVIL AND MARY ANN
LOVE AND MARY ANN
LIFE AND MARY ANN
MARRIAGE AND MARY ANN
MARY ANN'S ANGELS
MARY ANN AND BILL

Writing as Catherine Marchant
HOUSE OF MEN
THE FEN TIGER
HERITAGE OF FOLLY
MISS MARTHA MARY CRAWFORD
THE SLOW AWAKENING
THE IRON FAÇADE

Autobiography
OUR KATE
CATHERINE COOKSON COUNTRY

For Children
LANKY JONES
*OUR JOHN WILLIE
*MRS FLANAGAN'S TRUMPET
*MATTY DOOLIN
*GO TELL IT TO MRS GOLIGHTLY

and published by Corgi Books   *available in 1989

Catherine Cookson

Fenwick Houses

CORGI BOOKS

FENWICK HOUSES
A CORGI BOOK 0 552 08353 4

Originally published in Great Britain
by Macdonald & Co. (Publishers) Ltd.

PRINTING HISTORY
Macdonald edition published 1960
Corgi edition published 1970
Corgi edition reprinted 1970 (twice)
Corgi edition reprinted 1972
Corgi edition reprinted 1973 (twice)
Corgi edition reprinted 1974 (twice)
Corgi edition reprinted 1975
Corgi edition reprinted 1976
Corgi edition reprinted 1977
Corgi edition reprinted 1978 (twice)
Corgi edition reissued 1979
Corgi edition reprinted 1980 (twice)
Corgi edition reprinted 1981
Corgi edition reprinted 1983
Corgi edition reprinted 1984
Corgi edition reprinted 1985
Corgi edition reprinted 1986
Corgi edition reprinted 1987
Corgi edition reprinted 1988

This book is set in 10pt. Plantin

Corgi Books are published by Transworld Publishers
Ltd., 61–63 Uxbridge Road, Ealing, London W5 5SA, in
Australia by Transworld Publishers (Aust.) Pty. Ltd.,
15–23 Helles Avenue, Moorebank, NSW 2170, and in New
Zealand by Transworld Publishers (N.Z.) Ltd., Cnr. Moselle
and Waipareira Avenues, Henderson, Auckland.

Set, printed and bound in Great Britain by
Cox & Wyman Ltd., Reading, Berks.

Fenwick Houses

CHAPTER ONE

I KEEP my eyes closed when Sam and the doctor come into the room for they expect to find them closed, and I can think better with them closed; think of the strange washed feeling of my mind, for it has just been catapulted out of hell. This feeling takes some getting used to, for I have been in hell such a long time ... twenty years, and twenty years is a lifetime any time, but when it begins when the body is young and crying out to live it spreads itself into an eternity.

I was just sixteen when I realized that priests don't know everything. You don't go to hell because you sin, but because you love; and you haven't to wait until you die, either, to meet the Devil – oh no, he is your neighbour, I should know. Yet should I not say rather that I lived next door to evil as distinct from the Devil? For the Devil, poor soul, like myself isn't all bad. He is to evil as a commissionaire is to the film showing on the screen, someone you must pass before coming to the real thing. ... Sixteen and twenty are thirty-six. That is my age.

'Why can't she pull round?'

That is Sam's voice, rough, kind, squeezing under the bedclothes and patting at my body in soft, soft tones. Bringing comfort, always bringing comfort ... kind Sam, dear, dear Sam. Sam, who is made up of love and sacrifice.

That doctor thinks he knows everything. Doctors do. He is not even bothering to whisper. Why is he so sure that I can't hear him?

'Well, it's up to her now, but under the circumstances she'll likely take this way out, just slip away. She won't want to face the battle again. Once they've been on the track she's been on all these years, they can't turn back.'

Thank you, Doctor. Somewhere far inside me I am laughing at the doctor.

7

'But I would help her.' Sam's voice again, deep and eager now, its tone like a compassionate hand with pity dripping from its fingers. Oh, Sam, you make my heart sore. . . . But that doctor – Dear! dear! listen to him.

'I'm afraid, Sam, your's isn't the help that is necessary for her survival, she must find the help within herself. You know, when you feel you are no longer any use either to God or man, you give up. How long has she been in a coma this time?'

'Fifteen hours.'

'They'll likely get longer, and she'll go out in one of them.'

Thank you, Doctor, thank you, its nice to know anyway.

'Could the bullet have affected her brain, do you think, Doctor?'

'No, Sam, it went nowhere near it, and the wound healed beautifully. No, she just wants to go and nobody can stop her but herself.'

Nobody but myself . . . nobody but myself. I have the power of life and death. I am greater than Father Ellis now, greater than a priest. I can command myself 'Go' and I will go; I can say, 'No more agony, no more body longings, or bottle longings, and no shame of both.' Constance wrote, 'Shame is the fire that cleanses the soul.' She must have thought a lot about it to write that at seventeen. But her shame was one kind and mine another. My shame didn't cleanse my soul, it burnt it up; shrivelled it up like fried bacon skin. Yet once it was done I laughed again – most of the time anyway. Thank God for laughter. They used to say I had a lovely laugh. Listen. . . . Hear me? . . . There's my laugh, echoing over the fells, over the river . . . The river. If I could open my eyes I could see the river.

Well you can open them now for they're gone. Go on open them. It is daylight and the sun will be on the water. Open them and look. Don't be afraid for you can close them again and slip away at any time. Didn't he say so?

The sun is blinding, dazzling; I can see nothing but light. It hurts, but I want to see the river. . . . There, there it is, like a string of herrings, all scaly and shiny. That's how our Ronnie used to describe it when we were children and stood looking down on it from the fell. 'It's like a string of herrings,' he would say. Were we ever children? Of course, we were. Move your eyes and look there, right across the valley. Don't look at

8

the jumble of new red roofs, look past them, over Bog's End. Go on, lift your lids, look right up . . . high up. There it is, the fortress of pain wherein you were a child and you learned to laugh, only it looks nothing like a fortress, it's just a solitary little street called Fenwick Houses. Six of them, six of the ugliest, two-storey, flat-faced houses man could devise. Why did Mr. Fenwick place them up there, on such a height, with the end one pushing its nose almost into the wood? And why did he cut down the trees to give the front windows a clear view across Fellburn, right to Brampton Hill on the opposite side of the valley, and place the back windows so that they could suck in the wide expanse of sky that roofed the fells and the river?

When I'd asked this question of my dad, he had said, 'Because old man Fenwick had a spite in for people, for only beggars or blasted fools would stick out a winter in Fenwick Houses.' Yet he has stuck out forty of them, right from the day he married. And he's no fool and not quite a beggar. Well, I can give thanks for one thing . . . I was born up there, and ran out my childhood years like a wild thing in the woods and on the fells, and plodged in the river and laughed with the rock-trapped waters. If I listen hard enough I can hear myself laughing. I can see myself running down the hill to the river, our Ronnie after me, Don Dowling by his side, and Sam, fat and wobbling, coming up in the rear.

O to laugh again. To laugh. To laugh. . . .

'I can race you, I can beat you . . . whoopee!'

'Got you!' Ronnie's hand gripped my arm and wrenched me round, and I fell on my face and he fell on top of me and Don on top of him. Don's weight seemed to knock me through the earth and break all my bones and I wanted to cry, but laughed until they got up. Then I did cry, yet laughed at the same time, and Sam, seeing my tears, started to cry, too.

Sam was only three, I was five, and my brother Ronnie two years older. Don Dowling was the same age as Ronnie, and Don and Sam were brothers, and for years I thought they were my cousins and I called their mother and father Aunt and Uncle.

The Dowlings lived next door to us in number eight. We were the third house in the road, number six. On the Dowlings'

9

other side lived the Browns. They were old, really old, although Mr. Brown still went to the pit. They had two daughters who were married, and every Sunday these daughters came back to tea, and always without fail, or at least so it seemed to me then, they carried a new baby up the steep hill. I mustn't have been far wrong, because my mother said Sunday was the noisiest day of the week with the Brown squad racing around the street, for they never, like us children, made for the fells and the river. Mother said it was because they had been bred cooped up in the town and were afraid of open spaces.

Number twelve, the end house, was empty. It was often empty. On the other side of us in number four were the Pattersons. They had no children, and were funny because they were not Catholics. Everybody who wasn't a Catholic was funny. In number two, the first house, lived the Campbells. Cissie Campbell was three years older than me, and later I went to school with her. All the men in Fenwick Houses worked in the pit, and all the families were Catholics except the Pattersons, and everybody knew everything about everybody, so everybody knew that everybody feared being stood off.

When I heard the term 'stood off', I had a picture of a giant grabbing my dad by the seat of the pants and flinging him through the air to land in the roadway outside the colliery gates. Then I would see him sitting on his hunkers, his bait tin dangling between his knees, and on each side of him stretched a line of men, all sitting in the same position. To this picture I would add another. It would be that of my mother taking a heaped-up plate of dinner and standing over my dad, saying, 'There, lad, get that down you.' The sight of dad tucking away would make me happy again, and I would fling my arms about myself and jump off the floor, and everybody would laugh and say, 'There, she's at it again.'

The day our Ronnie and Don Dowling jumped on me was not the first thing I can remember. My first memory was of waking up one night and hearing Aunt Phyllis and Uncle Jim fighting next door. Their room was next to mine on the other side of the thin wall, and in later years if I strained my ears I could hear every word they said. But this night the sound of Uncle Jim's high, angry voice frightened me, and I cried out, and mother came in and gathered me into her arms. And as she marched with me out of the room, she said to Dad, as he stood in the doorway in his shirt, dusting the sleep out of his eyes, 'It's disgusting.' I was picking up words then, and for days I went around saying, 'It's dis . . . custin.'

As I grew I gathered knowledge, if unwittingly, from the rows between Aunt Phyllis and Uncle Jim.

Our house was a happy house because my mother thought of nothing but our welfare and filling our stomachs with good food. Clothes didn't matter so much. These she patched and darned and cut down and re-made. But the table did matter, and she was extravagant in this way.

Dad was of a happy, easy-going nature. He was a good two inches shorter than mother, and he adored her. I can see him now putting his arm about her waist and pulling her to him, saying, 'If you're all right, lass, there's nowt wrong in Heaven or earth.' And that was true for him. Even being stood off didn't hold the terror for Dad that it did for other men, for so great was his faith in mother that he felt she would find ways to provide for our needs. He had a saying, 'Keep it up,' and he would apply this to most things in life. To jokes until they became boring, to laughter long after it had ceased to ring true, but also to kindliness and to fantasies. Even when I was twelve I still believed in Santa Claus, for each year, as Christmas approached, he would regale us with this benevolent gentleman's kindness and generosity. Ronnie would play up to him, as we wrote letters to Dear Santa, and when our Ronnie read his out we would all double up with laughter. One such letter brought him a crack along the ear from my mother, for after asking for impossible and silly things, he finished up by saying, 'and, dear Santa, will you please put a man in Miss Spiers's stockin.' Miss Spiers was the spinster who had taken the end house, and from her first day in it it became evident that she didn't like children, particularly boys.

I knew that my Aunt Phyllis was jealous of my mother, and when I looked at them together I couldn't understand how they came to be sisters. It was years before it was explained to me that they weren't sisters at all. It had come about in this way. My grandmother died when my mother was a year old, and my grandfather married again. There were no children of this marriage. When my grandfather was killed in the pit, my mother's stepmother too married once more, and my Aunt Phyllis was born. My mother was three years older than my Aunt Phyllis, but looked ten years younger because she had a happy face. The house next door was where my mother was born, but when her stepmother died she left a will leaving all the furniture to my Aunt Phyllis. My mother was married at the time, and she told me, years later, that she hadn't minded my Aunt Phyllis getting the furniture; but I think she had, because in the first place it had all belonged to her own mother and father.

I knew from a very early age that my Aunt Phyllis loved Don and didn't love Sam. Sam was always getting smacked and pushed around, and he was put to bed without a light. And he used to raise the house and Aunt Phyllis wouldn't go up to him – she called it training. But we always knew when Uncle Jim came in, for we heard his heavy steps on the stairs, and we knew he had lifted Sam up. Then one day I saw a funny thing in Aunt Phyllis's. I dashed unannounced into her kitchen, and there she was sitting with her feet on the fender, her skirt tucked up above her knees, and in her lap was Don, and his mouth was at her bare breast. She jumped up so quickly that Don fell on to the floor. Then she went for me for not knocking and said 'Get out!' But as I was retreating through the back door she called me in again and gave me a big slice of cake. She was a good cook in the pastry line, but she was never generous with her food like my mother. And then I remember she told us both to go out on the fells, and I forgot the incident until years later.

The happiness of our house was such that at times it became unbearable. In class, when I would think of our kitchen, I could smell the bread baking and see the face of my mother as she dished out a meal. I could even smell the particular meal I was visualizing, and this would bring the saliva dripping from my mouth, and there would come over me a desire to shout and yell for joy. This being impossible, I would hug myself. But always when I hugged myself I wanted to leap from the ground, to let free a strange kind of feeling from inside of me. This feeling had nothing to do with the earth, but seemed to find its metier when I was in mid-air or when, as in dreams that came later, I flew through the air.

One night as we sat round the table eating our usual big tea, our Ronnie, gulping on a mouthful of food, looked across at my mother and said, 'Did our Christine tell you she got the cane the day?'

'No.' My mother leant towards me. 'What did you get the cane for?'

I looked down at my plate and, moving my bread around the dip, said, 'She said I was dreaming.'

'You weren't paying attention,' said my mother. 'That's your biggest fault and you've got to get over it.'

'What were you thinking, hinny?' asked my father, with a twinkle in his eye.

I returned the twinkle and said, 'Home, and this.' I pulled my nose down at my plate. Then we all threw ourselves this way and that, rocking with laughter, until my mother said, 'Now, now, get on with it.' Then she added, 'If you don't pay attention, you'll never be clever.'

Somehow I didn't care if I wasn't clever.

To share in our happiness, or rather, I think, to make it complete, there was Father Ellis. Every week, winter and summer, Father Ellis came up the hill to visit us. It was mostly on a Friday. Sometimes in the summer he would call in twice during the week, because he used to cut across Top Fell to visit Mrs. Bertram in her little farm in the next valley. But always he would have a cup of tea and a great shive of hot, lardy cake with butter on it. I always hurried home on a Friday so that I could sit close to his side and listen to him talk. Very often I couldn't understand half of what he was saying to my mother and dad, but I always got a feeling of comfort from his presence. And from looking up into his face I learned to appreciate beauty, for he had a beautiful face. He was young, and eager, and full of life, and brimming over with humour. This humour took the form of jokes, nearly always against himself or the Church, and Pat and Mick were the two figures on whom he based his kindly derision. I loved Father Ellis with a love that outshone every other affection in my life at that time, as did many an older girl. And he had a special love for me I knew, for we never met but he took my hand and said something that warmed my being.

Father Ellis never stayed so long in Aunt Phyllis's as he did in our house, and it was a sore point with her. Although she never came into the open about it she would make such statements as, 'Gallivantin' about, that's all that one does, leaving Father Howard to do the work. Talk's all he's good for!'

Then one day Uncle Jim went to the priest about Aunt Phyllis. I was about eight at the time, and I remember her coming into our kitchen. Her face drawn and grey, she stood confronting my mother, saying, 'Going to the priest! Telling the priest that, the filthy swine.' My mother had pushed me out of the door with the order to go and bring Ronnie to his tea, and that night I was woken again with the voices coming through the wall. And when about a foot from my face something crashed into the wall, I jumped out of bed and stood on the mat biting my lip, not knowing what to do. And as I stood there I heard the front room door open downstairs.

My mother and dad slept in the front room. Ronnie slept in the bedroom across the landing, and I had a tiny little room to myself. I was just going to get back into bed when I heard Aunt Phyllis's door crash closed and I went to the window and looked out. We never drew the curtains as no one could see you at the back except the birds swinging across the sky. I peered down into the yard, then over the backyard wall, and saw the dark, hunched figure of Uncle Jim striding fellwards. Then from next door came the sound of Sam crying, and this rose into a quick crescendo punctuated by the sound of slapping. Aunt Phyllis was smacking Sam's bottom. But why? Sam couldn't have done anything. He was only frightened of waking up in the dark. I found it impossible to get back into bed so went out on to the landing. Ronnie's door was closed, but from the bottom of the stairs came a gleam of light and I knew that my mother was up and had lit the lamp in the kitchen. As I crept down the stairs I heard her voice saying, 'Go after him, Bill,' and my father answering, 'No, lass it isn't a thing a man wants to talk about.' Then he said, 'Some women don't want a man. Phyllis is made that way. The only thing she ever wanted was a bairn, and just one bairn at that. She'll drive him mad. But he was wrong to go to the priest, for now she's put up the couch for him in the front room.'

As I reached the kitchen door, Sam's yelling reached even

a higher pitch, and I saw my mother strike the table with her fist as she said, 'But why has she got to take it out of the bairn?' I gave a shudder with the cold and they both swung round startled.

'What you up for, child?' demanded my mother.

'I couldn't sleep. They woke me. It was a bang against the wall. And, oh, Mam' – I stuck my finger's in my ears – 'she's still walloping Sam.'

'Come away in here and have a drink of tea.' My father gathered me into his arms and sat me on his knee before the fire, and, leaning forward, he poked the dying embers into a glow again. When my mother handed him a steaming cup of tea he did not immediately take it from her, but putting up his hand he touched her shoulder, covered with an old blue serge coat that she wore over her nightie, and never has any music held such depth of feeling or voice such sincerity as his as he murmured, 'Lass, we should go down on our bended knees and thank God that we match.'

For answer, my mother thrust the cup into his hand, saying, 'Bill! Talking like that! We've got big ears, me lad.' I knew the big ears were meant for me. 'Little pigs have big ears,' was a frequent saying of hers when she didn't want Dad to talk in front of us. Now he only smiled gently, and pouring some of the tea into his saucer he blew on it for me before I drank.

The following day I waited for Sam coming out of the Infants, and taking him by the hand I led him home. When we were half-way up the hill, Don's voice hailed us, and we stopped and waited for him. And when I wouldn't join in a race down to the river he walked behind us, chanting in a teasing voice:

> 'Sam, Sam, the dirty man,
> Washed himself in the frying pan,
> Combed his hair with a monkey's tail,
> Scratched his belly with his big-toe nail.'

I could feel Sam's hand getting stiffer and stiffer within mine. Then suddenly he tore himself from me and, swinging round, sprang on Don.

Don, even at this age, was big and stolid, and the result was that poor little Sam seemed to bounce off him. Anyway, he

15

fell on his bottom in the middle of the road, and when I solicitously went to pick him up, he turned on me, too; then scrambling to his feet, he ran off, not towards home, but on to the fells. When I was about to follow him Don's arms went about me and pinned me to him, my back to his chest. And his voice was still laughing as he said, 'If you'll come down to the river with me I won't touch him when I get in; if you don't I'll belt him.'

I went down to the river with him. When we reached it, he decided to plodge, and with a 'Come on!' ordered me to take off my shoes and stockings.

I was nothing loath to do this for I loved plodging, but we had a special place for plodging and this wasn't it. Here the river wound round the bend, and the curve was strewn with rocks, which if you were agile enough you could use as stepping stones, but beyond the rocks the water tumbled and frothed. It was too deep for plodging. When Ronnie stood in this part it came up to his shoulders, so when Don, gripping my hand, pulled me on to the stepping stones, I cried, 'Eeh! no, Don . . . not down there! It's too deep.'

Although I had played by the river since I had played at all, I was still unable to swim. The reason for this was simple; my mother had forbidden me to go into the water with the boys other than for a plodge. Sometimes when they swam I would stand on the bank yelling and laughing and shouting at them as they dived and plunged and larked about. Even Sam at six could swim, and for a bathing costume he had a pair of little white pants that kept slipping down and which were sometimes pulled down purposely by Don who would pretend it was just – carrying on.

I had strict orders from my mother that I was never to go into the water with the boys, and that if they went up to Pollard's burn I hadn't to go with them at all. I knew that this was because a lot of boys gathered at Pollard's burn at the week-end and swam with nothing on. But now Don was pulling me towards the deep water and I screamed at him to stop, for already the bottom of my dress and knickers were wet, and the water, spurting from between the stones, was stinging my legs like pins and needles.

My arms about his waist I cried, 'Don! Don! Let me go back.'

He stood perfectly still in the water, and looking down at me, he said, 'Well, if I do, will you promise never to wait for our Sam any more?'

'Yes . . . yes, I promise, Don.' I would have promised anything to get out of that swirling water.

'Swear.'

'I swear, Don.'

'Cross your heart.'

I released one trembling arm and religiously crossed my heart somewhere in the region of my collar bone. But now, having given him the assurance that he wanted, he did not let me go back towards the bank but, his face becoming stiff, he said, 'You heard me mum and dad row last night, didn't you?'

I looked at him and nodded once.

'It's none of your business.' He grabbed me roughly by the shoulder.

'No, Don,' I said, 'no, it isn't.'

'I'd like to shoot me dad . . . string him up.'

'Don!' My horror and amazement made me forget my fear for the moment, and I gasped, 'I like your dad, he's nice.'

'You!'

Petrified, I felt myself being pressed backwards and was on the point of screaming when our Ronnie's voice, coming from the bank, shouting, 'What you think you're up to? Let her go!' surprised Don so much that he did let me go, and I overbalanced and, yelling my head off, fell on my back into the water.

I hadn't time to go under before Don's hands gripped me, and, pulling me upwards, he dragged me to the bank, where Ronnie, already in the water, demanded angrily, 'What you think you're up to, eh? Frightenin' her!'

'I wasn't frightenin' her, we was just playin'.'

'Playin'! She was cryin' . . . scared.' He turned his head towards me. 'Weren't you?'

I gulped, but did not answer him. Instead, I said, 'Me mam'll pay me . . . look at me pinny!'

They neither of them looked at my pinny but stood staring at each other. They were both of about the same height, only Ronnie wasn't half as thick as Don. The next moment they

17

were rolling on the ground, punching and using their knees in each other's stomachs.

'Give over! Give over!' I yelled at them. 'Oh, give over!' And when they didn't I turned and ran, and never stopped until I reached the kitchen, there to cry out that our Ronnie and Don were fighting.

But my mother took no notice of this, only of my wet state. And stripping me, she said, 'You'll go to bed without any tea for this.'

Then the river and the fight were forgotten Even sending me to bed was forgotten, for my dad came in, and from the first sight of his face my mother knew what he was about to tell her.

She stood at one side of the kitchen table and he at the other, and, putting his bait tin slowly and definitely down and speaking to it, he said, 'I wonder if it'll be the last time I'll use thee, lad?'

I saw my mother swallow twice before she said, 'How many?'

'Over a hundred,' he replied.

My mother's eyes moved down to the table, across it, then came to rest on the bait tin, on which my dad still had his hands. Then throwing up her head and putting her hands behind her back to adjust the strings of a fancy little apron, which she had made herself out of the skirt of a summer frock and which she usually wore from a Friday tea-time until Sunday night, she exclaimed, 'Well, and now we know. So we can get on with it.'

And as she went about, putting the water into the big tin bath that stood before the fire, she talked of her plans for the future as if they had been long arranged in her mind. 'You can apply for a bit of that land at the wood edge for an allotment. That'll keep us going for veg, anyway.'

I watched her disappear into the scullery and heard the bucket being dipped into the washhouse pot, and as she poured the steaming water into the bath she announced, 'And I'll go back to Mrs. Durrant's.'

'Will you, lass?'

My dad had already divested himself of all his clothes except his short pants.

18

'Yes. She said that if I ever wanted work I had just to go and tell her.'

My mother had been in service at Mrs. Durrant's on Brampton Hill before she was married, and although she had left the place over eight years now, there still occasionally came a parcel of clothing from her late mistress.

My father stepped into the water and began to soap himself, and when the time came for my mother to wash his back, she said, comfortingly, 'Don't worry. We've still got our breath and a bit of spunk left.'

She had hardly finished speaking when the door opened and my Aunt Phyllis came in. Seeing my father in the bath she turned her eyes away from him, and her voice coming in rapid jerks she addressed my mother, who was once more at the table.

'What we goin' to do? This is the end. They'll never start again. It's only an excuse to shut the pit down. It's old.'

My mother turned to the oven and, taking a big, steaming earthenware dish from the shelf, said, as she passed my father, 'Watch yourself, lad,' and she placed the dish in the middle of the table before answering my Aunt Phyllis. Then deliberately she turned and, making a motion of drying her hands on the hessian oven cloth, she said quietly, 'We'll all have to do the best we can then.'

'And what's that? . . . starve?'

'We needn't starve, we've got our hands. There'll be some kind of work for women.'

'You'll go to Mrs. Durrant's, I suppose. Well, I can't see meself going skivvying for anybody, and what's more I'm not going to either.'

'That's your business.' My mother still went on quietly with the drying motion, and there was a silence in the kitchen except for the plodging noise my father was now making in the water. Then my Aunt Phyllis said in thin, steel-like tones,

'He'll get hissel' away and find work, there's other towns besides this, there's bound to be work some place.'

My father now turned his head over his shoulder and, looking at my Aunt Phyllis asked, 'You thinking about going with him, Phyllis, then?'

For answer my Aunt Phyllis gave him one long look, before

turning on her heel and going out, slamming the door after her. . . .

My mother went to Mrs. Durrant and got three mornings' work a week. My father did as she bade him and took a piece of ground on the outskirts of the woods, and we had always plenty of taties and things, with the result that our table remained the same. The smells of cooking perfumed the house, and nothing was changed for at least three years, except that we couldn't send our shoes to the cobblers and my dad did them and the nails stuck through and tore my stockings.

But there were more men lining the bridge at the bottom of the hill where it crossed the river. Some sat on top of the wall, some sat on their hunkers with their backs to the wall, some dangled sticks with string on and played at catching fish, and some did catch fish, but on the sly, for they would get something if they were caught fishing without a licence in the river.

For coal my father went to the tip and brought back bags of slack, and at first my mother had her work cut out on baking days, until she got the idea of wetting the slack and putting it into tins. It fell to our Ronnie and me to gather the tins.

Next door they did not fare so well. Although my Uncle Jim had come in with Dad in the allotment, his heart was never in the work, and I heard my dad say he dug as if he was using a spoon at a tea party. This was odd because I also heard Dad say that there wasn't a better hewer in the pit than my Uncle Jim.

Hardly a day went by but my mother set up Don and Sam to a meal, and so they became to me like our family, until one day this procedure was brought to an abrupt stop.

There had been a lot of talk of late between my mother and Aunt Phyllis about Don, doctors, and hospitals. It was all very mysterious until one evening Don joined us by the river. We knew Aunt Phyllis had taken him to the doctor's because Sam had told us. Sam, Ronnie and I were at our usual pastime, they at swimming and I at plodging. Don hailed us as he came running down the hill, and when he stood on the edge of the bank he could hardly speak for lack of wind and excitement, and when we gathered round him he told us excitedly that he was going into hospital. 'And you know what?' he said. We

20

waited in silence, our eyes fixed on him, 'I'm going to be split up, there and there.' He made two clipping movements with his forefinger up his groins, and when my face screwed up in horror, he said, 'That long.' His fingers on his groins measured about nine inches, and I felt my stomach heaving in horror at the thought of what he would have to endure.

That night I said to my mother, 'Poor Don is going to be cut up, Mam,' and she said, 'Nonsense. Who told you that?' 'He did.'

She went away mumbling, yet I thought I made out what she was saying. Yet I knew that I couldn't have heard aright, for what I imagined she said was, 'Good thing if he was.'

Don went to hospital, and after a few days he returned, covered in glory. Somehow it had been very nice while Don was away, because Sam was different. He talked more, laughed more, he had even told a Pat and Mick joke at the table, and my mother choked on her food as much in surprise at Sam telling a joke as at the joke itself. But once Don came back Sam was quiet again.

On the afternoon he returned we made an expedition, not to the river, but into the wood to gather blackies, for it was blackberry time and my mother wanted to make as much jelly as she could. But we were some time getting started on our picking for we were all listening open-mouthed to Don's description of the hospital and the things that had happened to him there. He got so excited in relating what had taken place that nothing would stop him from illustrating it, and when he lay down and started to perform an imaginary operation on himself, Ronnie threw cold water on the whole proceedings by saying, 'Oh, get up man, and don't be so daft, you would have been dead if they had done that !'

Don got up and without further words we started our picking, but I sensed that he was huffed at our Ronnie not believing him, and I felt sorry for him. I didn't like it when people didn't believe me, and didn't laugh when I told a funny joke. It made me feel silly, and I knew that was how Don was feeling. So I started picking near him, and when quite close I whispered, 'I believe you, Don.' He looked at me, then taking my hand pulled me away round the bushes, and there he whispered, 'Do you?'

I nodded, then emphasized, 'Yes, I do.'

My hand was still in his and quietly he drew me away until we were in a tangle of blackberry bushes, and then he whispered, 'Look, lie down and I'll show you what they did to me.'

'Me?' I said. 'Lie down?'

'Yes, I'll show you what they did to me in the hospital.'

He pressed hard down on my shoulders and I shrank away from him, saying, 'No, no, I'm not going to lie down. I believe you, but I'm not going to lie down.'

There was a look on his face that filled me with a sort of jerky fright. My stomach was reacting as if I was receiving a succession of shocks, it was jumping within me.

'Lie down.'

'Not, I'll not.'

'You will, I'll make you.'

'I'll shout for our Ronnie.'

His eyes darted to the height of the bushes, then with a fierce thrust he knocked me backwards and the next minute I was yelling with the pain of the brambles as they seemed to pierce every part of my body.

It was Sam who reached me first and pulled me up, then our Ronnie, coming on the scene, said, 'You would fall into something. And where's the blackies?'

The few blackberries that I had in my can were lost among the brambles now, and I began to cry.

'All right, all right, don't bubble. Come on.'

Ronnie's words were tender. Ronnie was nearly always tender with me, like I was with Sam. The three of us together were joined with a harmonious thread, but Don was the needle through which the thread was drawn, and its point was vicious, and I was to learn within the next few hours just how vicious.

We were sitting in the kitchen, my mother, Dad and myself, when I heard my Aunt Phyllis come into the scullery. I knew it was her before I saw her for she always rattled the back-door latch.

When she stood at the kitchen door we all knew something was wrong, for her thin lips lay tight upon one another and had caused a little puff of flesh at each side of her mouth, as if she was in the act of blowing up a balloon.

'I want a word with you, Annie.'

My mother looked at me, then said, 'It's about your bed-time.'

'I haven't washed, Mam.' I was looking at my Aunt Phyllis.

'Oh, well then, go and have your wash now.'

I went past Aunt Phyllis as she stood in the scullery door-way and something seemed to fall from her face, something hard and malevolent, and it pressed on me and drove my eyes away from hers towards the floor.

The clean water bucket in the scullery was empty, so I took it down to the bottom of the yard and put it under the tap, then turned the tap slowly on. For some reason or other I didn't want to return too quickly to the house, the reason was mixed up with my Aunt Phyllis's look. When the pail was full to the top and I knew that I would have to empty some out before I could carry it up the yard, my mother's voice came sharp and harsh from the doorway, crying, 'Christine!'

I walked slowly up the yard. My mother was waiting for me at the back door, and she looked at me steadily for a moment before her hand dropped to my shoulder, and without a word she guided me into the kitchen. My dad was standing on the mat and my Aunt Phyllis near the table, and when my mother led me into the room she turned me so that I faced my Aunt Phyllis. Then she said, calmly, 'What were you doing in the woods this afternoon?'

I lifted my eyes to hers without moving my head, and said, 'You know, Mam, getting blackberries.'

'What else did you do? Did you play with Don?'

'Play with Don?'

'Yes, that's what I said, play with Don.'

I looked at her and considered. Could what had happened behind the bushes be considered as play? I didn't think that it could, and I said, 'No, Mam.'

I heard the air being taken up through my mother's nose, and in the beam of the fading sun that slanted into the kitchen my whole attention became riveted on the golden hairs that quivered on the inside of her broad nostrils. I had never noticed before that she had hairs on the inside of her nose. She jerked my thoughts back to the matter in hand by saying, sharply, 'Christine, pay attention!'

'Yes, Mam.'

'What were you doing in the woods this afternoon?'

23

'Only pickin'—'

'You know you weren't, you were doing bad things . . . naughty things!' Now Aunt Phyllis was leaning over me, and her face looked dirty, as if it hadn't been washed for a long time. But my Aunt Phyllis was always washing herself and doing her hair. I stepped back away from her face, and said, 'Eeh, no, I wasn't! I never . . . I don't!'

It was Dad's hand that steadied me. Sitting down he called me to order.

'Now, hinny, don't worry, you've only got to tell the truth. I promise you you won't get into trouble, you won't get your backside smacked.'

There was no laughter in my dad's eyes nor in any other part of his face, and this, like a douche of cold water, brought it startlingly home to me that the matter was serious, very serious. If my dad wasn't laughing with any part of his face there was something very wrong. So I turned from him and, looking at my mother, I said, 'I never done anything naughty, Mam. Don took me behind the bushes. He wanted me to lie down so he could show me about the operation, and I wouldn't. . . .'

I felt my dad's fingers pressing on my hands, and when I looked back at him he was looking across the room to my Aunt Phyllis, and he said quietly, 'What do you say to that, Phyllis?'

'I say she's a little liar.'

'Well, it's up to us to say the same about Don, isn't it?'

'Look, I know my Don, he wouldn't have come home in that state if he had been telling a lie. He was upset, I've never seen the lad so upset, disgusted I would say. Surprised and disgusted at her. You've always given her too much rope . . . running mad about the fells like a wild thing.'

'That's our business, Phyllis, how we bring up our bairns.' It was my mother speaking, her voice tight and steady. 'And I'm telling you here and now that I don't believe a word of it. If you had said it was Cissie Campbell I might have believed you, but—'

'But not when it's her, oh, no!' Aunt Phyllis's tone was deriding. 'Well, let me tell you, if she was to go down on her bended knees before a priest this minute and tell him that she didn't do it, I wouldn't believe her, so there. And that's my last word on the matter.' She turned her gaze on me again,

24

then most surprisingly she said, her voice laden with bitterness, 'You and your silly laugh.'

The kitchen door and the back door had banged before any of us moved, then my mother with her fingers linked tightly together came to me and, kneeling down so that her face was on a level with mine and my dad's, she said to me softly, 'Christine, pay attention. . . . Tell me, did you . . .? Now don't be frightened, just tell me if you did or not. . . . Did you take your . . . your knickers off when Don was there and . . . and . . .' Before she had finished her struggling words I cried, 'No! Mam, no! You know I wouldn't do that.' Her hand covered mine when it was resting on my dad's knee, and she said, still quietly, 'I thought you wouldn't.'

My mother got to her feet and went and looked out of the window, and after a few moments she said, 'This is going to make things awkward.'

'Aye,' said Dad, 'it will for a time, but it'll pass over. Lads get funny notions; he's at a funny age. Try to think of that, Annie.'

My mother still kept looking out of the window as she said, 'I've never liked Don, and now I know why.'

Dad made a sound that wasn't a laugh but tried to be as he said, 'Well, she's returned the compliment: she doesn't like ours.'

He didn't say which one of us my Aunt Phyllis disliked, but the pressure on my arm as he automatically pulled me nearer told me. And I remember the surprise I felt, for whenever I went into the house next door I was always nice to my Aunt Phyllis. I had never answered her back, not once, and I had never been cheeky to her – oh no, that was the last thing I would have dreamed of – and I always noticed when she had something new and would say, 'I like that, Aunt Phyllis,' although very often I didn't know what the things were for. And when I would go in to my mother and say excitedly, 'Aunt Phyllis has got a new tablecloth, Mam, silky it is,' or, 'Aunt Phyllis has a new ornament, Mam,' she would make no comment whatever, but always tell me to get on with this or that, or go out to play. And because of my mother's attitude I felt that I was the only one who noticed my Aunt Phyllis's nice things, so besides being surprised I felt hurt to know that she didn't like me.

But even all this upset was obliterated from my mind the next day when Fitty Gunthorpe was thrust on to my horizon. Fitty lived in a caravan with his father on a piece of spare ground at the edge of Bog's End. He was a man six foot or more tall, thin and gangling and subject to epileptic fits. He was known to everybody as Fitty Gunthorpe, but he was also known to be quite harmless and very fond of animals. At times I had met him in the wood, and he aroused no fear in me. He had a little dog forever at his heels – they said the dog was never parted from him night or day. It was the sight of the dog that inspired the wish in me to have one of my own, and I had mentioned this to my father and had received a vague promise of 'Aye, I'll look out for one.' But it wasn't the dog but a rabbit that brought Fitty Gunthorpe into my life.

I was never one for lying in bed in the mornings. Often I was out of bed and had been down to the river, just to have a look, while my mother was getting the breakfast ready, and was back in the house before Ronnie stumbled downstairs, his knuckles in his eyes and his mouth agape. And when I would say to him, 'Oh, Ronnie, the river's lovely this morning,' he would reply, 'Oh, you, you're barmy, up all night.'

Some mornings I went into the fields or the wood to pick flowers to take to my teacher. There was always something to be picked at different times of the year, cowslips – not butter-cups or daisies, they were too common – catkins, wood anemones, ferns, bluebells and may, beautiful scented white may.

This particular morning was bright golden, and soft and warm, and the birds were all singing. I could distinguish some of them by their song: the lark, of course, for its voice shot it into the heavens, and I could tell the difference between the thrush, the blackbird, and the robin. But this morning I did not run up the street or hug myself and leap from the ground at the sound of the bird song as I sometimes did, but went into the wood and made my way to the place where yesterday I had been with Don, for it seemed to me that I would find something there that would bear out that I had spoken the truth, and then my Aunt Phyllis would believe me. But the only evidence that I found was three blackberries lying close together on a clear piece of sward. They were laden with dew and were sparkling like jewels. They should have been able to prove in some way that Don pushed me into the bushes and upset my can, but I knew that they couldn't, and I turned away on to the path. And there I saw Fitty Gunthorpe. He came up to me, his mouth agape and smiling a welcome. The dog was at his heels. He wore no hat, and his hair was longish and brown and wavy like a girl's. It did not seem part of him, but looked like a wig.

'Ha . . . hallo,' he said.

'Hallo,' I said.

'Lo . . . lovely m . . . morning.'

And I smiled at him and said, 'Yes, it is.'

The dog took no notice of me, and they both passed by, taking the path by which I had entered the wood. This was the lower path. It started above the last house in our street and if you kept to it you would come out on the hill that looked down on to Bog's End and the spare piece of ground where the caravans were. I did not want to go that way this morning so I took a side track which led to the upper path. I think we children had made many of the tracks in the wood, and we knew them as well as we did our own backyards. The wood itself was a continuation of the hill on which Fenwick Houses stood, and the hill was tree-studded to its summit and way down the other side, too. The upper path ran in a zigzag fashion towards the top of the hill. In parts the trees were sparse, and where they let in the light the grass grew and rabbits sported. We called these various open spaces bays. There was the little bay, the big bay and the tree bay. The tree bay was my favourite, for it was the smallest sward of grass and was set in a complete circle of trees, not in rigid formation, but nevertheless enclosing the space in a rough ring. It was an enchanted place to me, and I liked it best when I could come here on my own. When I was with the lads we were never quiet.

I had to cross the second path to get to the tree bay, and it was when I reached the path that I heard the cry. It was small, a squeaking, intermittent yet linked in a continuous, pitying yelp. I scrambled over a bank of rich moss, bright green and close woven, then through the trees and to the bay. I knew the cry was that of a rabbit, and before I saw it I was already shivering with pity. The men, to supplement their tables, were catching rabbits, setting traps for them. They would set them at night and come early in the morning to clear them. I'd never seen the traps but I knew, from listening to Dad, all about them. But I understood that they were mostly set around the perimeter of the wood, for the rabbits came out to feed in the fields. This was the heart of the wood and somebody must have set a trap here. Then I saw the poor creature, and the sight riveted me to the spot. I could feel my hands coming slowly up to my mouth to still the scream. The rabbit was not struggling against the weight of a trap, but against the weight of a tree, a big tree, for one of its back legs was nailed to it. I hid my face, then I knew I was running, and thought I was running away through the wood again, and seemed surprised when I felt the rabbit's quivering body under my hands. The leg was all torn and bleeding, and when I pulled madly at the nail and the poor thing squealed loudly I began to moan. The sound reminded me of a man who had been knocked down by a car in the market last year. They had lain him in a shop doorway and he made moaning sounds. The next thing I remember was that I was running through the wood finding my way more by instinct than by sight, for I was blinded with a flood of tears. When I came out of the dimness of the wood and into the morning sunlight on the street I tore to the house, and there pushed everything before me, doors, chairs, little obstacles, and flung myself, not on my mother, but on my dad, crying, 'Dad! Dad! Come on. The poor rabbit, the poor thing. Oh, Dad . . . Dad.'

I had knocked some fried bread out of his hand and the grease had gone across the tablecloth, and my mother exclaimed, 'What on earth's up with you, child? Look what you've done. What's the matter?' Then as if attacked by a thought that had suddenly frightened her, she pulled me from my dad and, shaking me, said, 'Stop it! Stop it! What's happened?'

'A rabbit, a rabbit, a poor rabbit!' I gulped and swallowed and choked before I could voice the horror that I had seen. 'Nailed, somebody's nailed it to the tree. It's back leg, and the blood all over it.' I turned up my palms to show the blood, and Dad, who was now on his feet, said, 'Where?'

'In the bay, Dad, up at the top.'

Stopping only to put his coat on, for nothing would have induced him to go outside the door without his coat, he hurriedly followed me into the street. I ran on ahead all the way, but when we reached the bay he was only a few steps behind. Now it was he who went ahead, and then, slowly, I approached his back, he ordered me sharply, 'Stay where you are!'

I saw his arm moving in a pumping motion, but he did not fall back with the nail in his hands as I had expected. Then I saw him grope in his pocket and bring out his knife. He paused with it in his hand, then called sharply, 'Christine! go away, go away into the trees.' I turned and, putting my fingers to my ears, ran to the end of the bay.

It was not long before I heard him behind me, the rabbit was in his hands, it was dead. There was blood on its neck and it had only three legs. I fell flat on the ground and pushed my face into the wet grass, then my stomach seemed to rise through my backbone. I felt my spine drawn up in a curve, something like the hump of a fell, and then it seemed that my whole stomach came through my mouth.

I didn't go to school that day.

It was my mother's morning for Mrs. Durrant and she took me with her, and when we reached the bridge at the bottom of the hill, it seemed to be blocked by men. They weren't sitting on their hunkers or leaning over the parapet, but they were gathered together in a group. We had reached them before I realized they were listening to my dad, and it was the first time I had heard him swear. I couldn't see his face now, but I knew by his voice that it would be long and hard, for he was crying, 'If I could find the bugger who did this, I'd nail him to the bloody tree with me own hands. The bloody sod! What it's done to my Christine remains to be seen.'

I was aware of two things at this moment, my dad was using bad language and my mother was doing nothing to stop him. We rounded the circle of men as if they were all unknown to us, even the man in the centre. Some moved to make way for my mother, and as we went towards the hump on the bridge, I heard one man explain angrily, 'Let's go and find Gunthorpe,' and I had a picture of Fitty's face with the morning light on it, saying, 'Hallo.' I could see the dog close pressed against his boot and ragged trouser leg, and I was filled with a feeling which I can put no name to, just that it was a sort of sorrowful bewilderment. Fitty had always appeared a part of the wood to me, he was as natural to the wood as were the trees, yet he had nailed a rabbit to one of them; at least I had said so.

I felt so upset that the beauty and elegance of Mrs. Durrant's house was lost on me. I could not see it because I was all the time seeing a rabbit with pain-glazed eyes.

Mrs. Durrant herself came into the kitchen, and as she bent over me to stroke my hair she smelled nice. And with her hand on my head she turned to my mother and said, 'How lucky you are, Ann.' Then looking again at me, she added, 'You can't tell if it's gold or silver, I have never seen anything like it.'

As Mrs. Durrant went out she paused by my mother and asked with a laugh, 'What will you take for her?' My mother answered with another laugh, 'not all the tea in China, Ma'am.'

Mrs. Durrant had no children, but she had a lot of money and a big house and nice clothes, and that day my mother brought a big parcel back home, and a basket of food, but I couldn't be happy about either the parcel or the food.

When we got back at half-past one there was a man standing at the door, and he took off his cap when he spoke to my mother.

'You Mrs. Winter, ma'am?'

'Yes,' said my mother. 'What is it?'

'I'm John Gunthorpe.'

'Oh!' said my mother. 'Will you come in?'

He was tall like Fitty, and his hair was thick, but it was very white. His face and hands were clean, with a scrubbed look, and though his clothes were old and there was a patch on his coat pocket, there was a cleanness about them, too.

'It is your husband I want to see, missis,' he said.

'He should be in at any time. Will you have a cup of tea? I am just going to make one. It's hot work coming up the hill.'

'No, thank you, missis,' he said. He moved from one foot to the other, twisted his cap into a roll and stuck it under his oxter and looked at my mother, and she at him. Then he burst out, 'The child was mistaken, Mick wouldn't do a thing like that. He loves animals . . . he's crazy about them. He lives for nothing else.' He poked out his head at her. 'He's not an imbecile, ma'am. He has fits but he's not an imbecile.'

'No,' said my mother.

'If it weren't for his fits you know what he would have been?'

My mother said nothing, and he went on, 'A vet, that's what he would have been. And then to say that he did that, nail a rabbit to a tree.' He shook his head slowly. 'And that lot of ignorant, big-mouthed louts comin' storming to me van. They would have lynched him, missis. Do you know that? Just another spark and they would have lynched him. They've got time on their hands, nowt to do.'

I was staring at him transfixed when he came to me and, bending his long length over me, said softly, 'Me bairn, my lad didn't hurt the rabbit, try to believe that. Somebody did, some cruel man but not my lad, will you try to believe that hinny?'

I moved my head once slowly in answer, then I watched him straighten up again and say to my mother, 'Where will I find him, missus – your man?'

'He'll be on his allotment, or you'll likely meet him coming back up the hill at this time.'

'Thanks, missis, I'm obliged.'

He jerked his head at my mother, then looked at me once more, and his look was kind, so kind that I wanted to cry. And I did cry, I cried on and off all day. And when I was in bed that night I was sick and my mother had to come and clean me up.

CHAPTER TWO

THE days moved on and the rules and formulae on which childhood is based formed a skin that covered up the scar on my mind made by the rabbit. This in turn had overshadowed Don Dowling's lying, at least for me, yet I could not help but notice that the incident was still to the fore in my mother's mind, and also in Aunt Phyllis's, for they did not speak. My Uncle Jim and Dad still worked together on the allotment and there was no rift between them. I still went up into the wood and down to the river, always now accompanied by Ronnie, or by Sam when he could get out. But I did not jump or hug myself as I used to, in fact, I did not feel joy again until Christmas Eve. And then the sight of Dad putting up the coloured chains across the ceiling, and of my mother taking out of the box in which they were replaced each New Year the fragile glass swans and balls made of coloured glass brought the leaping feeling back again, and forgotten magic from past Christmases rushed at me and I flung my arms about myself and leapt in the air.

Dad was standing on a chair tying the last coloured fan in the chain to the picture rail. Mam was on her knees, kneading dough in a great earthenware dish, the one she used for double bakings. They both stopped what they were doing, looked at me as I stood laughing at them, then looked at each other, and they, too, laughed. Then my mother said a funny thing. 'The time has come,' she said, 'to end this. I must go into Phyllis.'

'Aye, lass, that's right. Good will and peace to all men.'

The kitchen was filled with such warm happiness that I only had to put my hand out to touch it. I felt I could scoop it up in handfuls from the air. I knew that I was drawing it down into my chest with long sniffs up my nose. At last I lay on the mat, my bent arms coupling my head, and stared through the little brass rods that supported the steel top of the fender, the fender that I had cleaned that morning with whiting and ashes, at the white-heated bars, behind which the fire glowed a steady, fierce red. I wasn't thinking, I wasn't even breathing, or so it seemed for I was so still. I was only feeling . . . feeling comfort. And when a child feels comfort, it feels security, and with security, love. And I had so much security that I was swimming in love.

It was some time later. I was still lying on the mat, but on my back now, looking up into the ceiling of entwined colour, because now my view of the fire had been obscured by the loaf tins my mother had placed on the fender before she had gone next door to make it up with Aunt Phyllis. But she was not gone more than a few minutes before she was back again. She came in the front way, through the front room and into the kitchen, pulling her coat from around her shoulders as she did so, and making straight for the scullery, and on her way she said to my dad, 'Here, I want you a minute.' Her tone roused me from my dreaming, and I sat up and watched Dad follow her.

'She's near mad,' I heard my mother say. Then her voice fell and became a mumble. But Dad's voice was loud as he replied. 'Well don't say she hasn't asked for it, lass. To my mind it's long overdue, and I have an idea who the woman is an' all.'

'Sh! sh!'

The kitchen door was pulled close and I turned my gaze to the fire again. The bread had risen well up over the tins, and the paste of one of the loaves was drying and cracking, and so, taking a clean tea-towel and a piece of cloth I covered the bread over, and when some minutes later my mother came from the scullery she applauded my action and gave me a pat on the head as she said airily, 'You're learning, hinny.' Then she added, 'How would you like Sam and Don to come in with us the morrow?'

She had placed Sam first, and it was only of Sam I thought as I answered, 'Oh! yes, that would be lovely, Mam. . . . For dinner and tea?'

'Yes, all day. And the morrow night we'll have a bit of jollification.'

33

'Oh, Mam.' I flung my arms round her waist and drew into myself more happiness. It was Christmas, and tomorrow poor little Sam would be in our kitchen all day and I would make him eat everything and see that he laughed. I did not give a thought to my Aunt Phyllis and her trouble.

The rift was closed between my mother and Aunt Phyllis, but a rift that was never to close opened between Aunt Phyllis and my Uncle Jim, and as the months built up into years the rift widened. My Uncle Jim, I gleaned, had a woman in Bog's End, yet he still continued to live next door. Whenever he earned an odd shilling or two above the dole or beyond the means test he would throw the money on the table and my Aunt Phyllis would pick it up, and they never spoke.

The woman in Bog's End kept a little shop and, out of curiosity one day, I went in and bought some sweets. She was just the opposite of Aunt Phyllis, being round and fat with a happy face, and she spoke to me nice and put an extra sweet in the bag. I liked her, and when I came out I wished Aunt Phyllis would die, so that my Uncle Jim could marry her and Sam could have a nice mam.

Sam spent more time in our house that he did in his own, and Aunt Phyllis didn't mind. But if Don came in and Aunt Phyllis heard him through the kitchen wall she would call him to fetch water or wood, or just to come into the house.

I was about eleven when Cissie Campbell drew to my notice something that should have been evident before. 'You can't move a step without them lads,' she said. Perhaps this was jealousy on Cissie's part, for neither Ronnie nor Don would have anything to do with Cissie, and Sam was too young for her notice. But her words set me thinking, although I remember that, as usual when confronted by the smallest problem, I wanted to shelve it. Yet I did give this statement some thought, for as far as I could ever work myself up into a state of annoyance, I was annoyed, and by the fact that I seemed always to have to walk in the middle of a triangle, with one of them at each corner, Ronnie, Don and Sam. Going to school, coming back, running down to the river, darting through the wood, they were there. I knew why our Ronnie was always with me, for I heard my mother saying to him one night, 'You must never leave her alone with the lads, you hear? Now understand what I am saying to you. Never leave her alone.' And he had said, 'Yes, Mam.'

My mother had said 'Lads', but I knew that she just meant Don, for she would leave Sam and me together in our kitchen while she slipped down into the town. But she would never leave me alone with Don.

From the time I became aware of this pressure around me I had a desire to thrust my way out, but the desire had no strength and, as in other things, in this I took the line of least resistance.

It was when Ronnie was thirteen that he began to argue. He had always been a great talker, but as Dad said he never knew when to stop. At this age his talking became aggressive, and he became restless, chafing at the days until he could leave school and perhaps get set on, above ground, at the Venus pit, which, even while it was standing off older men, was still setting on young ones.

It was about this time that he started a funny game. We had an old dictionary and he would open it at any page, and with the aid of a pin and closed eyes choose a word. Then he would start talking about the word and telling Dad all he knew about it, and Dad would try to keep his face straight. Sometimes he went to the library and came back with thick books, which he would throw with a clatter on the table. Many of the books he never read, not even the first page, for the subjects were as foreign to him as would have been books in French or German. There was one word though that the pin picked out which really did catch his attention, and he did read the book that he got from the library on this subject, although when my dad picked the book up he laughed and exclaimed. 'My God, he's not going to tell me he understands this.' The subject was evolution, and in some measure Ronnie did understand it, and one day he brought forth my awful admiration even while I was astounded at his temerity of daring to argue with the priest.

It was Friday tea-time, and Father Ellis was on his weekly visit, and work or no work my mother still greeted him with the slab of lardy cake, although the week after my father came out he admonished her saying, 'No, no. Now we'll have no more of this . . . a cup of tea and that is all.'

My mother had spoken to him in the same tone she used

to us, as if he wasn't a priest at all. 'Get it down you,' she said, 'and let it stop your noise.' He had laughed and got it down him.

My dad liked Father Ellis although he was often chided by him for not going to mass on a Sunday; he wouldn't take the excuse that his clothes weren't decent enough. I heard Dad comment on Father Ellis one day, saying, 'He's a priest as God and meself would have them.' This linking of himself to God added to my father's importance in my eyes and gave Father Ellis the prestige usually allocated to angels. And here we were this Friday, all of us around the table, and we were listening not so much to Father Ellis as to our Ronnie.

He had brought my mother's mouth agape by saying flatly there was no such thing as the Garden of Eden; he had brought my eyes popping by talking about chimpanzees and orang-outangs and gorillas. At one point he became embarrassed, but recovered himself and went on, grimly this time, about ape men and prehistoric men, whatever they were. My father's face was straight, but his eyes were alive with laughter and I knew he was finding difficulty in suppressing it. Father Ellis's face was serious, and he looked deeply impressed as if he was drinking in every word that fell from Ronnie's lips, and when finally and quite abruptly Ronnie stopped and dug his thumb into the palm of his hand as if making a full-stop to his oration, the priest nodded thoughtfully at him and said in a deeply serious tone, with not a hint of laughter in it, 'You're right, you're right.' Ronnie came back, bumptious and arrogant: 'Yes, I know I'm right, Father, and them what doesn't believe in evolution are ignorant.'

He cast a defiant yet scared glance around the table, but nobody spoke except the priest, and he said, 'Well I for one believe in evolution, quite firmly. Now look, let's get it down to ordinary level and ordinary meaning. For instance, take Mrs. McKenna, you know; her who sings above everybody in church.'

All our faces answered this with a smile, and Father Ellis followed the smile from one to the other and brought us all into this discussion by saying, 'Now you're a sensible family, there's not a more sensible one. Now ask yourselves, would the good God have made Mrs. McKenna just as she is, feet, hands and all? No, when he first made her she was as bonnie a thing as ever stepped out of Paradise, but evolution has done this to her. She's got worse and worse until she is, as you know, a bit out of the ordinary, God help her. Now mind, I'm not blaming her and don't any one of you speak a word of what I've said, do you hear me? But I'm just using her as an illustration. She is a good woman, God bless her, although she has a voice like a corn crake.'

We all tittered, all except Ronnie. He sat there, straight of face, and there was a deep furrow between his brows, and he screwed in his chair before leaning towards Father Ellis and saying sharply, 'It's no use, Father, turning it funny and going on about Mrs. McKenna, she's no illustration. We all likely started like Mrs. McKenna and—'

'Ronnie, be quiet!'

It was my mother now, brought out of her bemusement at the talking on such a thing as evolution and horrified that a son of hers should speak so to a priest. She could use any tone she liked to Father Ellis, but then she was grown-up.

'And don't you dare interrupt the Father,' she cried. 'Name of goodness, what is things coming to?'

Ronnie's lids were blinking now and his tone was much more modified as he put in, 'But I read it, Mam, it's all in my book. And it's true, I know it's true.'

'Take that!'

It wasn't a hard slap, it was just a reproving slap across the ear, but it brought Ronnie quickly to his feet. He stood for a moment looking ashamed, and Mam's hands went out to him apologetically, but he brushed them aside and went into the scullery.

The great debate had come to an end. Father Ellis got to his feet, shook his head, patted my mother's arm, winked at Dad, and went into the scullery, with me at his heels.

'Come on, walk with me down the hill,' said the priest to Ronnie. 'There are things you can't get elders to understand.'

Ronnie was standing with his head bent, looking at the boiler. He turned and grabbed up his cap from the back door and went out, preceding the priest, which was very wrong, but under the circumstances could be forgiven him. Once clear of the house we walked abreast, then Father Ellis, putting his arm around Ronnie's shoulder, laughed, 'Don't look so downcast, Ronnie.'

'I'm not downcast, Father.'

'No, you're only annoyed and boiled up inside. Right?'

'Right.'

He didn't add 'Father' and I bit on my lip.

'About this evolution, Ronnie . . .'

Before the priest could go on Ronnie came to a stop and exclaimed, 'I was right, Father.'

'Yes, you were and all.' The priest drew him gently on again, but now his voice sank to a confidential note. 'But man to man, Ronnie, I ask you, do you expect me to explain the theory of evolution to you in front of your mother and dad and the like, and in five minutes? It is a wide subject, deep and wide you must confess, and they have no interest in it whatever at their age.'

He spoke of my mother and dad as if they were very old, but he was the same age as my mother – thirty-two. Dad was three years older but looked much more, that was with being down the pit so long.

We walked in silence for some yards, then Ronnie started again, and he used the tone which he used when he was going to go on talking for a long time. 'About the Garden of Eden, Father. . . .'

'Look . . .' Father Ellis almost pushed him into the ditch, then grabbed his shoulder and pulled him straight again, before throwing back his head and laughing. 'We will have to go into it all another time, right into it, head first into the Garden of Eden, but at the present minute I'm up to my eyes in work. I should never have stayed so long in your house but your mother makes one so comfortable that the time flies and all thought of my duties goes out of my head. But I promise you one of these days we shall get down to evolution and the Garden of Eden. Now I've got to hurry away. But listen, Ronnie, don't you talk about evolution in the kitchen for you'll get them all mixed up – not that I'm suggesting you're mixed up. No, you go on reading about evolution or about anything else you can find in that book of yours, but don't annoy your mother with it.'

He gave Ronnie a gentle punch with his fist then, cupping my chin in his hands, he shook his head saying, 'Here's one who doesn't bother about evolution. Do you, Christine?'

'No, Father.'

'You're too busy living, following the wind in the trees and the voice of the river.'

I wasn't quite sure what he meant, but I replied, 'Yes, Father.'

I expected that Ronnie would be sullen when the priest had gone, but instead he grabbed my hand and, laughing, ran me over the field towards the river, and when we reached the bank and sat down with our feet dangling above the gurgling water, he said to me without looking into my face, 'Do you think I can talk good, Christine?'

'Oh, yes, Ronnie, I love to hear you talk.'

He turned his face quickly to me. 'You do?'

'Yes, I think you're clever, oh, so clever.'

He turned his eyes away and looked across the river and said, 'Some day I will be clever and I'll talk and talk and talk, and I'll make people listen to me. Do you know what I want to do?'

'No.'

He laughed and, turning and kneeling at my side, he grabbed my hand, saying, 'I can always talk to you. I can tell you things. Well, I'll tell you what I want to do. I want to tie people in chairs so that they'll have to listen to me. In the middle of the night I wake up thinking things and nobody wants to listen, so I tie lots of people in chairs, Mam and Dad, Uncle Jim, Mr. Graham' – he was the schoolmaster – 'Aunt Phyllis. Oh, yes, Aunt Phyllis.'

'And me, Ronnie?'

'No, never you, Christine, because you listen. Will you always listen to me, Christine?'

'Yes, always, always.'

That summer the heat was intense and water became scarce, and for only part of the day it ran from the tap in the back-yard. By each evening I would feel so hot and sticky that I would beg my mother once again to let me go in the river with the boys. Ronnie had said he would teach me to swim. But Mam would have none of it.

'You can plodge and that's all,' she said.

So I would plodge in the shallows, shouting across the distance to where the boys sported in the deeper water. They would dive like turtles, the water spraying up like a fountain

39

when they disappeared, then their heads, black and shiny, and their faces running with the cool water would break through a fresh surface. On and on they would go, and I would think, 'Oh, if only. . . .'

At night we didn't go to bed early but sat around with all the doors and windows open. Dad used to sit on the front step reading aloud from the paper while my mother sat at the front window doing her mending or knitting; never did she sit down with idle hands. Gists of his reading stuck in my mind. The Dionne Quins were born, a man who had started to make bicycles with a capital of only five pounds was now a millionaire and they had changed his name from Morris to Nuffield. There was a woman found in a trunk in some station cloakroom, and there had been a lot of jollification over the King's jubilee.

I knew about the jubilee because they had had one or two tea parties in the town, but we hadn't had anything at Fenwick Houses. There had come a tentative suggestion from Mrs. Brown that something should be done for the bairns. 'What,' said my dad, 'and have a means test on the cakes?' Also from his reading I remember there was a man called Hore-Belisha, and he had something to do with lamp-posts, and this made my dad laugh. Then there was another man called Musso who had attacked the poor Abyssinians. Dad said it would be our turn next, and this worried me during a lot of hot, restless nights.

A number of times that summer I walked over Top Fell down to Bertram's Farm with Father Ellis, and Mrs. Bertram always gave me a cup of milk, then asked me, 'Was that nice?' And I always said, 'Yes, thank you.' She had the idea that I was hungry, but I was never hungry. I had only to dash into the house gasping, 'Oh, Mam, I'm starvin',' and my mother would say, 'Well you know where the knife is and you know where the bread is, if you can't help yourself I'm sorry for you.' But I was well aware that this practice wasn't prevalent in Fellburn at that time, and not even in Fenwick Houses, certainly not next door in my Aunt Phyllis's, for both Sam and Don always came in with me when I said I was hungry and always went out with something in their fists.

It wasn't the drink of milk that I looked forward to on these walks with Father Ellis to the farm, but the fun we had.

To my mind he was as good fun as our Ronnie or Sam. I never, even in the vaguest way, coupled Don with Sam, Ronnie and fun, although he was as much my constant companion as the other two.

Once we were on the fells proper, Father Ellis would give me a start, then race me to a tree, or taking my hand he would run and leap me into great leaps, higher than I could jump when I flung my arms round myself. On some of the leaps I could see over the far fells and catch glimpses of the entire town. Sometimes he would tell me a Pat and Mick story, and sometimes I would tell him one, and we both laughed long and loud.

One day, for some reason or another, I had missed him, but I knew he had gone to the farm and I went to meet him. The sun was going down and I stood on the top of High Fell straining my eyes into the dazzling rose and mauve light trying to make him out against the shades on the hills. But I could see nothing, for the sun was making my eyes water. Yet I remember I didn't turn my face away from the light. I was so high up that I felt on top of the sun, and as it slipped over the brow of the hill yon side of the river it seemed so near that I had but to bend forward, put out my hand, and I could press it into the valley beyond.

Blinking, I turned, blinded with colour, to see just a few feet away from me Father Ellis. He was standing looking at me, and I cried joyfully, 'Oh, hallo, Father.' But he didn't speak, he just took my hand and turned away and we walked homewards. I thought he was vexed, somebody had vexed him, yet he didn't look vexed, and then he said in a voice which he only used in confession and never on the fells, 'Christine, how old are you now?'

'Eleven, Father. I was eleven on April the twenty-sixth. You know I was born the day the Duke and Duchess of York were married. It was a nice day to be born, wasn't it?'

I looked up at him and he smiled and said, 'There wasn't a better.' And then he went on, 'But now, Christine, you're a big girl and you must give over dreaming.' He gave a little gentle wag to my hand. 'You must do practical things. You understand what I mean?'

'Yes, Father,' I said, but I wasn't quite sure in my mind.

'You must help your mother with the housework and things in the home, for she works very hard.'

'Oh, I do, Father. I do the brasses every Saturday morning, and the fender – oh, the fender, Father.' I smiled up at him. 'It's awful to do and takes so long to get bright.'

'Yes, I know you do things like that, but you must do even more. You must learn to cook and do all the housework, and sew, and always keep busy.'

'I'm a good sewer, Father, but I don't like patching.'

He laughed now and said, 'No, you wouldn't like patching.' Then he stopped, and looking down at me again with a straight face, he said quietly, 'But you'll remember what I said and try to put your mind on everyday things?'

'Yes, Father.'

I knew what he meant – I was always being told to pay attention and stop dreaming. But I liked dreaming, I liked to lie in bed and float away out of the bed. Not that I didn't like my bed and my little room, and not that I didn't think our kitchen the finest kitchen in the world, but I just wanted to go off somewhere. Where, I couldn't have explained, it was just somewhere. I came near to a vague understanding of this feeling the following spring.

Following the hot summer it was a hard winter, there was a lot of snow, with high winds and great drifts and thaws and freezing, and this pattern seemed to go on for ever. I wasn't very fond of the snow, for my hands, even with gloves on, would become very cold while playing snowballs, and I hated to be rolled in the snow. Our Ronnie knew this and never pushed me into it, nor did Sam, and Sam could have because, although he wasn't tall, he was strong. But Don, at every opportunity, pushed me down and tried to roll me in the snow. This often ended in a fight between Ronnie and him.

One day the fight became grim and Sam joined in, not to help his brother but to help Ronnie, and later that evening I heard Sam getting a walloping and knew Don had told on him. It was during this bitter cold time that I first noticed my mother walking slower. When she came up the hill she would stop once or twice, and as soon as she got in she would sit down. This was unusual, for she never sat down unless it was in the evening. She would never let me carry the bags of groceries, saying they were too heavy for me, nor had she ever let anyone else carry them. But one day she came in and Sam was with her, and he was carrying the big bass bag. It was nearly as big as himself and when he dumped it on the table she looked at him with a smile and said, 'Thanks, Sam.' And Sam's reply was an unusually lengthy one for him, for he said, 'That's all right, Aunt Annie, I'll always carry your bags for you if you like.'

My mother's smile broadened, and she patted his back and said, 'Go in the pantry and cut yourself a shive.'

He turned eagerly away, but then quickly looking back at her said, 'I didn't do it for that, Aunt Annie.'

'No, no, lad, I know that. Go on and don't be so thin-skinned.'

Christmas came but it did not seem so happy this year. The eons of time passed until one morning I knew it was spring. The sun was hard and bright; I had run up to the edge of the wood and there through the trees I saw a wonder-ful sight. There had been no snow for weeks, but sprinkled around the roots of the trees was something that looked like snow. As far as my eye could see there was this sprinkling of purity white, each drop separate from its fellow and divided within itself, and each part shining. I took in a great gulp of air. I wanted to share this wonder with someone, someone who needed wonder, and who needed wonder at this moment more than my mother, for she was tired. And so, dashing back down the street, I flew into the kitchen where she was on the point of lifting the big black frying pan from the fire, and clinging on to her apron I cried, 'Mam, come up to the wood and see something, it's beautiful. It's been snowing in the wood.'

She turned very quickly and looked down at me with a surprised, almost frightened expression. Then she said sharply, 'Don't be silly, child, it hasn't snowed for weeks.'

Now I laughed at her and said, 'It has, Mam.' I turned my head to where Dad had come out of the scullery, his shirt neck tucked in and soap on his face ready for a shave, and after looking at my face for a moment he said to my mother, 'Go on, lass. Leave the pan, I'll see to it.'

'What!' she exclaimed. 'Don't be silly.'

Now my dad came forward looking as if he had grown old

43

overnight, for the soap had formed a white beard, and taking the pan from her hand he whispered, 'Keep it up.' Then nudging her, he added, 'Go on.'

She looked at me impatiently. 'Oh, come on,' she said, straightening her apron and clicking her tongue.

Her attitude didn't dampen my spirits and I danced before her up the street and into the wood. Then from my vantage point I stopped, and when she came and stood by my side I pointed and she looked. Then her hand came slowly round my shoulder and she pressed me to her.

And as we stood like this, gazing spellbound at the first sprinkling of anemones, I said, 'They seem glad to be out, Mam, don't they?' Her hand drew me closer and she said, 'Yes, hinny, they're glad the winter's over.' Then much to my surprise she didn't turn homeward but walked quietly on into the wood, her arm still around me.

At one point she turned and looked back, and I did, too, wondering what she was looking for. Then she did a strange thing. She went down on her hunkers like my dad did and, taking me by the shoulders, she gazed into my face, her eyes moving around it as if looking for something, like when I've had a flea on me, and pressing my face between her large, rough hands she exclaimed softly, 'Oh, me bairn.' Then she said a thing that was stranger than her kneeling, yet not so strange, for I understood in part. 'Keep this all your life, hinny,' she said. And she ended with something which contradicted a daily statement of hers, for she said, 'Never change. Try to remain as you are, always.'

Now that was a funny thing for her to say for she was forever at me to 'Stop dreaming' and forever saying 'Come on, pay attention'. And hadn't Father Ellis too said that I would have to pay attention. But now she was telling me never to change.

The tears were rolling over the red part of her cheeks and dropping straight on to the grass, and I was crying, too. But it was a quiet crying. Then getting quickly to her feet, she wiped my face round with her apron, then wiped her own and, jerking her head up, she laughed and said, 'Eeh! that frying-pan. Your dad makes a mess of everything. Come on.' And she took my hand. But we didn't run out of the wood, just walked quietly.

The spring got warmer and warmer, and everything was beautiful, until I came up the hill one day with Cissie Campbell. She had left school now and had got a job in Braithwaite's the big grocery shop on the High Street that supplied most of Brampton Hill, and she had got very swanky all of a sudden and spoke down her nose. It was just after we had crossed over the bridge and one or two of the men had called, 'Hallo there, Christine,' and I had said, 'Hallo' back and called them by their names that Cissie said, 'I've got something to tell you.' Her voice had dropped to a whisper and she brought her face close to mine. 'You know last Saturday afternoon?' I couldn't remember anything particular about last Saturday afternoon, but I nodded and said, 'Yes.' And she went on, her voice dropping even lower, 'Well, you know what happened? You wouldn't believe it but I was coming across Top Fell, I hadn't reached the top, I was just at that part near the stile where the bushes are, you know that narrow cut?'

Again I nodded.

'Well, I met Father Ellis there and you know what?'

I shook my head now and there was a long pause before she said, 'He tried to kiss me.'

I stopped dead, my eyes stretching upwards, my mouth stretching downwards, even my ears seemed to be stretching out of my head.

'You don't believe me?'

'No, I don't.' I backed from her as if she was the devil himself. 'You're wicked. Priests don't kiss people, not girls. Eeh! Cissie Campbell.'

'He did, I tell you, and I run away.'

'You're lying and I'll tell Mam about you. He's . . . he's holy. My dad says he is the best priest in the world.'

'You promised not to say anything.'

'I didn't.'

'You did.' She was advancing on me now. 'If you dare tell your mother do you know what I'll do?'

I backed again, staring at her all the while.

'I'll tell your mother what you and Don Dowling do down by the river.'

'D . . . D . . . Don.' I was spluttering now, and a little fear was creeping like a thread through my body, vibrating on a memory from the past. 'I've never done anything with Don, never.'

'Yes you have, he told me. And I'll not only tell your mother but I'll go to Father Howard and tell him. And you won't half get it from him if I tell him all Don Dowling told me, so there.'

The many dangers that involved me through Don was security enough for Cissie, but as I watched her stalking away up the hill, her bottom wobbling, I wasn't thinking so much of Don and what he had said about me, but of Father Ellis, and my mind kept repeating, 'He didn't do it, he wouldn't do it.'

The Sunday following this incident my father came into my room very early in the morning and whispered, 'I'm off to mass. Your mother's going to have a lie in this morning, she's not feeling too good. Wouldn't you like to get up and get the breakfast under way?'

I got up and went downstairs and into the front room. Mother was sitting up in bed and she gave me a warm smile as I entered.

'You bad, Mam?'

'No,' she said. 'I took some medicine last night and I've got a pain in my tummy, that's all.'

'Oh.' I let out a long sigh of relief, Epsom Salts always gave me a pain in my tummy.

After getting dressed I set the table for breakfast and then did the vegetables for the dinner, and after Dad came back and breakfast was over I washed up and did the kitchen. With all this I was too late for the ten o'clock mass, the children's mass, so I went to eleven o'clock.

The church was different at eleven o'clock for it was full of grown-ups and all the men seemed to stand at the back while there was still some empty seats at the front. I was sitting behind a pillar and the only way I could see Father Howard was when I craned my neck, and I did crane my neck as he began his sermon, for without any leading up he yelled one word at the congregation.

'Immorality,' he yelled, and then there was such a silence that you could hear people breathing. I did not understand anything of what he said at first until he began to talk about the girls and women of the parish. 'Babylon isn't in it with this town,' he cried, 'and I'm not referring to the prostitutes in Bog's End. They carry out their profession in the open, they don't hide behind religion, nor have they the nerve to come to mass and the sacraments with blackness in their hearts that even they would be ashamed of. This parish has become such that it isn't safe for a priest to walk the streets at night.'

I knew without names being mentioned that the priest Father Howard was referring to was Father Ellis. There was another priest younger than Father Ellis, called Father James, but he did not have a nice face nor a nice voice like Father Ellis. And I also knew that Cissie Campbell had wanted the priest to kiss her and she wasn't the only one, for lots of the grown-up girls were always hanging round him.

When the mass was over and I was going up the side aisle I saw my Aunt Phyllis walking in the throng up the centre aisle; her head was high but her eyes looked downwards, and she had the appearance of someone wrapped around with righteousness. When she saw me outside she seemed surprised and asked, 'Have you been to this mass?' And when I said 'Yes' she said, 'Ah well, I hope it's done you some good.'

Later the whole town was talking about Father Howard's sermon, but neither Dad nor Mam asked me anything about it.

The following year, nineteen-thirty-five, our Ronnie and Don Dowling left school and both started at the Phoenix pit. Dad said it would not make much difference to us as they would dock it off his dole, and they did.

There hadn't been much laughter in our house for some months until one night, sitting at the table, I began to eat slowly, toying with my food, my whole attention concentrated on the thought that had been coming and going in my mind for some long time past. And now, being unable to contain myself any longer as to the truth of Aunt Phyllis's remark, I suddenly raised my eyes and, looking across at Dad, said, 'Have I really got a silly laugh, Dad?'

They all stopped eating and stared at me, then one after the other they began to laugh. My mother first, her body shaking before she would let her laughter loose, Ronnie's mouth was wide and his head back, and Dad, with his two hands clasped on the table, leant across to me – I was now laughing myself – and shaking his head slowly he said, 'It's the best laugh in the land, hinny. Never let it fade ... never.'

That night Ronnie came into my room. I don't know what time it was, I only know that a hand on my shoulder startled me into wakefulness, and I couldn't see anyone in the dark. But then I heard Ronnie's voice whispering near my ear, 'Ssh! it's me.'

I turned on my side in an effort to get up, but his hand kept me still, and I asked, 'What is it? Is Mam bad?'

'No,' he murmured, 'I only wanted to talk to you.'

I screwed my face up in the dark, then said, 'Talk to me? What about?'

'Oh, lots of things,' he whispered. 'I miss you, Christine, now that I'm at work, and we never seem to go anywhere without Sam or Don.' He paused, and although I could only see the dark outline of him I knew that we were staring into each other's eyes. Then, with a little gurgle of merriment in his voice, he asked, 'Have you been worrying about what Aunt Phyllis said that night about your laugh?'

'No,' I lied; 'only I would stop laughing if I thought it was silly.'

'It isn't silly, it's as Dad said, you've got a lovely laugh. And you know somethin', what I heard the day?'

'No.'

'It was when we were on the wagons. Harry Bentop – you wouldn't know him but he's seen you. Well, he said, "By, your sister's not half a smasher, she's going to be the prettiest lass in Fellburn." How d'you like that?'

'Me?'

'Huh, huh.'

I hadn't thought about being pretty. I knew that I had nice hair, everybody said so, but pretty. . . . It was nice to be thought pretty, it was something that I would have to think about, really think about. So went vague thoughts in the back of my mind, but what was bringing me into full wakefulness was a puzzling, bemusing thought, a thought that was there and yet wasn't. It was more of a feeling, and the feeling said that my mother wouldn't like our Ronnie to be here talking to me in the middle of the night.

'I'm sleepy,' I said and, turning abruptly round with a great flounce, I faced the wall.

Some seconds passed before I heard him padding across the room, and although I strained my ears I didn't hear the opening of the door, but knew he was gone by the relieved feeling inside of me.

I could not get to sleep now. Was I going to be the prettiest girl in Fellburn? Did the lads in the pit talk about me? But most of all my mind was groping around the question of why Ronnie had come into my room in the middle of the night to tell me this, why hadn't he told it to me in the kitchen, when Dad and Mam weren't there?

That week-end Ronnie brought home a puppy. He said its name was Stinker, that he would pay the licence and it could live on scraps. This last was to assure mother that it would be no bother as regards food. And lastly he said it was for me. My delight in the gift overflowed from my body and filled the house, and as I took Stinker into my arms, a love sprang up between us that was to make us inseparable until the day he died.

When I was fourteen I asked my mother if I could go to the baths. A number of the girls from school had joined a swimming club, and I had a great urge to learn to swim. I remember she considered thoughtfully for a moment before saying, 'No, Christine, I don't think it wise.'

'But why?' I asked, 'all the girls go, and I'm the only one that can't swim. Ronnie, Don and Sam can swim like ducks and there's me, I have to plodge on the edge. Oh, Mam, let's.'

Again she bowed her head as if considering, then said, 'Not yet awhile, hinny, leave it for a year or so.'

A year or so. In a year or so I'd be old and working, and not wanting to swim. But I didn't upset my mother with my pleading, for she wasn't herself these days, she spent a long time sitting in the lavatory at the bottom of the yard, and when she came into the kitchen she would huddle close to the fire and her face would look grey and drawn. But sometimes for weeks she would be all right, and I would get her to walk in the wood with me, and draw out her laugh with the fantasies I made about the trees. I would point out the oak

49

and say, 'There it goes making its breadcrumb pudding again.'
This was when it threw its brown, crumbly flowers out in the
spring. Or I'd bring in a spray of horse chestnut, and day
after day give a commentary to her on its unfolding. When
from its scaly brown cloak there peeped a pale reddy-brown
nose, I would turn from the kitchen window where it was
stuck in a jar to cry, 'Look, Mam, it's turned into a ballet
dancer.' And she would come and stand near me and look at
the silver down-engulfed thing straining away from the
brown cloaks that endeavoured to keep it covered. When on
the next day the ballet dancer would be gone, leaving only two
deep olive green leaves, one dangling in folds from a stalk
where the down disappeared at the touch of a finger, so fine
it was, I would continue my story. But she wouldn't, I noticed,
look so much at the wonder of the opening chestnut bud as at
me. In the middle of my narrating, if I turned and looked
up at her it would be to find her eyes riveted on my head,
and the soft, warm, comforting light in them would bring
my attention wholly to her, and I would fling my arms around
her waist and lay my head on her shoulder – now I could do
that, for I was tall for my age. On such days as these I was
wrapped around in a warm comforting glow.

When some months later I again put the plea of learning to
swim to her, she shut me up quickly with a snapping reply, and
I went out and down to the lavatory and had a good cry.
When I returned to the scullery I knew that my father had
come in, and that she had been telling him, for I heard his
voice saying quietly, 'Don't be afraid for her, God has a way
of looking after his own,' and I stood in some bewilderment.
What was she afraid of? Why should she be afraid for me just
because I wanted to learn to swim? Other girls learned to
swim and their mothers weren't afraid for them, at least, I
didn't think so. It should be the other way round; she should
be afraid because I couldn't swim and would likely drown in
the river if I fell in. Her attitude to this matter was very
puzzling. Then one Saturday morning, when I was wrapped
around with the warm glow again and the smell of baking in
the kitchen, she began to talk to me. Not looking at me, she
told me that I mustn't go off on my own with any boys.

'But I don't go around with boys, Mam, you know I don't.'
I was slightly huffed. 'Only with Don and Ronnie and Sam.'

There was a long pause, before she said, 'Well, never go out with Don on your own, always see that Ronnie goes along.'

I didn't want to go off with Don on my own, anywhere, or at any time, but did this rule apply to Sam? So I said, 'Not with Sam, either, Mam?'

'Oh.' She straightened her back. 'Oh, Sam is just a boy.' And she turned and looked at me and smiled warmly at me as she added, 'Sam's all right.'

Well, what was there to worry about? I didn't want to be alone with anybody, only perhaps Stinker when we went over the fells or into the wood. There were times when I was happier with Stinker than with anyone else I could think of. With Stinker as my sole companion I felt free; the closed-in feeling that I had in the company of Ronnie and Don fled and I felt lighter, able to run or sit if I wanted to without the restricting touches of their hands or contact with their bodies.

I had a sense of guilt when I felt that our Ronnie's presence, too, was irksome to me, for I had a nice feeling for him, at least during the day. But not at night when he came creeping into my room and woke me up because he wanted to talk. This had happened twice since that first night, when he told me I was pretty.

Then one day I went to the wood to take, so I told myself, my last walk, for on the morrow I was starting work. This business of starting work held no joy for me, for I was going into Mrs. Turnbull's draper shop. Father Ellis had got me the job. I was to start at quarter to nine in the morning, and four evenings a week I would finish at seven o'clock, but on Saturday it could be eight or nine, all according to custom, Mrs. Turnbull had pointed out. Wednesday I finished at one o'clock. Mother comforted me by saying it might lead to better things. What, I couldn't see, as there was only another girl and Mrs. Turnbull in the business. And the other girl was new, too.

Aunt Phyllis said I was lucky to get a job at all when there were dozens of girls with 'something up top' who would have jumped at the chance, but there was nothing like finding favour in the priest's eyes. And now, she had added, and this was in the absence of my mother, I might stop acting like a wild thing and grow up and have some sense. I knew

51

she was referring to Don and Sam following me about, and I wanted to say to her that I didn't want anybody to follow me about, I would rather be on my own, but I had strict orders from mother never to be cheeky, not to anyone, but particularly not to Aunt Phyllis. When speaking about Aunt Phyllis my mother always finished with, 'She has enough on her plate.'

And so I walked in the wood with Stinker at my heels. He seemed to feel the coming breach, too, for he didn't scamper about among the undergrowth but walked with his tail between his legs and his head cast down. He was taking his cue from my feelings. I went through one bay after the other, and it was when turning to make my way home again from the tree bay that I saw Fitty Gunthorpe.

When I had come across him in the wood following the incident of the rabbit I had run to get out of his way, but now I didn't run, for as on the morning that I had been riveted to the ground at the sight of the nailed rabbit, so I was equally riveted now, for Fitty was looking at something in his hand. It was a small bird. It was bare and had been plucked clean. If it had been large I would have known he had killed a pigeon and was going to eat it, but this was a small bird, too small to eat. Its body looked the size of a tiny mouse. It lay on its back in his great palm, its two spidery little legs sticking up into the air.

As if coming out of a trance Fitty took his eyes from the bird and looked at me, then he dropped it on to the ground, so quickly that it seemed as if someone had shot it from his hand, and he flicked his hand twice as if to throw off contact with the poor thing. Then coming towards me with slow steps, his eyes darting from my face to Stinker, who was growling now, he began to jabber. 'I didn't ... Listen ... listen, I found it. It wasn't me, I've done nothin' to it. ... You're the one that s ... s ... said about the r ... rabbit ... aren't you?'

I could only stare unblinking into his face. He was standing an arm's length from me now, and I was terrified. Then he frightened me still further by flinging his arms wide and crying, 'You've ... you've got to listen, see. I found it. I tell you I found it, it was still warm. Somebody's plucked it, not me, not me. I swear by Christ, not me!' Then his manner changed, and his voice dropped to a whining whisper, as he pleaded, 'Don't say anythin', will you? They'll say it was me. It wasn't me. Please, for Christ's sake, don't say anythin'.'

I backed from him, and when he cried again, his voice breaking as if on the verge of tears, 'Don't, will you?' I shook my head in a sickly daze and whispered, 'No, no, I won't.' Then I turned and went out of the wood, not running, yet not walking. But when I reached the top of the street, away from the shadow of the trees, I had my work cut out not to fly into our house and cry, 'The poor bird! the poor bird!'

I said nothing about the bird to anyone, not because I was thinking of Fitty, but because I was seeing his father's face as he had looked at me all those years ago. . . .

Next morning I presented myself at a quarter to nine at Mrs. Turnbull's shop. Dad had gone with me to the bridge, and before leaving me he had grinned down at me, saying, 'Well, lass, you are on your own now, life starts from this mornin'. Away you go now.' With a pressure of his hand he pushed my reluctant body across the bridge, and now here I was, confronted by Mrs. Turnbull and meeting, for the first time, Mollie Pollock.

Mrs. Turnbull was a short woman, and very fat. She seemed to me to be all large bumps, and strangely enough Mollie Pollock too was short and fat, but her fat didn't appear like bumps, it was more like molten flesh, pouring continuously from some central point of her body, for ever mobile.

Mrs. Turnbull informed us both abruptly and without any preamble that we had a lot to learn and we had better get started. The shop had two compartments but only one entrance. Into the second compartment she led me, and placed on the counter, apparently all ready for me, were numerous boxes, some holding cards of buttons, and others, a jumble of coloured tapes and bobbins of thread. My first duty was to get these all sorted out and counted, and to label anew the boxes, which had their place in a high framework that formed the dividing wall of the shop.

There was no window in the second compartment, only a skylight, and I found my eyes drawn to this time and again. The first hour seemed like an eternity, and I had my work cut out not to take to my heels and fly out of the place, for I felt I couldn't breathe. The air was thick, the smell was thick, it was what I called a calico smell.

At eleven o'clock Mrs. Turnbull brought me a mug of cocoa. This, too, was thick and I couldn't drink it. All morning I sorted buttons, tapes and threads and wrote labels, and the latter didn't suit Mrs. Turnbull, my writing was too large and sprawly, and a number of the labels I had to do again. Also I had spelt button 'buttin'. She was very sharp with me about this.

My dinner hour break was from quarter past twelve until one o'clock; it took almost twenty minutes hard walking from the shop to our house, which left only a few minutes for a meal. My mother asked me somewhat anxiously how I got on, and I could not dispel the hope in her eyes by telling her the truth, that I hated the shop, so I just answered weakly, 'All right.' Dad patted my head and said, 'There, lass, it's a new world.'

Yes, indeed it was a new world.

By the end of the week it was decided that I must stay in the town for my dinner, so Mam put me up a packet of sandwiches. I told her I could sit in the back shop and eat them, and this I did for the first two days of the new arrangement, until Mollie whispered to me in passing one morning, 'I'm bringin' me dinner an' all, but I'm going to have it in the park. You comin'?' Instinctively, I nodded, 'Yes.' And a feeling of excitement arose in me at the prospect of being able to sit in the park without being accompanied by any one of the boys.

From that dinner-time Mrs. Turnbull's shop took on a lighter shade. And the credit for this was due solely to Mollie, for she, even at sixteen, was a character. But she was a character my mother would certainly not have liked me to associate with, had she known how Mollie spoke.

There was very little swearing went on in our house. Outside, men swearing was as natural as a 'God bless you'. But women who swore were not nice, and I had been warned not to stand and listen to women who talked like this, as the lads would do.

But here was Mollie, swearing and cursing with nearly every other word she spoke, and it did not stop me from liking her. The strange thing about it was I found myself wanting to laugh as I listened to her, although I must admit her opening comment on our employer not only startled me but almost choked me, for I was swallowing a mouthful of meat and bread at the moment Mollie exclaimed in a doleful tone, 'Doesn't fat-arse Turnbull give you the pip?'

When she had thumped my back until I had spat out the meat, I sat up on the bench and we looked at each other, then we burst into gales of laughter. From that moment we were friends.

She informed me that this was the fifth job she'd had in a year, and if she lost this her mother would bash her brains in. Moreover, that she had only got it because her sister lived in Norton Terrace and was respectable, her husband being a bus driver. Mollie herself lived in Bog's End and was one of eleven children. Her father, when in work, was a ragman. But now, as she said, everybody was in bloody rags, so business was at a standstill.

It was strange that I could sit listening to Mollie swearing and cursing and not once think, Ech! she's awful, or Eeh! she's bad. Mollie was a natural swearer – there are such people who space the words into their own language and so colour it. It is, in a way, a gift, and she was the only one I ever met who had it, for when Cissie Campbell said even 'Damn and blast!' something would curl up inside of me against the repulsive sound, but not so with Mollie, Yet, nevertheless, I did not take Mollie home, for I knew immediately what my mother would say. She would find no entertainment or charm in Mollie's language, and I had no doubt about what would have been her attitude had she known that I was listening to it every day.

Sitting on the park seat in the bright sunlight one dinner hour, Mollie turned to me and said, 'Eeh! Christine, you know, you are bonny.' I felt my cheeks broadening with pleasure, but I denied the statement, saying, 'I'm not really, it's only me hair,' and I tossed over my shoulder one of my two plaits. 'It isn't only your hair,' went on Mollie, 'your hair's got nowt to do with it really, it's your face. The shape of it, and your eyes.' Then she leaned back against the park seat and, hanging her hands over the rail, she surveyed me and exclaimed, 'My God! what I wouldn't give to have your eyes. I'd run bare skinned round the bloody shipyard for them. Y'know what?' She had come up close to me now, lowering her voice, 'You could marry a bloody duke!'

When my laugh rang out, she shook my arm, saying, 'I'm not jokin', Christine,' although she was herself laughing, 'honest to God, you could! Coo, if I had your face, Fellburn wouldn't see me backside for dust.'

Now I was laughing louder and louder, and, warming to her theme, Mollie ranted on telling me what she would do if she was me.

That night I lit a new candle and stared at my face in the small mirror on top of the chest of drawers, the only article of furniture, beside the single bed, which the room would hold. My face looked waxy and pale and somehow far away. I moved nearer to the glass and stared into my eyes, but they didn't seem to stare right back at me, they looked dreamy, and I gurgled to myself, 'They're not paying attention.' And my eyes weren't paying attention to me, they were looking deep inside me, right into the place where my dreams were. For now, strangely enough since I had started work, I was dreaming more and more. In the mornings, surrounded by tapes, bobbins and bales of flannelette and drill, I released myself from the shop and went straight up through the fanlight into my dream world, the dream world which held the river and the wood and fells, and . . . someone. This someone who was big, yet had no definite outline. He was no one that I knew, not even Father Ellis, but he was someone beautiful to look upon, someone who spoke with a soft voice, a caressing voice, some-one who kept saying, 'Christine, oh, Christine.' And this someone had no resemblance to our Ronnie, oh no, none what-ever, although Ronnie kept saying, 'Christine, oh, Christine.'

There had lately come into me a fear when I heard our Ronnie speaking my name like that, and he was doing it more and more, for he was always wanting to talk to me in the night. He had never touched me or sat on my bed. He just squatted on his hunkers by the side of the bed and talked and talked in whispers. Yet fear of his visits was growing in me and I was terrified lest my mother should find out, for somehow I knew she would blame me. Yet I kept asking myself, why, why should she?

I had been at Mrs. Turnbull's a year when I got a shilling a week rise, which brought my wages to eight and sixpence, and because of this I was detailed to do a job for which I had no taste. This was going round the other shops in the centre of the town and taking note of their prices. If they were selling winceyette at one and threepence three-farthings a yard, Mrs. Turnbull would alter her card to one and three-pence-farthing. She was the first of the cut-price shops, I think.

It was on one of these distasteful excursions that I ran into Don. He wasn't in his working clothes, but had on his good suit and looked very big and hefty and, I noticed for the first time, somewhat handsome.

'Where you off to?' he asked, surprised to see me out.

When I told him he laughed and said, 'Well, she's got her head screwed on all right, I must say that for her. Look, come on and have a cup of tea.'

'No, no, I can't, Don,' I protested; 'I've got to get back, she'll raise the roof if I'm late.'

'Let her.' He was looking at me from the depths of his dark eyes. I could almost feel the gaze coming out of them, sharp and piercing, going through my clothes, right through my skin.

When I turned away, saying again, 'No, Don, I can't,' he pulled me back without moving a step. He just reached out with his great arm, and there I was, standing where I had been a second before, looking at him. Then without any leading up, as was the custom with lads, even this much I knew without having had experience, he said, 'This is as good a place as any to tell you, you're goin' to be me girl.'

I strained back from him, unable for a moment to say anything to this straight statement. Then vehemently I declared, 'Oh, no, I'm not, Don Dowling!'

At this he laughed and sang softly, 'Won't you come home, Bill Bailey?' then added, 'That's how you said that. Oh, no, you're not, Don Dowling! Well, I am, and you are, Christine Winter, do you hear?'

There were people passing us in the street now and looking at us, and he turned me about as if I was a cloth doll and led me down a cut that gave on to the town boat landing. I wriggled in his grip and cried, 'Don't be silly, Don, leave go!' But he took no notice until we were standing on the empty landing, the river flowing coldly by, and then he said, without any laughter now, 'I'm sick of this. What does

57

your mam expect? Does she think you're going to end up in a convent? And there's your Ronnie an' all gettin' as bad as her.'

'I don't want any lad. And Mam says I'm too young, I'm only fifteen. ... Anyway,' I added with some spirit, 'you'll not be my lad, Don Dowling.'

'Now look here, Christine,' his voice was softer now, 'don't take that line. I know it's not you talkin', you want to come out with me all right, but it's your mother, isn't it? God damn! you've got to come alive sometime, she's got to let you come alive.' Now his voice fell to a low, angry tone as he finished, 'She can't keep you in blinkers all the time.'

'Leave me go, leave me go!' I pulled away from him. 'My mother doesn't keep me in blinkers. And I don't want a lad, you or anybody else, so there!'

I turned from him and again he was blocking my way, and now his voice and manner changed once more and he was pleading, his words running into one another. 'Look, Christine, don't be mad. I'll do anything for you, anything, and I won't always be down the pit. No, by God! I've got something else in view. I'll have money some day, Christine, and I'll dress you up.' He spread his hands, making an outline about me but without touching me. 'Only be nice to me, Christine, let me see you alone sometimes.'

I had never before heard him plead, and it didn't seem like him, and I could have felt sorry for him, but I said, and quite firmly, 'I don't want you for a lad, Don. Why, you're more like me brother.'

'All right,' he said, his voice definite, 'I'll be your brother. Only don't keep avoiding me. I'll play the brother – anything you want.'

'But, Don, don't be silly, you can't.' I was trying to get past him as I spoke, and suddenly he brought me close to him, and with his face almost touching mine he muttered, 'But Ronnie does, doesn't he? He plays the brother all right. Oh,' he gave me a shake, 'don't tell me what I know. And when we are on, there's little Sam – dear little Sam. You don't mind sneaking off into the wood with Sam, do you? And don't tell me he's still at school and only a kid. Aye, he's only a kid but he's all eyes and quivers where you're concerned.' He shook me again, and then exclaimed, 'You've played fast and loose with the lot of us for years and it's finished.'

58

'Let me go, do you hear, let me go! If you don't I'll tell Aunt Phyllis.'

This threat brought his head up and he emitted a hard laugh. 'You'll tell Aunt Phyllis, and do you know what she'll say? She'll say you're a liar, she's always said you were a liar, and she'll go to your mother and she'll tell her to stop you from running after me and trying to trap me. Go on, tell Aunt Phyllis.'

'Here, what's up, what's he doing to you, lass?' The man's voice seemed to come out of the water, and when I turned my startled gaze towards his head which showed just above the landing stage the appeal in my eyes brought him up quickly and across the landing, crying, 'Leave her be!'

When Don's hold relaxed on my shoulder and he turned round to confront the man, my legs seemed too weak to hold me and I staggered a moment before turning to run. The last I heard as I dashed up the alleyway was the man shouting, 'You try it on an' you'll find yersel' in the river.'

I wanted to tell my mother of the incident but I was scared, for she would surely go into Aunt Phyllis and then there would be a row and Sam wouldn't be allowed to come in. Strangely enough it was this last that stopped me from confiding in her. Sam's only refuge was our house, for never a day went by but Aunt Phyllis's hand and voice were raised against him, and more so of late because she knew that when he came out of school he met my Uncle Jim. Uncle Jim was now living openly with the woman in the sweet shop, and it was to Sam that he gave the money for Aunt Phyllis, and always when Sam put the money on the table Aunt Phyllis pelted him with questions, then usually accused him of telling lies like his father, and the result of this would be Sam getting his ears boxed.

I doubt, too, if I had told my mother everything, whether she would have believed me utterly, for that night Don came into our kitchen and he acted as if nothing at all had happened, in fact, as if we were on the best of terms. First of all he joked banteringly with Ronnie, saying, 'You'll never believe it, Ronnie, but old Threadgold is putting me up for deputy. He says I've got all it takes.' Then, turning to my mother, he said, 'In five years' time I'll be a manager, how about that for success, Aunt Annie? And all due to the boy's brains.'

Ronnie laughed, as did my father, but my mother only smiled and said, 'Well I suppose there's stranger things happen.' Then just before he took his leave he said to Ronnie, 'Did you hear Father Ellis's running a social a week come Saturday?'

'No,' said Ronnie. 'Who told you?'

'Jonesy asked me did I want any tickets, and I bought a couple.' Then turning from Ronnie, he looked straight at my mother and with a disarming smile he said, 'Will it be all right for Christine to come along, Aunt Annie?'

My mother blinked twice, then lowered her gaze quickly to the mat before turning to me. The look on my face must have puzzled her for she replied neither 'Yes' nor 'No', but left the decision to me, saying, 'Well, it's up to Christine. If she wants to go to the social, she can.'

'We'll all go.' Ronnie had stood up.

'That's settled then,' said Don. He gave a nod that included us all. 'So long.'

'So long.'

As soon as the door had closed on him I turned to my mother, saying hurriedly under my breath, 'I'm not going to the social.'

'Why not? I thought—' She looked at me closely.

'I just don't want to go.'

'All right, all right, me girl, if you don't want to go you needn't.'

I knew she was puzzled, for I had been on to her for some weeks to let me go to the dances that were run in the schoolroom on a Saturday night, and of which I had heard from time to time such glowing and romantic accounts. A social, of course, was different. At a social, because of the old people and the very young, you played whist and games and just had a dance or two. Don had been clever in picking on a social. Don was clever altogether. His cleverness at this moment filled me with fear – who would have thought that only this morning he had acted like someone mad on the boat landing?

That night Ronnie came into my room again. It wasn't so very late and I wasn't asleep, and he sat on his hunkers by the bed and whispered, 'What's up, Christine?'

'Nothing,' I said. 'What makes you think that?'

'There's something wrong. I saw your face when Don was on about the social. Has he been at you?'

I could see the outline of him bending forward, and when his hand came on to my shoulder I shrugged it off, moving over to the wall, and I turned the conversation by saying, 'Look, our Ronnie, if me mam knew you were coming in here she would get mad.'

'Why should she, I'm doin' nothing? Good lord' – his whisper was intense – 'can't I just talk to you?'

His words sounded so reasonable that I felt silly. Silence fell between us, heavy and thick as the gloom in the room, and then he whispered, 'Don't think I'm sayin' anything against Don, but keep clear of him, Christine. Promise me. Do you hear me?'

'How can I promise when I don't know what you mean,' I stalled, knowing full well what he meant, and also knowing there was no need to extract a promise from me.

'Don't go out with him alone, he's wantin' to take up with you. Do you like him?'

'No, and you know I don't.'

I heard him sigh. Then after a pause he said, 'But that could only make him keener. He likes them hard to get, makes him feel tough. And he is tough, he might make you go out with him.'

I hitched myself up in the bed and my whisper carried all the conviction in me, 'I'll never go out with Don Dowling, never. And you can tell him that if you like.' After a moment I felt him rising, and then he whispered, 'Good night.'

I wondered if my mother would be surprised if I asked for a bolt on my door, and my last thoughts before I went to sleep were, 'Don't be silly, you can't ask for a bolt on the door. . . .'

In spite of all my protests that I didn't want to go to the social, I went after all. Two things contributed to my final decision. One was the pressure of Ronnie, and the other, which more than weighted the balance of the scales, a dress which my mother brought back from Mrs. Durrant's. It was an evening dress of pale blue velvet, and when my mother held it up before her I exclaimed in admiration, 'Oh! don't cut it up, Mam, wear it.'

'What!' my mother exclaimed, 'with no back to it?' She

61

glanced merrily at Dad. 'That would be the day, wouldn't it?' He nodded but declared gallantly, 'There wouldn't be a bonnier back shown at the do.'

There was a lot of laughter, followed by a lot of talk about just how she was going to alter the dress. The result of her handiwork was something quite beyond my dreams. She made the neck what she called 'low'. This meant that the line came below the nape and allowed my gold crucifix that had belonged to my great-grandmother to lie just below the hollow. The sleeves did not reach my elbow and were trimmed with minute flowers she had unpicked from the original belt. The skirt was full and reached below my calves, and the bodice she made in a wrap-over style. Why she chose this shape I didn't question. There was at the time nothing to question. It was Don who said, some years later, 'She even padded your front so we wouldn't know you had breasts.'

I had asked Mrs. Turnbull if I might be let off early on the Saturday night, and this privilege she grudgingly granted. Mollie, too, wanted to come to the social, but she would not let Mollie off.

At six o'clock I dashed out of the shop and through Fellburn and up the hill, and I was panting and red in the face when I reached the kitchen. My mother had all my things ready and she followed me up to my bedroom. There was as much excitement as if it was for my wedding.

When later I stood in the kitchen turning myself round before Dad's gaze I had a mighty surge of pleasurable happiness. I was for the first time acutely aware of myself as a whole, I had a body that did justice to my face and hair, and the feeling felt good.

There was a softness in Dad's eyes that was almost moisture as he gazed at me without speaking. Then he said softly, 'Lass, you're a picture come to life.'

'Oh, Dad.' I shook my head at him, but nevertheless felt greatly pleased, not so much with the words he had spoken as with the depth of feeling with which he uttered them.

Ronnie, standing by the table, had said nothing, and this was taken for brotherly indifference. He was wearing a blue serge suit which my mother had got him last year through the store club, and now the sleeves were a little too short, although my mother had turned down the cuffs as she had also done

62

the turn-ups of the trousers. Yet he looked nice; he looked like my dad must have looked at his age, but already he was much taller than Dad.

My mother was once again adjusting my dress and patting the folds into place when there came a tap on the outer door, and she shouted 'Come in'.

Don came in, followed by Sam. Don had on a blue serge suit and it looked new. He was wearing, I noticed, new shoes, too, and over his arm he carried his mack, also new. Everything about him looked so startlingly new that an exclamation was forced from my mother, and she said, 'Why, Don, aren't we smart the night! Has your ship come in?'

He moved the mack from one arm to the other, straightened his tie and said, 'Not a ship yet, Aunt Annie, just a little sculler.'

I saw Dad look at him. Our Ronnie and Don received the same wage; we were in a better position altogether than Aunt Phyllis, yet our Ronnie could not have a new suit.

As Don answered my mother he did not look at her but at me. Although I was standing sideways to him I knew that his eyes were moving all over me, yet he never said a word. It was Sam who, coming and standing in front of me, looked up into my face with a look that was to grow and deepen with the years, and hurt me with its tenderness and frighten me in a particular way with its adoration. Now his eyes tight on mine, not on the dress, he said in awe-laden tones, 'Eeh! Christine, you look lovely.'

I did not deny this as I had done to Dad, or would have done if Don or Ronnie had said it, but I answered him softly, 'Do I, Sam?'

'Aye,' he nodded, and then he looked to where Dad was standing near the fire, and my father and he smiled at each other knowingly.

'Well if we're going we'd better be moving unless we want to meet them coming out.' It was our Ronnie speaking and somewhat impatiently. I walked into the front room, my mother following, and there she helped me on with my coat; then turning me round towards her and flicking an imaginary speck from my shoulder and adjusting the cross on my neck, she said softly, 'Enjoy yourself, lass.' Yet her tone did not convey the meaning of the words, rather it held a

63

warning, but she continued to smile. Then accompanied by Dad, too, now, I followed Ronnie and Don.

Self-consciously I stepped out into the street and there, at her door, stood Aunt Phyllis. I smiled at her but she did not return my smile. She could see most of my dress through my open coat, yet she didn't make any comment on it, but looking towards Don, she snapped, 'Mind, I'm not waitin' up all night for you.' Then seeing Sam standing behind me and in front of Mam and Dad on the step, she said, 'Come on in here, I've been looking for you.'

I walked away down the street between Don and Ronnie. At the corner, leaning against the wall with two or three other men, was Mr. Patterson from next door. He was chewing a long piece of straw, and he pulled it quickly from his mouth and exclaimed, 'By! Christine, you're a smasher the night. Off to enjoy yersel'?'

'Yes, Mr. Patterson, I'm going to the social.'

'That's it, lass, enjoy yersel' when you're young. You're old afore you know it. Life flees. We're nowt but Feathers in the Fire.'

As we walked on Don muttered under his breath, 'Feathers in the fire. Old afore you know it. He makes me sick. That lot were never young. It won't happen to me.'

Ronnie, leaning across me, inquired jokingly of him, 'What are you going to do, take monkey glands?'

'Aye, monkey glands it'll be, but in the form of money. Money is all the monkey glands a feller needs. Money will keep me young, I'll see to that.'

Ronnie's eyes were narrow now, and he looked Don up and down before saying, 'Well, it looks as if you've had your first dose. Where did you get the windfall to buy that lot?'

Now Don's head went back and he moved it in stiff, slow movements from side to side. 'That's my business. I gave you the chance last week to be in on a good thing, but no, didn't want to dirty your fingers.'

Ronnie's face was stiff now and his voice resembled a growl as he said, 'I'm not gettin' meself into trouble doing any shady business.'

'It's not shady; it's business, but it's not shady. If you buy somethin' for threepence and sell it for sixpence that's business, there's nowt shady about it.'

'All right, have it your own way but—'

'Look. Are you going to this social or a boxing match, just let me know?' The words sounded cool; my tone was a grown-up tone. I felt grown-up, the dress was having an effect. Anyway, my attitude checked them both for they hesitated in their walk and laughed. Then, as if both of the same mind, they suddenly grabbed my hands and ran me down the hill as if we were children again, and in this moment of anticipation and excitement I did not resent the feeling of Don's hand in mine.

Just before we came in sight of the bridge they jerked to a stop and as I billowed out from them like a balloon about to take off I wrenched my hands free. Then I, too, came to a halt on the sight of two lads – no, lads is not the right word, young men can only describe them. It was these two young men who had halted Don and Ronnie. They were surveying us from a rise just off the road. They were both dressed in grey flannels and sports coats and wound around their necks were long scarves.

To wear woollen scarves in the height of summer seemed ridiculous, yet they did not look ridiculous; in fact I thought it was we three who must be appearing ridiculous for they both were looking at us through narrowed lids in a scrutinizing, weighing-up fashion, as if we were some oddities that they could not really make out. But I felt no feeling of resentment that they should look at us in this manner, rather my feeling was one of interest, for in a peculiar way the taller of the two seemed to be known to me. His face was pale; what colour his eyes were I could not see from this distance, I only knew they were bright and dark. His hair was brown and had a slight wave in it, and his body was thin, very thin, and he was as tall as Don.

When we had passed them Don spoke. 'They make me sick,' he said, sneering.

I turned my eyes swiftly to our Ronnie as he endorsed this in much the same tone.

'Who are they?' I asked.

'Cissies,' replied Don, 'from Brampton Hill. They're still at school and they wear them scarves to let you know it. I would like to swing them by their scarves, I would that.'

'You mean college?' I said, with a spark of interest.

'Call it what you like it's still school, and these are the types that get the jobs with the money. My God!' he spat into the gutter, and I closed my eyes for a moment and gave a little shiver.

Ronnie, sensing my feelings, put it cheerfully now, 'Ah well, let's live for the night. Away to the social and the high life of Fellburn.' He laughed and was about to link my arm when he thought better of it, thinking that whatever he did Don would do the same.

Ten minutes later I was standing at the school-room door being greeted by Father Ellis.

'Christine! Well, well.' His eyes looked me over. 'A new dress. Did . . . did your mother make it?'

'Yes, Father.' I was feeling now slightly embarrassed, for he had not lowered his voice and it had attracted the attention of most of the lads standing just within the doorway. They were buttoning and unbuttoning their coats. Among the eyes that were looking at me were those of Ted Farrel. Ted had been 'a big boy' at school when I had just left the infants, and I had always liked the look of him, and seeing him now close by and not with the width of the church between us, where I glimpsed him on a Sunday, I found that my opinion hadn't changed.

I turned my face away from the eyes and looked at the school clock. It said twenty-five past seven. The social would go on until half past ten. Three hours of enchantment lay before me. . . .

At half past nine I was back home standing in the kitchen looking with desperate eyes at my mother. Ronnie was standing with downcast head. The sleeve of his jacket was hanging off and he was bleeding from the nose and a cut on the chin.

'What ... what in the name of God's happened?' asked Dad.

Mam had said nothing, and I burst out crying and ran upstairs. In a few minutes she was with me and she pulled me up from the bed where I had flung myself and helped me off with my dress. She never spoke until she had folded the dress and put it away in the bottom drawer. Then drawing me down on to the side of the bed she took my hand in hers and said quietly, 'Tell me about it, lass.'

With my eyes cast down and my head moving from side to

side I muttered, 'It was Don, he didn't want me to dance with anybody else. A boy called Ted – Ted Farrel asked me and Don said if – if I danced with him again he would . . .'

'Go on,' said my mother.

'He – he would make him so's his mother wouldn't know him.'

'What did Ronnie do?' asked my mother. 'Did he know of this?'

'He – he . . .' I found I couldn't say that Ronnie, too, had warned me not to dance with Ted Farrel. How could I explain to her the grip on my arm as we went stumbling round the room, and him whispering, 'Now look, I'm tellin' you, our Christine. Don't you encourage Ted Farrel, for he's got a name. He's no good, and there'll only be trouble.'

'Where did they fight?'

'I – I don't know, I think it was near the boiler house. I saw Ted go out with two pals and then Don said to our Ronnie, "Come on".'

'Where was Father Ellis in all this?'

'In the whist. Somebody told him and he came out and stopped them, and . . . Oh, Mam!' I fell on her neck, 'everybody was looking at me, as if – as if . . .'

'There, there. Look – look at me.'

When I raised my eyes she said, 'Do you like Don, even a little bit?'

'No, Mam. No . . . no!'

She drew in a deep breath, then exclaimed, 'Thank God for that. I knew you didn't as a bairn, but girls change you know, and often in their teens they . . . well, they . . .'

'I could never like Don, I – I'm afraid of him, Mam.'

Her eyes tightened on mine and she said sternly, 'Don't be afraid of him, that's what he wants. Don is not a good boy, Christine. There's something, I don't know what it is, but there's something I can't fathom about him.'

I knew what she meant, and when she said next, 'You must keep out of his way as much as possible,' I didn't reply but asked myself somewhat wildly how I could do that, living almost in the same house with him?

Sensing my feelings, my mother said, 'I know, lass, it's going to be difficult.' Then she added, 'And we don't want any open rift if we can help it. Aunt Phyllis is a funny customer,

67

I know, and she would try the patience of a saint, but she's got a lot on her plate. She's a very unhappy woman, so we don't want to make things worse for her. Just you keep him at arm's length, and whatever you do don't let him see you're afraid of him.'

We looked at each other in the flickering candle-light, then her hands came out and cupped my face, and as she stared at me her eyes grew very soft, and bending forward she kissed me on the mouth. This was a very unusual gesture. I kissed her every night before going to bed and also before going out in the morning, but it was on the side of her cheek, and when she kissed me it was on my cheek, but this was a special kind of kiss and in that moment I felt that I must always be good and never, never do anything that would hurt her.

CHAPTER THREE

I REMEMBER the day I left Mrs. Turnbull's. It was a day in October, nineteen-thirty-eight, shortly after Hitler over-ran Czechoslovakia. I knew about this from Dad's talk, for I did not read the papers. He had been very concerned about this man called Hitler, but now, seemingly, the man had got what he wanted and everything would settle down. Anyway they had stopped digging trenches in the London parks.

Mollie, on the other hand, took a great interest in the news-papers and gave me her verdict, day by day, on the headlines. I knew that she was disappointed there wasn't going to be a war. A war for Mollie meant excitement and all the lads in uniform.

She was talking, this particular morning, in whispers and with some regret about the latest news, saying, 'Eeh! by, me ma had some fun in the last war. She keeps me in stitches sometimes with the things she did. And she had some chances an' all. She was a bloomin' fool not to snap one of 'ems up, sergeants and the like. And then she had to go and marry me da. That was a case of must. By, I've learned somethin'. If there was another war no bloody tatie peelin' private would get me, I can tell you. I mayn't be a Greta Garbo but I've got me head screwed on the right way. By, I have. Me ma's taught me a lesson, and the squad she's got.'

'Wouldn't you marry a pitman?'

'Pitman? Not me. No bloody fear. Pitman!'

I looked at her out of the side of my eye and said with a little laugh, 'I thought you liked our Ronnie?'

She gave me a sly look back, dug me in the ribs and said, 'Likin's one thing, marryin's another. If he won the pools now, I'd have him the morrer.'

We both burst out laughing, then covered our laughter

hurriedly as we heard Mrs. Turnbull coming out of the other shop. I remember I turned from a shelf to look at her and my mouth fell into a gape, for behind her stood Dad. He came straight towards me, his cap moving nervously between his hands, and said, 'I've been talking to Mrs. Turnbull' – he nodded his head back at her – 'you'll have to come home, lass, your mother's taken bad.'

I said nothing, I did not even apologize to Mrs. Turnbull for my hasty exit, but, running out to the back, I grabbed up my coat and hat and joined Dad in the shop. And there, Mollie, before Mrs. Turnbull could speak, asked, 'Will you be comin' back?'

It was my dad who answered. 'I don't think so, lass, not yet. Me wife's very ill, she'll be in bed for some time.'

Mrs. Turnbull moved with us towards the door, where she said, 'I'm very sorry, very sorry indeed, Mr. Winter.' And turning to me she finished, 'Your situation's waiting for you when you can come back, I'll see to that.'

'Thank you,' I said, and hurried into the street. And there gabbled my questions at Dad: What was the matter? When did it happen? How did it happen? What was it? She was all right when I left this morning.

Apparently my Aunt Phyllis had sent someone to the allotment for him, and when he got back he found my mother in bed – she had knocked on the wall for Aunt Phyllis. Aunt Phyllis had already sent for the doctor.

'But what's wrong?' I asked.

Dad moved his head quickly in a shaking movement as if trying to throw something off, then exclaimed, 'It's her stomach, there's something wrong with her stomach.'

I ran before him up the hill, and burst into the front room, to be greeted by Aunt Phyllis with the command, 'Be quiet! control yourself.'

When I stood by the bedside looking down at my mother, she seemed so much older that it could have been ten years since I last saw her instead of three hours. She did not speak but patted my hand twice; then my Aunt Phyllis moved me out of the room and followed me through to the kitchen, and there she said, 'Now you'll have to get your hand in. And not before time an' all. She'll have to be looked after. She should go to a hospital. But then she always thought she knew best. Now come along and get your things off and finish this washing. She was in the middle of it and it's a heavy one.'

As if in a dream, I took off my hat and coat and put on an apron. When I look back it seems I never took that apron off.

After two weeks in bed my mother seemed brighter and talked of getting up, but she did not get up, not for many weeks. Every night before I went to bed she would pat me on the hand and say, 'The morrow I must put my best foot forward, I can't lie here for ever.'

But in the morning she was always very tired again.

Dad hardly ever left the house except to sign on and go to the allotment, and he would help me with the work, but was no good with the cooking, though he would offer advice, saying, 'Your ma did it like this.' Yet no matter how hard I tried to follow the way Mam did it I always seemed to use twice as much stuff, and the result would be nowhere near as nice as when she had made it.

The money did not go so far either, and this was worrying us all. Although my money was not coming in, Dad could get no more from the unemployment exchange because Ronnie was still working; and then, too, we not only missed my mother's few shillings, but all the odds and ends she brought down from Mrs. Durrant's.

Every day Aunt Phyllis came in and washed my mother and made her bed, and sometimes my mother would say, 'Oh, Phyllis, you shouldn't trouble, I can manage on my own.' But she never told her not to come. And, moreover, every day my Aunt Phyllis told me in some way how badly I was managing.

One day when she was passing through the kitchen as I was dishing up the dinner she cast her eyes down on the cabbage which was a bit watery, and said, 'If you give that a shove it'll float away.'

To her astonishment, and to mine also, our Ronnie, who was standing by the hearth, turned on her, exclaiming, 'Leave her alone, Aunt Phyllis, she's not me mam and she's doing her best.'

Aunt Phyllis, in the act of walking away, stopped in her tracks, turned slightly and looked at Ronnie, and such was the expression in her eyes that Ronnie's head dropped before it and he turned gauchely towards the fire again, while Aunt Phyllis muttered something under her breath which I could not catch. But what she made sure I did catch was her parting shot, for at the kitchen door she turned on me almost in a white fury and exclaimed, 'By! you'll have something to answer for.'

As the outer door banged I turned to Ronnie, the pan still in my hand. 'What in the name of goodness have I done now?' I asked. 'All because the cabbage is a bit watery. Oh, I'll squeeze it again.'

I was flouncing back into the scullery when he caught my arm and said soothingly, 'Take no notice of her. The cabbage is all right. That woman's mad, she should be locked up. There'll be trouble with her one day, you'll see.'

Don and Sam came in every day to inquire after my mother, yet Don never went through to the front room, he always stayed in the kitchen. But he never managed to get me alone, nor did he manage to meet me outside, for whatever shift he was on I arranged to go for the shopping when I knew he would be at the pit.

Sam would sit by my mother's bedside as long as he was allowed, until she would say, 'Well, Sam, you'd better be trottin',' or until he heard Aunt Phyllis yell, 'Sam! You Sam!' Often he would say to me, 'Can't I do anything for you, Christine, get coal in or anything?' And nearly always my answer was, 'No, Sam, thanks; Dad's got it.'

The doctor's visits were spaced more widely apart now, which made Dad angry and he exclaimed one day, 'He'd be on the bloody doorstep if he could get his seven and a tanner each time. He'll get his bill.' And then he ended, 'My God! it makes you wish there was a bloody war, for then there'd be no shortage of money. They'd be crying out for us then.'

The week before Christmas my mother came into the kitchen and it was a time of rejoicing. I felt so happy that I seemed to do everything right; even the pastry I made turned out light and fluffy, and this caused the first real laugh there had been in the house for months. The world seemed to be right again. Dad put up the chains, Mrs. Durrant sent mother a big parcel of food, and Mollie came to see me and told me that she had left the shop for she couldn't stand it without me.

I had been surprised to see Mollie at the door, and I had invited her in after whispering to her, 'Don't swear, will you?' and she hadn't sworn for half an hour. I saw that my mother liked her. Then Stinker came in and, wanting to be friendly, put his paws on her leg and tore her stocking. At this she exclaimed in dismay, 'Oh, you bugger! And me best pair.' Then giving a laugh she ended, 'That's another bloody one an' eleven gone down the drain – cost price, too.' She gave me a push. I glanced at my mother and saw that her face was surprised and straight, but Ronnie and Dad were almost convulsed.

Mollie soon took her departure, and Mam asked me, immediately the door had closed on her, 'Does she usually swear?'

'No, Mam,' I lied. I knew that my mother did not believe me.

Christmas over, Mam's energy seemed to flag again, and one day I found her crying and she said, 'Go down to Father Howard and ask him if he will kindly say a mass for me.' Then she drew her purse to her and, counting out five shillings in sixpences and coppers, added, 'You'd better take this with you. Offer it to him, but he may not take it.'

Her request sounded so ominous that I hurriedly put on my hat and coat and went out. There was a cold wind blowing but the coldness of my hands, feet and face could not in any way compare with the coldness I was feeling round my heart. My mother was very ill; she was getting up, but this did not hide the fact that she was very ill.

Even in the biting wind there were men lining each side of the bridge and they called out to me and asked how she was.

The nine o'clock mass was just finishing and I saw Father Howard in the vestry. I made my request and offered him the five shillings, which he took quite casually and laid it on a shelf as if it were of no account.

When I returned home, Mam said, 'Well?' She did not ask if he was going to say the mass for her but ended, 'Did he take it?' I nodded silently and she said somewhat bitterly, 'My God!'

From this time on I started to go to mass every morning, even when there might be a chance of Don waylaying me. I went to Our Lady's altar after each service and begged her to spare my mother. And she answered my prayers, for in the months that followed my mother gradually regained her strength and, though she could not lift anything heavy or do housework, she resumed the cooking and became something of her former self. . . .

Then it was my birthday, 26th April. For my birthday present my mother had made me a coat. She had unpicked and turned a coat that Mrs. Durrant had sent down and had passed the hours, when she had to keep her feet up, by sewing the whole of it by hand. It was a beautiful coat, tight at the waist and full in the skirt, and I could not wait to get it on. Our Ronnie bought me a scarf, and Sam, who never had any money except for the odd copper my mother slipped him, carved my name with a penknife on a round piece of oak, with holes pierced in it so that it could be hung up like a picture. I was delighted with his present, and my pleasure pleased him greatly I could see. Don bought me nothing, and that also pleased me, for I did not want to have to thank him for anything, although during the last few months he had said nothing to me that anyone else could not have heard. Aunt Phyllis, Don and Sam were invited to tea. My Aunt Phyllis refused on some pretext or other, but Don and Sam came, and as we all stood in the kitchen looking at the lovely spread my mother had managed to make, Don moved to where his mack was lying on the head of the couch and from under it he brought a parcel, and, coming to me, put it into my hands, saying, 'Here's your birthday present.'

I tried to smile and mumbled some words of thanks. And then he said, 'Well, aren't you going to open it?'

My mother had not spoken, but she took the scissors from where they hung on a nail at the side of the mantelpiece and handed them to me. I cut the string and opened the parcel to reveal a green leather case. It was in the shape of an oblong box, and when I lifted the lid my eyes popped in amazement. It was a dressing-case, complete with bottles and jars, and the inside of the lid was fitted with glass to form a mirror. There was even a little case which held a manicure set.

I raised my eyes from the gift and looked at him and said, 'Thanks, but – I can't take it.'

He turned away and sat down at the table, saying, 'Don't be silly.'

My mother and Dad were standing one on each side of me now looking down into the box, and my mother said clearly, 'This must have cost a pretty penny, Don.'

'Aye, I'm not saying it didn't. Nobody's arguin' about it. Are we going to start eating, Aunt Annie?'

'Christine's not used to gifts like these. . . .' My mother stopped and everybody moved uneasily. Embarrassment filled the room.

We all came under it except Don who, swinging round in his chair, faced my mother, saying, 'Look, Aunt Annie, I didn't steal the money, I worked for it. I've got a job on the side. She needn't be ashamed to take it.'

'What's this job you've got on the side, Don?' asked Dad quietly, as he took his seat at the table and motioned us all to be seated.

'Selling things, Uncle Bill,' said Don. 'I do odd things for Remmy, the second-hand dealer, you know, I sell things for him.'

'What kind of things?' Dad was not looking at him but at my mother as he took a cup from her.

'Oh all kinds, junk and such. There's a car in at present. I wouldn't mind going in for it meself. He only wants twenty quid for it.'

'Put that down,' said my mother quietly.

I was still standing with the dressing-case in my hands. 'But, Mam . . .'

'Put it down. We'll talk about it later.'

As I sat down at the table Don, looking at me, exclaimed with a laugh, 'I didn't buy it to 'tice you to make up, your skin's fine as it is, isn't it, Aunt Annie?'

My mother was still pouring out the tea and she did not look at Don as she answered, 'Yes, it's quite all right as it is.'

My birthday tea that had promised to be a joyful occasion turned out to be only a stiff, rather ceremonious one, where everybody said 'Thank you' and 'No, thank you' and nobody laughed much except Don.

Our Ronnie, I saw, was furious, and after tea, as we all sat round the fire, I could not bear the stiffness in the atmosphere any longer, and so I said to him 'What about that funny rhyme you made up about Miss Spiers. Go on, read it.' I turned to my mother. 'It's funny, Mam,' I said. Then again turning to Ronnie, I urged, 'Go on, read it. You said you would after tea.'

'Yes, go on,' said my mother.

Somewhat mollified, Ronnie pulled from his pocket a piece of paper and, glancing self-consciously around the room, said, 'It's called "The Prayer of Mary Ellen Spiers".' Then he gave a little laughing 'Huh!' before he began:

O Lord, she said, look after me
And don't make me like the likes of she,
Who, next door, in dark sin abounds
A lipstick, rouge and film hound.

O Lord, I beg, look after me
Who only ever imbibes tea;
Not like others with drops of gin,
Which is the stimulant of sin.

O Lord, I beg, take care of me
From all those men who go to sea;
Shield me, I pray, from their winks,
And don't blame me, Lord, for what I thinks;

And from those men who swarm the air,
Fair bait I am for them up there.
If I am not to become a flyer
Work overtime, Lord, on . . .
    MARY ELLEN SPIERS.

From actors, Lord, protect me proper,
Or else I'll surely come a cropper;
Keep my dreams all dull and void,
And lock the door, Lord . . . on Charles Boyd.

Let me not mix, Lord, I pray,
With poets and writers of the day;
Keep my hands from their craft,
And stop me, Lord, from going daft.

And when I die, O Lord, remember
My life has been one grey December;

76

I ain't never had men, wine or beer,
And, O Lord, ain't I bored down here.

Don, Sam and Dad were roaring before he had reached
the last verse, and even Mam was making a vain effort to
hide her amusement, but she admonished him, 'You shouldn't
write things like that, 'tisn't right. Poor Miss Spiers.'

'Oh, Mam, it's only fun.'

'Poor woman,' said Mam again; then she turned to Sam
and said brightly, 'Come on, Sam, sing us a song.'

Sam was nearly fourteen. He was growing but still had a
shy reticence about him, and now he put his two hands between his knees and rocked his shoulders from side to side as
he protested, 'Eeh! no, Aunt Annie, I can't sing properly.'

'You've got a lovely voice, lad. Come on, sing something.
That one you were humming the other day.'

He turned his head sideways and glanced up at her, asking
shyly, 'Which one was that?'

'Oh, I don't know. It went like this.' She hummed one or
two bars, and he said, 'Aw, you mean "You May Not be an
Angel"?'

'Aye, I suppose that's it. Come on now, on your feet.'

Lumbering from his chair, he turned it round and, holding the back for support, he began to sing. His voice was clear
and true and pulled at something inside of me.

The song finished; we clapped and clapped, that is, all
except Don, and he, laughing, said, 'He's got a cissie voice.'

'Nothing of the sort,' said my mother sharply, 'he's got a
beautiful voice, a tenor voice. Sing again, sing something
else, Sam.'

Sam shook his head and was about to resume his seat when
I put in, 'Go on, Sam, sing another. Sing that one I like, "I'm
Painting the Clouds with Sunshine".'

He looked at me and said, 'I don't know all the words of
that one but I'll sing, "That's My Weakness Now", eh?'

The title and his shy look struck us all as very funny and
once again the kitchen was ringing with laughter, and when he
began, he himself could hardly get the words out for laughing. The tears were running down his cheeks, and as I looked
at him I thought, Thanks, Sam, for he more than anyone else
had made my birthday party.

77

Later, when Don and Sam had gone in next door, the dressing-case remained on the sideboard and we had a discussion about it as we sat round the fire.

'There's nothing much you can do,' said Dad, 'without causing trouble.'

'But I don't want her to have it,' said my mother.

'And,' I put in, 'I don't want it either.'

'Give it back to him,' said Ronnie, angered again at the thought of the present, and though Dad was for letting things rest as they were, he said, 'But that's the finish, mind, you'll take nothing from him again.'

'I won't use it,' I said; 'it's there for him when he wants it.' But later, when I took the case upstairs and looked at it under the light of the candle, I thought, 'Oh, if only I could use it.' It was so beautiful. If only Dad or Mam or Ronnie had bought it for me . . . or Sam. Sam who never had a penny.

I went to bed and, strangely, it was of Sam I lay thinking, Sam and his nice voice. He would be leaving school this summer and he wanted to get a job on a farm if he could. There was little prospect of that hereabouts, but he had said to my mother he wouldn't mind going away, although, he had added, he would miss us all very much. Sam was nice. Thinking of him brought no conflict to my mind, not like when I thought of Don or even our Ronnie.

I don't know how long I had been asleep before I heard Ronnie's voice saying, 'Christine, I want to talk to you.' He hadn't come to my room for months. I thought he had got over all that silliness of wanting to talk to me in the night, but now he was whispering, 'Christine . . . Christine.'

'What is it?' I said.

I was sitting up hugging the clothes around me, and he repeated, 'I want to talk to you.' He put his hand out to me, but I pressed away from him. I could see his face, for the night was light; it was white and his eyes were shining darkly.

'Don't use that case, will you?'

'Of course I won't, I've said so. Why did you wake me up for that?'

Screwing about on his hunkers he bent nearer to me, saying, 'I could kill him when he makes up to you like that. You don't want him, do you?'

'No, I've told you. And look, our Ronnie,' I exclaimed in

78

low rapid tones, 'if Mam or Dad knew you came in here there would be something to do, I'm telling you.'

'Why?' His voice sounded huffed.

'Don't keep saying "Why?" You know you shouldn't be . . .'

'What harm am I doing, anyway?' he put in. 'I just want to talk to you.'

'But what about?' My voice sounded as desperate as I felt.

'Oh, heaps of things. I can't talk to anybody else, and we should be able to talk now. I want to talk about all kinds of things. Us, for instance – yes us, and . . . and God . . . man, the world, the devil, and the flesh.'

I knew that in the last bit he was quoting Father Howard's Sunday sermon, but as he said 'flesh' his hands came on to me and his voice changed to a sort of trembling groan as he whispered, 'Move over and let me sit near you, just on the top . . . just on the top.'

'No, no!' I pressed myself against the wall; then springing up and on to my knees and holding the quilt in front of me, I gasped, 'Get out, our Ronnie; if you don't I'll yell for me mam.'

Slowly he drew himself up from his hunkers, and with his hands outstretched he began to plead, 'Christine . . . Christine, honest to God, I meant nothing. I just wanted to sit against you. Honest.'

'Go. Go on . . . get out!'

'You've got to believe me. Look, I won't ever touch you again. I just want to be with you and talk to you. Can't you see?'

'Go on. If you don't I'll shout. I will, mind. And if you come in again I'll tell me mam. Go on.'

His face took on such a look of sadness that I almost felt sorry for my attitude, but when the door closed on him I flew to it and jambed a chair under the knob, then rushing back into bed I covered my head with the bedclothes and prayed, 'Holy Mary, Mother of God, pray for us sinners, now and at the hour of our death, amen. Holy Mary, oh please, please don't let our Ronnie come in again, don't make me have to tell me mam. Oh please! please!'

Next morning I went to mass and to the side altar, and there I implored Our Lady to protect me. Against what I did not say, I just asked her to keep me a good girl, to keep my thoughts and mind pure and never to let me do anything wrong.

Just when I passed over the bridge before ascending the hill I met Don. He stood dead in front of me, searching my face in an exaggerated fashion, then exclaimed, 'No makeup? Mam's forbidden it, eh?'

I felt very tired and somehow unable to do battle with him. Instinctively, I knew I had to fight the same battle against him as I had against Ronnie, and the thought, for the moment, had ceased to be terrifying and was just a dead weight on my mind. Quietly I replied, 'I'm not old enough for make-up; I'll use it some time.'

'Well, don't wait too long. By the way, I'm coming in to see your mam and dad shortly.'

I raised my eyes just the slightest. The house was always open to him, why should he make a statement like this?

Then he said, 'Any idea what I'll be after?'

I shook my head. 'No, none.'

'Now, now, don't be coy, the come-hither stuff doesn't suit you, Christine. You want me to put it into words? All right, I'll tell you. I'm going to say "Uncle Bill and Aunt Annie". I'm going to do it proper like, I'm going to say to them' – he now struck a pose before going on – ' "Will it meet with your approval that I take your daughter out, courtin' like?" '

My heart was pounding now and I said, tersely, 'You can save yourself the trouble, Don, and you know it. I thought we had finished with all that.'

The laughter slid from his face and his big mouth seemed to shrink until it looked like Aunt Phyllis's. Then he said quietly, 'I've behaved meself, I've kept me temper, I've done everything according to the book and even that doesn't suit you. Well, I'll do as I said. I'll ask, and if they don't approve then I'll do it in me own way ... the courtin', I mean. So make up your mind you're for me, Christine. I've always known it, and I'd put you in the river afore I'd let anyone else lay eyes on you.'

Under his fixed stare and his words, which were bringing a feeling of terror spurting up in me, I stood as if hypnotized, until a snuffling and a joyous yelp at my legs told me that Stinker had come to meet me, and I turned to him as to some kind, normal human creature and, heedless of my good coat, I stooped down and gathered his warm wriggling body up into my arms. As Stinker's tongue licked his welcome on my face I thought of what my mother had said, 'Don't show him you're afraid,' but I was afraid, and he knew it. It was impossible to feel as I did inside and it not to show in my eyes, but with an effort I brought out, 'You're mad, Don Dowling, quite mad.'

His next words made me more terrified than ever, for he said quite calmly, 'Yes I am, Christine, you're right there. I am mad where you're concerned. I'm stark, staring mad. I think I always have been.' Then putting out his hand he pushed Stinker's head roughly aside away from my face, and his tone had altered when he said, 'Don't let him lick your face like that, I can't stand it.'

'Leave him alone!' Suddenly I was angry, and because I was angry I had courage. 'Who cares what you can stand and what you can't stand? You're nothing but a big bully, Don Dowling. And don't you push him like that. And don't speak to me again.'

I marched away and he made no effort to stop me, but I knew he was watching me. As I neared the house my steps became slower and I put Stinker down. My courage had ebbed and fear was flowing over me again and I wanted to be sick.

When I got in my mother asked if anything was wrong and I said no, I was just cold. And I was cold, I was cold all through. I went upstairs and peered into the little square of mirror and my reflection brought me no comfort. I wished I looked like Mollie. At that moment I longed to be all Mollie, fat, merry and comfortable. As I stared at myself I got a sort of insight into my character and I knew that although I looked bonny, inside I was ordinary, and somehow I knew that my main desire was to remain so. I wanted to feel comfortable and easy, I wanted my days to be without turmoil or stress. Perhaps I would have taken a different attitude, a pride in my looks, if I had not been vitally aware that it was these very looks that aroused that something, that terrifying something, in both our Ronnie and Don.

Three days later Stinker was missing. At times he would go on the rampage, but whatever time of the year it was, the approach of darkness would find him at the back door. But this particular night there was no scratching or barking, and when nine o'clock came and he had not returned, Dad put his coat on and went on to the fells calling for him. He would not let me go with him. He was out for almost an hour, and when he returned he asked, 'Is he in yet?'

I shook my head.

Next morning I was up at dawn searching the woods. My steps seemed to be directed towards the tree bay, and when I reached it I almost vomited my relief. There was no tortured body nailed to the tree this morning.

I returned home relieved yet crying, and Dad said he would go down to the pound and see if anyone had picked him up as a stray and taken him there. When he returned, it was to say that Stinker was not in the pound.

That afternoon when Sam came out of school we searched the fells together, looking over crags and down narrow, shallow crevices near which we used to play when he was a puppy. And lastly the river, perhaps someone had pushed him in the river. What a silly thought, he could swim like a duck. As I plodded up from the river bank to the house again, Sam walking silently by my side, I was overwhelmed by a sense of loss. I had not really realized before that Stinker was not just our dog, he was my dog. The lads could call him until they were hoarse, but he would never obey them unless I gave him the word, and his greatest joy was when he could sneak upstairs and curl up on my bed. He did not manage this often as Mam did not believe in dogs lying on beds.

When he could not be found my thoughts turned to Fitty Gunthorpe and the maimed rabbit and the plucked bird. The two poor things seemed now to link up with Stinker and I cried and shuddered alternately. Then Fitty Gunthorpe faded into the back of my mind and into his place came Don, and this for no other reason than my remembering his rough handling of Stinker the other morning and my reaction to it. Unreasonably, I began to say, 'He's done something just to spite me. It's him . . . I know it's him.'

Then on the Thursday night I had to revise all my ideas and for the only time in my life I wanted to shower my gratitude on Don Dowling. So grateful was I that I almost threw myself at him and put my arms round his neck and kissed him, for he came up the backyard shouting, 'Christine!

Christine! look what I've got.' And there, on a lead of string, was Stinker, a rather thinner Stinker, but Stinker.

Down on my knees on the scullery floor I kissed and patted and hugged his shaggy head to me, and he wriggled his body all over me in joy at our meeting. Then I cast grateful eyes upwards to Don as my mother asked, 'Where on earth did you get him, Don?'

He was scratching the back of his head and looking down at Stinker and me as he replied, 'Just a mere piece of luck, Aunt Annie. I happened to go through Spillers Cut, you know where the taggerine yard is, and I heard a yelp, and something about it reminded me of this scallywag here. So I went in and put my head round the door of the shed, and there he was, tied up in what had been a horse-box. He nearly pulled a partition down when he saw me. The taggerine bloke said he had come in with some kids a couple of days before. He said he had left them all playing together in the yard and when he came back they were gone and the dog was tied up. He was waiting for them comin' back to claim him. He had fed him what he could, he said.'

'Oh, Don.' My gratitude was in my voice and eyes as I slowly stood up and said, 'Thanks. Oh, thanks.' I was about to add, 'I'm sorry I was so nasty,' but checked myself in time. Yet at this moment I was sorry, I found I was even liking him a bit.

He smiled down at me, saying, 'I thought it would put you on top of the world again having him back. You've been going round like an accident looking for an ambulance.'

I laughed shakily. 'I felt like one, too.' Then because his eyes were on me, I lifted Stinker up into my arms and went into the kitchen.

Life seemed a little more tranquil after this event. Don was nicer, our Ronnie left me alone at night, my mother continued to improve, at least I thought so. In fact she led me to believe that she was very much better because she said to me one day, 'You'll soon be able to go back to your job, lass.' Yet she gave no time limit. But I was in no hurry to return to Mrs. Turnbull's.

It had been a wonderful day for washing. I had got up early and had the washing done and everything dried and damped down ready for ironing by tea-time, and this had pleased her and she said, 'By, lass, you'll make a grand housewife before you're finished.' Then suddenly changing her tone she added, 'But I don't want you to have this kind of life. You've been made for something different besides washing. When you get married I hope you'll have one of them washing machines and a Hoover for the mats.' Suddenly her laugh was joined to mine and she said, 'Well, I know I'm daft. If you have a Hoover you won't have clippie mats, will you, you'll have carpets.' She nodded and ended, 'Aye, you'll have carpets, you'll have a house with carpets, all right.'

It was a lovely prophecy, and it made me feel happy.

She was sitting in her chair by the open door, her knitting in her hands, and she said in a tone that was warmly conspiratorial, 'What about having a cup of tea afore they come in, eh?' I nodded. One of the luxuries of her life was a cup of tea and a piece of fruit cake.

I had just mashed the tea and put the pot on the hob when I heard Aunt Phyllis's voice coming through the wall, and to it was joined Don's. They both seemed to be yelling, but not at each other. Going swiftly into the scullery where Mam, her hands pressed tightly into her lap now, was straining her ear towards the backyard, I whispered rapidly, 'They're on at Sam again, Mam. What's he done now I wonder?'

Mam shook her head, then whispered back, 'He's just this minute got in from school.'

We had not long to wait before we knew the trouble. While Dad was in the scullery washing his hands Sam came creeping in from the back door. His eyes were red and his face was swollen with crying. He did not look at my mother or me but went straight to Dad and, rubbing his finger along the outside of the tin dish in which Dad was washing, he fixed his gaze on the muddy water and said almost in a mumble, 'Uncle Bill, they're going to make me go to the pit.'

Dad reached out for the towel, then asked, 'When's all this come about?'

'Just the day,' said Sam.

'Did you tell them you wanted to go to a farm somewhere?'

'Aye. Yes, I've been on about it all the time, but our Don came in the day and said he spoke for me up top.'

84

Sam was still looking at the water and still moving his finger back and forth on the outside of the dish, and Dad looked down at him for a moment before turning away and saying, 'Well, you'll have to look at it this way, Sam. Jobs are as scarce as gold dust. Some would say you're very lucky to get a chance of a start, although I did hear' – now he turned and looked at my mother – 'I did hear they're signing some men on again.'

My mother took her interest from Sam and said eagerly, 'They are?'

'Aye, not here but further afield, but it's a good sign. I'm going down first thing in the morning to have a talk with Lambert and see if there will be any chance.' He looked up at the ceiling and exclaimed, 'It'll be funny going down again, like starting a new life.'

I looked from Dad to Sam. Sam's head had drooped lower, he was no longer looking at the water but down to the floor. I went to him and put my arm round his shoulders, and Dad's attention was drawn to him again and he punched him playfully on the head saying, 'It's not really bad, Sam, you get used to it. You won't believe it, but I felt the same as you when I started. Thirteen I was and couldn't sleep for nights.'

'But, Uncle Bill, I'm . . . I'm . . .' The tears were in Sam's eyes again as he looked at Dad and he could not bring himself to say, 'I'm frightened of the dark,' but we all knew what he meant.

'Come and have some tea.' It was my mother speaking now. 'I've got some lardy cake.'

After tea Sam stayed in our kitchen until Aunt Phyllis's voice yelled from the backyard, 'You, Sam!' and when he was gone my mother said, 'Poor little beggar, and him scared without a light.' Then getting up from her chair and pushing the seat level under the table, she said, 'That's that Don.'

Neither Dad nor I made any comment.

Later that evening I found it impossible to sit quietly with my mother and so went upstairs, then came down again and walked from the front-room window to the kitchen window. The house felt airless and I had a sudden longing for a sight of the river. 'Do you mind if I take a walk, Mam?' I said.

'No,' she said hastily, 'You look peeky. It's this heat. Where do you think of going?'

'Just down to the river,' I said.

'You wouldn't like your dad to come with you?'

'No, no,' I shook my head quickly.

'Then go out the front way,' she said.

This was so that Don, if he was in the kitchen or in his room which looked on to the back as mine did, would not see me making for the river.

I did not even go upstairs to tidy my hair, I just slipped off my apron and went quickly out of the front door. I walked sedately down the street, around the corner and on to the fells proper. But once I was hidden behind the rise of the land I began to run and did not stop until I had reached the river bank, and there, looking down into the water, I kept drawing in deep gulps of air. Then I decided to go along the river as far as the bend. It seemed years since I had been to the big bend. The river was all bends but the big bend was where it turned sharply and rounded the foot of Brampton Hill. It was a good two-mile walk from where I was now, but it was not yet twilight and I knew I could do it and be back before dark.

I decided to cross by the stepping-stones further along and walk on the other bank. The path there was mostly clear, and it was prettier than on this side.

When I came to the stones I saw a couple with their arms around each other. They were both standing on the same stone. It was not very big and would hardly hold them, but they clung together laughing at the water rushing noisily round their feet. When the girl turned her face towards me I saw that I knew her. Her name was Edna Stace and she had been in my class. She and her boy friend made for the bank, and I said, 'Hullo, Edna,' and she said, 'Hullo, Christine.' That was all.

Jumping quickly from one stone to the other, I hurriedly crossed the river, and when I stepped on to the far side I did not look back at them but went on, feeling somewhat embarrassed and strangely very lonely. It was a feeling I had not experienced before. It was as if there was nobody in the world who loved me, and as I walked I thought, 'Fancy Edna having a lad.'

Later on I passed two men fishing and an elderly couple out for a walk, then I saw no one else until I reached the big bend. It was lovely at the big bend. The river was wider here and had not the tumbling turbulence of the narrower stretches, and rising steeply from the other side was Brampton Hill, the side of it that few people saw, and on the top of the hill there were railings, and inside the railings were trees. These were the grounds of some of the big houses of Brampton Hill. I could see from where I stood that there were gates let in to some of the railings and pathways leading down to the river. I sat down and rested on the bank for a while and, looking up towards the houses I couldn't see, I wondered what it would be like to live in one of them with a garden that bordered on the river. Well, didn't our houses almost border on to the river? But those railings with the gates in them spoke of something different from Fenwick Houses.

As I sat a mist came from nowhere and began to spread itself evenly over the water, like butter under a hot knife. It covered the river and I rose to my feet knowing that the heat of the day was over and soon it would turn surprisingly cold. I walked much quicker going back and had almost reached the stones again when I saw, crossing them, a young man. In the first glimpse I recognized him. He wasn't wearing a scarf this time, but it was one of the two young men who had watched Ronnie, Don and me running down the hill the night we went to the social. He stepped off the last stone as I reached the bank and we looked at each other. He looked the same as I remembered him, pale-faced, with dark eyes almost black in this light. And as he looked at me he did not blink and my eyes fell before his gaze. And then he spoke. 'Good evening,' he said. It was strange but I found myself stammering as I replied, 'Good evening.' Then although I had no intention of running I almost leaped across the stones, and when I got to the other side I had to take a firm hold of myself to stop myself from scampering away like a rabbit. 'Don't be silly,' I said, 'he'll think you're daft.'

I did not look across the river but I knew for certain that he was standing watching me, and so I walked as sedately as possible, with my head up and my arms swinging just a little. I had to stop my legs from striding out for, being long, they inclined to big steps.

I kept up my sedate walk until I rounded the first bend, because from here he could not see me. Then I almost jumped as I glanced across the river, for there he was walking nearly parallel with me on the other side. He smiled and caught my glance. But I did not smile back, I kept looking straight ahead, and even when I came to the bank below our houses I did not look across but turned up the hill. And when I reached the top my heart was beating rapidly. But, strangely, I did not feel lonely any more.

People were sitting on their doorsteps getting the cool evening air and they said, 'Hullo, Christine. By, it's hot isn't it?' 'Yes,' I said, 'it is.' I found speaking difficult, for my throat seemed tight.

'Where did you go?' asked my mother.

'The big bend,' I replied.

'All that way?' she said. 'Aren't you tired after that washing the day?'

I shook my head. I had never felt less tired in my life; my body was afloat, my heart was now leaping and bouncing within me; all I wanted to do was to get upstairs into my room and into bed and think and think.

When at last I found myself between the sheets I buried my head in the pillow, and in the deep darkness his face came up clearly outlined. He was beautiful . . . lovely, and I had not only seen him twice, I had been seeing him for years, for his was the face around which I had dreamed my budding dreams. That night going down the hill, I thought I had seen him before, and now I knew that in some strange way he had always been familiar to me. Turning on my back I lay staring out through the window to the star-laden sky. He was under that sky and somewhere quite near, and he was thinking of me. I knew he was thinking of me. That last look had told me that he would think of me all night and all tomorrow.

I sat quickly up in bed. Tomorrow night I would walk to the big bend again, and if he spoke I wouldn't be silly, I would speak back. But tomorrow night was eons of time away – I couldn't see how I was going to live until tomorrow night. . . .

Tomorrow night came after a day of ironing and doing bedrooms. The day had been much cooler, and by half past six the sun had gone in and it was not such a nice evening. Then after the meal was over and I had washed up and trying to keep all excitement from my voice, I said, 'I'm going for a short walk, Mam.'

She raised her eyes from her patching and said, 'All right, lass.'

Ronnie was sitting by the table and he had lifted his head quickly when I spoke, and I thought for a terrible moment he would say he was coming with me, but to my relief he did not. He dropped his eyes to his book again. He was always reading, always getting books from the library, but since the night I told him to get out of my room he had not talked to me as he used to, and was short with me – sometimes he wouldn't look at me for days.

I slipped on my coat and went out, and when I reached the end of the street I stopped myself from running – I must walk sedately, he could be anywhere on the river bank. Then my walk was halted. What if he wasn't there? I felt sick and my steps became slower as I neared the river.

As far as I could see along both banks I was the only one out for a walk. I continued up to the stones, across them and along the far bank. I stood as I had last night looking up at the gardens across the river. Once again I saw the mist come over the water, and tonight it brought an immediate chill, and the chill was on my heart, too. Slowly, very slowly, I walked back to the stepping stones. I crossed them and made my way along the other bank and did not see a soul until I was nearly below our houses, and then across the meadow on the other side came the black-coated figure of Father Ellis. In my present state of acute disappointment I did not want to speak even to Father Ellis, but he had recognized me over the distance and waved to me, so I waited until he reached the far bank and then we shouted over to each other.

'How are you, Christine?' he called.

'All right, Father,' I called back. I was not all right, I felt I would never be all right again.

'I'll be over one day next week.'

'Oh good, Father, Mam will be pleased.' Father Ellis was not on our district now, but he visited us at odd times. Since that Sunday when Father Howard had delivered his notable sermon on morality the two young priests had been moved from district to district. About every month there was a change round, and it was whispered that things were not happy in the presbytery.

'Hasn't it been hot?'

'Yes, Father.'

'Is your mother any better?'

'Yes, Father, quite a bit.'

'Oh, that's good. I say a prayer for her every day.'

'Oh, thank you, Father.'

'You're growing tremendously, Christine. It's ages since we had a walk ... we must have a walk and a chat, like old times.'

'Yes, Father, yes.'

'Well, good-bye, Christine.'

'Good-bye, Father.'

He went away, waving his hand, and I turned up the hill from the river.

The next fortnight I walked back up the hill every night. Inside I felt sad and lost and lonely, and my mother thought I was sickening for something. 'You're doing too much,' she would say; 'this kind of work is too heavy for you. All that washing. You weren't cut out for it.' I looked at her and smiled and asked, 'What about you?' and she had replied, 'I'm different, lass.'

This answer made me feel more lonely still.

In the weeks that followed only two things of any note happened: Don Dowling got a car and Father Ellis lost his temper with our Ronnie. This latter happened on his promised visit. He saw a book on the dresser and he went and picked it up and, holding it up at arm's length, said, 'Who's reading this?'

Our Ronnie, coming out of the scullery buttoning up his shirt, said firmly, 'I am, Father.' The priest looked at him across the room for a moment, then at the book, and as he placed it back on the dresser I could see that he was making a great effort to be his jovial self as he said, 'Well, Ronnie, no offence meant, but I don't think you're ready for Martin Luther yet. The mind needs training before you read such things.'

'Why?'

Ronnie's question was snapped out, and in it was a challenge, and from that moment they began to argue, and when my mother interrupted and said, 'Enough of that!' Father Ellis raised his hand and said, 'No, Mrs. Winter, leave him alone, let him go on.'

I was setting the table and buttering the bread, and most of their talk was far above my understanding, but I remember being amazed that our Ronnie knew so much, and my attention was caught when he said, 'But we are told, Father, that Satan was a fallen angel, he had been cast out of heaven, yet we're told that heaven is the reward of good people. Can you explain how Satan ever got in? And is there a power which can turn good people into bad in heaven?'

As Father Ellis was about to reply, Ronnie, with what was to me awful temerity, put in quickly, 'And you say God didn't create evil, but we are told that God created everything and there is nothing that wasn't created by him, then where does evil come in?'

Father Ellis's voice held real anger now as he replied, 'I can't answer your questions in a minute. It has taken scores of great men a lifetime to ponder them, but if you want to find the answer to these questions I'll help you. But there's no need for you to attack the Church and God Almighty himself because of your limited intellect.'

'Oh, Father, I'm sorry.' My mother was wringing her hands, and she looked threateningly at Ronnie as she said, 'When your dad comes in I'll have something to tell him.'

'There's no need, Mrs. Winter. We all go through these phases, but we don't get so angry about them, that's all.'

Father Ellis did not stay long, and when he had gone my mother, her hands in her lap, sat helplessly looking at Ronnie. And then she said, 'Well, lad, you've asked for a catastrophe the day.'

'Oh, Mam, for heaven's sake be your age. This is nineteen-thirty nine, you're not struck down dead the day if you talk back to a priest.'

He got up and marched out, and my mother turned and looked at me. I felt the same as she did: things happened when you went for a priest. My mother was very superstitious and she had handed it on to me: I never cut my nails on Friday, nor walked under a ladder at any time, and if there were knives crossed on the table I uncrossed them quickly and made the sign of the cross so that there would not be a row in the house; if a picture dropped, or we heard a cricket on the hearth we knew it was a sign of a death, and if one person died in the street two others would be sure to follow, so for days we waited for catastrophe to overtake us.

Then Don Dowling drove up to the front door in his car. It was an old one but it had been done up, and he tooted the horn so loudly that it brought the whole street out. Aunt Phyllis was at her door making no effort to hide her pride in her son, while my mother and I stood side by side on our step.

'I didn't know you could drive, Don,' said my mother.

'Oh, I've been practisin' for some time, Aunt Annie. Come on, get in. And you Ma.' He beckoned his mother.

But both Aunt Phyllis and my mother shook their heads. Next he turned to me saying, 'What about it?' But I backed a step into the passage, and gave a little laugh as I said, 'No, not me Don, I'm petrified of cars.'

He did not press me further. Then under the admiring gaze of the entire street he drove the car away, round the top corner, down the back lane and on to the main road again.

As we watched the car disappear down the hill my mother, feeling that the occasion required something of her, turned to Aunt Phyllis and said, 'By, he's getting on, isn't he?' And Aunt Phyllis replied, 'Yes, and nobody to thank but himself and his own brains. And this is only a beginning, he won't be much longer in the pits.'

My mother said nothing to this but turned indoors, and when we reached the kitchen she said to me, 'Now mind, Christine, don't you go out with him in that car.'

'As if I would,' I said. We looked at each other, then resumed our duties.

And so the days went on with a dull sameness, and I wondered if this was going to be my life forever, and I began to long to get a job. And then I saw him again – the young man.

What made me open our front door at that moment I don't know. I was cleaning the room out. There was no need for me to open the door but I opened it to look out into the street, and there he was, walking towards me. He had a walking stick in his hand and was evidently making for the wood. One minute he was in the middle of the road, the next he was standing on the pavement right opposite me, and I could not see his face for a silvery light that was floating before my eyes. But I heard his voice saying, 'Why, hallo.' And when I said 'Hallo' back, the mist cleared and I saw him.

'We meet again.'

I did not answer. Our eyes had not moved from each other's face.

'It's a beautiful day. I was going for a walk in the wood.'

'Oh,' I managed to say.

'Do you live here?'

I inclined my head.

He was going to speak again when my mother's voice came from within. She wasn't calling me, just carrying on the conversation where we had left off before I opened the door. His eyes moved from my face and looked behind me. Then he said in a low tone, 'Will you be walking by the river tonight?' I lowered my gaze and forced my voice to say, 'Yes, I'll be going that way.' 'Good-bye,' he said. 'Good-bye,' I replied. But he did not go, and it was I who made the first move. I turned about, took hold of the door and shyly closed it. Then stood with my back against it, my hands holding the front of my dress. My heart was racing, and not only my heart but every vein in my body was moving to a kind of throbbing pain. I could even feel the blood in my legs as it went down the veins.

I began to sing. I finished the room in a blissful daze, and my mother, putting her head round the door, said, 'By, you are painting the clouds with sunshine and no mistake. I've never heard you sing like that for a long time.'

At half past six I was on the river bank. There had been no time stated but he was there waiting for me, just below our houses at the spot where I used to plodge. He came forward quickly with no sign of embarrassment, no gaucheness or buttoning of coat, no shuffling of feet or fumbling with words. We stood for a moment looking at each other as we had done that morning, then he asked softly, 'What's your name?'

'Christine,' I said, 'Christine Winter.'

'Christine,' he repeated. 'It suits you. Mine is Martin Fonyère.'

His name had a foreign sound and I could only describe it to myself as Fon-year.

'Where would you like to go ... Christine?' My name sounded like music coming from his mouth. It had never been spoken like that before.

'Along the river bank.'

'Well,' he smiled, 'that won't cost much. And I admire your choice, it's a lovely walk.'

My body shaking, my feet all sixes and sevens, I stumbled over a tuft of grass before I had gone half a dozen paces, and when his hand came out and steadied me I wondered what he must think of me not being able to keep my balance on level ground. Once I was steady he took his hand away and did not touch me again until we were crossing the stepping stones, when his hand came naturally to my elbow as he guided me down on to the first stone. Then he took my hand and helped me over as if I had never crossed them before, and when we reached the other side I longed intensely for his fingers to remain on mine. But he released his hold and we walked side by side but not close.

By the time we reached the big bend not only my heart but all that was me was entirely lost to this creature, this wonderful creature. He was not a boy like either Don or our Ronnie, yet he was not much older, perhaps twenty. But in his talk he appeared more of a man than even my dad did.

Father Ellis was the only educated man I had ever talked to, but Father Ellis's fluency of speech and charm of manner were as candlelight to the sun when compared to – to Martin's. I found his name dancing through my head, shutting out even the remarks he was making.

We were standing on the bank looking up at the gardens of Brampton Hill when his voice recalled me sharply to him. He was laughing as he said, 'What are you dreaming about?'

I wanted to say, 'You and your name,' but I only looked at him and returned his laugh.

'Do you often dream?'

Again I wanted to say, 'I always dream when I'm happy,' but what I said was, 'I haven't much time to dream.'

'Tell me about yourself.'

It came so easy for me to tell him, not about myself, for there was nothing to tell, but about my mother and Dad and our Ronnie. I did not mention the Dowlings. When I finished he did not make any comment, nor did he tell me about his life, only that he was staying with friends on Brampton Hill and that he had just finished at Oxford.

The long twilight came and the mist floated around us as

we walked back in the gathering dust, and I cannot remember what we talked about, but when we reached the bank below the houses he caught hold of my hand and said urgently and in a different tone from that which he had used all evening, for now it was so intimate it caught at my breath and held it, 'Don't go yet, Christine.' Our faces were close, our eyes drawing something trembling from the other's. I swallowed deeply and murmured, 'I . . . I can't. I must go, they'll be waiting for me. My brother may come down to look for me.'

His grip on my hand tightened and he asked, 'When can I see you again?'

'Tomorrow,' I whispered. 'I could get out at six.'

At this he frowned slightly, then said, 'I'm committed for tomorrow evening, most of the time anyway.' Then pressing my hand even tighter he added, 'But I'll try to make it, although if I'm not here by seven o'clock don't wait. But I'll be here without fail on Sunday night, sixish. All right?'

Our faces remained stationary, then his eyes dropped to my lips and I felt a heat passing over my body.

'I . . . I must go.'

'Good night, Christine.'

As I backed away from him he still held on to my hand.

'Good night, Martin,' I whispered. Then with a little tug I released myself and, forgetting to be sedate, I ran up the hill, and I had to resist the temptation of flinging my arms around myself and leaping into the air for the old ecstatic feeling was in me as never before.

As I came to the corner of the street I ran into Sam and something in his eyes brought me to a halt. 'What is it, Sam?' I asked, smiling my happiness down on him. He dropped his head and moved his toe in the dirt of the road, before he asked, 'Who's the lad, Christine?'

My heart missed a beat, and in the space there rushed in thoughts of our Ronnie and Don, and just for a second I was filled with dread; I remembered Ted Farrel.

I bent towards him and pleaded, 'Sam, don't say anything, will you, not about me being up the river with anyone?'

He lifted his eyes to mine and said, 'No, Christine, I won't say anything.'

'Promise?'

'Aye, of course I do.'

I touched his hair lightly with my hand before going on up
the street and into the house singing not, 'I'm Painting the
Clouds with Sunshine' ... but, 'Oh! tomorrow, tomorrow,
tomorrow; oh! Martin, Martin, Martin.'

Saturday started hot. By noon the heat was almost unbearable, everybody was saying it was the worst yet, as if the heat
was a form of epidemic.

I was preparing a salad when Don came into the scullery.
He was all dressed up and he said in a quiet, even nice voice,
'Will you come for a run to Whitley Bay the night?'

'Thanks, Don,' I answered quite pleasantly, 'but I can't
leave me mam.'

His face darkened just the slightest and he said, 'What, not
for an hour? I'll ask her.'

'No.' I put my hand on his sleeve, and the pleasantness went
out of my voice now as I stated flatly but firmly, 'It wouldn't
be any use, I wouldn't go anyway.'

His whole attitude changed in a flash and he stood looking
at me and grinding his teeth together until I heard the crunch-
ing. Then he growled, 'You won't have the decent way, will
you? You always make me get on the raw, don't you? It seems
to give you a kick.'

'Don't be silly,' I said.

'Silly, am I?'

'Yes, of course you are. I don't know what you mean ...
on the raw.'

'You don't, eh? You're so innocent. Well, you will some
day, and that's a promise.'

The door slammed and for once his threats did not leave
me trembling and apprehensive.

Nothing could touch me today, no fear of Don Dowling
or our Ronnie or anybody in the world. I bent down and
rolled Stinker on to his back where he was sitting near the
wash-house pot. We had a secret, Stinker and I, for last night
I had smuggled him upstairs after Mam went to bed. I did
not dare transcribe my need of him into thoughts, but deep
down I knew I wanted to hold something.

Stinker lay in ecstatic calmness as I scratched his tummy,
and my mother, coming into the kitchen, said, 'You'll have

that beast as daft as yourself afore you're done.' She laughed, then asked soberly, 'What was he after?'

I went on scratching Stinker as I said offhandedly, 'Oh, the usual.'

'He never gives in,' said my mother. And she added, 'That frightens me.'

It usually frightened me, too, but today, like Stinker, I was experiencing ecstasy; it was an armour surrounding me.

Across the dinner table our Ronnie said, 'I'm going to Windy Nook to see a cricket match, you comin'?'

'No thanks,' I said; 'it's too hot to sit out all that time.'

I saw a shadow pass over his face, and he did not take his eyes off me as he added, 'You can sit in the shade.'

'I don't feel like it. I'm a bit tired and I've had enough of the heat without sitting out in it, shade or not.'

After he had left the house, stamping out without saying good-bye to anyone, Dad exclaimed, 'I don't know what's come over that lad lately. He never used to be short-tempered. It's all these fandangle books he reads, stuffing his head with things he can't understand. He'll find he's got enough to face in life without piling on the agony. But he can only live and learn like the rest of us.'

Around the middle of the afternoon the heat became unbearable, and it being Saturday and the house all cleaned and nothing more to do in the way of work except meals until Monday morning, my mother said she was going to have a lie down. And she added, 'Why don't you put yourself on the bed for half an hour and open a window wide. It'll be as cool up there as anywhere.'

I was sixteen and joy was throbbing in me and my mother was telling me to lie down – only women who were worn out with families and grinding housework ever went to lie down in the afternoon. When Mam saw the look on my face she gave a little laugh and said, 'Well, lass, you look so white and peaky. But no, I don't suppose you want to lie down.' Then, as if to afford me some pleasure, she ended, 'After tea we'll have a bath. We needn't put the pot on, just a few kettles. We'll have it afore Ronnie gets back.'

I made no comment. After tea I was going to the river.

When she had gone into the front room I did go upstairs. I stood by the window and looked down on the silver thread of water twisting its way through the valley bottom. In just over three hours I would be on its bank with Martin – that's if he could get away. Oh, he must get away, he must. If I did not see him tonight I would die. I could not wait another day before seeing him. I put my arms round myself and hugged my joy and trepidation to me.

At six o'clock I was ready. I had changed all my clothes and was wearing a blue cotton dress with a square neckline, and on my face I had rubbed, for the first time, some cream from one of the jars in the dressing-case. The irony of using Don's 'sprat to catch a mackerel' to beautify myself for another boy did not strike me at the time. I only knew I wanted to smell nice. And I had tied my hair back with a ribbon, and now I was ready.

I was going for a walk, I told my mother. She nodded, and as I went to go out she said, 'And what is that nice smell you've got on you?'

'It's soap,' I lied, 'one of the tablets I got for Christmas.'

The heat had not lifted, and in the short time it took me to get to the river bank I felt sticky all over. He wasn't there. Well, it wasn't anywhere near seven o'clock yet. I'd walk a little way along the bank but keep myself in view from this spot. My heart was beating wildly, and at the same time I felt sick with apprehension in case he should not come.

I lost count of the times I walked that particular stretch of bank; and when the market clock struck seven I could actually have vomited in the river. There was still tomorrow night, I consoled myself, but tomorrow night was as years away – there was all tonight to get through. And tomorrow night the bank would be lined with couples; it always was on Sunday nights. Saturday night it was rarely you saw one couple or even a man fishing. Saturday night in Fellburn was picture night, or dance night, and the men who fished during the week usully went to the bars on a Saturday night; it was also a general club night. Tonight we would have had the river to ourselves, the world to ourselves. I wanted to see no one and hear no one but him, and he had not come.

I walked slowly up to the stepping stones, across them, and in a sauntering gait made my way to the big bend. By the time I reached it my hair was damp on my forehead, there were beads of moisture round my lips and my dress was sticking to my shoulder blades.

I sat down on the bank and looked at the water and there came over me a longing to drop into its inviting coolness, and this thought brought a faint resentment against my mother. Why had she not let me learn to swim? If I could swim I wouldn't have this sticky, awful feeling now. Then I chided myself strongly for daring to feel like this about Mam, Mam who was so good, so kind, so wonderful to me. I knew the reason now why she hadn't let me learn to swim, and knowing Don Dowling I should be grateful to her, and knowing our Ronnie, too, I should be grateful to her, although she knew nothing about that.

My eyes were drawn swiftly up from the water by the sound of laughter coming from a garden on top of the Hill. There was no one to be seen but I knew there were several people in that garden and I began to wonder what they were doing. Was he there? Was he laughing? I got to my feet and began the long walk home.

I passed one couple, they were sitting on the river bank and the boy was taking the girl's shoes off – they were going to plodge. This sight hurt me so much that I could have cried, and I had to tell myself not to be silly. What was wrong with me anyway? There was no answer to this.

As I came nearer home I was loath for my walk to come to an end. If I went into the house and he should come after all and not find me? The thought was agony. Then I came opposite the place where the lads used to bathe. There were the bushes where they had hung their clothes and the well-worn path they had made leading down to the river. On this side of the river there was also a wide clump of bush, but the river path skirted this. But now I noticed for the first time another path that went through the thicket and down to the water's edge, likely a fishermen's path, and just to give myself something to do to lengthen the walk I took this path. Within a few steps the walls of the shrubbery widened to form a small clearing with a number of grassy hillocks with the grass well worn in parts, and I guessed, with a blush at the thought, that this was where the courting couples came. They would be screened from both the river and the other pathway here.

The river seemed very low at this point, for below the bank there was about six feet of its bed showing in sand and gravel. It looked like a little beach and so inviting. Within a second I had slipped over the bank and was sitting on it. Here, much nearer to the water, the thought came again, Oh, if I could only swim. I imagined what it would be like to feel the water flowing over my body. Well I couldn't swim, but there was nothing to stop me plodging. This at the moment seemed a poor substitute, just something that bairns did and, at my age, something to be spurned, but, nevertheless, I took off my stockings and shoes and, lifting up my dress well above my knees, I walked slowly into the water. It was cool, smooth and soothing, and I went back and forward kicking my feet gently. It came just below my calves and the longing for the feel of it about my legs became so insistent that I was drawn further in. But I had no intention of going actually near the middle for that was where the deep part was. When the water was well above my knees the bottom was still visible, so I tucked my dress a bit further up and cautiously moved forward, making sure with each step that I could still see where I was going. When the water had almost reached my tucked-in dress, the bottom disappeared and I came to a sharp halt. There, with my feet on it, was the browny, golden washed shelf of rock on which I was standing, then, as if it had been sliced by a sharp knife, it ended abruptly and the water beyond looked black and forbidding. This was the deep part.

One minute I was looking down into it and the next my head was jerked upwards and joy raced through me as I heard a voice calling, 'Ooh . . . ooh! there.' He wasn't hailing me from the river bank but from half-way up the fell beyond. He must have come by the short cut over Top Fell. He had stopped and was waving, not with one hand but with two, and I answered in the same way. Throwing up my arms high above my head I waved them. I had forgotten for the moment where I was and in my joyous excitement I stepped forward. It seemed as if I jumped into the water feet first, and I heard myself screaming as I jumped. The water closed over my head and I sank swiftly into a cool green light, and I was swallowing this light in great gulps and it was choking me. My feet touched something hard which acted like a spring-board and I felt myself rising, and when my head broke through the surface after what seemed endless terrifying seconds, my arms and legs began to thrash wildly, and I spluttered and screamed before I went down again. Then once again I came up through the green lighted water, and now my panic told me that if I once more sank into that greenness it would be for good. And I did, but there was someone with me this time, holding me, pushing me, dragging me, turning me about. Never in my life had surprise been greater than when I found myself moving backwards through the water looking up at the sky. And when I was lying on my back on the little beach that I had left only minutes before, and bending over me was Martin, his hair flat on his head, his breath coming in great gasps and the water running down his bare body. Then the sky was blotted out and a blackness came over me and the next thing I remember was being on my face and water spurting from my mouth, and I was sick and Martin was holding my head. I felt humiliated and ashamed beyond all comprehension – that I should be sick in front of him.

'God, you gave me a fright. What made you go in when you can't swim?'

I wiped my mouth on the skirt of my sodden dress and shook my head slowly.

'How do you feel?'

'All right.'

He turned my face towards him and, looking into it, said, 'You don't look it. Turn round and lie still.'

I did as he bade me and as I turned over I noticed he was wearing bathing trunks. Before I could turn my glance away from them he touched his thigh and remarked casually, 'I was reckoning on having a dip later, but had to take it sooner than I anticipated.' He gave me a little smile, then added, 'I'm going across the river for my clothes. I won't be long. Lie still.'

I watched him walk into the water and with an effortless movement lie upon it, and in a moment or so he was rising out of it and going up the far bank. I saw him bundle his clothes together and tie them on his head with his belt. If I had not felt so limp and shaken I would have laughed at the sight of him swimming towards me.

When he came out of the water I pulled myself up into a

sitting position and watched him loosen his clothes and lay them on the bank. It was at this moment that a great shiver ran through my body and it brought him to my side.

'You're cold,' he said.

I shook my head.

'It's the shock. Look, take off that dress, it will dry on the bushes in no time, and put my coat round you.'

'Oh, no, no.'

He had made this preposterous suggestion so casually that my protest sounded silly even to myself, but even so I said I had better go home and get changed. He dropped on his knees at my side and his eyes compelled mine to look into them as he said softly, 'Don't go home, Christine. Take my coat. Go behind the bushes and take off your dress. It will dry in the sun in ten minutes, but you mustn't let it dry on you, you'll likely catch a chill that way.'

Without uttering one more word of protest I took his coat, and with his assistance climbed up the bank and went behind the bushes into the little clearing, and there, with a feeling that I was committing a great sin, I took off my dress and quickly slipped my arms into his coat, and not only buttoned it up but turned the collar up over my neck. Then in a small voice I said, 'Will you hang it up for me?'

He put his head over the bank and stretched out his hand and I handed him the dress. I was afraid to stand up, so I tucked my feet under the coat and clasped my knees with my hands. And when he said, 'Can I come up?' I answered, in a voice hardly above a whisper, 'Yes.'

He sat on the grass but not near me, and although I did not look at him I knew he was wearing his shirt. I began to part my hair with my fingers and wring the water from it, bending forward as I did this so that it would not wet his coat more than it had already done.

'Let me.' Although he was shy in the request his tone and manner took away from the proceedings any awkwardness that I might have felt. When he whipped off his shirt and began to dry my hair with it I wanted to make a protest, saying, 'Oh, it'll get wet,' but I didn't. I sat quiet as his hands rubbed my head gently back and forth. He was kneeling at my back and I could feel the warmth of his bare legs through the coat. The feeling of fright and exhaustion was passing and I was becoming consumed with a feeling of wonder, and I was aware for the first time that this feeling was wonder. I had experienced it in minute doses before: on that morning when I had taken my mother to see the first anemones in the wood, and the time I watched the sticky buds of the chestnut opening; and there was another time when, after having received communion, I had felt for one fleeting second that I held God within me. But these occasions had just been minute particles of a whole, and this was the whole. My body was warmed with it, glowing with it, and my heart was ready to burst with it, when he pulled my head back against him and, bending above me, looked down into my eyes. And I looked up into his. With a quick movement he was kneeling in front of me, his arms were about me and we were breathing into each other's faces. For one long second he held my look, then his lips were on mine, and the wonder burst from my heart. For the second time that evening I almost sank into oblivion, and for the second time I became afraid. For I was being kissed, really kissed, for the first time in my life, and I had no experience with which to judge the intensity of it. But I knew that I was a little frightened. With an effort I eased myself away, and once again we were looking at each other. And then he laughed, and, taking my hands in his, he pressed them to his chest and said, over and over again, 'Christine . . . Christine . . . Christine.' I found his voice as intoxicating as his kiss. Like a runner pausing for breath, he gasped as he flung himself down, and I was relieved for the moment of the bewitchment of his countenance as he pressed his face into my side.

'You know the first time I saw you?' His voice was muffled.

I nodded as I said, 'Yes, near the bridge.'

'You were with two friends, and I thought if ever I'd seen beauty and the beasts, this was it. You looked like something from another world, and I fell for you in that second. It was the last day of the Easter vac, and I cursed myself for having to go back. By the way, who were those two?'

My mouth was smiling as I said, 'My brother Ronnie, and Don Dowling. He lives next door.'

'Which was the big one? Your brother?'

'No, the other one.'

'I'm glad of that anyway. I hated them both on sight.' He

pressed my arm to him. 'But the big fellow, I remember, looked as if he would like to murder me.'

I found I was able to laugh at this, and I said, 'He likely did.'

He pulled my face round to him and demanded hotly, 'He wants you?' Then before I could make any answer, he said, 'Of course he does, he'd be a fool if he didn't. Do you know how beautiful you are, Christine?'

The reply on my lips was the usual one that I would give to any lad that had made such a statement, 'Don't be so silly,' but I never said it. I accepted the tribute gladly and smiled my thanks. I think, for the first time in my life, I was happy with what I was. Happy isn't the right word, in that moment of delight I was grateful for my face.

I still had my legs tucked up under the coat, and I was feeling stiff, and when I made a movement to ease the strain, he said, 'Stretch your legs out;' then laughed, 'I've seen legs before, you know.'

He made things so easy and natural, but still I found it embarrassing to look down the length of my bare legs. They looked very white and shocked me somewhat, and this set my thoughts working. But although I was conscious of what they were saying I would not allow them to enter into this paradise. Most firmly I kept at bay thoughts of the occupants in the house at the top of the hill across the river. Yet I could not keep out fear. But it was a sweet fear. . . . I didn't want him to kiss me again for a little while, so I began to talk.

All kinds of things were happening to me for the first time tonight. I had Ronnie's urge to talk, and strangely enough I found myself talking about him. But not so strangely, for there was a desire in me to impress Martin in some other way than with my looks, and to talk of our Ronnie was the only way I could do it, for there was no topic I could discuss except cooking and housework for I couldn't talk about the wood or the river. These were my feelings and I had not the power of words with which to translate them.

But what did my talking result in? Only a slight feeling of pique when I realized Martin was amused by what I was saying. And when he said, 'And what books does Ronnie read?' I couldn't think of one title. Then to my aid came the incident of the day when he had answered the priest, and I said, with an assumed casualness, 'Oh, well, books like "Martin Luther".'

Instantly, I saw that he was impressed, and for the first time his tone held a note that was not nice, there was something, was it condescension as he said, 'Well, well, so we've got traitors among us. Your brother is a boy after my own heart.'

'Father Ellis didn't think so,' I laughed.

'You're a Catholic, Christine?'

I nodded.

'And your brother reads Martin Luther? I can see why the priest didn't like it.' He seemed amused.

'Are you a Catholic?' I asked shyly.

His head went back and he laughed, 'Good Lord, no!' Then he said softly, 'Oh, I'm sorry, Christine, I didn't mean it like that. I'm nothing. I'm searching, like your brother's doing. He must be if he's reading Luther.'

His mood changed and he exclaimed, 'Luther! A summer night like this, the most beautiful girl in the world – and you are you know – a flowing river, and here we are talking about Luther. . . . Let me look at you.' He pulled me round to face him. 'I want to look at your face, all the time, forever. You're like a star on a dung heap.'

As his eyes washed my face and his fingers outlined the curve of my mouth, I felt I was going to sink into the glory of oblivion – or was it of living – yet at the same time a pocket in my mind, the pocket that was holding thoughts of my mother and Dad and our Ronnie, was now urging me to get up and get my dress and go home. So much did my thoughts clamour that they burst their confines and I heard myself whisper, 'Will you see if my dress is dry?'

He gave a deep, soft laugh, then said, 'All right,' and springing up he went to the bushes. I saw him lift my dress in his hands, and then he called, 'It's slightly damp on the other side, I'll turn it over.' In a second he was at my side again. 'Look at me,' he said, and when I did so he added, 'I don't want to take my eyes off you.'

There followed a pause, during which I became filled with awe. That I, Christine Winter, could find such favour in the eyes of this god, this god from another planet.

'It's going to be a long, beautiful summer, Christine.'

I, too felt it was going to be a long, beautiful summer, and when his arms went about me I made no protest, but just leant against him. I had no urge now as I had a little while ago to ask questions: where did he live when he wasn't visiting on Brampton Hill, or at Oxford? Or where he was going when he left Brampton Hill? Or whether now he had found me he would stay on Brampton Hill? I had no desire to have an answer to any of these questions, for he had said, 'It's going to be a long, beautiful summer.'

The twilight was deepening, and soon it would be dusk and I must be home before dark, and I hated the thought of leaving this spot, of ever moving out of the circle of his arms. It did not seem the slightest bit out of place that he was wearing only bathing trunks, for I was used to the sight of our Ronnie and Don and Sam in bathing trunks. What I wasn't used to was the sight of my own bare legs against theirs, yet now, as I looked down towards my feet, I felt not the slightest embarrassment, only an intense joy at the contact of Martin's instep across my foot.

Then I could no longer look down at my feet, for he had turned my face towards him again and was holding me close, and there descended on my mind and body and all the world a stillness, and within the stillness I lay awake. What followed was inevitable, nothing could have stopped it, for I had no strength within myself to combat such a force, my religion and upbringing were as useless as if they had never existed. I was sent soaring into the heavens, higher than any bird, and when I floated down to earth again I was crying. Unrestrainedly and helplessly, I was crying. My arms, bare now, were about his neck, and I sobbed out this bewilderment of feeling. Then as quickly as my crying had begun it stopped, and I wanted to laugh. I made a small sound like a laugh, and it broke on a hiccup, and in a moment we were both laughing into each other's necks. I wanted to laugh louder and louder. I felt bodyless, there was nothing left of me but laughter. And this told me I was gloriously, ecstatically, blissfully happy. I was drunk with the wine of creation, oblivious for the moment to everything but bliss. And then the heavens opened and God spoke.

'CHRISTINE!'

My name thundered over me, and went rolling along the

river, and instinctively I broke away from Martin's arms and buried my face in the earth.

'CHRISTINE, GET UP!'

I shuddered and trembled and raised myself a little way on my hands, and from under my lids I saw Martin's feet turn swiftly towards the edge of the bank, then drop to the beach where his clothes were.

I put one hand and groped wildly for the coat, but could feel nothing. Then my dress descended on me, and Father Ellis's voice cried, 'Cover yourself, girl! Before God, I cannot believe it's you!'

In a mad frenzy of fear now, I pulled the dress over my head, but I still remained kneeling on the ground, terrified to get to my feet. Father Ellis's black-clothed legs were before me, the high polish on his black boots seemed to pierce the dusk. Then they turned from me and moved towards the edge of the bank, and his voice, rasping out in command, cried, 'Come here, you!'

Ironically now I was praying. Oh, Blessed Virgin Mary, don't let him say anything to Martin. Please! Please! don't let him. Then his voice cut through my agonized praying mind, yelling, 'Come here! Come here, I say.'

I raised my eyes and saw Father Ellis jumping down the bank. Then on the dull sound of pounding feet I staggered up and, going to the edge, I saw something that stripped the night of wonder and brought my god low, for Martin was running along the bank in great leaping strides and, almost as swiftly, Father Ellis was after him. But I was praying again, 'Don't let him catch him! don't let him catch him!' for I couldn't bear that Martin should suffer the indignity of being dragged back here by Father Ellis, not that he would allow himself to be dragged anywhere. I had a terrifying picture of him striking out at the priest.

Lowering myself quickly down the bank, I got into my shoes and stockings, and when I again stood up it was to see Father Ellis coming towards me – alone.

I have not the power of words with which to describe the mixture of feelings that were raging through me as I stood with my head bowed waiting for the priest's approach. I only knew that they centred around a great humiliation, and I wanted to die, to drop down dead on the spot.

I was looking down once more on to the shiny black boots, but they were some distance from me, and the distance the priest had left between us spoke to me of my degradation in his eyes more plainly than his words had done. The seconds ticked by and he did not speak, and I found myself swaying as if I was going to faint. And when he muttered in a strange voice, 'I just can't believe it. You . . . you, Christine. . . . How long has this been going on? Answer me!' The last words were said in a tone he had never used to me before, more like a bark, and I muttered, 'Just tonight, Father.'

'How long have you known him?'

How long had I known him? All my life, from the minute I started breathing he had been there. This wonderful, pale-faced, beautiful-voiced god. But could I answer now, 'Two nights,' or 'a week,' or 'since just after Easter'?

'Answer me.'

'Just . . . just a short time, Father.'

'How short?'

I couldn't bring myself to say 'Two nights', for it now seemed an impossibility that there had been so much love crammed into two nights, so I muttered, 'A week.'

'God! God!' The priest's exclamation sounded like deep swearing, and my shoulders sank down, dragging my head with them.

'What's his name?'

I paused, trying to gain the strength to refuse to answer, but it was useless. 'Martin Fonyère, Father.'

'Where does he live?'

'On . . . on Brampton Hill.'

'There are lots of people living on Brampton Hill, I want his address.'

My body seemed almost bent in two, so deep was my shame.

'Do you hear, Christine?'

'I – I don't know, Father.'

He did not speak again for some minutes, but I could hear his breathing, quick and hissing in the quiet around us. Then he said abruptly, 'Come along home.'

My body jerked up straight, and my eyes seemed to jump from my head to his grey face, and I repeated, 'Home, Father?' Then I gabbled, 'You won't tell me mam?'

'She must be told. Have you thought of the consequences of this night's escapade?'

'But, Father—' I had stepped towards him – 'you can't tell me mam, she's bad . . . ill, you know she is, and she doesn't know anything about . . .'

'All the more reason why she must be told.' His voice was cold now, dead sounding, without feeling.

'No, Father, no! . . . Please! please! Oh, don't tell me mam, please!' In desperation, I flung myself on the ground at his feet and grabbed hold of his trouser leg, and as I touched it, I felt his flesh recoiling from my hand as if it had been stung, and his voice was loud and angry once more as he cried, 'Get up!'

'No, Father, no! I won't move from here, I won't! You can't tell her. I'll drown meself, I will! I will! You can't tell her!'

'Leave go!' He put down his hand to remove my fingers, but before it touched me, he quickly drew it away again, and with a tug from his leg he freed himself. Then again standing some distance from me, he said, 'All right, I promise I won't tell her, but on one condition.'

I raised my tear-misted eyes to his now unfamiliar face, and then he said, 'You will never see that man again.'

My stomach retched, my heart seemed to turn over. Never to see Martin again, never to hear his voice. I couldn't, I couldn't promise, not at this moment I couldn't. A little earlier as I had watched him fleeing before the priest, in that brief moment perhaps I could have promised, but I couldn't now, and I said, 'I can't, Father, I can't.'

'Very well then, come home.'

When I got to my feet, my body seemed dragged down, as if I was carrying a bucket of coal in each hand, and my legs would not obey me and walk. I felt myself swaying and I muttered, 'I – I feel faint, Father.' As I felt myself falling, I sunk down to the ground but willed myself not to faint, and in a few minutes I got to my feet again.

I kept my eyes turned from the priest and made to walk on when his voice stopped me.

'Go home,' he said, 'I won't tell your mother anything yet. I don't believe you don't know where this man lives, but I'll find him quite easily, I have ways and means, and he must marry you right away.'

At this I turned wide, startled eyes on to his face, but found I couldn't say anything, not a word, for to my amazement I saw through the fading light that Father Ellis was crying, and at the sight a sorrow pierced me very like the day I had seen the rabbit nailed to the tree. Flinging myself about I ran stumbling and sobbing along the bank, and when I crossed the stones it was to meet our Ronnie. He pulled me to a stop and stared at me before exclaiming angrily, 'Where d'you think you've been to at this time of night? Mam's worried stiff.' Then looking me up and down he added, 'Good Lord! what's happened to you?'

My sorrow broke loose and burying my face in my hands, I cried and spluttered, 'I – I fell in the river – and – waited until – until my clothes dried.'

'Aw, never mind.' His voice was soft, softer than it had been for a long time. 'Come on,' he said. The instant I felt his arms going round me, I tore myself away from him like a mad thing, and, running as if my very life depended on it, I made for home.

CHAPTER FOUR

My mother said, 'You're ill, girl, you must see the doctor. That tumble into the river frightened you, and this is the after-effects. You look like a ghost.'

'I'm all right,' I said.

'But you're not, lass. You look like death, and you're not yourself in any way, and you're not going to go walking by that river by yourself at night again.'

'Oh, Mam!' I exclaimed hurriedly, 'I like walking by the river.'

'Well, then, you'll let Ronnie go with you.'

'No!' The tone even startled myself, and, coming to me, she looked into my face and said, 'What is it, lass? I've never known you to be like this. You're not frightened of all this war talk, are you?'

War talk. What did the war talk matter to me, with my own war raging inside me?

'War talk?' I said. 'No, of course not.'

I mustn't have sounded very convincing, for she added, comfortingly, 'There won't be any gas in this war, that's if it comes, and God knows it looks very much like it. They saw what gas did in the last one. They've learnt something, they won't act like mad animals again. Although that Hitler seems like a maniac.'

War, war, digging trenches and air-raid shelters and getting fitted for gasmasks, in their silly little boxes, and people storing in food, buying up everything they could, and men in different trades being stood off because they couldn't get the material with which to carry on their jobs. Everybody waiting for the war to start. Our Ronnie saying he was going to join up and looking at me as he said it. Don Dowling saying they wouldn't get him. Anyway, pitmen were exempt if they worked at the coal face. Then yesterday my mother sending me with her wedding-ring down to the pawnshop in Bog's End to get a little extra money to buy tin stuff to store away . . . just in case, as she said. Then going to Woolworths and buying her a ring there. This all unknown to Dad, for she said he wouldn't have stood for it. Her little duplicity pleased her, I saw, yet I could take no part in it. I could take no part in anything that went on in the house or outside, for I was dead.

I had gone down to the river bank on the Sunday night and walked and walked its length between the stepping stones and the big bend several times, but he hadn't come. There had been another couple lying in the green hollow, surrounded by the bushes, and our Ronnie had come looking for me again and demanded roughly, 'What you doing prowling the bank? You after a lad?'

He had gripped my arm and I had wrenched it angrily away from him, crying, 'And if I was it's none of your business!' And he, like Father Ellis, had looked amazed for a moment, before saying, 'Well, I thought you could have got one without going on the prowl.' As I have said the river bank was given over to the courting couples on a Sunday night and to groups of lads and lasses out for the sole purpose of clicking. But as we neared the house his tone had become solicitous and he inquired softly, 'What is it, Christine? There is something up with you. Can't you talk to me about it?' It was the only time during the past week that I was tempted to laugh.

Every night I went to the river, and if I had to go into the town during the day I made my way round to the better-class shopping centre at the foot of Brampton Hill, my eyes searching all the while.

The following Saturday night I stood in a warm drizzling rain looking up at the gardens on the hill across from the big bend and praying, 'Oh, Martin, Martin, please come. I'll die if I don't see you. I will, I will. Oh, Martin, Martin! Please God make him come. Oh, Holy Mother, answer my prayer.' Yet as I prayed I knew he wouldn't come. But even with this knowledge deep inside me, I kept asking, 'Why? Why?' He surely must come if only because of the fact that I needed him and wanted to see him, to hear him, to be pressed close to him and feel his eyes moving over my face, feel his look burying itself in me. And then there was this frightening urge of my body that I had to fight each night. ... Oh, Martin! Martin!

As I turned homewards I saw through the drizzle a figure coming along the river bank, but there was no leaping of my heart and I didn't think, 'That's Martin', I knew who it was. The black felt hat, the black mackintosh, the black trousers and the black boots. When Father Ellis stood in front of me I did not lower my head this time, I kept it level, but I turned my gaze away and looked over the river.

'Well, Christine?' His voice was one that I recognized. There was the old kindliness in it. I did not say, 'Hallo, Father,' I made no remark whatever, yet I was glad to see him and I longed for him to speak, for when he did he would give me some news of Martin. Perhaps he would say he had refused to marry me. And would it be any wonder? All beauty, all magic stripped from our lives by a compulsory order to marry.

I walked on and the priest turned and walked by my side. We had gone a considerable distance before he spoke, and then it seemed it was with an effort that he asked, 'Have you seen that man again, Christine?'

'No, Father.'

'Were you speaking the truth when you said you didn't know where he lived?'

'Yes, Father.'

'I made a boast last Saturday night that I'd find him. Well, I haven't been able to. Apparently there is no one of that name living on Brampton Hill, even visiting there.'

The leaping of my heart, the turning of my stomach, brought me round and I gazed on him and protested, 'But he does live there, in one of the houses that have the gardens backing on to the river.'

'You mean Fell Close or The Rise, and round about there? I have access into most of those houses, he doesn't live there. What is more I would recognize him again in a moment.' He was standing looking down on me now, compassion in his face, and he asked, 'Oh, what have you done, Christine? Let's hope God is merciful to you.'

I pressed my hand over my mouth and cried, 'Oh, don't start on me, Father, not again.'

'All right, all right. But I want you to promise me something, Christine.'

I stumbled on, taking no heed until he said, 'I want you to promise to come to mass every morning for the next three months.'

My eyes looked vacantly ahead as I muttered, 'I can't get every morning, Father; there's too much to see to in the house.'

'Well, when you can.'

He crossed the stones with me, and as we reached the bottom of the river bank, below our houses, Ronnie came down the hill and Sam with him. Before they reached us the priest had left me without even a word of good-bye. But he waved his hand to them and they waved back.

When they came up to me, Ronnie remarked, 'He's in a hurry the night.' Then taking my arm, he said, 'You come on up home and get to bed, you look as if you are in for something. You're mad, out in this drizzle.'

I said nothing but let him lead me up the hill. Sam, on my other side, said, 'I've made you another plaque with your surname on it, Christine,' and before we reached our door and I fainted, I remember thinking, 'Kind Sam, nice Sam.'

'But I assure you, Mrs. Winter, she is pregnant.'

'But . . . but, doctor, she can't be!'

'I understand it must be very difficult for you to take it in, but I assure you that that is her condition.'

I stood in the little room off the surgery getting into my clothes. My hands were shaking so that I couldn't fasten them up. Then for almost the sixth time since the doctor had joined my mother, I heard her explain, in high amazement, 'But, doctor!' Then, her voice in a terrible whisper, she exclaimed, 'But how can she, she never goes out with anyone, she's never been with anyone?'

The buttons were slipping away from my fingers as if possessed of a life of their own, and there was a pause before the doctor spoke again. 'She has had intercourse, Mrs. Winter.'

Every organ in my body was shaking with terror, and as automatically I smoothed the front of my dress over my stomach, my fingers drew sharply away from contact with it. Inside there was something vile and awful, a thing that was bringing horror into my mother's voice. I pushed myself towards the door, and when I entered the surgery, my mother stared at me as if she had never seen me before, and I noticed her reactions were similar to those of Father Ellis. She kept her distance, she even stepped back from me. When the doctor opened the door and we had passed out she still did not come near me, and we walked all the way home separated by an arm's length. And she uttered not a word until she got into the kitchen. Then sitting down in a chair by the table, she dropped her head on to her hands and burst into passionate weeping. Helplessly, I stood watching her, the tears raining down my face. And as I stood like this the back door opened and my dad came in from the allotment, accompanied by Ronnie, who was on back shift. The sound of their entry aroused me from my stupor, and I made to go upstairs when my mother, without looking at me, put out her hand and said, 'You stay here.'

Immediately on entering the kitchen Dad exclaimed, 'What's up?' Then going to my mother he asked anxiously, 'What is it, Annie? What's happened?' He looked from one to the other, and my mother, drawing herself up by the aid of the table, said, 'You'd better know sooner or later. There's a reason for her sickness these weeks, she's going to have a bairn.'

'Bairn?' The look on Dad's face could have been comic. His lips were drawn back from his teeth and his eyes were lost behind the pushed up flesh on his cheeks. But Ronnie's look was not comic. The colour had fled from his fresh-coloured face and his eyes looked terrible, fearsome and full of loathing, and he yelled right out loud as if he was on the open hillside, 'No! God, no!' Dad came slowly to me and, taking my hand gently, said, 'Look at me, lass.'

And when I could not look at him he dropped my hand exclaiming, 'Christ Almighty!' And my mother repeated, 'Aye, Christ Almighty.' Then Dad, turning to me again, said sternly, 'Who's the fella?' But before waiting for my answer he swung round to my mother, crying as if I wasn't there, 'But I've never known her to go out with a lad.'

'No,' said my mother, in dead sounding tones, 'she's had

no need. You haven't far to seek. It's been coming for years. I've seen it coming for years and dreaded this moment.'

These words brought my head up and a wave of protest through my body and I cried, 'It wasn't him, not Don Dowling.'

'What!' My mother was staring at me. 'Then who was it?' The deadness had left her voice and now she looked angry, threateningly angry, as she demanded, 'Who was it? Where have you been?'

I cast my eyes towards our Ronnie, and Dad turned to him and said, 'Go on out.'

Ronnie went out, but he backed from the room and his eyes never left my face until he had passed through the door and into the scullery.

Dad now going to the scullery door pulled it shut, then he joined my mother and, side by side, they stood looking at me.

With my hands gripped tightly together and my eyes fixed on the floor, I said, 'It was a boy I got to know.' I did not wait for them to ask his name but continued, 'They called him Martin Fonyère, he lives on Brampton Hill.' I still did not believe what the priest had said that Martin did not live on the Hill.

'Then we must have a talk with him.'

I raised my eyes when Dad spoke, and what I saw on his face was too much for me, for there, untouched, was his love still shining but threaded now with pity and compassion. I turned slowly about and leaning against the wall I buried my face in the crook of my arm and sobbed helplessly. . . .

It was a week later and Martin Fonyère had become someone who had never existed, at least to my mother and Dad. My mother was becoming frantic to find him and make him marry me before the scandal became obvious, and at this moment she had just returned from Mrs. Durrant's. Mrs. Durrant had lived on the Hill for years and she knew nearly everybody of any importance there. My mother had confided the whole business to her and she had suggested that the most likely place to find this elusive fellow was The Grange, for a number of young men were staying there, and not to ask for an appointment but to take me and go boldly up there and ask for Colonel Findlay.

I cried and protested but I could do nothing to deter her, and so, standing in a flame of shame, I found myself on the wide steps of The Grange listening to my mother asking to speak to this Colonel Findlay.

The colonel was tall and thin and never stopped moving about as my mother spoke, and although he scared me with his blustering my mother remained unperturbed, answering him calmly, saying, 'I'm not accusing anyone, I'm just asking you if you have anyone staying here by the name of Martin Fonyère and could we please speak to him?'

'There's no Martin Fonyère here,' said the colonel. 'I have two nephews staying in the house at present and my two sons. There they are on the tennis court. Here.' He lifted a sharp finger and beckoned me to the window. 'Is the young man you are seeking among those?'

I looked out of the great window on to the tennis court and the four men jumping about. Not one of them was anything like Martin and I shook my head slowly, and without waiting I walked towards the door. The colonel was speaking again to my mother asking her who had told her to come here.

As I stood just within the door waiting for her I found myself looking at a picture on a side table. It showed a group of children, three boys and two girls; they were about fourteen years of age and were all sitting in a row on a balustrade and the second one from the end was Martin Fonyère. As clearly as one would recognize oneself in a mirror I knew it was he. The long, pale face, the brown hair, that penetrating, dark, intense look already in his eyes. It was Martin, and this was the house where he had stayed. What relation he was to the people here I did not know, but what I did know was that the Colonel had been aware of us even before he had seen us, and in a flash of insight I knew I had Father Ellis to thank for this. His diplomatic investigations had been broadcast to this house as a warning against coming trouble . . . Catholic priest trouble. Priests had the power to bring about unusual things, even the power to force a man from Brampton Hill to marry a girl from Fenwick Houses, or at least ensure her of support.

My mother's steps were behind me and I moved forward into the hall, and if I wanted any further proof that this was the house where Martin had lived I had it as I came face to face with a young woman. She was much older than me, perhaps twenty-two or three. She stared at me as if wanting to remember my face forever, and as I looked back at her I thought, 'You were likely his girl before he met me, and hope to be again.'

'Eileen!'

It was a sharp voice calling from the stairway and the girl slowly drew her eyes from me and walked away. Then the colonel opened the door and let us out, and my mother said, 'Thank you.' But he said nothing.

War was declared but it made no impact on our house, I had already dropped the bomb that had blown our peace to smithereens. My mother seemed to have thrown off her illness and become possessed of an energy that enabled her to search and inquire. And I did nothing to stop her, for I was numb inside and not caring what happened to myself or to anyone else. This feeling was dominant in me until the night our Ronnie spoke.

My mother had come in from one of her visits to Mrs. Durrant. I was upstairs at the time, but my door was open and I heard her remark, 'The earth couldn't have opened and swallowed him up, he must be somewhere. If he was in the town somebody must have remembered him.' And then I heard our Ronnie say, 'Perhaps he never was.'

'What do you mean?' said my mother.

'It's only somebody she's made up.'

'Oh, lad, I wish it was, how I wish to God it was. But she couldn't, she hasn't made up the bairn. And if it isn't Don, and she says it isn't, who could it be?'

'Have you ever thought of Father Ellis?'

My hands went to my mouth and almost stopped my breathing, then I was on the landing, down the stairs and in the kitchen before my mother had repeated for the second time an agonized 'No!' It was a high 'No!' like a wail, and as her voice drifted away I almost sprang on our Ronnie, crying, 'You! you devil you.' Then turning to Mam, I screamed, 'You can't believe him. It was Martin Fonyère. There is a Martin Fonyère.'

Our Ronnie's eyes were like slits and he was apparently unperturbed by my onslaught, but his voice was bitter as he brought out, 'What about the night I met you on the river bank with him, and he scuttled away? Shortly after that you were in this state, you passed out. Explain that.'

'You! you wicked devil. What if I tell Mam? What if I tell Mam?' I was spluttering in my rage, and as I spluttered a voice warned me to be quiet, warned me that my mother had enough on her plate without telling her this thing about our Ronnie that would surely drive her mad.

I swung round to her, crying, 'Mam, believe me, for God's sake believe me, there is a Martin Fonyère.'

'Well, it's a funny thing, lass, nobody has seen him but you.' My mother's voice was quiet and tired now, and at this moment I remembered Sam. 'Wait!' I cried. 'Wait a minute.' I dashed out through the scullery, down our backyard, into the backlane, up Aunt Phyllis's backyard and, bursting open her door, cried, 'Where's Sam, Aunt Phyllis?'

She was sitting at the table with Don, and they both rose to their feet together.

'What's up?' asked Don. I shook my head, still looking at Aunt Phyllis, and demanded, 'Where's Sam?'

'Upstairs.'

'Get him.' I had never spoken to her in this fashion in my life, but she seemed not to notice and called, 'Sam! You, Sam, come down here.'

Within a minute Sam was in the kitchen, and to his astonishment, and certainly to the bewilderment of Aunt Phyllis and even of Don, I grabbed his hand and ran him through the two backyards and into our kitchen.

Thrusting the bewildered boy in front of my mother, I almost glared at him as I said, 'Sam, tell Mam what I asked you to promise not to tell anybody.'

He turned startled eyes upon me and said below his breath, 'About – about the lad, Christine?' I nodded quickly.

Sam looked at my mother and said very slowly, 'I promised Christine not to let on that she was out with a lad, Aunt Annie.'

As if a great load had been lifted from my mother's back she sat down in her chair and pulled Sam towards her.

'You saw Christine with a lad, Sam?'

'Yes, Aunt Annie.'

'Can you tell me what he looked like?'

Sam glanced back at me and I said, 'Tell her, tell her everything, Sam.'

'Well,' Sam said, 'he was tallish like, Aunt Annie.'

'As tall as Ronnie?'

'No, taller, like our Don. But thin, he was very thin and he had brown hair.'

'Is there anything else you remember?'

'He wore nice clothes, Aunt Annie.'

'Where did you see him with Christine?'

'They were walking along the river bank.'

'When?'

'Oh, one night a few weeks ago, that time it was very hot.'

'Thanks, Sam,' said my mother, and when Sam turned from her I put out my hand and touched his shoulder. I was unable to speak but my eyes spoke my thanks. Then I turned on Ronnie and, looking him full in the face, I said, 'I'll never forgive you for this, not as long as I live.' I went upstairs again and threw myself on the bed and cried and sobbed until I couldn't breathe, and felt that I would choke to death. Then the door opened and my mother's arm came round me for the first time in weeks, and I turned and clung to her, crying, 'Oh! Mam, Mam, I'm sorry.'

As she patted my head she kept saying, 'There now, there now. Tell me all about it, how it happened.'

It was odd that she had never asked that in the first place. And so, sitting side by side on the bed, I told her everything, or nearly so, and we were near again. Then she said, 'Come on downstairs and we'll have a cup of tea.' And she pulled me up from the bed. But as we got to the door she stopped and, jerking her head towards the bedroom wall, she looked at me and stated, 'They've got to know sooner or later.'

My mother made it sooner, likely thinking to get it over and done with. It was the next afternoon that she told Aunt Phyllis. I did not know she was going to tell her then, and I was at the table rolling out some pastry when I heard the commotion. It was coming from Aunt Phyllis's yard, but the next minute when I glanced towards the window I saw Don come tearing up our yard, my mother after him, her hand outstretched as if trying to catch hold of him.

When he appeared at the kitchen door I was standing ready waiting, for in this moment I had no fear of him. Strangely,

I felt strong and fortified against him. The sight of me standing thus halted him, and my mother pressed by him and stood in between us. And her voice was loud as she cried, 'Now, Don Dowling, this is nothing to do with you.'

'No, begod! no. No, it isn't.' He turned on her with a terrible smile. 'No, you saw to that, you padded her all over, her bloody breasts and everything, in case anybody looked at her. You're to blame for this if the truth were told. You wouldn't let me have her. Oh, no. Oh, I knew what you thought, I wasn't good enough, and now some bugger has given her a bellyful and skedaddled. And in a way I could laugh, laugh like hell at you. . . .'

On my mother's cry of 'Get out!' he turned his face from her but did not move, and he looked at me. His eyes were hooded with a dark light, and from it I could feel pouring malevolence so powerful that I seemed to smell it, it was like a stench. And when I thought of this later I told myself it was my imagination and my inborn fear of him that had created this illusion, for whereas I had felt no fear of him while waiting for him to enter the kitchen, from the moment he spoke I began to tremble, so that my mother intervened again, crying, 'If you don't get out this minute I'll let you have this.' She swung round and grabbed the poker and advanced threateningly on him. One thrust from his great hand and she would have been on her back. But he did not lift his hand, he simply let his gaze linger on me for a moment longer, then said on a grating laugh, 'The town will be full of soldiers in a week or two, I'll tell them where they can be supplied.'

'You! . . . You! Get out!' My mother actually brought the poker down on him, but he side-stepped and thrust her aside as if she were the weight of a child. Then, turning on his heel, he went out.

Slowly my mother moved to the fireplace and put the poker back into the hearth. I sat down by the table and rested my head on the palm of my hand, and she came and stood beside me and in a trembling voice she said a comforting thing. 'Don't shake so, lass,' she said; 'he can do nothing to you now. You have taken it out of his power, and for that I could even say "thank God", for I'd rather see you in the pickle you're in than married to him.'

'The reactions to my condition were many and varied, and we had more visitors to the house in the next few weeks than we'd had in years, on one pretext or another. But it was my Aunt Phyllis's reactions that amazed me most. She was civil to me, even kind. And I worked it out that this attitude was due to her being relieved of her jealousy. No longer was I acceptable to Don; there was no danger now that at any moment I would take her son from her. But later I think she even wished he had got me, for he was creating a name for himself among the women in Bog's End that outdid that of the soldiers. He and I did not meet for some weeks, and so I did not know whether or not he would have spoken to me, even in abuse. But Ronnie and I met every day – it was impossible sometimes not to rub shoulders – yet he never opened his mouth to me. Mam was kind and understanding, and as the days went on I became thankful for her sake that the war was on, for people were more concerned with the day-to-day news of it than they were in the shame I had brought on her. Only Dad remained the same. Yet not the same, he was more loving and considerate of me than ever before. As for Sam, he followed me around, saying little but always there, his kind eyes telling me that to him I was still Christine, the old Christine.

And what about myself? I laughed no longer, I could not even smile. At night, up in my room in the candlelight, I looked at my swelling body and had not even the strength to hate it. Quicker than I had fallen into the river I had fallen into life and I was stunned by it. I could not even find the heart in me to condemn the perpetrator, although I knew that Martin had not only run away from the priest, but had scuttled away from the house on the hill, aided, no doubt, by the colonel. In spite of all this I longed to see him, and the longing was at its height when I lay down in bed at night. For hours my eyes would stare through the window at the dark sky and my heart would be talking to him, pleading with him to come back. There was no call to him from my body now, that was taken up with the thing inside me. I did not think of it as a baby, but as something I would have to suffer and carry for the rest of my life because I had sinned, and grievously. I did not have to see the look in Father Ellis's eyes, on his odd visits, to know this. The terrifying thing was I knew with an absolute certainty that if Martin were to come back and the occasion to sin presented itself to me again I should be powerless to make any resistance. And this knowledge revealed to me more than anything else how weak I was where I loved, how weak I was altogether for I could not even hate properly – Martin, our Ronnie, or anyone else – at least not yet.

The war had been on six months, people had stopped sleeping in the air-raid shelters every night, and the song of the moment was 'We're Going to Hang Out the Washing on the Siegfried Line'. One morning early, about four o'clock, Dad came up to my room and woke me saying he would have to go for the doctor for Mam. By nine o'clock that morning my mother was in hospital. Three days later she died saying, 'Christine, my Christine. Oh, lass, oh, lass.' And the world went on with its business of fighting, but our house became a thing apart, like a deserted planet. The rooms seemed much larger and completely empty, and Dad turned into an old man within a week, and instead of he being my prop I now became his. I could not believe my mother had gone, and I cried unceasingly for days, but Dad did not cry. He seemed to be dried out, and the fact that I became worried about him took my mind somewhat from myself and also made me forget, at least for intervals, the fear of the coming event, the fear of giving birth to the baby, the fear of the pain that would rend me in two, as Aunt Phyllis had described it to me.

Dad was working again, and he and Ronnie were on the same shift. For hours at a stretch I would have the house to myself, and I would be so lonely at times that I wished I was with my mother. I never left the house unless I had to, and then I tried to arrange it when Ronnie would be indoors, thus giving me less time to suffer his silent condemnation. And though I was thankful that people now had less time to be concerned with the scandals around them, when Mrs. Campbell became a regular visitor to my Aunt Phyllis's kitchen, as also did Miss Spiers from the end house, I did not have to think deeply to imagine the gist of their conversation.

I was getting so big now that I did not want to be seen. I had no pride within me to keep my head defiantly high, and my laugh that could have sustained me, or at least formed a façade about my true feelings, was dead within me. So, with no attempt to titivate myself up, I would go down into town to get the groceries. And on one such visit I ran into Mollie. She must have been aware of what had befallen me for otherwise she would have made some comment on my rotund figure, but she seemed very pleased to see me, even delighted, and wanted me to go and have a cup of tea with her. She told me she was working in the munitions factory, and ended, 'What do you think? I've got a place of me own, two rooms and a kitchen By! I wouldn't call the Queen me aunt.' Then she had grabbed hold of my hand and said, 'Come and see me, Christine, will you? It's 21B Gordon Street.' And I smiled at her and promised I would. She must have felt a bit awkward with me for she had not sworn once.

Christmas came and added to the nightmare of my existence, for at this time I seemed to miss my mother more than I had done immediately after she died. As for Dad, his sorrow and loneliness were such that I wanted to cry every time I looked at him. How Ronnie was affected I did not know, for he showed the same taciturn face which had become usual with him.

By the end of March my body was so distorted that I became sick with the sight of it. Only when you have a husband and are carrying something for him can your bloated and stretched skin take on the appearance of beauty, but when there is no one to call this thing 'ours' and it remains yours alone, it is impossible to see beauty in it.

At seven o'clock on a Friday night towards the end of March, as the air-raid siren screeched a warning over the town, a fiery pain brought my swollen limbs to a sudden halt. I was at the cupboard getting my coat before going over to the shelter, and I found myself transfixed, one foot forward, one hand outstretched, my mouth open and my breath seemingly stopped. When I managed to reach a chair I thought, this is it. I was alone in the house and I became terrified – Aunt Phyllis would be already in the shelter. But just then I heard footsteps hurrying up the backyard. It would be Dad. I kept my eyes on the door but it was Ronnie who came through it. He stared at me for a moment and I tried to speak, to tell him to go for Aunt Phyllis, but I could not for the pain had come

124

again. Then he had hold of my hand and he was talking, but gently: 'Come on, lie down. Oh, my God! To see you in a state like this. Oh! Christine.'

I realized that he was crying and some part of me outside of the pain was horrified at this and was yelling, 'No! no! I don't want him to be sorry,' for if he were sorry for me all the old business would start again. I remember pushing him aside and getting up and saying between gasps, 'Go and get Aunt Phyllis,' and of being surprised when, immediately, like an obedient child, he ran out of the kitchen and through the front door, which was the nearest way to the shelter, to bring her.

Eighteen hours later the child was born, and Aunt Phyllis had been right about the pain. It was a girl with a face the shape of Martin's, and I had no interest in it.

The next night Don Dowling came in roaring drunk and sang and shouted in their front room, and since I was lying in Dad's bed in our front room it was as if he was standing by my side. When Aunt Phyllis came in to see me she made no comment whatever about the oration, and the situation should have appeared weird but I was so weak and dazed that her strange attitude must have seemed simply part of the pattern of this awful, pain-filled thing called living. But when the nurse came in for the night visit she hammered on the wall, shouting, 'If you don't cease that noise I'll go and get a policeman.'

Aunt Phyllis was in our kitchen when this occurred, and shortly afterwards she went in next door and there was no more noise. Vaguely it occurred to me that she could have stopped it sooner.

It was the first of June, nineteen-forty, a beautiful day, warm and mellow, and the wireless was telling of the evacuation from Dunkirk. There had been no 'washing hanging on the Seigfried Line' after all. I was standing in the scullery doing the dinner dishes. Outside in the yard, in her pram, lay Constance. Why I had called the child Constance I don't really know, maybe because it expressed my feelings for her father, constant, ever constant, and alongside this love there was growing daily for this child I had not wanted another kind of love. Now, when I took her in my arms and fed her, I knew I was no longer whole, part of me was in her.

She had also brought a feeling of family back into the house; she had, I knew, eased my father's pain, and his love for her was as deep as, if not deeper than, the love he had for me.

Ronnie paid little attention to her – he would glance at her but never spoke to her or talked the baby twaddle that Dad did and which, strangely, I found it impossible to use – but to my growing concern he had once again turned his attention to me. He was all forgiveness and solicitude, and this solicitude did more to bring me back into an awareness of life than anything else, because it created in me the old fear. I was now sleeping upstairs again, and each night I dreaded a midnight visit . . . just to talk.

As I finished the dishes Sam came up the yard and stood by the pram, looking down on the child and touching her with his finger, and he turned and smiled at me through the scullery window. Then coming in, he said, 'By, she's bonnie, Christine.'

I smiled at him, there was no need for words with Sam.

'Where's Stinker?' he asked. 'I'll take him for a run on the fells.'

'I haven't seen him since the middle of the morning, Sam,' I replied; 'he should be in for his dinner, he's never this late.'

I was never to see Stinker again. He did not come in all day, and Dad, as he had done once before, searched the fells for him. On the Sunday, remembering where Don had found him in the stables, Dad visited them again, but there was no sign of a dog of any kind, nor had anyone noticed the children playing with a strange dog.

When he brought this news back I began to cry. 'Now, now, lass,' he said, 'you know what dogs are, he's gone on the rampage. In about three days he'll show up, tired and hungry. It's the nature of the beast.'

Three days passed and Stinker did not show up, and on Tuesday afternoon a man came to ask if he could see Dad. I told him he was down on the allotment. An hour later Dad came slowly into the scullery, the blue marks on his forehead where the coal had left its design were standing out visibly. He came straight to the point, patting my shoulder and saying, 'Prepare yourself for a bit of a shock, lass. . . . Stinker's dead.'

126

'Oh, Dad, no!' I sank down on to a chair and said in a whisper, 'Where?' and then, 'How?'

I watched him draw the back of his hand across both sides of his mouth before replying, 'He was drowned, lass.'

I was on my feet now. 'He couldn't drown, Dad, he was a swimmer, he couldn't drown.'

Dad filled his chest with air and let it out slowly before speaking again. 'He was drowned, lass, in a sack filled with bricks.'

I closed my eyes, then pressed my palms over them, but it didn't shut out the picture of Stinker in the sack full of bricks. Dad's voice was going on, rising in anger, but I only heard snatches of what he was saying, such as 'I'll make the swine pay for this. I'll find out before I die who did the day's work, by God! I will.'

Oh! Stinker. Poor Stinker, with his shaggy coat and his warm tongue and his laughing eyes. Oh! Stinker.

I learned later that the man who had come to the door for Dad had seen a man swing a sack into the river. But he was too far away to be recognized except that he was very tall. My mind had sprung to Fitty Gunthorpe again, but when I put this to Dad he said, 'Aye, I thought that an' all and I went round there, but Fitty's been evacuated for the last month.'

I was deeply affected, not only by Stinker's death but by the way he had died, and day after day I cried about him until Dad, looking into my white face one morning, said firmly, 'Now look here, lass, he's gone and he can't be brought back and you've got the bairn to see to, so knuckle to.'

He was talking to the mother of Constance, but I did not feel a mother, I felt in this moment a very young girl who had lost her dog. Stinker hadn't only been a dog, he had been a person to whom in the darkness of the night I had whispered my thoughts, my pain.

All the time I had been carrying the child I had, in a way, been free, free from the pressure of both Ronnie and Don, but now the pressure was back, heavy and menacing. With Ronnie, it was his solicitude, for which at any moment he might ask payment or, what was more likely, plead for payment, for I had unheedingly broken down certain barriers for him: I was no longer a virgin, there was no question of being raped by my brother. With Don, it was the insidious penetration of himself into my life through the wall that separated us. For hours he would sing loudly and practise on a guitar, playing the one tune over and over again. And then every third week, when he was on the day shift, around twelve o'clock at night or at whatever time he returned from the bars, there would start a gentle tapping on the wall. This would last from ten minutes to anything up to an hour. The more tight he was the shorter would be the duration. I began to wait for the tapping, knowing it would come, for I could never go to sleep until it finished. It took swift payment of my nerves, for at times the soft tap-tap became loud in my head, like a hammer beating on tin, and I felt I must scream at him through the wall or go mad.

Between the two of them, I had good reason for asking Dad to change rooms again, but had I told him the situation I doubt whether he would have believed me. More likely he would have thought my mind was affected. I could not even make Constance the excuse for a change of room, for the child slept anywhere, and she never cried except when she was hungry, and then I had only to lift her from the cot where it was wedged between the wall and the foot of my bed.

And now I was back where I had started, with Don on one side and Ronnie on the other, the only difference being they were no longer boys, they were both men. Of the two, at this time, I think I was mostly afraid of our Ronnie, and this fear came to the surface one Friday night when, after placing his board money on the table, he pushed three pounds towards me, saying, 'Get yourself something.'

I looked at him, then turned sharply away from the light in his eyes, that soft, pleading light that could turn my stomach. I did not touch the money, but said, 'Thanks, but there's nothing I want.'

'Dont be silly,' he said; 'you're letting yourself go and you're not to do that. Get yourself a frock or something.' He picked the money up and put it on the mantelpiece.

I left the money where it was. And there it remained until Dad came in.

'Whose is this?' he asked, touching the notes.

'Our Ronnie's,' I said, but gave no further information.

The next morning the money had gone, and I went down the town and bought a strong bolt and that afternoon I fixed it on my bedroom door.

CHAPTER FIVE

THE night following Constance's second birthday, in March 1942, Fellburn had the heaviest air-raid it had yet experienced. I was alone in the house, both Dad and Ronnie being on the night shift, and at the first sound of the siren I quickly gathered up the things I always kept ready and hurried across the road, with Constance in my arms, and down into the shelter. Dad had rigged up three bunks. Also there was a little oil stove and a cupboard made out of boxes, and if one could have slept without worry the shelter would not have proved a bad alternative to the bedroom.

I had just got Constance settled when from outside the door in the sandbagged passage I heard Sam's voice saying, 'You there, Christine?'

I opened the door for him, and he came in making, as usual, an excuse to cover his concern for us. 'Our shelter is already like the morgue. I hate to be in there by meself – I still can't get Mam to use it. Funny, isn't it, her so frightened and won't go in an air-raid shelter. She did at first, that's the odd thing.'

I nodded. 'Perhaps she's wise,' I said. 'If you've got to go you'll go, air-raid shelter or no.'

He turned his head slowly and looked at me in the light of the hurricane lamp, then as slowly turned his gaze down on Constance and, repeating a statement he had made a thousand times before, he said, 'By, she's bonnie, Christine.'

At this very moment the earth gave a mighty shudder and we both dropped on to our knees and threw ourselves across Constance. For quite some moments I could feel the trembling, and it seemed to run through me, and Sam, whose head was close to mine, smiled and said, 'Coo! a step nearer and it would have taken the skin off our noses.' Then he added, 'Look, she's still sleeping.'

There came another thud, more distant this time; then within a few seconds another one that seemed to fall softly. 'They're trying for the aerodrome,' said Sam. 'What the devil did they want to build an aerodrome up here for anyway? They should never put dromes near houses.' He sounded angry.

I smiled at him and whispered, as if afraid to raise my voice, 'But I thought you liked the air force. Weren't you talking of joining up?'

'I like the air force but not that aerodrome. It's too bloomin' near for my fancy. Anyway, when I do join up they'll know about it, for I'll go straight to the Air Marshal and give him a piece of my mind.' And he demonstrated with his finger and thumb how big the piece would be. Then went on, 'I'll tell him a thing or two he won't forget before I'm shot.'

It wasn't only what Sam said that was funny but the way he said it, and he was always using his dry humour to turn my thoughts from myself. And he succeeded in his aim once again for, moving from his side, I laid my head on the foot of the bunk for a moment and laughed. Then looking at him I said, 'You are an idiot, Sam.' He was looking at Constance and made no comment, but there was a little pleased smile around his lips.

He got to his feet now, saying, 'I'll just look out and see if the street's standin',' and by this I knew he was going to slip across and see if his mother was all right.

As I opened the door for him and watched him ease his thick body and broad shoulders out into the passage I wondered, and not for the first time, what I would have done during the past three years without him. He was just turned seventeen but he seemed much older, and so wise for a lad. One thing I was certain of, he was the most understanding of those around me, and that included Dad, for his understanding was not born of sorrow like Dad's and there was not a trace of condemnation in it. I'm sure that something within me, never very strong, call it my nerves for want of a better name, would have snapped under the strain of Don's persistent covert persecution and our Ronnie's insidious attempts to penetrate into my inner life, if it hadn't been for Sam.

Ronnie had now placed me in such a position that I could no longer turn on him in a temper, real or simulated, for he was so kind and patient . . . so patient. It was this patience that was wearing my nerves to frayed threads. Not the threat of raids and bombing or even Don Dowling's present form of torture, it was Ronnie, and his blatant desire I knew would be the end of me, if not morally, then in some disastrous way, should the situation continue for much longer.

Dad was blissfully unaware of anything wrong and he daily added to my strain by making such suggestions as, 'Go on, lass, go to the pictures with Ronnie. The bairn will be all right with me. You worry too much about her.' Or, 'Go on, let Ronnie go with you for the shopping and carry the things.'

One day, getting Dad by himself I said to him, 'Dad, I want to go out on my own, I don't want Ronnie or anybody else about me.' At this he had said, 'All right, lass, have it your own way.' But there had been a look of worry in his eyes.

I knew the reason for both the look and his tone. The air force was all around, lorryloads of blue-clad figures passed the door every day. I wanted to say to him, 'Dad, they hold no more interest for me than old Mr. Patterson next door,' but I knew he wouldn't believe me. I was nineteen and motherhood had caused me to side-step the unbalanced fat of the teens, and I had quickly developed a figure which brought whistles from the lorries and advances from more than one uniformed male. But it was always the new ones to the drome that made the advances, for it had got around that I was unmarried and had a child, and in some perverse way this seemed to give me a form of protection, at least in the daylight. I never trusted myself out of doors after dark for, as Aunt Phyllis crudely put it, the air force swarmed over the town at night like maggots on meat.

Sometimes lying awake at night I asked myself if I was a complete fool altogether, for I simply could not forget Martin. If I could get him out of my mind then perhaps I would meet some man who would accept Constance and marry me. On this thought I would always toss restlessly and end up by turning my face into the pillow and there see his face emerge through great clouds of multi-coloured mist and the desire for him would rise in me until, unable to bear it any longer, I would get up and pace the narrow length of my room. Or sometimes I would sit at the window for hours on end, wondering about him, where he was, if he was in the army, the navy or the air force, if he had been wounded. I could never think of him as being dead, for my longing told me I should meet him again ... I must. I was still young enough to imagine that all things are possible to them that hope.

One day I started a sort of mental game — I got the idea from a book our Ronnie was reading. It was dealing with the power of thought, and it told you that anything you wished for in life could be yours, if you made the desire strong enough. I remember laughing with some bitterness as I read this — there could be no desire stronger in anyone alive than the desire in me for Martin. The book gave a number of exercises that had to be done just before dropping off to sleep, and I did the exercises and played this game until I asked myself one night why Ronnie had been reading such a book, and it came to me, as it should have done at the beginning, that he was using the exercises to accomplish his desires as I was to accomplish mine, and from that moment I stopped doing them, but hope was in no way lessened in me.

Sam came back into the shelter saying briefly that everything was all right, but added, 'By! there's some fires blazing round about,' and as he sat down on the bunk he remarked, 'You know I used to be terrified of the pit, but now I think it's the safest place.' He was in his usual position with his hands hanging down between his knees, and he looked down at them as he stated, 'They say given the will you can get over anything in life, but you can't, not really.'

'Are you going to stay in the pit, Sam?' I asked.

'No,' he said. 'When I make a bit money I'm going to save like billy-ho for that piece of land I've always been on about. You know,' he went on, his eyes still cast down, but now with his head moving slowly from side to side, 'when I'm sitting at the end of that conveyor belt pushing the coal around I'm not seeing coal. Some pieces are taties, and the longish pieces carrots, and when along comes a piece that's nice and rounded I say "There's a grand turnip for you, that one's threepence, Mrs. Jones." '

I was laughing again, a real laugh. It started as a chuckle inside, then for the first time in nearly three years I was really laughing, really laughing, and Sam was laughing with me, his eyes on me now. And Constance slept all through the laughter as she had through the bombing.

'Oh, Sam,' I said, as I held myself, 'I've got a lot to thank you for.'

His kind mouth was smiling and his eyes had a gentle light. From his expression you would have imagined he had just received a gift of some kind. I knew as I looked at him that this was what he had been trying for during these past years, to bring my laughter back. Across the narrow space I put out my hand and touched his knee. 'Thanks, Sam,' I said. As his head drooped I patted him two or three times, and this reminded me of my mother. When unable to find words with which to express her feelings she would pat.

This moment of warm comfort between Sam and me was broken by a voice calling, 'Anybody there?'

Sam rose hastily and went to the door, and a man's voice said, 'Any of the Winters inside . . . the father?'

'No, only Christine.'

There was a pause, and I stood behind Sam and asked, 'What is it? Anything the matter?'

Again there was a pause; then the man said, 'I'm afraid, lass, your brother's been hurt.'

A stillness settled within me. Then out of it I heard my voice asking, 'Has there been a fall?' Although the war was on we pit folk would always associate accidents with the mine.

The man's voice came again. 'No, lass. It was the bomb that got the bridge.'

I was outside in the passage now, standing close to the man, and as I peered into his face I said, 'It couldn't be my brother, he's doing his shift. He left the house about an hour ago.'

'Well, lass, he's been recognized as Ronnie Winter. Where's your dad?'

'He – he's at work, Ronnie and him went out together. He's not . . .?'

'No. As far as I can gather there was a woman and two bairns and your brother. Can you come to the hospital?'

I looked at Sam, and he whispered, 'I'll see to her, go on.'

I picked up my coat and followed the man, and not until we were outside did I realize that he was in uniform and an A.R.P. warden.

A jeep was coming down the road and he hailed it and said

to the driver, 'Will you give us a lift to the footbridge, the main one's gone?'

'Get up,' said the man. 'Where you for?'

'The General Hospital,' replied the A.R.P. man. 'This lass's brother caught it.' His voice had taken on a sad intonation.

'Oh.'

I felt the man's eyes slip towards me for a second. I said nothing because I was feeling nothing.

When we reached the place where the bridge had stood there seemed to be crowds of people about; it was the same at the footbridge, and the driver said, 'Look, I'll run you down to Bog's Bridge and take you right to the hospital that way.'

'Thanks,' said the warden.

Ten minutes later I was in the casualty ward, and standing in a small cubicle by the side of a bed. On it lay Ronnie. His face looked very clean, as if it had been lightly powdered. His eyes were closed and I knew without being told that he was near death. As a thought rose up swiftly to the surface of my mind I cried at it, 'No! No, for God's sake don't wish that. How can you?' But I knew in my heart that I could and did wish that he would die.

Someone pushed a chair forward and I sat down, and someone else brought me a cup of tea but I couldn't drink it. I sat there for three hours. Towards the end of that time Ronnie opened his eyes and looked at me. There seemed to be no recognition in the look yet he lifted his hand towards me. But before my hand reached him his dropped back on to the counterpane, and I knew that my subconscious desire had been granted. Ronnie was dead, and pity and remorse and relief, but also love, yes strangely, love, now twisted my whole being.

A different nurse came and led me away into another room and she spoke to me as if I were his wife. 'Have you any children?' she asked.

After a moment I moved my head and she said, 'Well, don't worry, you'll be taken care of.'

Something loud within me yelled at her 'Shut up! shut up!' and when I shuddered she said, 'You mustn't catch cold.' I had to get away from her and her misplaced kindness or I would scream. A few minutes later a woman took me home in a car and I didn't thank her, but ran into the house and into the kitchen and retched my heart out at the sink.

Ronnie had been dead three weeks and Dad still kept saying, 'If only he had gone down that night.'

The mystery of how Ronnie had come to be on the bridge when he should have been down the pit was solved when Dad had come up the next morning. While they waited for the cage Ronnie had apparently said he felt off-colour, that he could not go down and must go back to bed. As Dad was telling me this there had come to my mind a saying of my mother's: 'The mills of God grind slowly, but they grind exceeding small'. Ronnie had been unable to get me alone, Dad was always there. I had no doubt in my mind that his illness was a ruse to be in the house alone with me, and he had paid dearly for it. Yet, now safe from anything he could do, or try to do, I could say, 'Oh, Ronnie. Poor Ronnie.' But I did not hide from myself the release from strain that his death had brought to me. There remained only Don Dowling, and now, oddly enough, since Ronnie's death, he had let up in his persecution. For the first time since my mother had threatened him with the poker he came to our door. Dad answered it and asked him in, and he stood in the kitchen expressing his sympathy in tones that sounded sincere.

'We had our differences, Uncle Bill,' he said, 'but we were pals from when we were lads.'

'Aye, that's true,' said Dad.

'You'll miss him, Christine,' he said to me.

He had spoken my name as if he had never stopped using it, and although his tone was most kindly I could not help but wonder what was behind the words 'You'll miss him, Christine.' But after that one remark he addressed himself to Dad all the time. He did not stay more than a few minutes, and when he left he said to Dad, 'If there's anything I can do, Uncle Bill, you've only to ask. I'm just next door, you know.'

There was no tapping through the wall now, there was no singing loudly or playing of the guitar, nor did he come again to the house for almost a month after this first visit. Then one day there was a knock on our front door, and when I went to it he said, 'Hullo, Christine,' and before I could reply he asked, 'Is Uncle Bill about?'

'He's in the kitchen,' I said.

'Can I see him a minute?'

He made no attempt to come in, and I did not ask him to but went into the kitchen and told Dad.

It was almost ten minutes later that Dad closed the front door and came back into the room. He had a parcel in his hand and he looked at me rather helplessly as he put it on the table, saying, 'Now don't go for me, lass, I couldn't do anything about it.'

'About what?' I asked.

'This.' He tapped the parcel. 'It's some butter and sugar and stuff.'

I sighed and closed my eyes for a moment, then said quietly, 'Dad, you mustn't start that, not with him.'

'I know, I know, lass.' Dad's tone sounded harassed. 'But what could I do? He's trying to be kind and he seems changed. I think Ronnie going was a shock to him an' all. We've got to give him a chance, lass.'

I did not answer, but went into the kitchen thinking, 'Dear God, dear God.' And Dad came after me, saying, 'And there's Phyllis, she's got nothing really, nothing but her bits and pieces. It's her that's to be pitied.'

Some time later an incident occurred which explained the many, and seemingly useless, bits and pieces that my Aunt Phyllis gathered about her. I was in Burton's in the High Street, upstairs in the china department, or what had been the china department before china, like everything else, became hard to get. Burton's was a sort of multiple store, with counters dotted here and there and goods displayed in arranged piles on the floor. It was just as I caught sight of my Aunt Phyllis's familiar back that my steps towards her were halted, for I saw her hand, which was holding a cloth bag at her side, gently pick up a small ornament and with a swift twist of her wrist slip it into the bag and she carried this out while looking the other way. The whole thing was so slick that I could not believe my eyes. I was only a few yards from her, and the next instant she had turned and was facing me, and she saw by my face that I knew what she had done, for she came towards me quickly, saying 'Come on.'

'But, Aunt Phyllis. . . .'

'Look' – she was breathing quickly – 'don't stand there with your mouth agape, come on.' She grabbed hold of my arm, but when I refused to be moved her whole attitude changed and she pleaded in a whisper, 'For God's sake, Christine, come on ... come on. I'll explain, I'll tell you about it when we're outside.'

I allowed her to lead me from the shop, but once outside I pulled my arm from her. We passed up the main street and were on the road for home before she spoke. Then she said, 'I've never done it before, honest. I don't know what came over me.'

I was shocked at the idea of her stealing and felt only contempt for her lying, and so there was little pity in my voice as I said, 'You have done it before, all those odd, useless things coming into the house for years.'

I had not looked at her as I spoke, but when she did not answer or deny anything I glanced sideways at her and could not help but be touched to see her in tears. I had never seen her cry, never, and now she was mumbling, 'I only do it when I'm worried, I can't help it. It's Don, he's on with a woman in Bog's End. She's old enough to be his grandmother, as old as me anyway. It's nearly driving me frantic. I only do it when I'm worried.'

In this, at least, I believed her; she only did it when she was worried. The knowledge, too, that Don had a woman came as a relief to me, and my tone was much more kindly as I said, 'All right, Aunt Phyllis.' Then I added, 'But if you're caught, just think what'll happen.'

'Sometimes I don't care if I am.' Her tone was so dead sounding, so hopeless, that I realized as I looked at her how true my mother's words had been. Aunt Phyllis was a very unhappy woman. She was not yet forty yet she looked an old woman. She had no joy in life except her elder son, and he, I was convinced, cared not a fig for her. It was Sam on whom she had thrashed out her unhappiness. It was he alone who showed her any consideration, and she could not find even a small grain of comfort in it for she had no love for Sam. I now thought, 'Poor unhappy soul, poor Aunt Phyllis.'

When I reached home and entered the kitchen and saw Constance turn from Sam and rush towards me with a cry of joy, and felt her little arms tighten about my legs and heard her voice cry, 'Mummy, Mummy,' I thought that after all I

138

had quite a lot to be thankful for. I had her, and there was no bitterness in my heart.

I hadn't been in the house long enough to put away the rations and the odd things I had bought in the town when there came a tap on the back door, and thinking it was Aunt Phyllis again, I called, 'Come in!'

It was Don who appeared in the kitchen doorway, filling its frame and making the room look small with his hugeness. At times he looked bigger than at others; when he was in a pleasant humour he seemed to swell.

He looked at me now and said 'Hallo, there,' and I said lightly, 'Hallo, Don.' Then he glanced at Sam who was getting up from the mat where he had been playing with Constance and said, 'You're cutting it fine, aren't you? You should be on your way.'

'Oh, I've time enough,' said Sam briefly, and his tone, I noticed, was not that of a younger brother to an elder, and such an elder, but he spoke to Don as to an equal, and his tone implied, if not an active dislike, utter disregard, and he made no move to leave the kitchen, for which I was thankful.

'Been for your rations?' Don nodded down to the articles on the table, and I said, 'Yes, I've been for the rations.'

'Well, there's no need to starve yourself, you know that, don't you?'

I was saved from making any comment on this by Constance pulling at Sam and crying, 'Come on, play, Uncle Sam, come on, play, and make houses.' She was trying to pull him towards her blocks again when Don's voice brought her little fair head towards him as, dropping on to his hunkers and facing her, he said, 'Come here and talk to your Uncle Don . . . I'm your Uncle Don.'

I found that my hand was gripping my forearm until it hurt, and as he put his hand out towards her a wave of faintness swept over me and I heard myself praying, 'Oh, Holy Mary, don't let him touch her!'

But he did touch her. His hand took hers gently from Sam's trouser leg, and he turned her towards him. It was with a glad face that she stood between his knees. They looked at each other, and he touched her under the chin and said, 'You know, you're a bonnie lass.'

It was a phrase that any north country man would have

used to a child, and Don's tone was that of any north country man talking to a child, but I knew that Don was no ordinary north country man. Some deep instinct told me to beware of even his kindest word. But it was obvious that Constance liked him, for she put out a finger and touched the small moustache that he was now growing, and at the feel of it she laughed. Then, with a sudden agile movement in one so heavy, he swung up from his hunkers with her in his arms and I rushed towards them as if saving her from some danger. My hand was on her to pull her away from him when his fingers touched mine. His eyes left her face and his gaze held me for a brief second, but in that time it was as if my temperature dropped by degrees, as if I had been suddenly thrust into a refrigerator. I took my hands away and turned from her, and he put her down on the floor again, saying, in the most pleasant fashion, 'Uncle Don will bring you something the morrow. What would you like? A doll?'

She nodded at him, laughing. 'A doll, like Patsy.' She went to the cupboard and pulled out her box of toys and, taking from it a doll, she held it up to him saying, 'Like Patsy.'

'Oh, it'll be bigger than Patsy – that big . . .' He stretched out his hands indicating the size. Then saying, 'Well, I must be off,' he turned towards the door, but when there, he looked back at Sam and remarked, 'You in with the deputy that you can afford to be late?'

Sam did not answer, but he turned and looked him straight in the face, and Don, saying nothing more, went out.

I found that I was trembling, shaking from head to foot. I looked at Sam but he would not meet my eyes and turned away and stood gazing into the fire until I said, 'You will be late, Sam. I'm sorry I was so long.'

He did not answer but made for the door, patting Constance's head as he passed her. He did not even say good-bye, and I remember thinking, 'Oh, if he were only as old and as big as Don and could fight him.'

Don brought the doll for Constance, but he did not follow up his gift with daily visits. Sometimes a week would go by before he came in, and then all his talk and attention would be for the child. It would have appeared to an outsider that I did not exist for him, had never existed for him. But I knew differently, and was afraid.

One day as I was making a detour from the footbridge towards the hill, with a bag of groceries in each hand and Constance toddling by my side, a jeep drew up and the driver, leaning forward, said, 'Hallo, there. Would you like a lift?' I was on the point of saying, 'No, thank you,' when I recognized the man who had driven me to the hospital the night that Ronnie died. He was not young, near forty I should say, with a plain, ordinary face, relieved by two small, very bright eyes. Before I could say 'Yes' or 'No' he had jumped down and picked Constance up and placed her on the seat, and, taking my bags from me, he helped me up into the car. And that was my second meeting with Tom Tyler ... Tommy, as I came to call him.

He put me at my ease with regard to any ulterior motive of his kindness by showing me a photograph of his wife and two children. He was from Whitley Bay, which wasn't so far away, and he told me of some of the things he got up to in order to get long week-ends home. He said that Constance reminded him of his youngest, only, he added most generously, his youngster wasn't quite so bonnie. But having said, 'They change as they get older,' he laughed and added, 'Not that yours will, missis.'

It was the first time anyone had called me missis and it made me seem very old and reminded me forcibly that I was a mother. Little did I dream that day that Tommy was to have a finger in my destiny, that a suppressed lift of his hand was to be the signal for the second phase of my life to begin. But before this happened an incident was to occur that brought Sam and Don at each other's throats, to be followed by a pit disaster which cast a shadow on Sam's character.

The first happened when Sam came in one day and said, 'Have you got such a thing as a sack, Christine? Old Miss Spiers has been after some coal. Me ma won't lend her our bucket and her's won't hold a shovelful. It would be easier for me if I could fill a sack and take it up.'

'We haven't such a thing, Sam,' I said, 'I'm sorry.'

At that moment the door opened and Dad came in, and he remarked, 'What you sorry about? What haven't we got?' He stood taking off his coat and Sam said, 'I was after a sack, Uncle Bill, to take Miss Spiers some coal along.'

'We haven't got one, have we, Dad?'

Dad stood silent for a moment, then said, 'Aye, we've got one, Sam, it's in the shed. I wrapped it up and stuck it back of the paint shelf thinking that one day it might give me a lead on Stinker. It's got a funny name on it, and I thought at the time, "You never know; if ever I see another one like that I'll know where this one came from." But now you take it, Sam, it's no use worrying about things like that now, there's much more to worry about in the world the day, with people dying by the thousand. Aye, it's no use harbouring bitterness. You take it, Sam. Will I get it for you?'

'No, Uncle Bill, I'll get it. And thanks.'

Our kitchen window looked down the length of the yard, and I saw Sam go into the shed and come out with a brown-paper parcel. I remembered the brown-paper parcel and my dad putting it there and saying, 'Leave that be, Christine. It's only rags I've put away for when I start paintin'.' I saw Sam take off the paper and shake out the sack, then I watched him spread it out on the yard, and from where I stood I could see the black painted marks on it, but not the words they made. Then I saw him turn and look swiftly up the yard. He saw me through the window and stared at me for a moment before picking up the sack and hurrying out. I heard his feet running up his yard and into the house, and within seconds his voice and that of Don's came through the kitchen wall, and to them was joined Aunt Phyllis's.

Dad and I looked at each other. Then Dad, going to the scullery, carefully opened our back door and stood listening. I joined him, and when Aunt Phyllis's kitchen door was pulled open the crack that it gave as it hit the wall sounded as if the wood had splintered. Then Don's voice filled the air, crying, 'You're bloody well mad!'

'Mad, am I?' I could not recognize Sam's voice, yet I knew it was he who was shouting, 'All right, I'm mad, but you're insane. This explains everything. I've always had me suspicions, but now. . . .'

'You're a bloody fool!' Don's tone had dropped and there was a conciliatory note in it as he said, 'Get inside.'

'Take your hands off me!'

'Come inside, will you, both of you, and stop that yelling!' It was Aunt Phyllis now, shouting from within the doorway.

'You bloody, dirty, mad swine!' I could not believe I was

listening to Sam, Sam of the quiet voice and even temper, and when his words were cut sharply off and there came only the sound of scraping feet I knew that they were fighting. I clutched at Dad and whispered, 'Oh, Dad, go on in and stop them, he'll kill Sam.'

I saw Dad hesitate; then he said, 'I don't know so much about that. Sam's as strong as a horse, and the other's bloated with beer and . . .' He stopped.

'But, Dad, he's only half his size.'

As the sickening thud of blows and heavy breathing came over the wall, Dad ran down the backyard, and the next second his voice came to me, shouting, 'Break it up! Break it up! Sam! Sam, do you hear, stop it! leave over!'

There was some more scuffling, and then Dad came into the yard again, pushing Sam before him. Sam's face was covered with blood coming from a split in his upper lip.

'Oh! Sam.' I led him into the scullery, saying, 'What's it all about? What's happened? You should never have started on him.'

When I poured the water into the dish he swilled his face with it, then took the towel from my hand and pressed it over his mouth. But he didn't tell me what the row was about, nor did he tell Dad. And I didn't inquire further. Anything connected with Don I naturally shied from. It didn't occur to me to connect the row with the sack.

Three months later there was an explosion in the mine and four men died. Others were dragged out just in the nick of time, and one of these was Don. He was three days in hospital, and Aunt Phyllis haunted the place night and day. Sam, too, had been in the explosion, but had got out without any ill effects from the gas. Yet the experience had told on him, for he seemed to have changed overnight and was quiet, even with me and the child. He was usually quiet, I knew, with every-one else, but with me he had always been at ease, and we generally talked and jabbered together. But following the accident he said little.

Part of the wood was still standing, the remainder had been hewn down by the air force, to enlarge their camp. But I often took Constance to the first bay, the only one left, and there we would sit on the grass and she would play and romp while I knitted or just sat and watched her. Often Sam would come with us. He had today. Constance loved him to come along because he played and gambolled with her, but on this day he didn't play but sat by my side, his knees up, his hands hanging in their usual position.

'Aren't you feeling well, Sam?' I asked.

'Aye, I'm all right,' he answered.

I said no more. It was well known that a man's first disaster always affected him. Some got over it quickly and used it as experience. But with others it left a mark, and I felt this one had done so on Sam. He had always been afraid of the dark, no matter how bravely he faced it.

Constance, being tired after so much playing, he gave her a piggy-back home, and he had hardly dropped her from his shoulders on to the floor when, without any knocking, the back door through which we had just entered was burst open and Don stalked into the kitchen.

In lowering Constance to the floor Sam had bent over backwards, but now, as if released by a spring, he shot up straight, and I was not mistaken when I saw a look of fear flit across his face at the sight of his brother.

'Ay . . . aye. We . . . ell!'

The two words were drawn out, and it seemed as if Don was singing them.

Sam did not speak, and Don, with no singsong inflection to his words now, said, 'You pleased to see me?' He took a step forward, but Sam did not retreat, he only said, 'What d'you mean?'

'What do I mean? You treacherous bugger! For two pins I'd brain you where you stand.'

At the sound of Don's threatening voice Constance gave a whimpering cry, and I gathered her swiftly up into my arms before saying, 'Now look, Don, I want no rowing in here.'

'Do you know what he tried to do?' Don was speaking to me but he did not move his eyes from Sam and his face was convulsed with such fury that it looked as if it would burst at any moment. 'He tried to kill me!'

I could not stop my eyes flicking in startled inquiry to Sam. Sam's face told me nothing, but there was no vestige of fear on it now, and he exclaimed, quickly, 'You're mad!'

'Mad am I? Well, you'll be a bloody sight madder by the time I've finished with you!'

'I don't know what you're on about.'

'Oh, no? I was almost gasping me last when we reached the air door. You didn't go through it and bang it shut, did you? Oh, no! If it hadn't been for Steve Moreton comin' back to see if we were all out I'd have been a gonner. And you told him you were the last, didn't you?'

'I don't know what I told him, I was overcome meself.'

'You were overcome yourself . . . you were so bad that they let you come straight home. You bloody . . .!'

As he made a lunge towards Sam I rushed in front of him, crying, 'No, you don't, not in here!'

Don drew in a deep breath, then exclaimed, 'All right, all right. Have it your way. Not in here, but I'll get him, one way or t'other, I'll get him. In a day or so he'll not be able to raise his head in this town again. Steve Moreton has a big gob and I'll see that he opens it. Aye, you treacherous bugger, I will.'

He swung about, and when I heard the back-door close on him, I looked at Sam and saw that he appeared about to pass out. He sank down on the couch and buried his face in his hands.

Dropping Constance on to the floor I went quickly to him and put my arm about his shoulder. 'What is it, Sam? Can I get you something? Don't worry, I don't believe a word he says, nor will anybody else. He's mad, as you said.'

Nor did I believe what Don had accused Sam of, because it was the greatest crime a pitman could commit. No pitman, even of the worst character, would leave another to die. In the moment of crisis when wits are scattered by shock there may be a temporary pandemonium, but I knew from Dad's talk and that of other men that no man down the pit would leave his mate if he was in need and every man became another man's mate in a disaster. A man would stick to another who needed help closer than a mother would.

Sam was moving his head back and forth in a despairing fashion and I repeated, 'Don't worry, nobody will take any notice what he says or Steve Moreton. You've only got to tell them your side of it and they'll believe you.'

Sam raised his face slowly from his hands and stared in front of him as he said quietly, 'Aye, that's all I've got to do. And I'll do it, and I'll keep doing it. It's only my word against theirs. There'll be a private inquiry with the club lot, I know, but I'll stick to what I've said. I was in a daze and I didn't know what I was doin'.' Then he turned his eyes to mine, and his voice was calm and without a tremor as he stated, 'But I did know what I was doing, Christine, I did shut that air trap on him.'

I felt my hand lifting away from him, and at the same time I became conscious that he was aware of this and immediately I put it back, more firmly than it had been before.

'I wanted him to die. I've been wanting him to die for years.'

'Oh, Sam!'

He was staring at me now, his eyes wide, but his voice was a whisper as he said, 'There's something wrong with him, Christine. He'd be better dead. He's bad, wicked . . . and I'm frightened. Not for meself I'm not, but . . .' He didn't go on, but the look in his eyes told me for whom he was frightened, and all I could say was 'Oh, Sam!'

'He should see a doctor, one of those psychiatrist men. He should have been seen to years ago. It's me ma's fault. . . . Oh, no, it isn't, not altogether.' He shook his head as if weary of its weight, then added, 'I've got to tell you this now, Christine. I've kept it to meself for years, but now, since you know what I've tried to do, I'd better tell you the lot.' His eyes moved away from mine, and he seemed to be staring at my hand on his shoulder. It was as if he was turning away from the words he was about to speak, as if he was sickened by them. He said, very low, 'Stinker – it was him who drowned Stinker, in that sack.'

I felt my stomach heave. My chin dropped on to my chest and I waited. And then he said, 'The rabbit in the wood that time, it was him who did that. There were more things that you didn't know about, birds and things. And it was him who hid Stinker that time he was lost. And you know why I'm afraid of the dark?' His voice was still low.

I could not speak.

'He used to push me into the bottom of the cupboard in the scullery whenever me ma was out, and poke things at me through the airholes. You know this dent in the side of my cheek here?' He tapped his cheek where there was a round

146

mark, with the skin a shade paler than the rest of his face.

Still I could not speak, and he continued, 'That was a steel skewer he jabbed through the hole. I was about four then. And he had another pretty trick. After me ma had finished the washing and cleaned out the boiler the iron would still be hot, and he'd lift me in there and pop the lid on. When me da caught him doing this to me he lathered him, and me ma and him had a row. She called it playing. I had burns on me feet and hands for weeks after one bit of playing. I tell you, Christine, he's not right.'

'But, Sam.' I was gasping as if I had been running up the hill. 'But, Sam, if he had died it would have been on your conscience all your life.'

'Aye, I know. When I heard he'd got out I was so relieved I went into church.' He was looking at the floor again. 'Father Ellis was there, and I told him about it in confession. He can't say anything, and I know you never would, but to everybody else I'll deny it.'

'Oh, Sam.' I put my arms around him as if he was a small boy and made an attempt to stroke his head, but much to my surprise he pushed me away and got up and went to the fire-place.

'What if he goes for you?'

'He won't, not now you know about it. He's got better ways of punishing people than with a punch. For all his bigness and brawn he's really afraid of a fight, I know that.'

'Why don't you ask for a transfer, Sam?'

He picked up his cap and went towards the door, saying, 'No, that idea's no good. Here I am, and here I'm staying. I'll see you later.'

He went out. I watched him go down the yard and listened to him going in next door, but there was no sound of raised voices.

I stared across the room without seeing anything in it, for I was once again looking at the rabbit and the bird and seeing Stinker's body in the sack.

'Holy Mary!' I went to my rosary box, which was on the dresser, and, taking out the beads which I had not touched for many a long month, I knelt down by the couch and began to pray: 'Hail Mary, full of grace, the Lord is with thee. Blessed art thou amongst women. . . .' And as I prayed I began to cry,

147

and when I cried, Constance came from the front room where she had wandered and she began to cry.

I got up from my knees and took her into my arms, and we were both crying when Dad came in.

'What on earth's the matter?' he asked.

'Nothing,' I said. 'I'm just feeling a bit blue.' To which he replied, 'Aye, we all feel like that at times. I've just heard something that I can't believe. They're saying Sam tried to save his own skin and left Don behind. That isn't like him, is it? That isn't Sam. I just wouldn't believe it, and I didn't put a tooth in it when I told them so. Would you believe it?'

'No,' I said. 'No, I'd never believe that. Why, it's a dreadful thing to say. People are wicked.'

Yes, people were wicked – God, how wicked – and strangely they didn't appear to suffer. It was others who suffered for them, and through them. There was a question here, a deep, deep question, and I was not even capable of scratching its surface, much less of trying to get at the answer – all I ever achieved when I attempted to probe any depths was a dizzying in my mind, and at such times I knew myself to be a clot, a blonde clot who could not think about things that really mattered, only feel about things that didn't.

CHAPTER SIX

It was at the end of March, nineteen-forty-four, a Monday morning, and I was in the middle of washing when Father Ellis called. He had for some time been assigned to this district again, but he did not call every week as he had done in my mother's time. The feeling that had been between us before the child came had not returned. Constance herself was a reminder of that night by the river, and I don't think either he or I ever met without some memory of it returning. And the memory would bring heat to my face and neck. I still went to confession to him, but I knew that I did not make a good confession, for I could not speak of the thoughts that were ever present in my mind and the longing of my body which I knew to be sinful, so because of this I did not often take communion. This was the reason for his visit this morning. He had not seen me at the altar rails of late and wanted to know the reason why. I gave him every reason but the right one, saying it was awkward with Dad's shifts, and that I had no one with whom to leave Constance.

'What about your Aunt Phyllis?' he asked. 'Surely she would look after her for an hour or so?'

I could not tell him that the very thought of letting the child go next door and come in contact with Don was terrifying to me. More so because Constance was fond of him. If she was playing in the front street and saw him coming up the road she would run to him before I could check her, crying, 'Uncle Don! Uncle Don!' and always he had some gift for her, large or small, and I could do nothing about it. After Sam had brought into the open the terrible trait in Don's make-up, I had taken a stand saying that the child was being spoilt and could have no more presents except at birthdays and Christmas. But Aunt Phyllis undermined my authority, for

she supported Don, saying, 'Let the bairn have the bit things.'
She was a strange woman, for had I allowed her she would
have treated Constance as she had Don when he was a child
and ruined her with extravagant affection, as she still did Don
even to this day.

While Father Ellis was standing on the step saying good-
bye, there came between us a flash of the old relationship as he
said kindly, 'You still miss your mother, Christine?'

'Yes, Father,' I replied. 'Sometimes I seem to feel her about
the house. In fact, I can't believe that I won't go into the kitchen and not find her there.'

He nodded his head, saying, 'Yes, I understand. She was
a good woman was your mother, and she loved you dearly.'
His words now brought the past into the present for they
seemed to say, 'And she would have lived for some time longer
but for the shock you gave her.'

'Good-bye, Christine . . . good-bye, Constance.'

'Good-bye, Father.'

He patted Constance's head as he went down the steps –
it was the kind of pat he would have used on the head of any
child. He had shown no interest in her from the first time he
had seen her on the day of her christening, and it seemed to
me that he had made up his mind never to have his feelings
rent again by showing affection for a child. Perhaps he
knew that he should never have allowed himself to single me
out; perhaps he had sinned. To a priest all children should
be alike, so that when they sinned they sinned against God
only.

Father Ellis's visit depressed me, and it set its seal on the
morning. Nothing seemed to go right. There were various
interruptions, and Constance started to complain of toothache.
Then as I was coming to the end of the washing Dad hurried
in, saying, 'I've just seen young Rex Watson, and he said they've
got some beef in and if you go down this mornin' he'll be there
and he'll see you get a piece . . . a good cut.'

I sighed with exasperation. No matter what cut we got,
we would only get rations for two, but Dad liked beef and
we'd had none for the last three weeks. He must have seen how
I felt, for he said, 'Aw, lass, all right, it doesn't matter.'

'I'll go,' I said, 'but what about the dinner?'

'I'll see to that, lass. What is it?'

'Stew, and I was going to make some dumplings.'

'Don't bother about dumplings, go on, get yourself off and see what's going. And anyway, it'll give you a break.'

I could have been amused at the break of going to the butcher's, but I wasn't in the mood at that moment to be amused at anything, so I simply went upstairs and tidied my hair and slipped a decent coat over my working skirt and blouse. Of late I had taken an interest in myself and used lipstick as a matter of course. I told myself I must keep tidy – Aunt Phyllis termed it getting myself up. She had remarked one day recently, 'You're gettin' yourself up these days, aren't you?'

I was now wearing my hair in a bun at the nape of my neck, and often would be greeted from passing lorries with, 'Hallo, Goldilocks,' which was better than, 'And her golden hair was hanging down her back,' which had been the usual salute, sung in all keys, before I had put it up.

The day was windy, cold and dull, and I remember as I hurried down the bank thinking, 'If it rains I'll never get those things dried indoors and they'll be hanging about all week.'

I was still thinking of the washing when I crossed the bridge and made for Clement Street where our butcher's was, but to reach the street I had to pass the air force supply depot near the railway station. Airmen and goods were shunted into this depot from the station. Two iron gates opened on to a great yard and sometimes I would see Tommy Tyler driving in or out or helping to load his lorry with boxes or pieces of machinery, for his job was that of a mechanic.

Today I saw him just inside the gates. He was talking to someone standing at the other side of his laden lorry. I was about four arm-lengths from him when I said, 'Hallo, Tommy.'

He turned his head quickly and his hand came up to give me a salute, then he checked it and turned his face from me, dropping his hand to his side again.

His attitude suggested he was speaking to an officer, and my hail had nearly made him put his foot in it. I had hesitated for only an instant and was going on when the man to whom he was speaking glanced casually round the corner of the lorry, and I found myself with one foot set in mid-air and the other glued, as it were, to the ground. It seemed a long time before my feet came together again, and when they did they were pointing straight into the yard and I was walking towards the lorry, and Martin was coming towards me.

What are human emotions? What are they made up of? Where do they come from? Does your heart really leap within your body? How is it that the sight of a face and a voice can draw from your being such a wave of thanksgiving that you know you are praying for the first time in your life. That you love God and want to sing His praises, for who but He could have kept hope alive, who but He could see through and beyond common sense which would have smothered hope.

'Why, Christine!'

That was his voice, as if I had heard it just a moment ago saying, 'You're like a star that's fallen on a dung heap.'

'Hallo.'

After nearly five years of daily, of hourly longing, all I could say was, 'Hallo.'

'You ... you haven't changed, I recognized you instantly. How are you?'

'Very well, thank you.'

Dear God. 'Very well, thank you,' when I wanted to throw myself into his arms and cry, 'Martin! Martin! Oh, Martin, you've come back. Oh, my Martin, I knew you'd come back,' and all I could say was, 'Very well, thank you.'

'Where are you off to? Have you a minute?'

Could I say I'm going to the butcher's, they've got meat this week? 'I've just slipped down to do a little shopping,' I said. 'Yes, I have a minute.'

'Ah, well.' He pulled at the bottom of his tunic and jerked his neck upwards out of his collar, and I saw that he was embarrassed, greatly embarrassed, and I wanted to cry, 'Oh Martin, don't be like that, forget that night. No, not that night, but forget that you scampered away like a frightened rabbit before the priest.'

'Come and have a drink.'

He took my arm casually and turned me about. 'Where do you usually go?'

He seemed to take it for granted that I frequented the bars. Well that was no slight, most girls did these days, nice girls. I was in the world but not of it. I had lived like a cloistered nun since last he had touched my hand. I had been dead from a moment after we had rolled laughing on the grass together.

'Anywhere,' I said, smiling at him.

'I know a place, quiet. Come on.'

He hurried me along as if time was important and there was little of it left, and, taking me up an alley, he pushed open a door which led into a passage and guided me into a room where a fire was burning brightly. There were half a dozen iron-legged and glass-topped tables and only one other couple in the room, an army officer and a smart woman with a heavily made-up face. Martin seated me in the corner with my back to the wall, and took his seat opposite to me.

'What are you going to have?' he asked.

I was about to say a lemonade but changed it to, 'Oh, anything.'

'Gin . . . gin and lime?'

Again I was going to say, 'Oh, anything,' but it was the smart woman's sidelong glance that made me say, 'Yes, that'll do, gin and lime.'

He was leaning with his elbows on the table, his face not far from mine, he was looking into my eyes as I remembered him doing that night, that night that was last night so near it was again, and in a whisper he said, 'Oh, Christine. I've thought of you often.'

'Have you?' My voice was soft, my whole being was soft and as wide as an ocean, and was flowing over him in great waves of love.

'Have you thought of me?'

I did not lower my eyes when I said, 'Yes, all the time.'

A little smile came to his lips as he whispered, 'I can't believe that. . . . You married?'

'Married!' I screwed up my face then shook my head. 'No,' I said quietly, 'I'm not married.' I did not say, 'Are you?' I knew he wouldn't be married.

'Well I bet you've been swamped with boy-friends.'

The conversation was not as I had imagined it would be, but perhaps he was just wanting to find out if I had a boy. I said without any subtlety, 'I haven't a boy-friend. I've never had one. . . . Well, only. . . .'

His face became straight and I watched him blink his eyes rapidly as he sat up straight in the chair. He was about to say something when the drinks came, and after handing me mine he clinked my glass.

'Cheers,' he said.

'Cheers,' I said, and tasted my first gin, which I thought horrible.

He was staring at me from across the table now, when he said under his breath, 'You mean to say you've . . . you've . . .' He dropped his eyes to his drink and twisted the glass between his fingers, and I could have finished the sentence for him, 'You've had no one but me?'

It was not in me to say 'I've had dozen of chances,' although it was true; nor yet to say, 'I've waited for years for this day, just to see you.' Nor could I say anything that would embarrass him further, not only embarrass but frighten him. A little flame of terror shot through me at this last thought. Whatever happened I must not frighten him away before he had seen Constance, for when he had seen her he would be mine forever. There was no thought in my mind of trapping him. I had no subtlety. My ideas were straight and simple, based, although I did not realize it, on the teachings of my religion. He was the father of Constance – there had been no other man near me. In my mind he was my husband, and when he saw his child there could be no doubt in his mind either. Yet I could not mention her name here. Perhaps I was a little subtle, perhaps a little cunning.

Still with the smart woman's example before me, I tried to adopt a casual tone which would put him at his ease, as I asked, 'What have you been doing all this time?'

I could see that his mind was not on his words as he tapped his uniform, saying, 'Flying, since the beginning.'

'Since the beginning?' My inflection must have implied how lucky he was to be still alive, and he answered this by saying, 'I've been one of the favoured. I'm in with Him.' He thumbed the ceiling and gave a little smile before adding, 'I'm on training duties now.'

'At the aerodrome on the fells?' I couldn't keep the eagerness from my voice. He shook his head. 'No,' he said, 'the Littleborough drome.'

The Littleborough drome was about ten miles away.

'Have you been back here long?'

'Four months or so.'

154

Four months and I hadn't seen him ... four whole months.

There followed an awkward silence, and he broke it by saying, 'Come on, finish that and have another.'

'No, thanks.' I shook my head and remembered the butcher's, but I did not say, 'I've got to go.' It was he, pushing back his sleeve and looking at his wrist watch, who said, ' 'Struth, I must be off I'm afraid. I was due in Littleborough at one. I won't make it now, but I'll have to go.'

He did not immediately rise but leant across the table, saying, 'It's been grand seeing you, Christine. We must meet again.'

'Yes. Yes, we must.'

He did not make any date and I became panicky inside. As I buttoned up my coat I heard myself saying rapidly, 'I can't get out much now, my mother died and I'm looking after the house.'

'Oh. ... Do you still live in the same place?'

'Yes.'

'I must look you up then.'

'Yes ... yes, do. Would you make it after seven o'clock?'

He gave me a look of startled surprise, then said, 'Yes ... yes, of course.'

We were in the street now, standing facing each other once again, and I knew he was going to leave me without making any definite date, and the panic screamed in my head, 'Ask him to come.'

'When can I expect you?' I asked sedately.

'Oh, well now.' Again he pulled at the bottom of his tunic, and I remember thinking the action wasn't far removed from the coat-buttoning one that the lads indulged in, and I had once imagined he was as separated from such gaucheness as was God.

'Any night could it be? You said after seven?'

'Yes,' I nodded.

'Well, what about tomorrow? No, you'd better say Wednesday. How's that?'

'Yes, that'll do fine.'

'Good-bye then, Christine.'

He held out his hand, and I placed mine in it and said, 'Good-bye, Martin.'

It was he who turned away first. Even his walk thrilled me

155

– the movement of his legs was more intoxicating than the gin that I had just drunk. My road lay in the same direction that he was taking, up the street and round the corner, but I let him get a start for he had not inquired which way I was going, and I would not see this as symbolical of the future.

I cannot tell you what my feelings were as I stood alone in that street. Not of joy, but definitely not of sorrow. Not full of new hope, but definitely not of despair. I felt no new-born courage, nor yet a chilling fear. I only knew that Martin was in my life again as I had known that one day he would be. That book of Ronnie's had been right. Desire something with all your heart and you'll get it.

When I got to the butcher's Rex Watson wasn't there – he had gone to his dinner – and Mr. Jameson said they had nothing but mutton. So I took our rations in mutton, and when I reached the house I couldn't remember having walked from the butcher's.

Dad was disappointed and said, 'Wait till I see Rex Watson,' and he had let the stew set on, but the burnt taste made no impression on me.

On the Tuesday night, with the house to myself, I washed my hair, bathed myself and did my nails, and on the Wednesday morning I practised making up my face, not heavily, but just enough to give me a touch of sophistication, for that is what I knew I lacked.

Sam, like Dad, was on night-shift, and for this I was thankful, for I would have had to get rid of him somehow. Not that he would have stayed once he had seen Martin, but I wanted no one here when Martin came, for it was absolutely necessary that I had him alone.

The last thing I did before getting myself ready was to prepare Constance for bed, but I did it as if she were going out for a special occasion. I curled her hair and did her nails and put her on a clean nightie, and every stitch on her bed was fresh. The only thing I couldn't do was make Ronnie's room, where she now slept, look like a nursery. I could do little with the house, the things were shabby, but everything was as clean as soap and water and polish could make it.

At five-to-seven I stood on the mat, my back to the fire, and wished that I smoked or drank or had some other means

156

of settling my nerves. At seven o'clock there was no knock on the door, but I heard Don Dowling's cough coming through the wall, and involuntarily I shuddered. Would he come in? But no. I knew his routine pretty well now. He would be off down to the house in Bog's End.

At half past seven I was sick in every pore of my body. During the eternity from seven o'clock I had never moved from the mat and now I felt I could collapse at any moment. Then there came the knock on the front door and I went to open it.

'Hallo.'

'Hallo,' I said.

He was in the front room, and I noticed his eyes flicking from the brass bed to the other articles of furniture that crowded the room. He had his cap in his hand and seemed ill at ease.

'Will . . . will I take your coat?'

Slowly he took off his coat and handed it to me and I laid it on the bed.

When he stood in the brighter light of the kitchen he said, 'I'm sorry I'm late. I thought I wasn't going to be able to make it at all.'

'Sit down,' I said. And as he sat down by the side of the table I asked, 'Would you like a cup of tea?'

'No thanks,' he answered, and gave a little laugh. I sat down, too. The table was between us, and so was something else. A great, solid awkwardness. He did not seem to possess the ease of manner and fluency of speech that I remembered.

His thoughts, too, must have been on how he remembered me, for he now said as he looked into my face across the space of the table, 'I thought when I saw you the other morning that you hadn't changed, but you have. You're better looking than ever, Christine. And you've grown . . . sort of filled out.' He again gave a little laugh, and I thought if Don Dowling had said these words I would have taken them as an insult, something bad, but nothing Martin said could be bad to me. Then he added, 'What have you been doing with yourself all the time?'

It was such a trite question that some small part of me that held the same vein of character that had run through our Ronnie cried voicelessly, 'Having your child and looking after it.'

157

The thought brought me to my feet, and I went to the fire and poked it, and as I poked I felt his eyes on me and I knew that I must come straight to the point, I must show him Constance. I placed the poker very gently on the hearth and, turning about, said, 'Martin, I've got something I want you to see.'

'Yes?' He was looking up at me, and we were about an arm's length away from each other, and I wanted to fling myself on him, and into him, never to come out as myself again.

'You sound very serious all of a sudden.'

'Would you mind coming upstairs?'

He was on his feet now, his face straight and not pale anymore but tinged with colour. His eyes were hard on me and he asked in a flat voice, 'What's this?'

I did not answer but led the way up the narrow dark stairs and into the bedroom where I had left a night light on.

I felt him hesitate on the threshold, and I turned and looked at him, and he came into the room. I had to close the door behind him before he could see the cot, and I could see that he was puzzled, even amazed at my action. And then he saw Constance. She was lying on her side, her hair no longer tidy but tousled about her head. She had pushed the clothes down from about her, and her pink nightie was rumpled around her waist. I don't know how long he looked at her, it might have been seconds or minutes, but when he turned to me his face was a deep dark red. He did not say, 'Now look here, you can't pin this on me.' Nothing like that. He had only to look on the child to know it was his – her skin, the shape of her face, her hair were all his. He turned fully to me and moved his head once from side to side, then dragged his lips between his teeth before speaking my name in a dazed kind of way.

'Christine.'

My eyes dropped before his gaze.

'Good God!'

I did not speak, I just waited for his arms to come about me.

'Christ!'

He was swearing like any man I knew, and because of it was nearer to my life.

'But, Christine . . . only that . . . that once.' The last word was just a whisper and he stumbled on its utterance, then slowly he put out his arms and drew me to him, and I lay

158

where I had wanted to lie for so, so long. And it was too much for me. I had rehearsed our meeting step by step and what would take place, and crying had no part in it, but now I was sobbing into his neck as if I would never stop. Yet, even at this moment, I told myself to be quiet in case they heard me next door.

His mouth was moving near my ear and he was repeating my name: 'Christine. Oh, Christine,' and by the depth of regret in the tone I was repaid a thousandfold for all I had gone through.

It was he who led me down the stairs, but we did not relinquish our hold on each other, and in the kitchen he again took me in his arms and soothed me, saying, 'Oh, my dear.' And when he asked, 'You waited all this time?' and I nodded my head dumbly against his coat, his voice sounded agonized as he muttered, 'Good God!'

He sat me down in the armchair by the fire, then pulling a little cracket forward with his foot he seated himself by my knees and held my hands tightly. And I looked down into his face, which seemed changed and full of trouble, and now it was my turn to comfort and I touched his cheek, and said, 'Don't look like that. It happened and there it is, and I'm not sorry, not a bit.'

Suddenly he dropped his head and buried his face in my lap, and the happiness I experienced as I stroked his hair was new, like the love that I had for Constance intensified a thousandfold. It had nothing to do with the body.

When after some time he looked up at me, he said softly, 'Christine, we have got to talk.'

'Yes, Martin.'

I did not want to talk. I just wanted to sit and hold him and he to hold me. I wanted to feel his mouth on mine; he had not yet kissed me.

'That night . . . by the river. . . .'

'It doesn't matter.' I smiled down at him with the compassion and understanding of all the mothers in the world, for now he was like a troubled child and I was not just twenty, I was old in wisdom. I did not want him to resurrect his humiliation, but he cut me short, saying, 'It's odd, but I've never been able to get you out of my mind. It is the only time I ran away in my life.'

'It's all right.'

'It isn't all right. It's been on my conscience for years. Not because I love you, you understand.' I nodded. And then he went on, 'But because I ran before that damned priest. He put the combined fear and terror of all the ages into me that night. He made his appearance at the wrong moment, for my uncle, Colonel Findlay, had been talking that very day about the power of the priests in this town. Apparently some time earlier my uncle's housemaid – she was a Catholic – married a Protestant in spite of the threats of the priest. The man had a mind of his own and wouldn't turn, nor say that the children would be brought up in the Church, and uncle said they were giving the girl hell.'

I gazed down at him. What was he trying to tell me? That he would not become a Catholic? That he was afraid of the pressure? I would give up my religion tomorrow, this minute. What did my religion matter to me if it meant losing him? Not all the Father Ellises in the world could make me feel differently. He was still talking.

'Then the very next day Uncle had a phone call from a friend at the other side of the hill saying that one of the priests was on the warpath looking for a fellow who had been—' He dropped his eyes from mine as he said, 'carrying on was the word used.' Then looking at me again he added, 'I wasn't carrying on that night, Christine, I loved you. It was the greatest experience of my life. I have never felt like it since. I meant to see you again – I remember what I said, "It's going to be a lovely summer" but I skedaddled home to France that very Sunday afternoon with a big push from Uncle.'

Again I stroked his cheek and said, 'I knew that was the house you had been living in. I knew that the colonel was some relation of yours.'

Slowly I watched him pull back from me and I tried to draw him towards me again, as I said, 'It's all right, I didn't say anything. My mother took me up, she made me go, and the colonel said there was no one of your name there. But I saw a picture of you with some other children. You looked just like Constance does now.'

Slowly again he pulled himself from my hands and stood up and turned his back towards me, and I said softly, 'I couldn't help it, Martin, I didn't want to go. It was my mother, she was so troubled.'

He did not look at me as he said, 'It isn't that, but they never told me you had been.' Then he asked a question. 'Did you see anyone else beside my uncle?'

'Yes, a young woman as we were going out.' I did not add that she looked as if she could have killed me. He sat down by the table, then got up immediately again and asked, 'Could I have my greatcoat, there's a bottle in there? I think I need a drink, Christine.'

I went into the front room and lifted his coat and held it to me tightly for a moment before taking it to him. From the inner pocket he pulled out a flask, and when I brought him a glass he said, 'Where's the other one?'

There was no need to be polished any more, so I replied truthfully, 'I don't drink. I thought the gin was terrible yesterday.'

He stared at me in a sort of puzzled, bewildered fashion, then filling the glass to the top he drank it in one gulp, and as he set the glass down on the table he repeated what he had said earlier, 'We've got to talk, Christine.' But now he added as if to himself, 'And I don't feel so badly about it now.'

My look must have held a question, for he touched my arm quickly saying, 'I don't mean about you. I'm referring to other things. We'll talk about them later, but now, Christine, something must be done. How have you managed all these years?'

His tone was so business-like that it changed him. He had become the officer, and I smiled softly as I said, 'Dad's good.'

He gripped my hand at this and exclaimed in a low voice, 'And you're good, you're so good — it's frightening.' He jerked himself upright now and his voice held the stiff note again as he said, 'But you must have money. I must make provision, we must talk about money.'

'Oh, money.' I not only shook my head, but shook my body as if throwing the word off, then shamelessly I put my arms about him and cried, 'Oh, Martin, Martin, don't talk about money, talk about us.'

Our faces were close, our breaths were mixing as they had done once before, then we were kissing and I was quite unashamed that it was I who had made the first move, though once I had done so there was no need to press further for it would seem that he wanted to eat me alive with his love. . . .

My body was at ease for the first time in years. It lay heavy on the bed, weighted down with content and the release that I longed for, and deep within my stomach there was the old gurgle of mirth. It could have been that we were once again lying on the grass ready to roll with our laughter. I had not cried this time. I felt I would never cry again; there was nothing that could make me cry. I told myself that if this love was snatched away from me within the hour, so intense, so solid was the feeling burning through me that it would take a lifetime to extinguish. His hands were moving lovingly over me and I was so unashamed that I was sorry it was dark, and then he whispered, 'Darling, darling, you're out of this world, they don't come like you today, high or low. You're a woman, Christine, a woman, and there are women and women. But you wouldn't know that. Listen, I want you to remember this. . . .'

I did not speak, only my heart repeated slowly, 'Yes, Martin, yes, Martin.'

'There's never been anyone like you and there never will. Remember that, will you, and I love you. I don't think I've ever stopped loving you. That's why – oh what does it matter. Wake up!'

'I am awake and I'll remember.'

At that moment there came a rap on the front door and I felt him stiffen. I stiffened myself, then said, 'Ssh! they'll think I've gone to bed.'

Whoever it was rapped three times before going away, and after that the enchantment was somehow broken and Martin said, 'I'm afraid I'll have to make a move, Christine, but God, how I'm loath to go. And we haven't talked, and we must talk, it's important that we talk.'

With my lips on his I silenced him saying, 'Tomorrow we will talk.'

Fifteen minutes later, after clinging together for another long moment, I let him out the front door into the dark street, which, as far as I could make out, was empty. Then I bolted the door and went straight upstairs and lay down again, and was surprised when I awoke and it was daylight. I put my arms upwards and stretched, then turned over on to my face and murmured, 'Martin. Oh, Martin,' and went to sleep again.

'I was awakened by Dad saying, 'Come on, lass, you going to sleep all day?'

I sat up with a bound, asking, 'What . . . what time is it?'

'Just on nine.'

'Nine o'clock!'

'Aye, nine o'clock.' He handed me a cup of tea, and as he left the room he said, 'It must have been that washing and all that running round. It used to tell even on your mother and you're not half her size.'

'Constance?'

'Oh, now—' Dad flapped his hand at me – 'she's all right. She came in to me over two hours ago and got me up. She's had her breakfast, so don't worry. You lie on a bit if you want to.'

'I'll be down in a minute,' I said.

'Now there's no hurry.' He went out, closing the door after him, and I drank the tea, then lay back. I felt rested as I had never known rest, I felt that I had been asleep for the first time in my life. I was purged of all weariness yet consumed with a delightful languor, and my body seemed to draw this feeling from my mind which was bemused with happiness. I was a young girl again, walking blindly in the white mist of love.

I hummed as I dressed, and in the middle of the morning Dad came in from the yard where he had been chopping sticks and, standing in the doorway, he said, 'It's good to hear you singing, lass. You look as if you've had a new lease of life. It's sleep you want.'

No, not sleep, Dad, not sleep.

In the afternooon Sam came in, and after a few minutes he too cast a closer sidelong glance at me and said, 'You got the spring feelin', Christine?'

I laughed, and answered, 'No, I just feel this way.' I had unconsciously misquoted a line from my favourite song and he nodded with a laugh, 'You're only painting the clouds with sunshine?'

As I laughed outright his face became straight and he stared at me. Sam had a much keener perception than Dad, and he asked quietly, 'Something happened, Christine?' I turned from him, then swiftly to him again. I wanted to tell him everything for I knew he would understand – Sam would always understand – but it was too new, too much mine yet . . . ours, so all I said was, 'I've got something to tell you, Sam, but later.' His eyes were still fixed on me, but being Sam he did not press to know what my something was. Sam could always wait. Sam had patience. I, too, had had patience, for five years I'd had patience and had waited, but now I had no patience left. The minutes could not pass quickly enough until Martin came again. His last words had been, 'We must talk.' They seemed reminiscent of our Ronnie's, but unlike his words, they left no foreboding.

There had been no definite time stated. 'Any time after seven,' he had said. He did not arrive until half past eight, and this time there was no awkwardness between us, for before we passed through the front room our arms were holding, and on the threshold of the kitchen we embraced with a fierceness that left us breathless. Gone was the gentle element that had been prominent in last night's loving.

When we let each other go he held me from him and said, 'I've thought of you all day, I haven't been able to get you out of my mind for a minute . . . a second.'

'And me, it's been the same with me. Oh, Martin.' I was on his breast again saying softly, 'I love you so, I love you so.'

We did not talk but went upstairs, and even hours later we still did not talk. It was as he was leaving the house for the second time he turned to me at the door and said, 'I really must talk to you, Christine, before we go on. There are things I must say. There are things to be straightened out.'

Just for a fleeting second a fear tore through me, and I gasped, 'You want me. You love me? You'll not leave me again?'

'Never. Never. It's all in your hands now. I'll want you as long as I breathe.' His mouth came on mine, hard yet tender. And after a moment he went on, 'But in the meantime you've got to live, and I want you to live . . . well—' he smiled – 'comfortably. You understand?'

I gave a soft chuckle and for answer fell against him. And time stood still once again. Then, taking me by the shoulders, he shook me gently, saying, 'Be practical. Look, take this.' He pulled a wallet from his pocket and out of it a thick wad of notes.

'No, no. No, I don't want any money, I'm all right.'

'Look, don't be silly. All these years. You must take this. It's nothing. I'm going to arrange about money for you.'

When he could not get my hands from behind my back to take the money he rolled it up and threw it into the far corner of the room, behind a chair, saying, 'Now you'll have to find it.'

'Oh, Martin.' Again we embraced, and then with the latch in his hand he whispered, 'The same time tomorrow night, or about it anyway. And then, mind—' He gripped my chin in his hand and, shaking my face, he said, 'We'll talk first, understand?'

I nodded happily. Then even once again he pulled me into his arms and murmured, 'There's so much to be said, we really must talk, Christine. Look, come out tomorrow night, to that pub where we went on Monday. . . .'

'No.' I shook my head. 'Come here. I promise you I'll let you talk as much as ever you like, and I'll agree with everything you say.'

'You mean that?'

'Yes, yes, my love.'

'God bless you.'

I had always considered 'God bless you' as a saying the prerogative of Catholics. It sounded funny coming from his lips, and there was something . . . a trace of sadness in it. And there was a touch of sadness on his face, too, as he took my hands and pressed them on to his cheek. Then he opened the door and passed out into the darkness. I did not watch him go but returned slowly into the kitchen, dazed and happy.

It was as I was about to go upstairs that I remembered the money. Gathering it up, I did not even count it properly, but guessed there was more than twenty pounds and thought: 'Fancy being able to carry so much money around with you.' When I got into my room I noticed with a start that he had forgotten his wrist-watch. I picked it up. It was a lovely watch and, I surmised, solid gold. I pressed it to my face, then, placing it on top of the notes, I laid them both in the bottom drawer of the chest. . . .

The next morning Don Dowling came in with a pound box of chocolates for Constance. Chocolates were rationed, and to see a fancy box was something unusual. Before I could do anything the box was in her hands, and when I said, 'Let me have it, Constance,' she put it behind her back, then ran away into the front room. And I turned to Don and said in a voice that I tried to keep ordinary, 'You mustn't give her things like that, Don. She's too young for them.'

'Nonsense,' he said. 'It's little enough she gets.'

'She gets all she needs.'

'You know, Christine, you sounded just like your mother then. You're getting like her.'

'I couldn't get like a better person.'

Before he made his next remark he rasped his great hand up and down the stubble on his cheek. 'That's questionable. You know, if it hadn't been for her . . .'

'Look, Don, I'm not going to discuss my mother with you.'

'All right, all right.' He wagged his finger at me. 'There's no need for us to fight, is there?'

I wanted to say, 'I'll fight with you as long as I have breath,' but I was afraid. I was not only afraid for myself and Constance, I was afraid for Sam. Whenever I had got Don Dowling's back up somebody had suffered. It had been the animals at first, the poor animals, then Sam and his burnt hands and feet. And still Sam, for there was a feeling against Sam in the town now. Don had done what he had promised. Even my dad was not quite the same to Sam. He had tackled him about the pit episode and Sam had denied it, but his denial had not been convincing, perhaps because I was present. I must not, I knew, add to the burden that was already Sam's, so I said evenly, 'It takes two to make a fight and I don't feel like it today.'

He laughed. 'Good enough. By the way, I bought a smasher of a car yesterday.'

'What can you do with a car,' I asked, 'you can't get petrol?'

'I look ahead, Christine. I'm always looking ahead. The war's on its last legs. I got this car for a hundred and twenty. The minute the war's over I bet I can ask three hundred for it. It's a Wolseley, dark blue, a beautiful job. I'm leaving the pit as soon as this business is finished.'

'Are you? What are you going to do?' I was rolling out some pastry.

'I'm going in with Remmy. I haven't done so bad already. I've got quite a little bit tucked away, you know.'

At this I wanted to retort, 'Then you want to give some to your mother,' for I knew Aunt Phyllis had to depend mainly on Sam to keep the house going, but all I said was, 'That's nice.'

'I've got ideas, big ideas. I'll even leave Remmy behind shortly.'

'Oh?'

'I was looking at a house on Brampton Hill the other day.'

In spite of myself my eyes swung to him and I exclaimed, 'Brampton Hill?'

'Aye, and why shouldn't I? Me and the likes of me are as good as anybody up there. Anyway half of them are empty now, and most of the others have been requisitioned and will go for a song. They won't have the money to keep them up – the present owners. Things'll be different after the war. By! they will that, and not afore time. It'll be a case of the mighty brought low.' He paused, then added, 'Anyway, I'll have to have a house some time, I'm thinkin' of getting married.'

I had turned to the pastry, but now again I was looking at him. 'Married? Who to?'

'Oh, just a lass.'

'Oh, I'm glad, Don.' And I was glad.

'Well, so long.' He smiled at me, then went to the front-room door and called to Constance, saying, 'What! you haven't opened them yet?' When he passed me again he remarked, 'You've got her scared – I told you you were like your mam.' He laughed teasingly, 'So long again.'

'So long, Don.'

I could not help feeling swamped with relief, for if I had thought about him in the last forty-eight hours it was to tell myself that he could not spoil my happiness in any way, and yet, knowing Don, I had still been fearful. And after all, there had been no need for fear, he was going to be married. It seemed that everything was working together for my good, the tide had turned at last. I sang, not under my breath, but right out loud, and I was carolling, 'You May Not Be An Angel' and thinking of Martin when Sam came in. I stopped immediately and greeted him with, 'Well what do you think of the news?'

He blinked an enquiring blink and said, 'I've never heard any, not since last night. I wasn't up for the eight o'clock.'

'I'm not talking about the wireless, but about your Don.'

A shadow passed over his face, leaving it with the blank dead look that even Don's name had the power to create, and he asked, 'Well, what about him?'

'Don't you know?'

'Apparently not the latest.'

'He's going to be married. Hasn't he told your mother?'

'He's going to be married?' Sam repeated each word slowly.

'Yes, didn't you know?'

'Who did he say he was going to marry?'

'Well . . . well when I asked him he just said a lass. But he's got somebody, hasn't he, in Bog's End?'

Sam gave me a long, concentrated look before letting his gaze slip away, and he walked from me and sat down by the table, and from there he looked at me again and said, 'The lass he's got in Bog's End is no lass, she's a woman near on forty and she's married and apart from her man.'

'But, Sam, he said a lass. It needn't be her, it could be somebody else.'

'Oh, God in heaven. . . .' Sam's voice drifted away wearily as he finished this phrase and, taking up his favourite position, his hands dangling, his eyes cast floorwards, he said, 'You better know this. You're the lass, Christine. You always have been and you always will be with him.' He turned his head slightly to the side and glanced at me.

There was a dryness in my mouth, and I wet my lips several times before I managed to bring out, 'You're wrong, Sam. He might have wanted me that way once but not since I've had Constance. He hates me for what I did.'

'He might have done, but he still wants you and he means to get you. He's never been baulked of anything he's wanted in his life, and the very fact that you're hard to get makes him all the more sure that he'll win. If you weren't that way, he would've dropped the idea of you years ago. It's the twist in him.'

'Sam, you're mistaken.'

'No, Christine.' Sam got to his feet and stood opposite to me, and he did not look like an eighteen-year-old lad but like a man much older than myself. And he talked like one as he said, 'I live next door, I know what goes on. Only the night afore last me mother was up when I came in off late shift.

She was crying because he hadn't come in and it near two in the morning. She said they'd had a row before he went out. It started about the woman in Bog's End, and he had said to her, "You needn't worry your head about her much longer for I'm going over the fence where I threw me cap years ago." And he had nodded towards the wall. It's funny, Christine, but I think me ma's as twisted as he is for she's more worried over him having you than she is the one in Bog's End.'

My voice was very small when I said, 'Well, he'll have his jump to no purpose. You know that, Sam, don't you?'

Now Sam stepped close to me and there was an actual tremor in his voice when he spoke. 'Listen to me, Christine. You've got to get away. That's the only place you'll be safe from him. Take the bairn and go some place. You'll get work. . . . And listen—' he held up his hand to stop me from speaking and added – 'let me finish. I've thought about this a lot. I've saved a little bit and I never spend half my pocket money. I can help you until you get on your feet. But you've got to get out. Your dad'll manage, and I'll talk to him and explain.'

'Sam . . . Sam, you listen to me. Come and sit down.' I took his hand and pressed him into a chair, and, sitting opposite him, I said, 'I've got something to tell you, Sam. Remember what I said yesterday?' He gave a brief nod and I went on, 'Do you remember the lad you saw me with that night by the river? You remember me grabbing you into the kitchen to tell me mam that you had seen me with that lad?' Again he nodded. 'Well he's come back. He loves me and I love him and we're going to be married.'

I don't know what reaction I expected from Sam to my news, I hadn't thought about it, but when, with his eyes fixed intently on me, he got slowly to his feet and, turning without a word, made for the door. I cried to him, 'Sam!'

On this he paused, and without looking at me, he said, 'I would still go away if I was you.'

Standing alone in the kitchen I had, for a moment, a feeling of utter deflation. I had thought I could talk to Sam about Martin, but he had no intention of listening to anything I had to say about him; that was plain. Then there was what he had told me about Don. Cap over the fence indeed! Yet who could have judged from Don's manner that he still wanted me. That he would want to hurt me for hurting him, yes, but not want to marry me. Fear was with me again. But I pressed it away, Martin would deal with him. In my mind's eyes I saw them together and I saw Don dwarfed by Martin's presence. Martin had something that could shrivel people like Don. A crisp word from him and Don would soon know where he stood with regards to me. Don could no longer frighten me with his subtle tactics. Martin had said that tonight we must talk. He would talk, I wouldn't be able to stop him tonight, I knew, and I would talk, too, and tell him about Don, and that would be that.

Martin did not come, and I spent the evening in a fever of waiting and the night hours in telling myself between doses that there would be a letter in the post for me. If there was not I wondered just how I would get through each hour until the night again.

There was no letter in the post. About eleven o'clock Sam came in, and for the first time in my life I snapped at him, for he began again to tell me that I must get away. 'Oh, don't be silly, Sam,' I said sharply, 'where am I to go?'

He turned his eyes away as he muttered, 'Well you said you've got this fellow ... if he's on the level he'll fix something.'

His tone made me angry and I exclaimed, 'Of course he's on the level.'

And then he asked with a sort of pleading, 'Christine, do this for me, will you? Go away for a little while.' And I replied, 'I can't Sam, there's nothing settled yet.' On this he barked at me in a very unSam-like manner, 'Well, don't tell me later on you wished you had.'

When in the afternoon I slapped Constance's bottom hard for getting on the chair and taking from the top shelf the box of chocolates, Dad said, 'That trick, lass, didn't merit that spankin'.' And he looked at me with a little twisted smile and, perhaps remembering my gaiety of yesterday, added 'Spring's soon over and summer comes.'

Yes, summer comes, but Martin did not come that night either and by nine o'clock I was pacing the floor like someone demented. At half-past ten I was retching into the sink. Knowing I would go mad if I did not sleep I took six aspirins, but even in the drowsy daze that these induced I was still waiting and calling, 'Martin . . . Martin.'

The following day I made preparations for that evening. If he did not come by eight I would go down to that bar and try to get news of him – I just could not stand another evening of pacing from the front room to the kitchen. But there had to be someone in the house with Constance. There was no one I could ask who would not want to know my business except, strangely enough, the Pattersons next door. As I have said before, they were the only Protestants in the place and because of this had always been divided from us. The fault lay not on the one side or the other. It would seem that the roads on which we were travelling to God were going in exactly opposite directions and therefore we never met. Mrs. Patterson had always been pleasant, she would always speak about the weather, or the news when we met, but we had never visited each other, even the war had not brought us close. The house next door could have been at the end of the street, so far apart were we. In fact I knew more of Miss Spiers at the top end and the Campbells at the bottom end than I did of the Pattersons. But it was of Mrs. Patterson I thought when I wanted someone to stay with Constance.

When I knocked at her door and made my request she did not seem in any way surprised and said, 'Yes, of course, Christine, I'll see to the bairn. Just let me know when you want to get away.'

By asking this favour of her I had broken down the barriers of years, and I think that she was pleased. She took it, anyway, as if it had been a daily occurrence that I should ask her to come into our house. I told her there might not be any necessity for it. I was expecting a friend and if she didn't turn up then I'd have to go and see her as she might be ill. How easily the stories come when the necessity arises, and you don't think of them as lies. The arrangement was that I was to knock on the wall if I wanted her.

At eight o'clock, my hat and coat already on, I knocked on the wall and Mrs. Patterson came in immediately, and so nice was she that her eyes did not roam around the place to see how it was fixed, but she sat down by the fire with her knitting and said, 'Don't hurry, Christine.' Even with anxiety rending my body I could spare a thought to think, 'She's nice.'

171

I liked her. For over twenty years she had been next door and I don't think I had given her more than a passing thought. And now I knew that of all the women in the street I liked Mrs. Patterson. I took my torch and said, 'I won't be long, not more than an hour.'

I was not used to being out in the black-out and, apart from the blackness which made the roads unfamiliar, I had the men to contend with. When I reached the High Street, time after time a light was flashed into my face and an invitation given to me. The first time it happened I ran, the second time I side-stepped the man. He was in uniform. The third time wasn't so easy. There were three of them abreast and they were laughing, and as I dodged off the pavement they dodged, too, this way and that. And then in desperation I yelled, and as they dispersed I heard one exclaim as if in amazement, 'Struth!' Three times I lost my way, but finally I came to the passage leading to the bar. When at last I pushed open the door and went round the black-out curtains and into the saloon, I stood blinking and dazed for a moment. I could not recognize the room that I had visited a few days ago. All the seats were occupied, people were even standing round the walls, and all the men were in uniform, R.A.F. uniform, and I saw at a glance they were all officers. It did not take more than a second to assure me that Martin was not there, and I told myself I had known he wouldn't be. If he could have got off he would have come to me at the house, perhaps at this very minute he was there. This thought brought a flurry to my mind. Why had I not told Mrs. Patterson the truth? Then the barman squeezed past me. He was the man who had served us the other day, and I touched his arm and asked, 'Have you a minute? Has Flight-Lieutenant Fonyère been in?'

The man screwed up his eyes and said, 'Fonyère? I don't seem to know anybody of that name, miss. But just a minute, I'll be back in a tick.'

He went into the saloon with a tray, and I walked past the door and stood against the wall, and from where I stood I could see into the bar. It, too, was packed, but there, right at the front of the counter, was Tommy, and the sight of him made me draw farther back along the passage.

When the barman returned he said, 'Now, miss, Fonyère you said, that was the name, wasn't it?'

'Yes,' I said. 'Flight-Lieutenant Fonyère. We were in the other day. Perhaps you don't remember.' He looked over his shoulder towards the saloon and said, 'Yes, yes I do now.'

'I . . . I had gin, remember?'

He gave a little laugh. 'I wouldn't remember you by your drink, miss – I sell some gins in a day, when we have it – but I remember you all right. I think though you're mistaken about the name. That officer's name was Belling. He was Flight-Lieutenant Belling.'

'But his name's Fonyère.'

'Well it could be double-barrelled, miss.'

'Yes, yes perhaps. But has he been in this evening?'

'No, I haven't seen him since he was in with you, miss. He's not a regular here. Why not try The Crown in the High Street? A lot of them go there. I've got to go now.'

'Wait. That man,' I pointed through to the bar. 'Mr. Tyler. Will you tell him that he's wanted outside for a minute, please?'

The man looked at me – it was like a sly dig – and if I had been capable of thinking of anything but seeing Martin at that moment my thoughts would have made me blush. Muttering 'Thank you,' I went out into the street and along to the bar door, my torch all ready to shine on it when it opened.

It was evident from Tommy's face that the request for his presence outside had caused him some surprise, but as soon as I spoke he said, 'Why, Christine, what are you doing up here?'

'I just wanted a word with you, Tommy.'

'Well, come on in and have a drink instead of standing out here in the dark.'

'No, thanks, Tommy, if you don't mind I won't come in. I just want to ask you something. You remember the other morning when you were talking to that officer?'

He did not answer, and I went on, 'I just wondered if you had seen him the day?'

Still he made no reply, and I said quickly, 'Don't you think me awful, Tommy. We are friends . . . we were friends before the war. We had lost sight of each other until . . . until that minute when I saw him talking to you.'

I heard Tommy clear his throat, and then he said quietly, 'Come on in and have a drink. Not in the bar. We'll go in the other room.'

'No, thanks.'

'I think you'd better.'

There was something in his tone that meant much more than the words he spoke, and when his hand came on my arm I allowed him to lead me a few steps down the street and through the door and into the Commercial Room. This room, too, I saw was full, but here they were not all officers, but a mixture of civilians and uniformed men and women. And Tommy, pushing his way through to a corner where there were a couple of spare seats near the wall, said, 'What do you drink?'

'Gin,' I said.

'Gin it is.' I watched him make his way to a narrow counter, which I guessed divided this room from the main bar. And when he came and placed the drink before me, he said, 'I didn't expect to be able to get a gin but your luck's in.' As I held the glass in my hands he said, 'Chin up.'

I did not drink politely but finished it at one go, every drop, and when I placed the glass on the table, Tommy, looking straight at me, said, 'I don't know anything about your business, lass, or what was between you and him, but I've got some bad news for you.'

My fingers were tight round the tubby little glass and his hand came out and, taking it from me, he moved it across the table. Then, putting his hand over mine, he said, 'He got his packet Wednesday afternoon.'

I saw the people in the room quite clearly. There were several groups all talking and laughing, and one fellow in the far corner was singing. He was imitating a popular crooner and the girl with him was covering her face and laughing.

'Now look. Look, pull yourself together, this is happening every day.'

All the voices in the room seemed very faint. Then above them I heard Tommy saying, 'And somebody else will be missing him the night. You shouldn't forget that, lass.'

I was looking at him and he was looking at the table, and I heard my voice repeating, 'Somebody else? There was nobody else. He had nobody but me.'

'Aye, well, it's nice for you to think that, all lasses do, and go on thinking it if it's any comfort to you, but, nevertheless, he had a wife and a couple of bairns.'

174

'You're lying.' My words were slow and my voice was heavy, deep and accusing, and I knew that I hated this man who was sitting looking away from me more than I did Don Dowling.

'I'm not lying, Christine. The Flight-Looey was married. His wife is living in Littleborough with her father. She's got quite a name in the W.V.S. in these parts. The bairns are evacuated some place, so I understand. Her family's well known, she's Colonel Findlay's daughter.'

'No! no!' I smacked away his hand as it came to comfort me again. It was the same action that Constance would use when in a tantrum and wanting her own way. Again I said, 'No, it's not true. I don't believe you.'

Although I had not moved from the seat I knew I was backing away from him, backing away from the room, backing away from all he had told me, all the terrible reality of the moment, reality and truth. For in a section of my mind I was seeing it all now, the whole jig-saw. But I wasn't controlled by that section, I was controlled by my feelings. This agony, this love and despair, and the knowledge of the torturous years ahead, the empty years into which I would be unable to bring any man to fill the gap Martin had left. The section was saying, 'You must have known this, you must have known there could be nothing between you and him, not really, other than a kept woman.' And I cried at it, 'No, I didn't,' but it said, 'You did. And it's a fact anyway, so face it. He never wanted to come up to the house, and when he did he wasn't for staying, it was you.' 'It wasn't,' I yelled back, 'he did want to stay. He loved me, I know he loved me.' 'If he had a wife he must have also loved her,' the voice insisted. 'Shut up! shut up! shut your big mouth. Go to hell, you ...!' God God. That wasn't me, I never even thought swear words. Oh, don't make me sick. Come alive. Listen to what Tommy's saying. . . . 'I can't, God Almighty, Jesus, Mary and Joseph, don't let it be true.'

'Look, lass, take a pull at yourself. I'll get you another drink.'

'Shut up! shut up!' I was saying it, yelling it. The people in the room were still clear, so clear that their outlines were sharply defined as if in light. But I wasn't concerned with them. I was concerned with Tommy and his lies.

'It isn't true, it isn't true. Shut up! shut up!'

Everybody was looking at me now, and my voice alone was filling the room, it was packing every corner. I made some effort to stop it, but when a woman took hold of my arm I screamed at her, and when Tommy's arms came about me I struck out with both my feet and my hands, and then the scream lifted me straight off the ground and I floated in the air. For a moment of time, so small a second would have been long in comparison, I felt the return of the ecstatic feeling I used to have as a child when I jumped in the air, and I screamed at it to 'Go away! go away!' and then there was nothing. . . .

I knew I was waking up, and as always when I had something unpleasant to face in the day I tried to hang on to sleep. But this was a different hanging on, a different sleep. It was deeper, and I was willing myself to die in it, yet not really aware of the reason why I wanted to die; but when, with the sureness of an incoming wave, awareness gradually forced itself to the surface of my mind I groaned, 'Oh God! Oh God!' My eyelids lifted and there was Dad sitting looking at me. It was daylight and I was in a strange room. I put out my hands and gripped his as I cried, 'Oh, Dad!'

'Now, lass, take it easy, you're all right.'

'Oh, Dad! What am I going to do?' I was asking him this question and he did not know what I was talking about. So he stroked back my hair and said, 'Now take it easy, take it easy.'

I pulled myself up in the bed and looked round the room and asked, 'Where am I?'

'Now, you're all right.' He was patting my shoulder. 'You remember Mollie, you know Mollie?' He was smiling and talking to me as if I was a child who had to be reminded of something ordinary to pacify her.

'Yes. Yes, of course I know Mollie.'

'You took bad and she happened to come along at the time and took you home. Then she sent a note up to the house and I got it when I came in.'

My mind was strangely numb. Although it told me that Martin was dead and he had a wife and two children, it did not seem to be real, not real enough to cause me pain, for after the moment of waking and realization, I had an odd, strange feeling of being shut off from myself. I was two people, one of me held my head and the other my heart, and the part with my heart had no feeling. I had an urge to use the part with my head, so I got up, pulling the eiderdown around me. Then gently pushing Dad to one side, I said, 'I must go home. There's the child.'

'She's all right. She's in with Aunt Phyllis.'

Aunt Phyllis meant Don.

'Where's my clothes?'

'Now look, there's no hurry. I'm going in the other room. Mollie will be back in a minute, she's just slipped out to get something. There's your things there.' He pointed to a chair. 'Now take it easy.' He patted my shoulder and went out, and I grabbed my things and pulled off my nightie, but as I did so, I realized it was not my nightie. I never had a nightie like this, this was silky and soft and frail, but much too short for me. I threw it on the bed, and within a few minutes I was dressed. As I picked up my coat and hat the door opened and Mollie came in.

'Feeling better?' She spoke as if there were no years between, no years when we had not been close friends.

'Yes . . . yes, thanks Mollie, I'm better.'

'Look, there's no hurry.'

'I've got to get home, there's the child. But – but thanks, Mollie.'

Ignoring the thanks, Mollie said, 'Well if you're bent on goin'' I'll get somebody to take you, but come and have a wash and a bite of breakfast.'

'No, thanks. No, thanks. I'll have a wash, that's all.'

'You'll have a cup of tea. Come on.'

Her briskness drew me into the other room, which I saw was a sitting-room, and through it to the kitchen where there was a modern sink with hot and cold water. There I washed my face and hands, and when I came back into the room she handed me a cup of tea, and another to Dad, saying, 'By the time you've drunk that I'll have a jeep at the door.' She had hardly finished speaking before she went out, and it would seem that she was as good as her word for a few minutes later she came back saying, 'He'll be here in a minute, it's a friend of mine. He'll run you home.'

When I heard the car pull up outside the house I got quickly to my feet, and Dad, taking me by the arm as one did a patient just coming out of hospital, led me on to the landing and down the stairs and into the street, Mollie, coming behind us, nodded towards the driver and said, 'This is Joe.'

The man nodded and smiled, then helped me up into the front of the jeep, and Dad, going round the other side, sat beside me and took my unresisting hand in his. I don't remember thanking Mollie, or the man who drove us, and in a few minutes I was home and in our kitchen again, and it looked quite different. I stood in the middle of it as if I had never seen it before, and Dad, helping me off with my coat, said softly, 'What is it, lass? What's happened? What's come over you?'

Like a child again I turned to him and, flinging myself into his arms, I cried, cried until I nearly choked, cried until he begged and implored me to stop, cried whilst Sam, having come in, held my head, cried while Aunt Phyllis said, 'This's got to stop. Get a doctor,' cried while Don, trying to thrust Sam away, grabbed my shoulder and yelled at me, 'Stop it! stop it! Tell us what's happened,' cried until the doctor came. From then on I went into a sort of sleep in which there were patterns, great patterns of colour, beautiful colours, and, like a thread weaving in and out and separating one colour from another, there were strings of words, and some said, 'We must talk, Christine,' and others, 'I love you. . . . You're like a star that's fallen on a dung heap,' and others, 'I'll want you as long as I breathe.' 'If I can get away I'll be here by seven.'

I was in bed a week and had no desire to get up. It was Mollie who stung me into life again. She had come to see me nearly every day. Sometimes she could only stay five minutes for, as she blankly put it, between men, cordite and coupons, she hadn't time to say, 'Whoa! there.' She had been sitting on the foot of my bed talking about what she meant to do when the war was over, and she could leave the munition factory, when she stopped and, leaning towards me, said, 'And it will be over you know, Christine, everything will be over. Life doesn't stop.'

I turned my head sideways on the pillow away from her eyes, and she remarked, 'Aye, that's what you're doing, looking sideways at life, and it won't do, you know. You've got to get back into the stream.' She hitched herself nearer to me, 'Look, Christine, you've had a dirty trick played on you, but you're not the only one, no, by God! not by a long chalk. You've got to remember that.'

My face was as stiff as my voice when, looking at her, I demanded, 'What do you know about it?'

'More than you think.'

'You know nothing, you're only guessing.'

'Tommy Tyler is a pal of Joe's and Joe's a pal of mine. Joe and me just stopped into the bar that night you were raisin' Cain, and what's more natural than Tommy should tell us after I got you round to my place. Look, Christine ...' She dropped her hand on mine where it was gripping a fistful of the coverlet, and then said, 'Them type are all alike. Why, I could tell you things that would lift the skin off your scalp.'

I pulled my hand away from her touch, and she straightened herself and said, 'Well, have it your own way, but I kept you this.' She opened her bag and took out a single sheet of newspaper saying, 'That's the front page of last Saturday's *Review*. Take a good dekko at it, and if that doesn't shake you nothing will.' She dropped it on the bed, then, getting to her feet, her tone changed and she said softly, 'I'll be in the morrow, so long.'

I did not speak, and even after the door had closed on her I did not grab up the paper, but lay looking at it, willing it to hold other than I knew it held, willing it not to tell me anything about him that would lessen my love for him. He was dead and I wanted to cherish his memory. That was all that was left to me, the memory of him. Slowly I drew the paper towards me and there was his face looking at me – his long, pale face with the dark eyes. He was in uniform, and next to him, also in uniform, was the woman I had seen in the hall of Colonel Findlay's house. Under the picture it said:

'Flight Lieutenant Fonyère-Belling and Mrs. Fonyère-Belling.
This photograph was taken the day Mrs. Fonyère-Belling was decorated for her outstanding service in the W.V.S.'

I read the column and a half, slowly lifting each word, as it were, from the page. It told me that Martin was Colonel Findlay's nephew, and that he had lived his early years in France, his father being of French extraction, but he had spent part of his holidays with his uncle and cousins. He had married his cousin in June, nineteen-forty, after a romantic attachment begun in childhood. He, too, had a distinguished war career and had been decorated for outstanding bravery. He had been transferred to Littleborough for a rest from operations. Whilst there he had been doing valuable work training young pilots. It was while instructing that his plane crashed into the hillside near Brooker's Fell. The trainee, too, was killed.

This information only covered the half column. The long column dealt with Mrs. Fonyère-Belling and her work in the W.V.S. and ended with the fact that the colonel had given up The Grange to the military for the duration of the war, and that since coming back north Mrs. Fonyère-Belling had taken a small house at Littleborough. She had hoped, after the war, to live with her husband in France.

Slowly I put the paper down. For the moment, Martin's personality had receded, swamped as it were by the weight of the woman staring at me from the page. This wasn't an obituary for Flight-Lieutenant Fonyère-Belling, but simply a few details about the husband of Mrs. Fonyère-Belling, and into my numbed body and brain came a feeling of pity. He had been as helpless against her love as I had been against his. I could see her face as I had seen it that day, the hate of me expressed in it was a gauge of her feelings.

Through the numbness that had enveloped me during the past week there had forced itself to my notice, again and again, a question, until I had to face it. And this question was: Why, living in the town, had I not heard of the marriage? They were prominent people. And Father Ellis ... that astute detective and tracker down of men who seduced Catholic girls, how had it escaped his notice? Or hadn't it? Perhaps he had known but had seen the uselessness of stirring up trouble. Of one thing I was certain, the marriage had been as quiet as she could keep it. It must have taken place in some other part of the country. It certainly hadn't taken place in Fellburn, or I would surely have seen a report in *The Review*.

The colonel, too, would have been all for keeping Martin clear of Fellburn, for undoubtedly he would know I had a child – Martin's child. It must have shaken both him and her when Martin was transferred back here, only ten miles away – she hadn't counted on the authority of the R.A.F. And Martin. He had understood everything that night I had told him about my visit to the colonel's. His words came back to me. 'I don't feel so badly about it now.' He knew then that he had been blindfolded and led gently into the Findlay fold.

Never had I thought that I could have pitied Martin – you don't pity a god. But Martin was no longer a god. I saw him as I saw myself. We both had one trait that had linked us together, weakness, a weakness that had strength only to indulge itself. Poor Martin. . . . I was still not capable of hating. . . .

The day I came downstairs it was Constance who took my hand. Talking to me as I did to her when coming down the steep stairs, she said with old-fashioned solicitude, 'Careful now, Mummie, careful.' And while Dad fussed around me in the kitchen, making me put my feet up on the fender and lean back in the armchair, she fussed, too. But their kindness could not warm me in any way.

The following day I took up the business of managing the house again, and such was my intensity in doing so that Dad kept cautioning me, 'Now lass, ease off. It's over-work that's got you where you are.' But now I was being driven by a thought, a terrifying thought, that made me look daily at the calendar hanging at the side of the mantelpiece under the scissors. It made me think in the night, 'If it happens I'll drown myself, I just couldn't bear that, not that shame again.'

Of those about me only Sam guessed at what had happened, but he could only guess. Perhaps he thought I had been given the chuck . . . and I had. Definitely I'd been given the chuck, but before being given the chuck I might have been given something else. Good God! No! No! No! No! No!

Towards the end of the third week I had a slight heaviness in the pit of my stomach and a sickly feeling, but then I often had a sickly feeling with a period, and it would present itself at any time, not just in the morning, so I waited, asking myself immediately I awoke, 'Do I feel sick?' And then one morning the answer turned me completely round in the bed and I dug my fists into the pillow. Sitting up, I whispered to myself, 'Sam will take care of her.' Dad might not live until she was able to look after herself, but Sam would take care of her. I got up and dressed, and going downstairs I took a sheet of notepaper and an envelope out of the chiffonier drawer, and on the paper I wrote:

> 'Dear Sam, Will you please look after Constance
> for me? I just can't go on.'

That was all. I sealed it, addressed it briefly to Sam, went back upstairs and placed it against the mirror. It was seven o'clock now. I got Constance up and dressed her, gave her her breakfast, then clasping her hand tightly in mine I took her next door to Mrs. Patterson.

Mrs. Patterson was an early riser, she always had most of her work done before nine o'clock in the morning, and she showed no surprise at seeing me at this hour, but she did look a bit taken aback when I asked her if Constance could stay with her until Dad came in at ten o'clock. 'Are you feeling no better?' she asked me.

'Yes, thank you, Mrs. Patterson,' I replied. 'I'm feeling much better.'

'You don't look it,' she said. 'Will you have a cup of tea?'

'No thanks,' I said. Then before I turned from her I added, 'Thank you, Mrs. Patterson, for your kindness. It's a pity we didn't get to know you years ago.'

She did not say anything but stepped out into the street and said, 'Look, Christine, won't you come in?'

'Mummie.' Constance began to whimper, and I said to her, 'Be a good girl and stay with Mrs. Patterson.' Then I walked quickly away down the street. But I did not immediately go to the fells, for Mrs. Patterson might still be watching me and become suspicious if she saw me going towards the river at this hour. I went down towards the bridge, and cut across to the river that way. I walked back along the river bank and in a very short time came to the place I was making for, the place where the lads used to bathe, the place where I nearly drowned, the place that was deep and into which Martin had come for me.

Well, if there was any coming together I'd soon be with him. As I stood looking at the water I saw that at this side, for quite some distance from the bank, it was rather shallow, and I did not want to be deterred — I was sensible enough to know that a plodge through the cold water to the deeper part might do this — so I deliberately walked along the bank towards the stones, across to the other side, and back along the far bank to the place where my life had begun.

The place where Martin and I had lain on the grass was all mud now and held no significance whatever. At the edge of the water I paused for a moment, taking stock of how far I had to go before I should come to where the shelf of rock ended, then I moved.

My feet were actually in the water when I saw a figure, like a tumbling boulder, come bounding down the hill opposite. The pattern was so similar to that which had taken place that summer night, the hair seemed to rise from my head. Then I saw that the running figure was Don Dowling, and now he was shouting at the top of his voice. To be dragged out of the water by Don Dowling was something I could not stand. This moment must wait. I stepped back on to the little beach and, stooping down, picked up a piece of driftwood just as his panting hollow came across the river, ordering, 'Stay where you are!'

I looked across at him, and in a voice that surprised me with its steadiness, I said, 'What's up with you?' This seemed to nonplus him for a moment. Then he shouted, 'What do you think you're up to?'

Now I was back in the game, acting as I always acted with him, and I cried, 'I'm out for a walk and I'm picking a piece of stick up. Is there anything wrong in that?' I held the stick out in my hand, and I saw him blinking as if not knowing what to make of me. Then he yelled, 'Stay where you are, I'm coming over.'

But before he took one step along the bank towards the stepping stones, I shouted, 'You can save yourself the trouble, I'm going into the town. I had to do some shopping and I just wanted to have a look at the river. What's up with you anyway?'

His face was screwed up and he was blinking again, and I turned about and climbed the bank, knowing his eyes were on me. I knew what had happened. Mrs. Patterson had suspected something and had gone to Aunt Phyllis's. I should never have taken Constance in to her. I should have left her in bed, she would have been all right.

When I came to the path I took the short-cut to the town, asking myself as I did so where I was going. But as I came towards the houses I knew. I was going to Mollie; Mollie would know what to do.

When I knocked on Mollie's door it was opened by a man. He was about thirty and tall, with black hair and eyes, and a voice that did not belong to this part of the country, a voice that somehow held the same timbre in it as Martin's. He had evidently just got up, and I murmured in embarrassment, 'Is . . . is Mollie up yet?'

'Ah.' It was a loud 'Ah' as if he had just remembered something. 'I know who you are. Come in, come in.' I sidled past him, and he closed the door behind me. 'Go on up.'

When I entered the sitting-room and saw Mollie was not there I turned to him, saying, 'I'm sorry I'm early.'

'Early?' he repeated. 'You're not early, I'm late. Sit down, sit down, that's if you can find a chair.' He swept a coat and pullover off a chair and, pointing to it, said, 'She won't be a minute. I thought it was her and she'd forgotten her key.'

On this I remembered that Mollie was on the night-shift. I did not say that I would go and come back again later, for I knew that I must see Mollie. So I sat down, and was glad to do so, for my legs were shaking beneath me. And the man said, 'Are your feet wet?' He was looking at my shoes and I made no effort to draw them away under the chair but said, 'Yes, I've been walking through the grass.'

'Ho,' he said again in that peculiar fashion, then added, ' "The dew is on the heather long ere it is light".'

There was a funny little twist to his lips. It was a smile that invited me to smile back but I just stared at him, wondering dazedly how he had come to know Mollie and that he seemed a bit funny, and it wasn't the kind of funniness that I would associate with laughter, not like Sam's funniness.

As he went into the kitchen I heard a quick step on the stairs, and the door burst open and Mollie came in, only to stop dead on the sight of me and exclaim, 'Why, hallo. . . . You're up early, aren't you, Christine?' And before I could answer she looked round the room, then called, 'You, Doddy, look at the bloody mess you've got this room in.'

The man appeared in the doorway, he was holding the stanchions at each side and he pushed his head forward. ' "Hail fair enchantress of the morning",' he greeted her, and she cried at him, 'Oh, stop your bloody chatter at this hour. You wouldn't feel so buoyant, lad, if your belly was full of cordite fumes like mine is. Get some tea on and stop your carry on.'

When the man disappeared she turned to me and said softly, 'That's Doddy. He's all right, he's a good lad but—' She tapped her brow with her finger. 'His name should be Potts not Dodds, he's so damned clever he's daft. . . . But what's up, Christine?' Her voice was low now, and I put my hands out to her and whispered desperately, 'I've got to talk to you alone, Mollie.'

'O.K. I'll get rid of him after we've had a cup of tea. My!' She looked down at my feet. 'You're wet.'

I did not answer her but bowed my head. And I felt her staring at me, then she turned and yelled, 'Don't be all bloody day, Doddy. For Christ's sake put a move on.'

The man came in carrying a laden tray, and as he put it on the table he looked at Mollie and said, with a smile, and still in his high, chanting voice, ' "Your words shame jewels, and in their twinkling—" '

'Oh, for God's sake, Doddy.' There was an unusual quiet appeal in Mollie's voice, and the man sat down, and with a solemn gesture raised his hand and said, 'So be it. 'Tis done. Drink your tea, girls.'

I gulped at the scalding tea, feeling that I must have some warmth within me for I had begun to shiver. Noticing this, Mollie said, 'Is there anything left in the cupboard, Dod?'

The man rose immediately and went into the kitchen, to return with a bottle which he handed to Mollie, and she, pulling the cup from my hand, emptied the contents of the bottle into it, then, scooping some sugar into the cup, she stirred it vigorously, saying, 'Get that down you.'

It tasted nice, much better than gin, and after a few minutes there was a comforting glow spreading through me and I felt my taut body relaxing. I saw Mollie covertly signalling the man to make himself scarce, then I heard the tap running in the kitchen and the splashing of him washing, and when he next came into the room he was fully dressed and I saw that he was an R.A.F. corporal. He stood in front of me, clicked his heels, saluted smartly, did a half turn and marched out. I saw that Mollie wanted to laugh, but she didn't, she just turned to me and said, 'He's a bloody fool, but you couldn't get a nicer one if you searched the globe. And what's more, he's harmless.'

'Mollie,' I grabbed her hands again, 'I think I'm . . . I know I'm . . .'

'Good God, no!' Mollie's voice expressed horror. What I had just inferred had really shocked her – I had thought she was the last person on earth who could be affected by anything of this kind. It was this that had brought me to her, and now she was shocked. But not for the reason that I surmised, as, to my relief, I soon found out, for, getting to her feet, she exploded, 'The dirty sod! the rotten, low-down—'

'It wasn't his fault.'

'Oh, for God's sake stop being like that. Have you no bloody spunk at all? Not his fault! He went with you, didn't he? He could have seen that you didn't get into this predicament. Not his fault! They're all the bloody same, but if they want to deal at the same market they should see you don't get landed with a bloody bellyful.'

I sat looking at her as she tramped about the room cursing and swearing. She wasn't to know that he hadn't really wanted to come to me, not at the beginning, and when he had come what had happened was entirely my fault, at least the first night. The second night, I knew he was mine forever, and the only comfort that remained of this whole business was the truth of that knowledge. I wasn't unaware that my condition could have been prevented, but how does one go about a thing like that? Did one take a big stick and beat at the gossamer strands of enchantment, demanding, 'What do I have to pay for this?' Mollie would know, and Mollie could take the big stick I felt sure, but I was not Mollie.

'What am I going to do?'

'Stop buggering about and get rid of it. Have you any money, anything saved up?'

I had nothing saved up but I had the roll of notes in the bottom drawer. There was twenty-five pounds and the gold watch which bore the inscription inside the back, 'To Martin, June 1st, 1942, Eileen.' A stiff, proper inscription. Not 'To my beloved Martin', or 'From your loving Eileen', just 'To

Martin ... Eileen'. It was like the picture on the front page of the paper. Yet she had loved him. But he had never loved her.

Although he had never mentioned her name to me, I knew this. Daily, over the past few weeks, this conviction had become stronger.

'I've got twenty-five pounds.'

'You'll need more than that. They're asking big figures now, thirty and more.'

'But what do they do?'

'It isn't they, it's a her. She'll take it away.'

I had imagined Mollie would know of some medicine, some stuff that I could take, I hadn't thought of having it taken away. My whole being curled up in revolt and I said, 'I don't want that done, Mollie. Isn't there anything I could take?'

'Nothing that is sure. Some of the stuff will skite the innards out of you and you'll still have the bairn. No, she's your best bet. Your only bet, for you can't be saddled with another. Tommy told me you knew him – the chap – afore the war. Does Constance belong to him?'

I looked at her. 'Yes.'

'Well, my God' – she let out a long breath – 'I've heard everything now. You must be clean barmy, Christine. A girl like you who could pick and choose among the best to let yersel' be bitten by the same bug twice. Are you completely green? Anybody would think you were soft.'

Yes, anybody would think that I was soft. And I was soft – soft, weak, squashy and sentimental. Nobody who wasn't soft would wait four years for a myth, and nobody, unless they were made that way, would stop a man from talking, talking money, and make him make love instead. Yes, Mollie was right.

'I'll go along this afternoon after I've had a bit of sleep and see Ma Pringle, and then I'll come up and tell you when she can do it.'

'And you may as well take a new-born child and bash its brains out against the wall as have an abortion. You sin even by contemplating it, and you damn your immortal soul by doing it.'

The words of a sermon I had heard Father Ellis deliver

a short while ago were in my ears, his voice was loud and clear as if he was standing in the room, and I felt a moment's terror, the quaking terror that only a Catholic feels when his immortal soul is said to be in peril. And this terror must have expressed itself on my face, for Mollie exclaimed, 'Now what's the matter with you?' and I heard myself muttering, 'I daren't go to that woman.'

'But you're willing to take stuff, it's just the same.'

Yes, it was just the same, but somehow different. If I took the stuff and it worked the child would come away in a sort of miscarriage, but to have it taken away was different. I couldn't explain to myself or Mollie, but I knew it was different, and because of the difference I knew I couldn't have this abortion. I heaved and ran towards the kitchen, and as I leaned over the sink Mollie held my head and soothed me, and not until I was in the room again did she say, 'You're thinkin' of the priest, aren't you? That's what comes of going to mass every Sunday. Me, I gave it up years ago. They weren't goin' to frighten the liver out of me. I'm laying me stakes on what's down here. Nobody's come back to show us the prizes they get for being so bloody good, so don't be such a blasted fool. But you were always a bit of a priest's pet, weren't you?'

A priest's pet! There rose in me for an instant a feeling of hate against all priests, particularly Father Ellis. If he hadn't come on us that night. If I hadn't laughed. If I hadn't led him to us with my laugh. If ... if ... A priest's pet!

Then Mollie spoke, quietly and comfortingly as she said, 'Think it over. Chew on it for a day or two. There'll be no time lost, and then we'll see what's to be done. But remember this, it's all the same to me whatever you decide on, you'll always be welcome here.'

One thing I've found in life, if there's not a cure for an ill, there's a solace provided, and Mollie was that solace for me, at least for a time.

I was four months gone and it could not be hidden any longer. The suspicions of those around me burst into the open and I was besieged from all sides. The scandal lit not only the street but the community of the church. They did not take into account that Cissie Campbell and a good many more were having the time of their lives, or so it was called, while their men were away, and that in certain cases children were being born when husbands had not been home for years. But they were married, they were sheltered by wedding rings, and if they were foolish enough to slip up once, and show evidence of their good times, they certainly did not repeat the mistake. Christine Winter had repeated it – she was a bad lot.

These reactions, strangely enough, hardened me. They dragged out from my depths some spark that enabled me to answer their stares with a straight look when I met them and put an air of defiance into my stride in passing. To these mothers and daughters who looked at me with a 'Dear! dear!' clicking of the tongue look, I wanted to shout, 'I have been with a man three times, and out of that I've had two bairns. You wouldn't believe it, would you? No, of course you wouldn't.'

Dad, I knew, was stunned and he kept saying, 'Why, lass? ... How? ... I never knew there was anybody.' These words had a familiar ring.

Sam, dear understanding Sam, even he looked at me as if I had changed into a different being and said, 'Good God, Christine, what's up with you, anyway?'

My Aunt Phyllis, I knew, said a lot but not to me. I heard her say to Dad, 'Well, it didn't come as any surprise.' Oh, you liar, Aunt Phyllis. But how happy you are, I thought.

And then came Father Ellis, rigid of countenance and frozen inside against me. He stood in the kitchen by the side of my father and stared at me and, after swallowing and breathing deeply, he brought out, 'May God forgive you.' And my mind cried back at him, 'And you, too.' And then he said something that freed me from all fear for a moment. 'And to think,' he said, 'this has happened when only a few days ago Don was down having a talk with me about you. He put the whole situation clearly to me. He didn't pretend to be a saint, but he's got this in his favour, he made a good confession, and then he told me what's been in his heart for years, to make you his wife. And now—'

'What!' I screamed the word at him, startling him and Dad. I screamed again, 'What!' Then drawing myself up, I faced him squarely and said, 'Father, I wouldn't marry Don Dowling if I had twenty illegitimate kids.' The words sounded raw coming from my mouth, and I would have termed the person I heard speaking them cheap and common. But this defiance was from the spark that was growing within me, it was not so much a spark of strength as of retaliation.

'You might do worse. You wouldn't have been—'

'Shut up!'

That I had startled my dad as he had never been startled before I could see, and, as my mother had punished Ronnie years ago for daring to answer a priest, so now my father stepped towards me, his face dark with anger, and he cried at me, 'Don't you dare speak to the Father in that manner, for as much as I care for you I'll raise my hand to you.'

But now the spark was afire and I turned on him and cried, 'Well, come on, do it.... Don Dowling! You'd know what Don Dowling is if you'd only open your eyes wide enough. Everybody in the town knows of his carry on, but there are lots of things that everybody in the town doesn't know. My mother knew. Oh, yes, she knew, and she tried to protect me from him. And Sam knows, and I know. Don Dowling!' I turned and confronted Father Ellis again and cried, 'I could have got rid of the child but I wouldn't, I remembered what you said from the pulpit. But I swear to you, Father, that if you side with Don Dowling and try to make me marry him, I swear to you that I'll have it taken away.'

My voice had dropped to a low note as I finished, and after a long pause, during which the priest looked at me as if he hated me, he said, 'There will be no need. Don could not be induced under any circumstances, I'm sure, to make his offer now.'

'Then we can thank God for that, can't we, Father?' I turned without haste and walked out of the kitchen and up the stairs, and when I got into my bedroom I stood gripping the knob of the bed and repeating, 'Don Dowling! Don Dowling!' I cast my eyes towards the wall and spat the name at it – 'Don Dowling!'

The fire within me was well alight and burning out the old Christine.

I was sitting in Mollie's house in the sitting-room. It was a bright afternoon, warm and sunny, and the room was tidy, even attractive. There was a tray on the table with a teapot on it, and the steam had ceased to come out of the spout, and the tea, I felt, would be very cold now. Mollie had made no attempt to pour it out since I began talking, nor had she interrupted me. It was odd for her, and when she got to her feet and turned her back to me I said, with a tremor in my voice, 'It didn't seem like me going for the priest like that, but I didn't swear at him as they're saying, and now Don Dowling has taken on a kind of halo, for it's all over the place that we were going to be married when he found I was going to have a bairn and it wasn't his. I could kill him, Mollie, I could kill him – I hate him, he has started the tapping again on the wall and he sings – sings filthy – oh, God Almighty.' It was not the first time I had thought 'God Almighty' but it was the first time I had voiced it, and it sounded repulsive and I got to my feet and began pacing the floor.

'Here, drink this. I've laced it.' Mollie's voice was cool.

I took the cup from her hand and swallowed it almost in one draught. I had got used, these past months, to the taste of whisky and I liked it. It not only warmed me, it did more. A glass of whisky could ease the pain inside of me and could make me think in a quiet way, 'Oh well, such is life.'

The whisky was like a stream of fire running down into my stomach, and I pressed my hand on the rising globe, then sat down in the chair again and turned my eyes towards the empty grate. I was changed. I knew I was changed. That tall, blonde girl who was nice in spite of having a child, nice inside, easy for Christine Winter to live with, even made as she was, more of feeling than of sense, and knowing she would have accepted Martin's wife and become his woman, she was still nice. But she had vanished, dissolved when a plane had hit a hill and out of the wreck had risen a new Christine Winter, and she wasn't easy to live with, except when her nerves were eased and her stomach warmed with a drop of whisky. . . .

Sam was coming down from the wood with Constance as I returned home. The child waved to me crying, 'Mummie! Mummie!' then ran towards me, holding out some flowers she had picked. As she thrust them into my hands she said, 'I picked them for you.' Then catching sight of one of the Campbell grandchildren she asked in the next breath, 'Can I go and play with Terry, Mummie?'

I nodded.

'You'll put them in water, won't you?'

I nodded again.

Sam followed me through the front room and into the kitchen and remarked, 'I'll make you a cup of tea, you look under the weather.'

I did not want any tea but I did not stop him making it. Then as we sat, one on each side of the table, the cups before us, he made this remark, 'I'm leaving, Christine.'

In spite of the worry that was eating me I was startled by his news and exclaimed, 'No, Sam!'

'I'm not going far but if I don't get away from there—' he nodded to the fireplace walls which divided the kitchens – 'something'll happen that we'll all be sorry for.'

'Where are you going?'

He raised his eyes shyly to mine and said, 'You'll be surprised,' and, nodding his head in the other direction, he said briefly, 'Mrs. Patterson's.'

'Mrs. Patterson's?'

'Aye, I've always liked Mrs. Patterson. She's always been kind to me. Many a copper she gave me when I was a bairn. The only other one who ever did that was your mother.'

'But she's a Methodist.' God! had I not got rid of myself altogether? Were fragments still sticking to me? Mrs. Patterson was worth a hundred of my Aunt Phyllis, and her a supposedly good Catholic. 'That was a daft thing to say,' I now put in. 'They're a fine couple. You'll be better off there.' I found I was relieved that Sam was still going to be near.

'Christine, I want to ask you something.' He was not sitting forward in his usual position with his hand hanging between his knees, but was upright in the chair looking straight at me. 'And I'll thank you not to laugh on the one hand, or go for me on the other, and no matter what you might think I'm doing this because I want to, because I've always wanted to. Will you marry me?'

I didn't laugh or go for him, I didn't even speak, but I dropped my eyes slowly from his fixed gaze and groaned inside, Oh, Sam, Sam.

'I know you don't care for me, not in that way, not as you did for him, but we get on together like a house on fire. We always have done. You know that. And I can't see meself ever wanting anything but just to be near you. Don't think I haven't tried to thrash this out of meself. I have, but that's how it is.'

He was talking as I had never heard him talk before about himself, and I kept groaning to myself, Oh, Sam, Sam.

'I was fifteen when it came to me how I felt about you, and I thought, Not me an' all, there's enough with our Don and their Ronnie.'

So he had known about Ronnie. Sam knew everything. No, not everything. He didn't know I was so changed that in the dark of the night when lost in the blackness of despair I searched for ways of hurting someone as I'd been hurt, and I never had far to seek. Taking Martin's watch from under my pillow I would grip it between my palms and see myself parcelling it up and sending it to her. Then out of the darkness she would rise with the little package in her hands and I would watch her open it. I would see her groping at something for support, then quickly search the wrapping for the post mark, and having found it, she would lift her eyes to mine and in her look I would find my compensation. She would have been paid back for her deception, I would be content.

But when the dawn broke I knew I could never do it. Even in the dark the old Christine would never have contemplated such a mean revenge, but I was changed. Everybody was changed.... Except Sam. Sam was unchanging. Sam was the kindest man on earth. Although he was only nineteen I thought of him as a man, for he was a man in sense. If Sam had made this offer some weeks ago when I had still been in ignorance of what had befallen me, then I would have accepted it, because to Sam I didn't appear bad. I knew that. But that road of escape into peace, and even respectability, was closed. Sam did not deserve what I had to offer him.

'And now that I'm on the face and making good money there would be no worry that way, and I'm savin' . . .'

'Sam—' I forced myself to look into his face – 'I like you better than anybody on earth; anybody—' I stressed the word – 'and if I could, I would marry you tomorrow and thank you Sam, thank you from the bottom of my heart for asking me.'

His face showed a mixture of pleasure and disappointment, and he leaned towards me and said, 'Well if that's how you feel, what's to stop you? I wouldn't . . . I mean . . . well, what I want to say is that we could go on just as we are until you felt different.' His hand came out and covered mine.

'I know what you mean, Sam, but I can't do it. Anyway you should be going around with some nice girl. You've never had a girl. I feel I'm to blame there, too.'

'I've always had a girl.' His other hand came out and my hand lay between his two rough palms as he said, 'There's not a better girl in the world.'

'Oh, Sam.' My head bowed in shame before his love. When his next words came to me I knew that I had no power to measure such love as Sam's, for he said quietly, 'And there's another side to it, Christine. Once you're married you'll be sort of safer somehow. Our Don's never spoken to you, has he?'

I made no movement, and he went on, 'But he talks, he talks to me ma, and he talks at me and that's bad, for you see I know every shade of him. It would have been better if he had come in here and gone for you, far better. You would have known where you stood, at least as far as anybody can know with him. But I feel all the time that he's brewing something. What, I don't know. You never know with him until it's done. But there's one thing sure, he'll have his own back.' He paused and nodded his head slowly as he said, 'It's funny but when a man's mad but harmless he's put away, yet when he's bad and harmful he's left to roam. Our Don is bad, Christine. I've said it afore. And bad isn't the right word for him, he's something more than bad. I feel sometimes the earth will never be clean until he's off it. That's why I thought it best for all concerned to put more space atween us.'

At this moment Constance came running into the kitchen and Sam got to his feet, and I got to mine and there the matter rested. Rested for years.

Sam went next door to live and my Aunt Phyllis blamed me and upbraided Mrs. Patterson. She went as far as to suggest that I had corrupted him and that the coming child was his. But what Aunt Phyllis was worrying over most was the loss of Sam's money, not Sam. She wouldn't have blinked an eyelid if Sam had dropped down dead, and I knew this, and Sam knew it. And, as Sam had warned me, Don never forgot. His repayment was to go on for a long time. It had started with the tapping and singing but now it took a more vicious form, and I had my first taste of it one Friday night a few days after Sam had made his home with Mrs. Patterson. It was just on dark, and Dad being on late shift I had locked up and was getting ready to go upstairs to bed when a knock came on the front door. I thought as I went to it, 'There's no light showing, the blackouts are all right' – a few weeks previously a warden had come to the door to tell me that a light was showing from the top of the blind. But there was no light in the front room now. When I opened the door there was a man standing on the pavement. He was in army uniform, a private, and all I could take in of him in the dusk was that he was thick-set and had bulbous eyes. But when he spoke I knew he was from these parts, perhaps the North Tyne.

'Hallo,' he said, and the 'O' was dragged and brought his lower lip out with it.

'Hallo,' I replied quietly. There was a pause, during which he grinned at me. Then he said, 'I'm right, aren't I? You're Christine Winter?'

'Yes. Yes, I am.'

'Aye, well—' his grin broadened – 'can I come in?'

I had the door in my hand. Instinctively I drew it closer to me and asked swiftly, 'What do you want?'

He gave a little laugh and replied, 'Well that's a question, isn't it? You'd better let's come in and I'll tell you.'

I pulled the door closer still and said, 'Me father's asleep, I'm going to bed.'

'Your father?' he repeated, and as he screwed up his eyes I asked sharply, 'Who are you?'

'Oh—' his voice had a cold sound now – 'it doesn't matter who I am. I was given your name and address. Seems like I'm not very welcome the night. But custom's custom I suppose? Still, I can come another time. I'd better book, eh?'

As if I had been prodded from behind I jumped back and banged the door shut, then staggering into the kitchen I stood with my face buried in my hands. Later, as I lay staring into darkness, I told myself I couldn't go on. Yet as I said this I knew that I was not strong enough to make an end of it. I even had to face the fact that if Don Dowling had not made his appearance on the river bank that morning I still wouldn't have drowned myself. I hadn't that kind of courage. I hadn't any kind of courage. The new Christine hadn't any more courage than the old one; all I was equipped with now was a kind of angry defiance. Yet I knew that I was going to need courage, for Don, as Sam said, was remembering. As the night wore on and I could not sleep there came over me a longing . . . an intense longing for a drop of whisky.

Following on this incident I was afraid to answer any knock on the front door, and when one evening a few days later, there came a sharp rat-tat I went upstairs and peered down from behind the blind on to the heads of two men, both in uniform, and thought stupidly, I'll kill Don Dowling. The rat-tats came at intervals over the following weeks and always at night when Dad and Sam were on the late shift.

I told Sam nothing about this, nor Dad. The humiliation was so great that I could not bear to speak of it. Besides, I was afraid of what Sam might attempt should I tell him. To help steady my nerves and calm, to some extent, my fears, I began fortifying myself in the evening with a glass of whisky. Two glasses, when I could afford it, ensuring me a night's heavy, dreamless sleep. If I had more than one during the day, which I sometimes managed at Mollie's, my tongue was loosened and I became confidential and found relief in talking, talking about anything. And Mollie listened and never said to me as she did to Doddy, 'For Christ's sake shut your trap!'

Whisky was scarce and I could only get it through Mollie, and she got it because she had a number of pals in the know. One particular evening I had been to Mollie's and when I came back I had a couple of glasses of whisky in my bag, and was comforted somewhat to know that I would sleep that night, a sound sleep, without thoughts bursting through and dragging me into wakefulness.

After Dad had bidden me good night and gone into the front room, I made the whisky hot and took it immediately, not taking it upstairs to drink as I usually did, and it got to work even before I was undressed, and as soon as I lay down I fell asleep.

How long I had been asleep I don't know, but I was roused by the sound of Don Dowling singing. I turned on my side and put my head under the clothes, but the insistence of his voice brought me on to my back again, and wearily I opened my eyes. He must be roaring drunk to sing in the street like that. Even with my room being at the back I could hear him clearly. I heard him banging on the front door, then his voice told me he was going through the front room and into the kitchen. I did not hear Aunt Phyllis speaking, but I could hear him yelling replies. Some time later there came the sound of his heavy steps on the stairs, then of his bedroom door crashing open and his voice almost in my ear yelling a parody on a well-known song, a dirty parody as usual. He raved on for about half an hour, then abruptly his voice ceased, and in the quiet that followed I went to sleep again, and I dreamed, as I had done often of late, that I was drowning, and it was always in the same place, in the river between the shelves of rock, and I never seemed to be surprised that the river was running through my bedroom. I had come to the point of the dream where I screamed and clutched at an invisible hand when I was brought sharply awake not only by the sound, but the feeling of someone in the room. I swung up on to my elbow, whispering, 'Is that you, Constance?' There was no answer. The room should have been in black darkness for I always left the blackout up now, but through my sleep-bleared eyes and muddled mind I took in the fact that I could see the sky. And then I saw something else, the great dark outline of a man.

As one tries in vain in a dream to shout for help, so now no sound escaped from my throat, but I scrambled up on the bed as swiftly as my heavy bulk would allow, and stood with my head grazing the ceiling and my back and hands pressed to the wall, and I knew before he spoke that it was Don.

'If you as much as make a sound I'll kill you.'

The scream wouldn't come loose.

'The Fenwick Houses' whore. I've come to be obliged. Any objection?'

His voice through all this was low, and it held none of the thick muddled tones of a man in drink. I knew he was solid and sober. 'You can't say I haven't been patient, I've waited a long time . . . years. Now I'll see your bloody bust that your mother padded, and more. . . .'

As he made a silent lunge towards me the scream ripped from my throat: 'Dad! Dad! Dad! Da . . . ad! Da . . . ad!'

I had turned my face to the wall and was clawing at it as I screamed, and when hands came on me and pulled me down on to the bed I still continued to scream until I recognized Dad's agonized voice yelling above mine, 'For God's sake, lass, what's the matter now?'

'Oh! oh! oh! Oh, Dad! Oh, Dad!'

'Quiet, and you, Constance an' all, be quiet. Quiet! I say. My God, the street'll be out. What's happened? Stay still until I light a candle.'

Shaking and sobbing, my gasping breath threatening to choke me at any moment, I pointed towards the window, and it was only then that he became aware that the blackout curtains were drawn and the window wide open. He closed the window and drew the curtains before lighting the candle, then said, 'Get back into bed.'

'No, no, I'm going downstairs.' I struggled into my coat, and with Constance hanging on to me I went down into the kitchen. He followed, saying in a different kind of voice now, 'Tell me what happened.'

I drew a chair up to the nearly dead fire and, crouching over it, muttered, 'Someone came through the window . . . a man.'

'A man?' he repeated. Then pulling his belt he went out through the scullery and into the backyard. In a few minutes he was back and his face looked grim and he asked quietly, 'Did you see who it was?'

I did not look at him as I said, 'No.' Had I said it was Don there was no telling what the consequences might be. But more than this, if he knew it was Don, Sam would know it was Don, and Sam must not know, not for sure. He would suspect, but that would prove nothing in this case.

'There was no ladder and the spout isn't near the window. I can't see how he could have climbed up.'

I knew without looking at him that he was working out the distance between Aunt Phyllis's back bedroom and mine. Ten feet separated them, and about three feet from each windowsill was a big staple which he himself had placed there some years previously. The clothes lines ran through these staples and through rings on the end of high poles fixed to the backyard walls, thus enabling the clothes to soar above the confined space of the yard and catch the wind from the fells. Anyone holding on to the gutter and having a large enough stride and being reckless enough into the bargain could make the distance between the two windows.

I knew that I must not allow Dad to put two and two together else there would be murder done, so I shamefacedly admitted about the soldier coming to the door.

I heard him mutter an oath, then as he turned away to go into the scullery he cut me to the heart by saying, 'Thank God your mother didn't live.'

It was as I drank the hot cup of tea he made me that I felt sick, and then a pain started that was like no pain I had felt before. When at four o'clock he said he would go for Aunt Phyllis, I stopped him and murmured, 'No, no. Get Sam to go for the doctor.'

I was in hospital at seven o'clock and before that afternoon I gave birth to a boy, and he lived an hour and I floated for days in a semi-lit world, uncaring, unthinking, unfeeling.

My first lucid thought was one of relief that the child was dead. I should have been grateful to Don Dowling.

CHAPTER SEVEN

THE war was over. 'Hip . . . hip! . . . hooray!' I hung over
Mollie's front room window sill, crushed between her and
Doddy, and waving my flag to the procession passing below.
Fellburn Victory Procession. Bands playing, lorries laden
with men and girls, and rows of couples joined arm in arm,
dancing along the width of the street.

'Conquerors – Conquerors – Germany lies bleeding.'

Doddy was at it again, and I turned my face to him and
laughed widely. And he went on, 'But the blood is yellow and
the victors will squeeze her as they did before, and there will
rise out of the juice another Hitler.'

'For God Almighty's sake, stow it, Doddy. If you don't
talk some bloody sense for a change I'll push you out of the
window, so help me God I will!' Mollie, too, was laughing,
and Doddy went on, 'But I'm merely quoting one, Sir Eric
Geddes. Hast thou not heard of his words, spoken at the end
of the last war? He was the man who conceived Mr. Hitler, for
didn't he say "We will get everything out of her that you can
get out of a lemon, I'll squeeze her until you can hear the pips
squeak".'

'And you're a pip-squeak if there ever was one. And for
God's sake don't push, Jackie, you'll have me in the street.'
Mollie was talking to the man behind her now who was lean-
ing over her back.

'Hooray! hooray!'

'Can that "sweet, red, soft kissing mouth" utter nothing
but hooray! hooray? And for what dost thou cry hooray!
sweet maiden?'

'Oh Doddy, Doddy, you are funny.'

'There, that's the end. Get off me back, Jackie, and let me
up.' Mollie gave a push with her large buttocks and finished,

'Come on, let's have a drink. Coo! I can't believe it. No more bloody cordite. Christine, come away in out of that. You and your hooray. . . . Come on. Come on, let's get the table set. The others'll be here afore we know where we are. What did you bring, Jackie?'

'A ham, a whole one.'

'Good for you.'

'And three tins of bully, a collop of butter, and a four-pound tin of biscuits. How's that for an entrance fee?'

'It'll get you in.'

'And you, Doddy,' demanded Mollie, 'what about the liquor?'

'It will flow out of the side door six o'clock as the bell tolls. The scullion he did promise me in good faith. Three pounds a bottle, because tonight is one of glorious victory. . . .'

'He wants a kick in the arse for chargin' that.'

'Doubtless, doubtless.'

The room was filled with high laughter and gaiety as the four of us set the table for the party. At one period Doddy and I put our heads together and sang,

> 'Maid of Athens, 'ere we part
> Give, oh give me back my heart!'
> Or, since that has left my breast,
> Keep it now and take the rest!'

I had learned this from Doddy, and when we finished we hung round each other's neck laughing.

'Stow it, you two.' There was a touch of irritation in Mollie's voice. I would not have Mollie irritated for the world, so I drew away and made an effort to stop my laughter and to straighten my face. And Mollie, looking at me, said, 'You get a whisky inside of you and you go daft.'

And Doddy, striking a protective pose, cried, 'Touch her not with your harsh tones, God's laughing in Heaven to see her so good . . . and happy.' His eyes looked kindly at me on these last words.

I went into Mollie's kitchen and began to put the cakes I had baked that morning on to the plates, and as I did so I warned myself, 'Quieten down. Quieten down and stop laughing with Doddy.' But it was difficult not to laugh with Doddy for he was a fellow you could laugh with and he wouldn't take it wrong. Doddy was a bit of a mystery. All Mollie knew of him was that he had been to college. He was possessed of a photographic mind, for he remembered all the poetry he had ever read. More often than not he spoke in poetry, little of which I could make head or tail of. Yet I knew behind his flippancy there was sense in everything he said. When I had a drink I enjoyed Doddy, when I hadn't he got a bit on my nerves.

It would seem on the surface he got on Mollie's nerves, too, for she was always on at him. But what irritated her most was that he had never asked to sleep with her. He would do anything on earth for her except apparently that, and Mollie was at present sleeping with Jackie. It was a funny set-up but no one said a word against Mollie. No, by gum, and they shouldn't either – I moved my head in warning down on to the plate of cakes – Mollie was one of the best. Where would I have been if it hadn't been for her? This house had become a haven in more ways than one, for when no one else could get a drop of spirits in the town Mollie could always be relied upon to turn up with some. No, Mollie was all right. And one day she would get Doddy. My head suddenly went back and I burst out laughing to myself at the thought of Mollie and Doddy together. Mollie with every other word a curse and Doddy to whom poetry was as the air he breathed, a necessity.

'Are you baking those bloody things all over again?'

'No, I'm coming, Mollie.'

'Stop laughing,' I said to myself. 'Stop laughing.'

As I entered the room Mollie was looking towards the outer door and crying, 'Listen to that. It's the bloody light infantry coming.' A moment later the door burst open and there poured into the room a number of men in uniform, both army and air force, and a crowd of girls, and they were all pals of Mollie's.

I never ceased to be amazed at the number of pals Mollie had. I knew none of these people and for a moment the old shyness in me overcame my whisky-stimulated gaiety, and in the pushing and shoving and the din of voices I was looking round for Doddy or Jackie when I came face to face with someone I did know.

'Why, hallo.'

'Oh, hallo.'

'Many moons, no see.'

I laughed, 'Yes.'

'Fancy meeting you here.'

'I know Mollie.'

'Who doesn't?' We laughed together.

He was looking me up and down as much as was possible in the crush, and then he said, 'Remember the fight with Don Dowling?'

My face fell and I said quietly, 'Yes, I remember.'

'Look, the lot of you, move round and sit down so's I can see what I'm doin'.' Mollie's voice was roaring above the din, and Ted Farrel, taking my arm, said, 'Where does she expect all this lot to sit, on top of one another? Anyway, I'm sitting next to you.' And he wagged his finger at me. Then asked, 'What's Dowling up to these days?'

'I don't know, and what's more I don't care.'

'Ah, that's it, is it?'

'You two know each other?' It was Mollie squeezing past us, and Ted said, 'I'll say. Done battle for this lady in me time. A war afore the war.'

Mollie looked from me to Ted and back again to me, and she laughed her hearty laugh as she said, 'It's a small world.' And then, 'What the hell am I goin' to do with this lot? I never asked all this squad, I know that. Twelve of us there was going to be and there must be thirty or more buggers here. Will we have enough to eat?'

'I doubt it,' I said.

'Then somebody will have to raid the stores, that's all.'

Later it was Ted who raided the stores. He was a sergeant and sergeants could get things. He took me in the jeep with him and parked me in a side cut while he went scrounging. He brought his efforts back in a sack, and we laughed long and loud on the return journey. Later that evening, room and seats being scarce, I sat on his knee with my arm around his shoulders and he with his arms tightly round my waist, and we sang and ate and drank. At eight o'clock when I remembered Constance I told myself just another half-hour.

When the half-hour was up Doddy was reciting, and everybody was talking and laughing and paying no heed. He was standing in the middle of the room and there were people sitting round his feet. He was more drunk than ever I had seen him. Sometimes somebody would shout, 'Ssh! let's listen to him.' And once in the lull he was saying, 'I come from Nottingham. But from where come the undying thoughts I bear?'

Then in another lull, with his arms wide, he stood looking at Mollie where she sat on Jackie's knee, and he cried:

> 'Haste thee, nymph, and bring with thee
> Jest and youthful jollity,
> Quips and cranks, and wanton wiles,
> Nods, and becks, and wreathed smiles.'

And Mollie cried back, 'Oh, go to hell with you, Doddy.' And he laughed. But when he was reciting some puzzling words which went:

> 'I am that which began;
> Out of me the years roll;
> Out of me God and Man;
> I am equal the whole,'

and somebody shouted, 'Can't somebody knock that bugger down? He's been on all the night,' it was Mollie who commanded, 'Leave him alone.'

'But doesn't he get on your bloody nerves?'

'He's tight, and that's the way it takes him.'

'God, what a way to be taken. Sit down and hug somebody, man!'

In the lull of talk, Doddy was heard quoting ' "Tis chastity, brother, chastity; she that has this is clad in concrete steel".' And there came a roar, and for a moment you couldn't hear anything but laughter, yet through it Doddy continued to quote his poetry. And it became too much for the man who had objected, and he got to his feet and threw a glass of beer into Doddy's face.

For a space of seconds there was a dead silence in the room. Doddy wiped the beer slowly and stupidly from his face, then like an avalanche Mollie turned on the man crying, 'Get out, you sod, you'll insult nobody in my house.'

'But, Mollie, he'd drive you bloody. . . .'

'Get out! I never asked you here. Get out and take her with you.' She nodded to the girl who had been sitting on the man's knee, and amid strong mumblings the couple left the house, and a flatness fell on the company. The old jollity could not be revived, and again I remembered Constance.

Going to Mollie, I said, 'I must be making for home, Mollie.'

'Aye, it's gettin' on, I suppose you must. Who's goin' with you? You're not very steady on your pins.'

With a silly giggle I was about to say, 'I'll manage all right,' when Ted Farrel, putting his hand on my shoulder, said, 'I'll see she gets home, never fear.'

So with his arms in mine Ted walked me home. Sometimes we sang and sometimes we laughed, and when we reached the corner of the street I stopped, saying, 'Now I'll manage.'

'I'll see you the morrow then?'

'Yes, Ted, the morrow.'

'Give us a kiss, Christine.'

'Wait until the morrow, Ted.'

'The morrow's a long time, Christine.'

'Not tonight Ted, the morrow.'

I pulled away from him. 'Good night, Ted.'

'Good night, Christine.'

I made an effort to steady my steps as I neared our door, then in the dimness I saw someone standing on the Patterson's step, and I knew it was Sam. He didn't speak, and when I said, 'That you, Sam?' he still did not speak, and I laughed and said, 'Good night, Sam,' then let myself into the house.

In the kitchen Dad was sitting waiting, and his look seemed to sober me a little, and as I pulled off my hat and coat I said, 'Don't say it, Dad, don't say it.'

'Do you know you've a bairn?'

'I think so, Dad, I think so.' My voice sounded high and careless.

'She's been crying her eyes out for you.'

'She's got to be left sometimes. I brought her up wrong, I never left her a minute for years.'

'You've no right to put on Mrs. Patterson.'

'Mrs. Patterson likes having her.'

'Mrs. Patterson likes having her so's she can turn her into a bloody Methodist.'

'If she grows up like Mrs. Patterson then she won't be so bad.'

'The next time you go out and stay out all day I'm goin' to put her in next door with Phyllis.'

I swung round on him, no careless touch to my voice now. I was rocking slightly and I held on to the table, but my speech was steady as I said, 'You do. You do that, Dad, and I'll walk out. There's nothing to stop me, y'know. I could take her and leave this house the morrow. You take her to Aunt Phyllis's just once' – I bounced my head emphasizing the 'once' – 'and I'll walk out. I can get a job, in fact I'm going to get a job in any case. If I stay here I'm going to get a job, but I'll get one quicker than you think if you take her into Aunt Phyllis's.'

I had beaten him and he knew it, and he turned from me saying, 'My God!'

For a moment I felt a great pity for him and tears welled up unbidden into my eyes, but they didn't fall. I wanted to go to him and put my arms about him and say, 'It's all right, I'm not going to go away. It's all right. And don't worry about anything else, I've had my lesson.' I wanted to say that, but I didn't for I wasn't sure of myself. I didn't know if I was going to go wrong, really wrong, or not. I was all sixes and sevens inside unless I had a drop, and then all I wanted was to talk and have a laugh.

Slowly I turned about and went upstairs and into the front room. Constance was awake and lying sucking her thumb as if she were a baby. At the sight of me she raised herself in the bed and I went to her and, bending over her, I said somewhat thickly, 'Hallo there, dear, kiss Mummie good night.' I swayed a little as I bent, and put my hand out to the bed rail to steady myself. Her face was outlined in the night light, her eyes were peering at me, then her little hand came on to my chin and she pushed my face from her as she said, 'I don't like you, I hate you, you smell nasty.' Then flinging herself round in the bed she covered her head with the clothes.

Slowly I straightened myself up, and blindly now, for the tears were running down my face, I turned about and went into my room. I was filled with anger and pity for my plight, a maudlin pity. I was nasty and I smelt. My God! I tore my things off and, getting into bed, I crushed my face into the pillow and sobbed, but strangely enough I did not cry myself to sleep. I was dry-eyed and sober when at last sleep came to me.

The next morning Dad woke me with a cup of tea, and as I opened my eyes the light pierced through my head like a sheet of flame and I covered my face against the glare, and Dad, sitting on the side of the bed, looked at me and said quietly, 'Lass, I'm worried to death about you.'

'Oh, Dad, don't start again.'

'I've got to talk with you, I can't see you going on like this. Every time you go down to that Mollie's you come back drunk. You who didn't know what the taste of it was like. What's got into you?'

'That's a daft question, isn't it, Dad?'

'I know, I know, lass.' His hand came on to my shoulder. 'But you're not going to alter things, you're not going to make them better by killing yourself. You're not made for drink, you can't carry it, and if you go on the way you've been doing lately, that's what it'll do, it'll kill you. Your mind first and then your body. I've seen it afore with certain women. And, lass, I'm sick to the heart.'

It was odd but I, too, was sick to the heart this morning, sick of myself and the memories of last night, not that there had been anything out of place, but the company in Mollie's from this distance seemed to be questionable – not my kind of company. But what was my kind of company? Men who talked posh? I'd had some . . . with interest! There . . . there I was thinking like Mollie's lot, so where was the difference?

'And you know something else?' went on Dad. 'Sam is worried about you. And it's him who looks after Constance, more than Mrs. Patterson, that is when he's not on shifts. I'll tell you something. I think Sam wants to marry you. Mind you, he hasn't said anything to me, but I can twig it.'

'Dad, keep quiet.' My voice was low. 'I'm not going to marry Sam or anybody else.' Yet why did I think of Ted at this moment? I could think of marrying Ted when I couldn't think of marrying Sam, yet I cared for Sam. But Sam roused nothing but tenderness in me, and I had sensed already that Ted could rouse other feelings, and it seemed a necessary ingredient of love that these feelings should be roused, for I was just twenty-two.

'Don't go to that Mollie's any more, promise me that, lass, will you?'

'No, Dad, I can't promise. Mollie's been a good friend to

me. But I'll promise to go steady. I won't repeat last night.'

'And you won't leave the bairn so often when I'm not in? I don't mind when I'm in and can look after her.'

'Yes, I promise that an' all. I won't leave her unless you or Sam's in.'

He sighed and patted my hand and rose heavily from the bed, and my eyes lifted with him and I realized that in the five years since my mother died he had become an old man. He wasn't fifty but he was stooped and his face was lined, and there was no life or strength in him, only the strength necessary to hew coal, which was a different strength from that required for living.

That afternoon I took Constance for a walk. She had apparently forgotten her tantrum of the night before. I had dabbed my clothes with scent to take away any smell of the stale whisky that might be hanging about them, and while we were in the town I called at Mollie's. The door was open as was usual. The place looked a shambles and nobody was there. I left a note on the mantelpiece to say that I wouldn't be able to come down this evening, but I left no message for Ted.

The following night we were sitting at tea, Dad, Constance and myself, when a knock came on the door. Dad went and opened it, and when he came back into the kitchen with Ted behind him I rose from the table, and my hands were trembling.

'Thought I would just look you up,' said Ted.

'Sit down,' said Dad. 'Have you had any tea?'

'No,' said Ted.

'Well sit yourself down and make yourself at home.'

I could see that Dad liked the look of this man. I could see that his mind was working swiftly. Aye, even as mine was. Ted knew that I had Constance. What else he knew I didn't know, but he had come in search of me. I felt, above all things at that moment, grateful.

We had tea, and then Dad said. 'Well now, if you want to go out just leave the bairn with me. She'll be all right.'

Ted and I looked at each other, and I went upstairs and made myself up with care and changed into another frock and put on my best coat. Later that night, in the dark, we stood at the corner of the street and Ted took me in his arms and kissed me, and we were both sober and I hadn't laughed much all evening.

Three days later he brought me news that his unit was being moved. Would I write to him?

Yes, I said, I would write.

'I'll soon be demobbed, but I'll get leave before then.' He looked steadily into my eyes, then he kissed me.

I would be looking forward to his leave, I said.

I felt shy and awkward like a young girl, but the hungry feeling inside me was not that of a young girl.

Dad was happy, happier than I had seen him for years. He liked Ted. I liked Ted. What did Sam think of him? Sam, to my knowledge, hadn't met him, but I knew that he knew all that he wanted to know. Dad had likely told him in the gentlest way possible, but Sam said nothing. He showed no change, except perhaps that he was a little more quiet with me than usual. . . .

It was a fortnight later that I received the first of the letters. It was not from Ted. The letter had no signature, but as I read the first horrible sentence I knew who had written it. The old fear, bursting like water from sluice-gates, swamped me and, turning my eyes to the wall, I could almost see Don, having timed the postman, watching my reactions as I read the filth and threats the page contained. Perhaps I should have done what the police are always telling you to do if you are unfortunate enough to be persecuted in this way, take the letter straight to them. But I could no more have done that than I could have read it aloud in the street. I could not even show it to Dad. Dad was happy, and although he didn't like Don and suspected him of many things, he would, I know, have found it hard to believe that he had written what was on this page. As for Sam, I had only to show this letter to him and he would know who the author was and there would be bloodshed and I feared for Sam, for I could never see anyone succeeding in hurting Don Dowling.

I was in no doubt as to why this letter had been written. Aunt Phyllis had seen Ted and me leave the house that night with Dad saying a cordial good-bye to Ted on the step. The purpose of this letter was to frighten me off, frighten me off Ted. Well it wouldn't. I knew what I was going to do with this letter – put it on the fire, and if any more came they would have the same destination.

When the second one came I opened it, spread it out on the table, then sat down and clasped my hands tightly as I read it. The text was even worse and I felt my stomach heaving and had to put my hand over my mouth until I reached the scullery. Faint and shaking I went upstairs and lay down on the bed and, burying my face in the pillow, I cried until I could cry no more.

The letters continued to arrive, but I never opened another but put them straight into the fire.

Ted was no great writer. His letters were stilted and told me little, only that he was thinking of me and hoping to get a leave. But when the time of the leave drew near he wrote to say he was unable to make it, and Dad began to ask, 'When's Ted coming? When does he say he'll be out?'

I had been getting a letter once a week from Ted, but now the intervals between the letters grew longer. Yet it did not worry me, it was July and soon, I hoped, he'd be demobbed, the Americans were wiping up the Japs.

I still went to Mollie's, and it fell to me to try and cheer her up, for Doddy had been posted to Dorset. He had stopped quoting poetry long enough to tell her that when he was demobbed he hoped to get a teaching post for a while, before going to America to teach there. He didn't want to stay in England. She had learned what she hadn't known before, which had explained a great deal about him. He was without people, his mother, father, uncle and two sisters having been killed in one of the big raids at the beginning of the war. Mollie had looked at me, the nearest I had seen her to tears, as she said, 'He wanted a mother and I was the nearest thing to it. He wanted some place where he could come and sleep when he could get away from the barracks, and this was as good a place as any. Mind you,' she had jabbed her finger in my direction, 'he did nothing underhand. He never promised anything or asked anything. He gave me back twice as much as ever he got from me, with all the things he did for me, fetching and carrying and the like. And now he's gone, he owes me nowt.'

'You've still got Jackie,' I said.

'Aye, I've still got Jackie, but Jackie knows no poetry. I don't know any poetry, and Doddy's bloody poetry used to get on me nerves.' She turned to me and added in a dead voice, 'But what I wouldn't give to hear him spouting away now. There'll never be anybody like him. I'll never know anybody like him again.'

I'd had Martin and she in a lesser way had had Doddy. Martin was now, and always would be, an ache in my heart, a loneliness to my nights, but Doddy would remain to her always an endearing memory, perhaps all the more endearing for it was without hope of fruition; the trying fruition of listening to Doddy for breakfast, dinner and tea and into the night . . . .

All during July I waited, waited and waited, and I heard nothing from Ted. I had written and asked him if anything was wrong, but he had not replied. I began to worry, and the thought was always in my mind . . . this mustn't go wrong. When he was demobbed he would have to come to Fellburn, because his home was in Fellburn. I had passed the house where he lived. It was in quite a nice part of the town, very respectable. I wondered what his mother was like and had a little dread at the thought of meeting her – if ever I did.

Then one morning I called in at Mollie's. I always went to a little shop quite near her with my sweet coupons. The woman had been more than kind when sweets were scarce and now, though they were still on ration, though a little more plentiful, I still continued to go there. It was just a short step to Mollie's, and although it was only eleven o'clock in the morning I expected to find her in for she had been off work for the past fortnight. She was having a well-earned rest she said. Anyway, Mollie could live quite well without an eight to six job. I was no longer shocked by this fact, nor was I put off going to her house knowing that my visits there did not enhance my reputation. I went in calling, 'Oo! oo!' my usual way of making my presence known. But there was no answer. There was no one in the sitting-room, and the bedroom door, wide open, showed me the unmade bed, and I saw there was no one there either. The kitchen, too, was empty except for a pile of washing up, but on the table was a note, which said simply, 'Be back in half an hour.' That would be for Jackie; Jackie was a long-distance lorry driver and his times were erratic.

I did not admit to myself that the primary motive of my visit was to learn if Mollie had heard anything of Ted. Mollie's many pals formed a sort of private telephone exchange, and she would hear things when nobody else would. Having decided to wait I thought I might as well make myself useful. I put my shopping bag and coat on the only chair the kitchen held, which was behind the door, and, rolling up my sleeves, I started on the dishes. When I had finished them and tidied the kitchen and there was still no sign of Mollie, I went to pick up my coat. It was then that I heard her step on the stairs, but what arrested me was the sound of a man's voice, and as the door opened and I heard it more clearly I straightened up, the coat in my hands, and said to myself, 'Oh!' What kept me where I was, hidden in the triangle of the joining walls and the open door, I'm not quite sure. Inherent shyness? or suspicion? or something that I was already aware of? – I don't know, but I stayed where I was, giving no indication of my presence, even when Mollie, for some reason that wasn't evident to me at that moment, cried, 'Anybody there?' I heard her move towards the bedroom then come towards the kitchen, and when she pressed her hand on the door my hiding-place became even more secure, for nobody coming right into the kitchen would have known I was there unless they went to shut the door from the inside or wanted to get the chair.

'Look, Mollie, have a heart.' Ted's voice was quiet and persuasive.

'I think it's a bloody dirty trick if you ask me. You've led her up the garden.'

'What! Me led her up the garden?' His voice had risen and sounded indignant. 'I like that, that's rich that is. Me led her up the garden? Aw, Mollie.'

'Well, you've made her think you're on the level, writin' and all that. What did you go up to the house for? Real first stage of a courtin' job that was, going to the house and meeting her dad. You knew she had the bairn?'

'Yes I knew she had one bairn and was quite prepared to accept that. But I didn't know she'd had two, and what's more had her card stamped into the bargain, and you don't pick that up, Mollie, from going with Boy Scouts. She must have been around some to get that.'

'That's a bloody lie, a downright bloody lie, she's as clean as a pin. You tell me the sod that said that and I'll. . . .'

'O.K. O.K. Don't bawl, but you're not going to deny she's had two kids, are you?'

'It was from the same fellow.'

'Oh, you can't tell me. And it's good of you to stick up for her. She's lucky to have somebody like you. But I've heard a thing or two lately.'

'Well you can take it from me they're all bloody lies.'

'No, Mollie, I can't take it from you, for some bloke even wrote to me.'

My hand was at my throat, checking all sound, trying to throttle down the pain.

'Then there's another thing. You know yourself she's got the makings of a soaker.'

'Well, you knew she was like that when you started the courtin' business, didn't you?'

'Aye, I did, Mollie, I admit it, but I thought I could cure that. But I didn't know all this other and I'm not a bloody fool altogether. I've seen too many blokes let in these last few years and it's not going to happen to me.'

'You'll go further and fare worse, I'm tellin' you that, Ted. Christine's all right. She's had a dirty deal. Her only trouble was she was too damn innocent; she was bound to be caught by some bugger.'

There came a silence, and I kept my eyes tightly closed as I wondered what I should do. Then Ted was speaking again.

'I'm sorry to have to tell you this, Mollie, because you're a wise bird and not likely to be taken in, but I think she's so damned clever that she's taken you for a ride an' all.'

'What do you mean?'

'The virgin stuff. You didn't know she'd been carrying on with her brother, did you?'

'What! Who the hell said that?'

'It was in this letter I got.'

'And you believed it?'

'When I found out all the rest was true, aye. Mind I didn't take it as read at first, I made inquiries, but when all the rest tied up with the letter why should I disbelieve that?'

'Whoever sent you that letter is a dirty bastard.'

'It's all the way you look at it. He was likely trying to do me a good turn, and he has, you've got to admit that, although she's a pal of yours.'

Scarcely breathing, I lowered myself silently into the chair. There was a buzzing sound in my ears now and I dropped my head, terrified that I was going to faint. I heard Mollie still talking, I heard Ted still protesting, then Mollie's steps came towards the kitchen. Just within the doorway I heard her stop. It must have dawned on her that I had been there – I was the only one since Doddy had gone who washed up for her. I heard her moving again, and when I judged she was at the sink I pressed the door slightly ajar and made a desperate motion with my hand for her to get rid of Ted. The sight of me startled her, and the flush of concern and pity on her face was too much for me and I had to ram my handkerchief into my mouth to stop the sound of my crying.

What she said to Ted to make him go I don't know, but within a few minutes the door was pulled open and her hands came to me and lifted me up. And when I was on my feet she held me and comforted me, saying, 'Don't, don't. You're the unluckiest bugger alive. Anyway, you're well rid of him. There now, there now. Come and sit down and I'll get you a drop of something. There now, there now . . . oh, don't give way like that. I tell you he's not worth it. None of the sods are worth it.'

A few minutes later she handed me a glass of whisky, and when I had gulped it I gasped and muttered, 'Le. . . let me have another, Mollie.' And she let me have another.

CHAPTER EIGHT

'I DIDN'T ask him for it.'

'You must have.'

'I tell you I didn't.' As Constance flung round and left the front room I looked at her indignant back. She appeared like a boy from behind, with her jeans and jersey and short-cropped hair. She was now fifteen and had left school two months and had a job in the electric component factory. I turned my gaze back to the piano standing ludicrously out of place in the corner of the front room. It was a second-hand one but it wasn't an old thing with fretwork and candle brackets, but looked quite up-to-date. I looked from it to Sam, and he, too, was staring at it.

'I thought you had brought it for her or I'd never have let it inside the house,' I said under my breath.

Sam put his fist to his mouth and bit sharply on one knuckle before saying, 'If I'd known she wanted one so much I would have got one. She never mentioned piano to me.'

'What will I do? Send it next door?'

'That won't be any good. Knowing him, he'll leave it standin' in the street, and it will only upset her. In the long run it would be you who'd get the blame.'

Yes, it would be me who would get the blame, as always. Not that I hadn't deserved it during these past ten years, but that was my business. I was always telling myself these days that it was my business and mine alone. What I drank I paid for. I worked hard for the money and, strangely, my labour was in demand. Years ago if you were fitted only for domestic service you weren't of much account, but now domestic servants were no longer domestic servants, but home helps, and so scarce were they around these parts you could demand as much an hour for cooking in a kitchen as for working in a factory. But most of the girls preferred factory work, so I made good money, money to pay for my drink. But in spite of my drinking I rarely neglected the house and had never, since the end of the war, neglected Constance, except perhaps on a Saturday night. No matter how I whipped my will to obey me during the week, Saturday night and the Crown back room were a weakness that I could not overcome. Nor did I want to overcome it, for this weakness was my only pleasure, and I looked forward to it from one week-end to the next. So I went on telling myself I did nobody any harm. In fact, I reiterated that most girls having had my experience would have gone to the bad altogether. I was well aware that most of the town considered I had already done this. The general opinion was that I was living with Sam, not openly, of course, but on the quiet, and who was to prove them wrong? He might sleep at Mrs. Patterson's and eat there, but he was never out of our house. And Sam, though no taller than myself, had grown into a very mannish looking man. He was attractive in a big-boned sort of way and had a pleasant face, and a voice that went with it.

Why hadn't I married Sam? For the simple reason that I was afraid to. It's all right saying that I should have gone ahead, that once married to him Don could have done nothing about it. But you see I knew Don. I knew him as well as I knew the dark places in myself. I knew that some part of him, a part that you couldn't put a finger on and define clearly, was mad. And the only protection I could give Sam was not to marry him. Not that I hadn't wanted to once or twice, and not that I hadn't wished he would ask me to live with him. Oh, yes, I had wished that. And it might have eased things for us both and made life more bearable for me; also it may have set up an opposition to the bottle. But apparently Sam didn't see it like this, and there was enough of the old Christine in me to prevent me leading up to it.

From the night Don Dowling had done me the service of bringing on a miscarriage we had never exchanged one word. We had passed each other on the road and I don't know whether he looked at me or not for I kept my eyes cast down at his approach. But he had never ceased to talk to, and beguile Constance. Quite early on I found that the more I smacked her and forbade her to go in next door the more she would go. I had talked to her quietly at first, then shouted and ordered, until Dad roared, 'This is getting you nowhere, you're driving her in there,' and at last I realized that this was true and so forced myself to say less and less. But as she grew older she sensed my feelings and started to hide the things Don gave her, until one day, making an effort to check this, I said casually, 'Why don't you show me the things Uncle Don buys you?' From then on she would show me what he had given her. She was about eight at the time, and with each year he bought her gifts to suit her age. And with them he bought her affection, and something more that made me sick at the mere thought of it – a kind of love that showed itself in her defence of him. 'Why don't you speak to Uncle Don, Mummie. Other people have rows but they don't keep them up for years like you do?' When she had said this I had asked her quietly, 'Do you like your Uncle Sam?' and she had answered, 'Of course I do. Of course I like Uncle Sam.' Then I had said, 'Do you like him better than Uncle Don?' At this she had screwed up her face and said, 'They're different, I can't explain. Uncle Sam's so quiet and Uncle Don's jolly. I like them both in different ways.'

The question of who her father was must have troubled her from time to time. She was about ten when she first put it to me. She had come straight from school one day and, throwing her satchel on the table and without kissing me as usual, she looked at me and asked point blank, 'Why aren't you married, Mummie?'

The question was so unexpected that I was lost for an answer and my mouth opened without making a sound. Then she said, 'Is Uncle Sam my father?'

I made plenty of sound now for, my voice seeming to come out of the top of my head, I cried, 'No, no, he's not. Your father died in the war. He was in the air force.'

'What was his name?'

My mouth hung open again, then I brought out, 'Johnson.' It was the name advertising flour on the back of a magazine lying on the table, and I added, 'Why are you asking all these questions?'

'Because I want to know. What did he look like?'

My voice was quiet now and weary. 'Like you, very like you.'

She seemed pleased at this, and she asked no more questions on this subject until two years ago. It was a Saturday night and it was summer. I had sat in the back room of the Crown until closing time. There was the usual Saturday night crowd and we had laughed and joked until we parted. Mollie wasn't there, Mollie was never there now. I must tell you about Mollie. But this Saturday night I felt particularly carefree and happy. This wasn't always the effect that drink had upon me now. At one time I could rely on it obliterating all my worries and transforming me, as it were, on to another plane where cares were non-existent and whatever future there was was rosy. Then for no reason for which I could account, every now and again the effect of whisky would be to make me want to argue and to pick a row with somebody, and this feeling would always be accompanied by a spate of swearing in my mind. I would think in swear words – Mollie's vocabulary wasn't in it compared with the words that presented themselves to me. The first time I felt like this I started an argument with one of the regulars, but she took it in good part, and because she took it in good part, I had the desire to lift my hand and smack her across the mouth. And this aggressive feeling had persisted, even mounted, as I made my way unsteadily in the dark up the hill, and when I got in and Dad greeted me with the look that he always wore on a Saturday night, I turned on him crying, 'And what the hell are you lookin' at me like that for? I'm drunk, and what about it? It's the only escape out of this bloody cage. Aye, it's a cage and you're the jailer. I would've been gone from this hole years ago if it hadn't been for you. I could have worked for her and made a home for her, but I was trapped here twixt you and Sam and that bugger next door.'

For the first and only time in his life Dad struck me, and the next morning I remembered most of what had happened and was bowed down with shame and resolved to take a strong pull at myself. But the next Saturday night I was in the back room again.

The second time the drink aroused an aggressive fury in me it was all directed against Don Dowling. Vaguely, I remember standing in the kitchen holding the bread knife and telling myself I would burst into the kitchen next door and take him by surprise and he wouldn't be able to lift a hand. I don't remember what stopped me carrying out this intent.

The night that Constance brought up my past again was a

Saturday night, but I was feeling happy and at peace with the world. I was crossing the bridge in the late twilight, humming to myself the song they had been singing in the back room earlier on: 'Now is the hour when we must say good-bye,' and then I saw Constance. She was standing talking to two girls and I saw her deliberately turn her back towards me. But that did not deter me from crossing over to her and demanding in words that I tried to separate, 'What ... what-you-doing-out at this time anight? Eh? Come on now, away home.' She did not turn and look at me as I mumbled my order, but the other two girls stared at me in a sort of surprised way. I was about to add, 'You, too, you should be at home in bed,' when Constance darted away. I gave an admonitory nod to the girls and walked on, trying to keep my gait steady as I knew their eyes were on me.

There was no evasiveness from Constance once I entered the kitchen; she was standing waiting for me. Her pale skin looked bleached and her brown eyes black and staring, and she greeted me with, 'You! ... you! You're a disgrace – acting like that on the bridge and Jean and Olive in my class. Oh ... h.' The 'Oh' had a weary sound and she followed it up with, 'I hate you. I hate you. Do you hear?'

Somewhere in my head words were gathering fast but I couldn't get them to come down into my mouth. It was as if there was a gap across which they couldn't jump. And then she said, 'There's something else I've learned about you. You had another baby, didn't you?'

All the happiness evoked by my kind friend the whisky was gone. Although I knew I wasn't sober I was filled with the pain that I endured when sober, only it was intensified now.

'You're a disgrace to everybody, you're no good. What Aunt Phyllis says is right, you've always caused trouble. You've separated Uncle Sam and Uncle Don and broken up her home, and now ... and now ... I won't be able to face them in class on Monday. I hate you, do you hear?' The last was spoken too quietly to be just the outcome of childish anger, it had the stamp of calculation and much thought.

The words had now jumped the gap and were in my mouth ready to fall on her in my own defence, but without a word I passed her and went into the scullery, and she went upstairs to bed, banging the door after her. Five minutes later Dad came out of the front room and, looking at me where I sat staring into the fire, he said simply, 'Well, what do you expect?' I gave no answer, I did not even turn to him, and he went back into the room and closed the door. But he closed it quietly.

After a restless night I heard her get up and go out to early mass, and when she returned I had her breakfast ready as usual. I was alone in the kitchen and didn't speak to her as I placed a plate with egg and bacon on the table. I had turned away to the stove when I heard her whispered 'I'm sorry.' I didn't say anything, but lifted the teapot and came back to the table, and then she was standing in front of me, her head bowed, and she repeated again, 'Oh, Mummie, I'm sorry.' In an impulsive movement she flung her arms about me, and I held her tightly to me, saying, 'It's all right, it's all right.'

'Oh, I'm sorry.'

'There's nothing to be sorry about.'

'I'm a beast and ... and I don't care what anybody says about you.'

I stroked her hair and looked over her head and out of the window towards the broad sky that covered the fells, and I thought, 'Neither do I.' But I knew that wasn't true. Then on the spur of the moment I made a decision and, drawing her down to a chair, I sat opposite to her and said, 'You're old enough to know what I've got to tell you. It's true I had another baby, but it was to ... your father.'

Her wet lashes blinked at me and her eyes widened, and I said, 'Yes, it was years after you were born. But he didn't know you had been born and he came back and ... and' — now for the supreme lie — 'we were going to be married. You see the war was on and things were difficult, moving about and one thing and another. I was to see him one night and he didn't come, he had been killed that day.'

'Someone said he came from the Hill ... Brampton.'

'He didn't come from the Hill, he came from France.'

Her lashes blinked again, and she said with something like pleasure. 'Then I'm half French?'

'No, just a little bit, he was half French.'

I looked at her and her quivering lashes. She was pondering this last news. She seemed pleased that she was partly French. It was odd but there wasn't a facet of her character that

I could trace to myself. She had the kindliness of Dad, and very much to the fore were traits that reminded me sharply of Ronnie, for she was always reading and scribbling. Her scribbling took the form of rhyming and making up songs. It was this that led to Don buying her the piano.

From that Sunday we came close together for a time, and I made a great effort to moderate my Saturday night diversion. If my effort had been accepted and let go at that, all might have been well and I may have improved steadily, but from the time I cut my visits to the back room of the Crown she and Sam became so solicitous that they never left me alone for five minutes. They combined to be kind, and their kindness oozed with protection, and it was the protection that I wanted to kick against. I wanted to throw my arms wide and press myself out of this second triangle in which I was living. Sometimes I thought I would go away and leave them all, but this never got further than a thought, for each in their different ways held me. I had no strength of character. I was still tied by my feelings, and so the monotony of my days went on unrelieved even by my hate of Don Dowling.

This monotony was bred, I think, because I was prevented from loving, loving with my body, and not because of lack of interest, for things were happening and swiftly. First, Sam left the pits and took over a smallholding across the river. Every now and again he had given Mr. Pybus a hand in his garden. The old man had four acres of land, two greenhouses and a four-roomed cottage. He lived alone, and when he told Sam he was going to sell and asked if he was interested it was as if he had offered him a goldmine. Sam had now been working at the coal face for ten years, and for the last three years had done a lot of overtime. He had saved the greater part of his money. One day he came to me more excited than I had ever seen him in his life and said, 'Christine, I'm going to buy Mr. Pybus's cottage and the smallholding.'

'You are, Sam?' I asked in surprise.

'Aye. Yes, I am that. And I'll make a go of it. It's what I've been waitin' for for years, praying for. Oh, Christine.' He had put his hand out and grabbed mine. 'Think, working in the open all day.'

'But won't you miss the big money, Sam?'

'I'd rather have a crust and fresh air and the sky for a roof than any fortune that could be offered me for working down the pit.'

And then he had turned from me and gone to the window and, looking up at the sky, had said softly, 'No more darkness.'

Sam did the business very thoroughly. He took out a mortgage on the house, then set about furnishing it. And he insisted on me going round with him to choose the necessary furniture. He bought most of it in the second-hand shops, and although he would say such things, 'Well now, I'll need some kitchen chairs, and a comfortable chair or two, and a table and a couch,' he seemed to have no preference when confronted with numbers of chairs and tables and couches but left the picking to me. I must say that I enjoyed furnishing Sam's house. But even before he went into it I was feeling the miss of him. And I remember wondering with a pang if he had got tired of his rôle as guardian; there was a limit to patience, even such as his. The break in the triangle that I had longed for had come about and I didn't like it.

Whether Don was riled by Sam's venture and was determined to show him, or, as he gave out, his side-line was doing so well that he could afford now to have only one job, and that a well-paying job into the bargain, he, too, left the pit. Whatever his new job was it was certainly of a leisurely nature, for his car was outside the door at all hours of the day, except when he would go away for a week at a time, buying, so I understood from Aunt Phyllis's loud chattering with the neighbours.

Then there was Constance and her rhyming. Since the piano had come into the house she was always picking out tunes and fitting the words to them. I wanted to suggest to her that she should take piano lessons but I couldn't bring myself to do it, for at times I wanted to smash the thing to smithereens. These times would be when, through the front-room curtains, I would see Don Dowling standing in the street talking and laughing with her.

Dad was very proud of her literary efforts and he said to her one day, 'Why don't you send them rhymes to the magazines, or write a song and try it in a song contest?' and she did, but she had them all returned with polite little printed slips. Every so often she sent out little batches, and the printed slips came again and again, yet she did not seem to mind these rejections. It was an exciting game to her, which occupied most of her spare time She didn't bother very much with the lads, and one day I thought I had found the reason, and the discovery filled me with such horror and hate that I think I became insane for a time. Anyway, I did more harm than good with my reactions.

I was doing afternoons at Dr. Stoddard's and didn't usually get in the house until six, but this day I had accidentally cut my hand with a glass and the doctor, having dressed it, insisted that I go home. It was about five o'clock when I got in, and I felt a bit sick and went straight upstairs with the intention of lying down. The sun at this time of the day was filling the room and shining on to the bed, and as I went to the window to pull the curtains, my eye was drawn down to Aunt Phyllis's back yard. There stood Don Dowling and Constance. Don had his arm round her waist and in his hand was a little box, and her two hands were round the box. It was as if hell had opened and engulfed me. Yet I did not seem to be taken by surprise. It was a case of 'And the things they feared came upon them.' This is what I had feared. I flew down the stairs and through the kitchen and to the scullery door, and there, gripping the front of my coat in an effort to steady myself, I called, 'Constance! Constance!'

There was no sound of running footsteps down the next yard, and as I waited, the sweat breaking out all over my body, I heard our front door open and she came through the front room into the kitchen. I glared at her across the length of the room.

'Where've you been?'

'Why?'

'Never mind why, where've you been?' I felt forced to ask the road I knew.

'Well if you want to know I've been talking to Uncle Don.'

'Talking! Where is it?'

'Where's what?'

'That box, where is it? What's in it?'

Slowly I watched the red flooding her face and her soft young mouth becoming tight as she said, 'Well if you know so much, you'll know what's in it.'

On this I rushed across to her, and gripping her by the shoulder, cried, 'Give it to me. Give it to me this minute.'

223

'She pulled herself roughly from me crying, 'No, I won't, it's my birthday present.'

She looked startled, and I saw her mouth drop open and her eyes widen and it came to me that she might not even be aware that he had had his arm around her. Perhaps I was putting into her mind things of which she had never even thought, but in my fear I could not stop myself from galloping on and I shouted, 'If I see him near you again, or if you let him touch you, I'll kill you, do you hear, I'll kill you.'

And now she blinked her eyes and peered at me through narrowed lids as if seeing me from a different angle. Then she gave an infuriating little laugh and said, 'Uncle Don's right again ... you're jealous. I asked him what the trouble really was between you and him and he said you were jealous because he threw you over after ... after the other baby was born.'

'Oh, my God!' I groaned the words aloud, and they seemed to drain me of all my strength, all my wild, angry strength, and when she said, 'Well, why else would you be going on like this? We were doing nothing!' I replied in a weary voice, 'Then if you were doing nothing why didn't you come through the back yard and into your own. I saw you from the bedroom.'

Her colour deepened and she said lamely, 'Well, Uncle Don knows how you go on if I'm in there, and so he told me to slip through the front way.'

Clever. Oh, how clever. The devil wasn't in it, he was an infant by comparison.

After this incident there came between us a rift, and daily it widened. If I had told Dad of my fears he would have been unable to comprehend, he would have thought that my mind had become twisted. It was not in him to understand such evil, such long-calculated evil as was in Don Dowling. And if I had told Sam he would have blamed himself for having moved away from next door. Though he came across the river nearly every day to see me, and this fact set Aunt Phyllis's tongue wagging afresh, he had not now any spare time in which to sit around, for he worked practically from dawn to dusk.

On one of his visits he must have noticed I looked unusually harassed, for he said in his casual way, that would have belied his words of any forethought had I not known him so well, 'You know, Christine, I was standing on a chair in the bedroom the other day fixing the sash at the top of the window and I could see the roofs of all the houses in the street and a bit of the top windows an' all. It was a nice discovery. I didn't feel so far away as it were.' He had then dropped into his old position, his hands dangling, and he seemed to talk to them rather than to me as he went on, 'If ever you wanted me and couldn't get across you could jamb something in the top of the window – I'd be able to see it – say a towel or something.'

I did not laugh at the suggestion but looked down at his head and replied slowly, 'Thanks, Sam, I'll remember. Who knows?'

Now I must go back to Mollie. She had played quite a part in my life and she was to play even a bigger part. The simple reason I didn't see Mollie any more was that she had married. Not Jackie, but a very respectable man, a greengrocer, a Mr. Arkwright. He was fifteen years older than her and had not been married before, and he didn't like me. It was really laughable when I thought of it, for whatever blame there was attached to Mollie's past he put it down to my influence. There was evidence of my sinning but none of Mollie's. I cannot think that she'd had any hand in forming this opinion, but apparently she could do nothing to alter it, and when she had to choose between becoming Mrs. Arkwright and respectability, which position I am sure she never dreamed would be her luck, or keeping our friendship, Mollie, being human, chose Mr. Arkwright. She tried to soften the blow by saying he was a bit fussy like and wanted her to himself for the time being. She had laughed and nudged me, but I couldn't see the funny side of it. I had met Mr. Arkwright three times, and he did not hide his opinion of me. In Mr. Arkwright's mind I was one of the fast pieces left over from the war. Moreover, when I had a drink I laughed a lot, which only proved to the greengrocer that he was right in his opinion of me. So Mollie and I no longer met in the back room of the Crown on a Saturday night. Nor had I been invited to the wedding. The excuse given me was that it was to be very quiet in the register office. And I wasn't invited to her new home. I liked Mollie; next to my mother, I think I loved her. She had been good to me, she had been my stay in my time of trouble, and her rejection of me hurt more than a little. It absolutely amazed me that she, of all people, could allow herself to be dominated by any man, and it seemed that she was paying a high price for her respectability. But that was the way she wanted it.

Then this particular week, because I had felt so miserable and down, I paid a visit to the Crown on a Friday night, which I had never done before. I had my week's wages on me intact as I had just left the doctor's. It was half past six when I entered the back room and I noticed immediately that most of the people present were not the Saturday night crowd. There were only one or two that I knew, the remainder being strangers.

I sat down next to a woman called Mrs. Wright. She was always a bit of a sponger and soon she was telling me her woes, and I was paying for her drinks. After my third whisky, one of which was a double, I stopped listening and I began to talk. I told her about my job at the doctor's, my clever daughter who could write poetry, which, I assured her, she would one day see in the papers, and I told her about my dear friend who had a farm – Sam's smallholding. At this point we were joined by a man and a woman from a table near by. The man I had seen before. I did not know his name but I knew that he often looked my way. He talked a lot and he laughed as he talked, but his wife had little to say. He stood a round, and then it was my turn. Someone went to the piano and we all sang. And this was the setting when the door opened and Mollie and her man came in. I was facing the door and I saw her immediately, and with the past lost in the thick vapour of four whiskies I hailed Mollie loudly, shouting, Oo! oo! there, Mollie Oo! oo!' She turned immediately in my direction and after a moment's hesitation she lifted her hand and waved. Then her husband, turning and looking at me for a moment, deliberately took her by the arm and led her to the farthest corner of the room.

Well, who did he think he was? That was deliberate, that was. He wouldn't let her come across, wouldn't even let her speak to me. Who did he think he was, anyway? I threw off my drink.

'What'll you have?' It was the man standing the round again. I looked at him and blinked, and in the act of blinking all my merriness seemed to vanish. I didn't like this man and I didn't like his wife, and I didn't like Mrs. Wright. I had

226

spent a lot of money on her tonight and I didn't like her. 'I'll have a whisky – large,' I said to the man.

'You won't, you know, unless you pay for it.' It was the wife speaking, and I turned sharply on her and said, 'I haven't seen you handing out much.'

'Well! Come on, Dickie. That's the limit, that is.' She pulled her husband's arm, and I mimicked, 'That's right – go on, Dickie. Go on before you stand your turn.'

'Now, now.' The man's tone was soothing, and I flung my hand wide and said, 'Oh! get yourself away or she'll hammer you when she gets you in.'

Mrs. Wright started to laugh, but I didn't join in. The piano had stopped and people were looking towards our corner, and although the words were whispered I heard a voice saying, 'You shouldn't take it unless you know how far to go. It's shameful. She'll turn nasty now.'

I rounded on the unknown speaker, yelling, 'Yes, I'll turn nasty if you don't mind your own bloody business.'

'Here! here! quieten down.' It was the old woman Wright pulling at me, and I pushed off her hand. Who did the lot of them think they were? They were all looking down their noses at me. I was a bad lot because I'd had two bairns. But there was Mollie over in that corner who had slept with a different man every week for the first year of the war – she had told me so herself – and now she was so respectable she wouldn't look at me – I wasn't good enough.

I was in the middle of the floor before I knew what I was up to and could not stop myself from advancing towards her.

'Hallo, Mollie.'

'Hallo, Christine.'

'Long time since . . . since we met, eh?'

'You'll have to excuse us, we're in company.' It was the husband talking, and I was about to turn on him when Mollie put out her hand towards him and said in the old tone that I recognized, 'Leave her be and let her sit down.'

'Not likely, you're not starting this. I've told you, and on it I stand firm.'

'Oh, firm Mr. Arkwright. Oh, goody, goody, Mister bloody Arkwright.' I heard a voice chanting and it didn't seem to be mine.

'Here! here! Now come on.' It was the barman, and he was

standing at my side with his hand on my shoulder trying to steer me away. But I flung him off, crying, 'You keep your hands to yourself, I'm sitting here.'

I went to take the seat near Mollie, when, as if risking his life to spare his wife the contamination of my touch, Mr. Arkwright stood in front of her. I looked him in the eye for a second, then my arm swept outwards and my hand brought him a slap across the face that resounded round the room and in some way brought me deep satisfaction, so much so that I went to repeat the action with my other hand. Then I was knocked backwards and would have fallen but somebody caught me, and when I was upright again I seemed to be surrounded by hands and faces, and I kept moving my head this way and that to get a look at the man as I yelled, 'Who d'you think you are, anyway, tinpot little greengrocer? Specked apples and rotten oranges in tissue paper.'

'Outside! outside!'

'Take your hands off me.'

'Get!' I was flung through the side door into the yard, and I seemed to bounce off the opposite wall. Then within a second I was back at the door hammering with my fists and yelling, 'You take me money, you've taken it for years, you dirty lot of swine. Who do you think you are?'

How long I shouted and pounded on the door I don't now, but when a heavy hand came on my shoulder and pulled me round and I faced the policeman I was past being intimidated. I can't remember what he said but I know that I disliked him, and I know that I swore at him and tried to knock him on his back. What followed is hazy. There were two police-women, and one said, 'If you don't stop shouting I'll throw a bucket of water over you.' I remember this quite clearly. I remember shouting at her, 'You try it, you Blue-Beat Betty.' I also remember telling myself to give over, but the shouting was in my head and I had no control over it. Then I can't remember what else happened before I fell asleep, only that I continued to hate the greengrocer.

When I awoke I thought I had died and gone to hell. There was a blinding pain in my head that prevented me from opening my eyes. But it was the smell that first suggested hell. I've always been allergic to the smell of urine, it has the power

228

to make me vomit. So the combination of the pain, the smell, and my bemused thinking suggested that I had died and was getting my deserts. I believed in my childhood, that whatever you disliked in this life, in the next you were given an overdose by way of payment for your sins, and my belief hadn't changed much. And then I opened my eyes. Never, to my dying day, will I be able to forget that moment. I had experienced the feeling of shame. Yes, I knew what shame was, flesh-curling shame, but this was something beyond, something deep and searing.

I looked up at the stone walls that enclosed me. At the top of one wall there was a small barred window. My dull, sleep-laden eyes moved down to a wooden structure in the corner. It was a lavatory pan. Next to it was a seat and a well-scrubbed wooden table. I looked down on the bed on which I lay. It had neither head nor foot, it was merely a platform with a mattress. I raised myself up and sat on the edge of it, and the 'Oh! God' that escaped from my lips was an agony-laden sound to my ears.

Oh! God, what had I done? I next looked at the blank wooden door in the middle of which was a dark grille, and panic swept over me, the panic of being enclosed in a view-less space. I dashed to the door but didn't hammer it, for as I stood with my face and body pressed to it I heard footsteps. I stared at the grating, and behind it the little door opened and a face appeared. It was a woman's face and she seemed surprised to see my face looking at her. She did not speak, but I heard a key turn in the lock and I stepped back. I was gasping for breath and had my work cut out to prevent myself trying to dash past her.

It was her voice that steadied me. It was a most ordinary voice and she spoke as if she had come into my room at home.

'Feeling better?' she said.

I could not speak. 'Sit down.' She pointed to the bed. 'I'll fetch you a cup of tea; I bet you've got a headache.'

I did not sit down, but moved a space from her, and I beseeched her, 'Please let me go.'

Her hand was on my arm and she said, 'Your case will come up this morning; it will come up first. There aren't many. You can go straight home after that.'

'But ... but ...' For a moment I was going to say, 'I have a little girl,' and then I changed it to, 'My daughter and my father, they'll be worrying.'

'They know, they know.'

She was patting my arm. She wasn't a day older than me, but her action reminded me of my mother, and it was too much for me. I broke down and sobbed helplessly. She sat on the bed beside me and talked. 'You know, you are too young to go on like this.' I felt her hand lifting the tangled hair from my brow, and was brought to greater depths of crying by her kindness. Then she said, 'I remember you as a girl. Oh, from quite a small girl. You used to go to St. Stephen's School, didn't you? I remember thinking that I wished I looked like you – you had such wonderful hair. You still have.'

Oh God, if she would only stop, if she would shout at me and go for me. I lifted my eyes to hers and asked, 'What ... what will they do to me?'

'Nothing. You'll get off with a caution and a fine. This is your first offence, isn't it?'

What a terrible sound that had, first offence. Oh, God in heaven, what had I done? WHAT HAD I DONE? I'd never be able to look Dad or Constance or Sam in the face ... And Don Dowling? The thought brought me curling up inside.

At half past ten I was taken up some stone steps and into the court. There were a number of people sitting behind a barrier and I knew without looking that Dad and Sam were among them. Also I knew that Constance was not present. For this, at least, I thanked God. Then across a narrow space I found myself staring at a stern-faced man with white hair and a short moustache. We recognized each other immediately. I was looking into the eyes of Colonel Findlay, and he was looking at the depraved creature who had tried to ensnare his nephew.

A policeman to the side of me began to speak, and his words filled me with terror.

'I was called to the Crown where I saw the accused battering on the side door. She was shouting and using obscene language and when I reprimanded her she turned on me and said ...'

Oh God! Oh God!

Next the policewoman was telling the colonel how I fought and struggled. I saw a woman sitting in the seat to the right of the colonel pass him a note. I watched him read it and nod, and then he was talking to me. But I was so sick with shame and terror that I could not follow what he was saying. The only words that penetrated to my agonized mind were: 'clean this town up . . . disgrace and example.'

The woman to his right passed him another note which he read somewhat impatiently before pushing it aside. And then I heard him say, 'Forty shillings' and something else before he added, 'six months'. For one agonized moment I thought he meant prison, and then I realized that I was on probation to keep the peace for six month Me, Christine Winter, who only wanted to love, was on probation for being drunk, using obscene language, and striking a policeman. Oh God! God! God!

The policewoman was taking me up the stairs once again and she held my arm gently as she said, 'Don't worry about him, he must be feeling his ulcer this morning.' Then there was Dad and Sam, and I couldn't look at them. I heard the police-woman's kindly tones whispering something to Dad. I couldn't hear what it was, but he took my arm and led me outside, with Sam on my other side. There was a taxi waiting and I got in, still with my head bowed. And I got out with my head bowed – it was still bowed when I stood in the kitchen. When I sunk slowly and dazedly into a chair Dad's hand came on my shoulder, and I dropped my face to my hands. I heard him mutter brokenly, 'I'll make a cup of tea.' As I heard him go to the scullery, I became very conscious of Sam, as if I hadn't seen him until that moment. When he drew my hands from my face I saw that he was on his hunkers, and his voice was warm and kind as he said, 'You're coming up to the house with me to stay for a while. You'll be away from it all there.'

'Oh, Sam, what have I done? What have I done?' I appealed to him. 'I can't remember half of it, just bits. I can't believe I . . .' My head dropped again. I couldn't believe that I had used bad language and struck a policeman. I could believe that I had got drunk and perhaps had hit out at Mollie's husband. That reaction would only have been natural, but to use obscene language, no. I had been swearing inside my head a lot of late, but it hadn't been bad swearing, just swearing. I gripped Sam's hands and said, 'Constance?'

'Don't worry about her, she's young and she'll come round.'

So that meant she had taken it badly. Well, in what way did I expect her to take it? My name would be a byword in the town now and she'd have to live it down. And there was Don. If in the past I had raised any doubts in her mind as regards the truth of Don's statements my actions last night would have wiped them completely away.

I did not go to Sam's house; I did not leave our house, even to go for an errand, for a solid month, and during this time Constance's condemnation was like a searing iron on my brain. It was silent, absolutely silent, and I had not the courage to break it. The first week she did not purposely look at me. When our eyes did meet at last I saw how deeply her pride was hurt. And to hurt the pride of the young is unforgivable. She went out more and I could not ask her where she was going. I was sick with dread in case she was taking jaunts secretly in Don's car. And my agony was of a high intensity, for I dare not now give myself the solace of whisky. Nine times out of ten it could make me happy and jolly and of a mind to cover the world with laughter, but there was the one time to be feared when it would bring forth a facet of character that in my sober moments I could not believe was a part of me. The strain told on me. My nerves became like tangled wires making my temper brittle, yet I could not vent my temper either.

Then on the fourth Saturday night Sam came in. I was sitting alone in the kitchen, not reading, not knitting, not doing anything, just sitting. And when he looked at me he didn't speak but drew from his pocket a miniature whisky. Standing it on the table within my reach, he said, 'Look, Christine, I'll bring you a drink if you'll promise me that you'll never go into the bars again. I'll see that you get a couple at least, every week-end, but you've got to promise me that you're finished with the bars.'

There was something shameful in this. Although I continued to sit upright my body felt as if it was being drawn into the shape of a bow. I wanted to say, 'Take it away, Sam, I can do without it,' but the yellow-gold glinting through the bottle made my tongue move in my mouth, and my saliva run in avid anticipation. Then I was leaning against him, crying into his shoulder, 'Sam ... Sam.'

So it came about that Sam would bring me two glasses of whisky every Saturday night, and an odd one during the week, and this went on for a year. Then I began, privately, to kick against this control. I was working again, domestic servants were so hard to get few questions were asked. And with money in my pocket the temptation when passing a bar was almost overpowering. I had promised Sam not to go in, but now I told myself that I hadn't promised him not to go in to an out-door beer shop. I did not put up any fight against the distinction, and so I began adding to my supply on the sly, but I saw to it that I indulged only in my room last thing at night before going to bed.

And what of Father Ellis in all this? Father Howard had died and Father Ellis was now our parish priest, and a very busy man. He did not visit us any more, but his new curate did, and I knew from the way he looked at me that he had been informed of my past. He did his duty by telling me constantly what would happen were I to die in a state of mortal sin and that I had better come to confession. He always put this as if he had private knowledge that my end was coming tomorrow. I was thirty-three and I did not feel my time was so near, though often and often I wished it was. Nor did I hold any resentment against this man, he was only doing his duty. That is, until one day when I saw him in the roadway laughing with Don Dowling and Constance. Then a great anger rose in me against him, for I felt that he should know the character of the man he was speaking to – with his supposed goodness he should surely be able to smell out the evil in Don Dowling. Yet there he was, condoning as it were Don's association with my girl. It was the first time I had allowed myself to think that word – association – in connection with Don Dowling and Constance, but now I knew he was giving her driving lessons and meeting her at work, and he was buying her more presents than ever. I knew this because each drawer in her chest was locked. My fear for her was no longer isolated but was not supplemented by a great hurt feeling at the unfairness of things, the unfairness that made her believe this man yet despise me. For despise me she did.

233

One day, after walking at a distance behind Don and her up the bank, and hearing them laughing together and seeing his hand on her shoulder, I entered the house boiling inside with rage. Yet I tried my utmost to speak to her with calmness, but my choice of words was not fortunate. 'Look,' I started, my voice quite level, 'I know I've got myself talked about in this town, but there's no need for you to go and do the same. You hardly go up or down that road that he isn't with you.'

She was taking off her hat, a long, woolly thing that they were all wearing now. It had a pom-pom on the end and, to my mind, looked silly. She swung it round by the pom-pom and, turning and confronting me squarely, she said in calm even tones, 'Don' – not Uncle Don – 'wants me to marry him.'

For a second I was struck dumb, then the fury inside of me burst, and I was torn in pieces, and each piece was yelling. I think I must have gone mad. I said so much but it sounded incoherent, even to myself. Then I saw her with the door in her hand and she half turned to me, saying with that same unruffled calmness, 'I don't believe a word of it. As for age, what's eighteen years? Yesterday a girl married a man twenty years older than herself, and in St. Margaret's in the old town.'

All the pieces that were me were sinking now into a feeble mass. 'Your Grandad won't allow it,' I said.

'Grandad can't do anything. I'm eighteen now and if I can't marry until I'm twenty-one, I'll wait, but if I want to marry badly I won't wait.'

'I'll . . . I'll get Uncle Sam over to you.'

She turned more fully to me now and her voice was laden with sarcasm as she said, 'Uncle Sam. Why don't you marry him and stop making Grandad the excuse? Living like you both do, you're not fooling anybody.'

The door closed on her and I dropped into the chair. 'Dear God! dear God!' Then I flung my arms wide. Couldn't I ever say anything but 'Dear God! dear God!' Even my protestations were weak and ineffective. What had 'Dear God' done for me? I must go to Sam, I must tell Sam. No, no; he would come over and go next door and God knew what the result of that could be.

I sat very very still for a long time, and there was only one

234

thought in my head: Would it be possible to kill Don Dowling?

The thought stayed with me all that night and all the next day until it wore a groove in my mind, and back and forwards in this deepening furrow there now followed one suggestion after another, one plan after another. But I realized each was impossible because of one vital flaw, contact. I had never spoken to him or come in contact with him for years. How was I, short of rushing out at him and stabbing him in the back, for I would never get a chance to do it from the front, how was I to accomplish this overpowering desire. It would have been easy had he frequented the house as he had done years ago, for then, my tortured mind told me, I could have poisoned him. One thing only was settled in my tormented brain: I would do it before I allowed him to marry Constance, for I knew he was using her as a weapon against me. The years that had gone were as days, so fresh was his desire for revenge.

Then something happened that brought me such relief, I almost became young again. Constance won a competition. It was run by a newspaper which offered a hundred pounds for the words of a song under the title of 'Hope'. In her excitement she forgot for the moment that there was anything between us, and she exclaimed as she held the letter containing the good news to her breast, 'I knew I would do it some day, I knew I would.'

Dad was over the moon and he asked her the question I had stopped myself from asking, 'What are you going to do with the money?' And she replied, 'Oh, I don't really know, Grandad. The only think I can think of is I've won something at last.'

The next day, about five o'clock, a knock came on the front door, and when I opened it standing in the street was a young man. He was not more than twenty. He was well made and had wide, grey eyes and he asked if Constance was in. I said she wasn't but she wouldn't be long. He was from the *Fellburn Review* he said, and would like to know how she had reacted to winning the song contest.

'Come in,' I said. When he was in the kitchen I asked, 'Would you like a cup of tea?' and in the most homely manner he answered, 'I would very much.'

So we drank a cup of tea together and I offered him a piece

of egg-and-bacon pie, which he took and ate with a relish that was a compliment to my cooking. And then we talked. I can't remember what we talked about but I knew I laughed as I hadn't laughed for a long time, and while we were laughing Constance appeared in the scullery doorway. I hadn't heard her come in, and I got swiftly to my feet and said, 'Constance, this young man's from the paper.'

He had stood up, and they looked at each other in silence and my heart leaped because I saw immediately that that was that. Just as quickly as it takes to say it. Somehow I had known from the moment I opened the door to him, perhaps the unseen part of me that was in her had responded in the same way.

I left them alone together with the excuse that I had to prepare the tea, and I went into the scullery, and there I stayed for quite a considerable time. When I came back with the laden tray they were talking as if they had known each other for years. Half an hour later he shook me warmly by the hand and Constance set him to the door.

When she was back in the kitchen I said to her, 'He's a nice lad, isn't he?' and she answered, but not too tartly, 'How should I know, I've only just met him?'

The next evening he was at the door again. There were one or two things, he said, he hadn't got quite right, and he had brought a couple of books of poems he thought she might be interested in. One, I heard him say, was by a man called John Betjeman, who was often on the television. As we hadn't television I had never heard of John Betjeman.

They sat at the kitchen table, and from the scullery I listened to her talking as I had never heard her talk. I'd never guessed she knew so much. She sounded to me very, very knowledgeable. And then she came out to me, her face bright and her voice low, and asked 'Did you iron my grey print . . .?'

I nodded and answered quietly, 'It's upstairs in your room.'

They went out together and I went upstairs and, falling on my knees, I prayed for the first time in years, asking God to bring something out of this association, and quickly. Not to let it be just a lad and lass affair with a dance on a Saturday night and the pictures now and again and nothing certain. I prayed that the spark I saw struck in the kitchen last night would fan itself quickly into a blaze and marriage.

Three months from the day they met they became engaged. It was the happiest moment I had known for years, there would only be a happier when I stood in the church and saw them married. The night they came and told me she flung herself into my arms and whispered, 'Oh, Mummie!' and I held her tightly and thanked God, and I looked over her head towards David, smiling my affection for him.

Later that evening when they had gone out I wanted to go upstairs and celebrate with the quarter bottle of whisky I had tucked away in the bottom drawer, but I resisted the temptation because not for the world would I imperil the existing harmony that now reigned between Constance and me – if she smelled the whisky on me I knew the dark, dull look would come into her face again and her happiness would be marred. God forbid, I thought, that I should mar it again. No, I would wait until bedtime.

Each morning I woke up with a very thick head and had difficulty in rousing myself, but I dared not take a 'nip of the dog that had bitten me'. I had rarely any difficulty in resisting this temptation, for I had nearly always finished up what was in the bottle the night before. These thick heads made me long for Sunday mornings, for then I could have a lie-in. This particular Sunday morning I lay in a drowsy state for quite a long time, for Dad did not wake me with a cup of tea on this one morning of the week. Then with startling swiftness I was brought awake by the sound of two well-known voices, first one and then the other. The thought that they were coming through the wall brought me upright in bed and the next minute on to my feet, and as I stood blinking dazedly I realized they weren't coming through the wall but from outside. Going cautiously to the window, I drew the curtains an eye-width apart and looked down. There was no one in our back yard, nor could I see anyone next door, but the voices were coming from there. And they were the voices of Don and Constance. My window was raised from the bottom a few inches, and I knelt on the floor and put my ear to the opening. The next thing I heard was Constance's laugh. But it was a shaky laugh, and she followed it by saying softly, 'Don't be silly.'

'I'm telling you, Connie, you can have what you like – a twelve hundred car – anything. I'm in big business now, and I'm leaving this God-forsaken hole.'

He said something more which I couldn't catch. Then again came Constance's laugh, and again she said, 'Oh, don't be silly.'

Don Dowling's job kept him away for anything from two or three days to two or three weeks now. This time he had been away more than three weeks, and this was the first knowledge I had that he was back.

'I told you, we're engaged.' Constance's voice came a little louder.

'Now, don't you start kidding me, Connie, you and that little whipper-snapper, it's laughable. That type of bloke never gets past reporting tea-parties and bazaars. You were made for better things, things that cost money. You know what I told you last year. I told you I would soon be able to give you anything – the world. Well, now I can. Listen.'

His voice dropped, and suddenly I found I was afraid to hear any more. I was sitting on the floor with my back to the wall and fear was swamping me again. I was sick with it. What if he did something? What if he broke them up? But he wouldn't. No, he wouldn't. I was forcing anger up through the fear and I turned it on to Aunt Phyllis, for she was in the house there listening to him trying to ensnare my girl, and knowing the reason why he wanted her. She was, I thought, as mad as him, or the other way about, for it was from her he had inherited what was in him.

I hurried into my clothes, my fingers fumbling and slipping the while, and when I got downstairs Dad was sitting at the table calmly reading the paper. And I went for him immediately saying. 'Did you know Don Dowling was back and has got Constance in their back yard?'

He looked at me closely, then said, 'But that's nothing new, lass, he's always talking to her. He must have just got back from his trip.'

'And what's he talking about?'

'Now, now, how should I know? What's upset you? Don's always talking, he's all talk. It means nothing.'

'It means he's after our Constance.'

His look now was long and pitying and his voice was soft when he said, 'Don't be silly, lass.'

'Oh!' I turned from him with a helpless gesture. Dad would not believe meat was rank until he saw the maggots crawling out of it.

When she came into the kitchen looking somewhat pale, I restrained myself from making any reference to Don. Neither did she mention his name. So the matter rested, uneasily rested.

It was May and the month of processions, and this particular Sunday night Constance was in a procession, and David, although not a Catholic, was going to Benediction to see her. At least, I understood that to be the arrangement until there came a knock on the front door. Sam, who had arrived just a few minutes earlier, went to open it, and when I saw him return with David I was startled into crying, 'What's happened? Where is she?'

'Nothing's happened. Constance is at church and I was going, as you know, but I thought I would just slip up and see you.' He was looking at me. 'There is something I want to talk to you about, but it would be awkward with Constance here.'

I heaved a sigh of relief, yet it did not clear my mind of anxiety. What could he want to talk about that Constance shouldn't hear? It couldn't be about his people, he hadn't any – for which I was heartily grateful – except an aunt who had brought him up and who had accepted Constance without question. I noticed he looked rather drawn and worried, and when he cast his eyes towards Sam I added, 'There's something wrong, isn't there? You can speak in front of Sam, he knows all there is to know about us.'

As I watched him draw an envelope from his pocket a sweat broke out on me, and before he handed it to me he leant forward and said, 'I'm going to let you see this letter because I feel you should know about it. It was slipped through the door when we were out. But it makes not the slightest difference between Constance and me. Please understand that. And I don't want her to know a thing about it. You seem to have an enemy, and with your permission I'll take it to the police.'

My hand was on my throat and I was crying loudly inside me, 'Not again! not again!' Then I was reading the letter. It was asking David if he knew that Constance was illegitimate? Did he know that her mother had had several men, including her brother, and was now living with the man known as Sam Dowling? Moreover, she was disease-ridden and had been brought before the court for being drunk and using obscene language.

The terrifying thought leaped at me from the page telling me that although only the first and last statements were true I had no way of proving to an outsider that the rest was lies.

'What is it?' Sam was standing at my side and he put out his hand for the letter, but I crushed it in my fist, and bowed my head. Then I heard Sam saying to David, 'Show me the envelope.' My head was still bowed when Sam said, 'Give me that letter.'

Slowly I opened my hand and he took the letter from it. There was no sound in the kitchen until Sam spoke again, when, touching my shoulder, he said, 'Stay where you are. I'm walking down the hill with David, I'll be back.'

Before David left the room he stood over me and in a very firm voice he said, 'Please believe me, Mrs. Winter, it makes no difference to me . . . none.'

I couldn't speak, and he went out.

About twenty minutes later Sam returned, and I was sitting where he had left me. His face looked darker and his voice was unsteady as he said, 'Don't worry, he understands.'

'Sam.' My voice sounded steady, yet I was trembling in every vein. 'Sam,' I said, 'if he breaks this up I'll kill him.'

'He won't break it up. David isn't so easily put off. He knows what he wants, and it will take more than a letter to frighten him off.'

'But it won't stop at letters, Sam. You know it won't. Look at me.' Suddenly I was thumping my chest and crying, 'All my life I've lived in fear of him. It's him that's ruined my life, not Martin Fonyère. I would have married you years ago if I hadn't been afraid of what he would do. He's tortured me for years. That isn't the first letter. He did the same with Ted Farrel, only they were much worse than that. And he sent men to the house. . . . You didn't know that, did you? He's tortured me for years one way and another, and I wasn't strong enough to stand up to him. I'm not made like that. But, by God, I swear that if he spoils this for Constance, and I repeat, I swear, Sam, I'll kill him.'

Sam said nothing for a moment, but sat down by the table and rubbed his chin with his hand. Then he said quietly, 'There'll be no need for you to do that, Constance'll marry

David, don't you worry.' Then as if to himself he repeated, 'Don't you worry.'

But I did worry, night and day, and the anxiety was too much for me. I was in agony all the time Constance was out of my sight. The only peace I had was when she was in bed or with David. I was standing in the front room at the window one Wednesday dinner-time waiting for her when I heard the quick tap of her heels on the pavement, and I moved to the door to open it when Don Dowling's voice checked me.

'Hullo,' he said. 'Where are you hiding yourself these days?'

'Oh . . . I'm not hiding myself, Uncle Don.'

Her 'oh' told me he must have surprised her.

'Uncle Don it is now? Why have I got my old title back?'

'Oh, I don't know. Habit, I suppose.' I heard her give a little laugh, then Don's voice again, saying, 'I'm bringing the car for you on Saturday, what about it?'

The tone to anyone else would have sounded playful, but to me it was laden with threat. There was a pause that I could not fill with any image in my mind until Constance's voice came sharply, saying, 'Leave go, Uncle Don, I've got to have my dinner. Oh, leave go!' And then I pulled the door wide. There, not a foot away, with his back to me he stood, his hands gripping Constance's arms.

'Take your hands off her!'

Slowly he turned and confronted me. I had never been so close to him for years, I had never looked into his face for years, I had always been aware that he was smart in his own way, so I wasn't prepared for the close-up of his face. It was bloated, and his hair was receding from his forehead. But it was his eyes that held me. They were very, very bright and bluey dark, not black. As if fascinated, I watched his lips draw back, and then he said, 'Well, well, Christine. Sober enough to talk after all these years?'

I reached out and, pulling Constance over the steps and thrusting her behind me, I cried, 'You've done all you can, Don Dowling, and now I'm warning you. You can frighten me no more. You touch her again and it'll be for the last time.'

His head went up and back, and he laughed. And on the high note of the laugh he cried, 'Christine Winter with spunk. My God! what will we be hearing next?'

I banged the door closed and hurried into the kitchen. Strangely enough, there was no reprimand awaiting me from Constance, for I saw immediately that she was afraid, and her fear was like a reflection of my own at her age.

'Sit down and have your dinner,' I said as calmly as I could, and when I placed the meal before her I added quietly, 'You could stay at the canteen and have your dinner after this, and David or your Grandad or your Uncle Sam would meet you coming back.' Even on what only a few days ago would have sounded like a preposterous proposal she made no comment.

The next morning, just before she went out to work, she said to me, 'I won't ask David to meet me, it would mean explaining things.' She did not look at me as she spoke and I couldn't say to her, 'David knows.' If he wanted her to know he was in the picture he would tell her himself, so I said, 'All right, your Grandad will meet you tonight.'

When I told Dad as briefly as possible that Don was pestering and frightening Constance and asked would he go and meet her, he was still unable to take in the full import of the situation, and he screwed up his face at me and said, 'But he's always been fond of her, lass. You must realize that.'

'This is more than being fond, Dad. Can't you see?'

He blinked his eyes rapidly as if he was at last beginning to see, and then over his shoulder he glanced towards the dividing wall and said, 'If I thought he meant anything I'd knock his bloody head through the road.'

'He does mean something, but don't say anything, at least not yet. Sam knows and David knows, and now you know. And you must believe this, Dad. Don Dowling is bad.' I pressed one closed hand tightly into the palm of the other to emphasize this, and he stared at me for a long moment in a bewildered fashion, then muttered, 'I've always known he wasn't the best. 'Twill be better if I don't come across him for a while.'

There was neither sight nor sound of Don for the next three days. I listened carefully to the sounds next door. When Aunt Phyllis's wireless wasn't blaring forth there came no sound of voices, only the sound of doors closing and her footsteps creaking on the stairs.

And then it was Saturday. David had rushed in about ten

o'clock to say he was being sent out on an assignment. It was a murder case, some place near Hartlepool, and he didn't know what time he would be back. If he was too late in getting home this evening to come up, he would be round first thing in the morning. Would I tell Constance how disappointed he was about the dance tonight?

'Yes,' I said. 'And don't worry, she'll understand.' And I patted his arm. 'It might be a big thing for you.'

He nodded and said, 'That's what I'm thinking. But isn't it awful somebody has to go and be murdered before you get a break?'

In the afternoon Constance washed her hair, then she washed some of her undies and ironed them, and it was as she stood ironing in the kitchen at the table near the window and I stood baking at the table in the centre of the room, going back and forward to the oven every now and then, that I talked. I talked about myself and Don Dowling. I told her right from the time I could remember, right from the time he held me in the river, and only once did she pause in her ironing and put her hand over her mouth. That was early in my talking when I came to the incident of the rabbit nailed to the tree. I told her about her father and how he came the second time, and how I wanted to do away with myself when I discovered I was going to have another baby. But I didn't tell her he had any relations on Brampton Hill. I thought it better not to. If there had been any chance of her meeting up with her half-brothers then I certainly would have told her about the colonel and his daughter. But as it was I thought it better to leave that page closed. But I told her about Ted Farrel and about the letter he had received and the letters I had received. I told her about the form of mental torture that went on for years with the knockings on the wall. I told her everything that concerned me and why I hadn't married her Uncle Sam. And I knew that she understood, especially this last, for there was a fear in her now, a fear that something would happen to separate her from David.

When my story was ended I felt very tired, suddenly very tired, and I dropped into a chair. I had a need on me for a drop of whisky, but when she came and put her arms around me and pressed my head to her, saying softly, 'Oh, Mummie! Oh, Mummie!' the need for the moment left me.

243

We were close, really close for the first time in our lives. And then it was she who talked, and as if she were the mother and I her daughter. This was no new feeling, for often in the last two years or so I had felt that she had already reached a maturity that would never be mine. The only thing that had developed in me through the years was my weakness.

That evening, after tea, Dad said, 'I'm going to slip down to the club for an hour. Harry Benger's interested in the allotment.'

'Our allotment?' I said.

'Aye.' He got up and put on his coat. 'I'm not gettin' any younger, I've been feeling lately I'm past it. Anyway, the vegetables we need we can get from Sam. Half the stuff I grow there I give away.'

I felt I knew the reason why he was doing this, and it wasn't because the allotment was too much for him. Soon we'd be needing the allotment as much as we had done years ago, for the pits, after a blaze of prosperity never before known in their history, were once again on the down-grade. It was a repeat of the nineteen-thirties. Whole pits were closing down. At any moment the Phoenix or the Venus might be on the list.

'I'll leave your supper,' I said. 'I'm a bit tired and I'll get to bed early.'

Neither Dad nor Constance ever remarked on my going to bed early. If they knew why I went upstairs so soon in the evenings they thought it better to say nothing. If I had to drink, then that was the best place to do it.

But I did not get upstairs early that night, because this new relationship between Constance and me kept me tied to the kitchen listening to her plans for the future. The wonderful plans for her and David. And then it was she who went upstairs first. She kissed me good night in a new way. Again as if I were the younger, she held my face between her hands and looked at me, and then she said something that gave me a thrill, like I'd never had for many a year.

'Mummie,' she said, 'you're still beautiful.'

'Oh! lass,' I said, disbelieving, but grateful.

'I wish I was half as pretty as you are. I've always thought it unfair that I don't look like you.'

I pulled her to me for a moment and, pressing her head into

my shoulder, I said quietly, 'Thank God you don't, lass. Thank God you're not like me in any way.'

'Oh! Mummie.' She moved her head slowly. 'I am, I'm like you in lots of ways.'

I put my lips on hers, then said, 'Good night, and God bless you. . . . God bless you and keep you happy,' I said.

I stood where she had left me, listening to her going up the stairs. I heard her open the door, and then I thought she had started to sing. It was a high note as if she had burst into song, and I smiled to myself. Then my smile vanished and became perplexed for a moment by the sound of banging in her room, as if something had dropped. There was nothing to drop that I could think of would make that thudding sound. I found myself standing at the bottom of the stairs listening. There was no sound now, and then I called, 'Constance!' And when she didn't answer I took the stairs like some frantic animal, for before I thrust open her door I knew what to expect. She was standing with her back pressed into Don's body, held fast by his great arm, and from her mouth dangled the ends of a tea towel. A loud unearthly scream escaped me and the spring was in my body when he checked it: 'Come any farther and I'll give her this.' This, I saw, was a razor very like the one Dad used.

'Go on downstairs.'

'As I backed slowly, he pressed Constance forward. Step by by step I went down the stairs and into the kitchen where a moment before I had kissed her with so much love. Suddenly I was helpless with fear, I had no strength to combat this man and I heard my voice pleading, 'For God's sake, Don, leave her be. Please! I'll do anything . . . anything, only leave her be.'

'Even kill me, like me God-damn brother.' He was smiling, but only with his mouth, his eyes were dead cold and terrifying. 'You've both been sittin' for years behind these walls, haven't you, wondering how you could do me in? And you haven't been able to keep it out of your face, yet you couldn't rake up the nerve. I've had you taped. I've always had you in the hollow of me hand, and I still have. Nobody does anything to Don Dowling and gets away with it, and you've done plenty, you bitch, you!'

'Don' – my voice was a thin, pathetic whimper – 'Don, I

245

tell you I'll do anything, anything you ask, only don't touch her.' I put my hand out towards Constance's petrified face, and he stepped back pulling her with him as he said, 'Thank you very much for nowt, Miss Christine Winter. You're still Miss Christine Winter. God, it's laughable. But where'd you get the idea I want you now? Christ! I'd as soon go with a midden bitch as I would with you. But this' – he jerked his arm tighter, pushing up Constance's breasts – 'this is you when I wanted you, and, believe it or not I'm going to play fair with her. I'm not goin' to leave her on the grass like you were left. No, when she's goin' to have the bairn I'll marry her. Not that I want a bairn, but she's goin' to have one. You know why? Because I want to see you on a grid-iron. You'd think after all this time I'd done enough to you to have me own back, but it's never been enough. But this'll satisfy me, for you'll feel it. . . . Aye, every time I touch her you'll know and you'll feel it like hell.'

He caused her bust to rise again, and a moaning sound came through the tea towel, and I began to gibber. 'Don, Don,' but as I did so I knew what I was going to do. I was going to dash through the front room and out into the street and scream blue murder. He would never use that razor. I was on the verge of making a move towards the front room door when he fore-stalled me. Lifting the razor to Constance's cheek and pressing the blade to her skin he cried, 'Another jerk like that and I'll mark her – I'll mark her for life.'

As I stood gasping and shaking before him he gave a grim laugh and added, 'You can do nowt – like always you can do nowt, an' I've got everything fixed, every step. I'm not letting you or any white-livered paper bugger man thraw me – not this time I'm not.'

At this moment there came from our back yard the sound of someone whistling softly and Don turned his head sharply to-wards the kitchen window. Then saying to me. 'Open the back door,' he pushed Constance towards me and once again I was walking backwards.

When I withdrew the bolt from the scullery door he called softly, 'In here Rox,' and in came a short man in a big, bulky coat. The man looked from one to the other then grinned and said, 'Well, well.'

'Keep an eye on her.' Don nodded towards me and then

moved back into the kitchen, and as the man came towards me I backed from him. This man had a round, chubby face and a fresh complexion. If you had met him in the street you would have thought he looked homely. He stared at me as he fitted his steps to mine and said coolly. 'So you're Christine Winter. Well, what d'you know?' Then coming into the kitchen and turning to Don, his tone taking on a curt note, he said, 'Come on, man, you've spent enough time over this.'

'She's got to be put out of action first.' Don nodded towards me again. 'She's generally blind about this time and sleeping it off, snoring. You'd have to be sober the night, wouldn't you, Christine?' His tone was mocking. 'That's just your bad luck for I'm going to give meself the pleasure of putting you to sleep.'

Like someone hypnotized I watched his tongue move over his upper lip as if he was licking something off it, then he went on, 'It'll be my last parting gift so to speak, for we won't meet again – Connie and me are off to faraway lands – aren't we, Connie?' He almost lifted her off her feet and I saw her eyes close.

'Well, hand her over,' said the man hastily, moving towards Constance, 'and get on with it if we want to make the docks the night.'

It was at this point that the key turned in the front door and I heard myself screaming, 'Dad! Dad!' There was hardly a second between my scream and Dad entering the kitchen, but he stopped dead just within the door and I knew by his face he couldn't take in what he was seeing. Then the full realization springing at him, he yelled in a terrible voice, 'Take your hands off her, Don Dowling, or before God you'll not live to tell the tale.' He was moving steadily towards him when the other man spoke again, and as he did so he pulled his hand from his pocket.

'Take it easy, Grandad, we're just goin'.'

'Get out of me way!' Dad brushed the man aside without even glancing at him.

'Dad!' I screamed at him as he had not seemed to notice what the man held in his hand. The man, too, was taken aback, but he said. 'Now look here, I don't want to get rough with you, so stop acting the bloody goat and stay put.'

Dad's arm came up in an ugly swing but before his fist had

247

descended on the man I saw him jerk upwards as if something had hit him in the chest, then he bowed his head, and then his shoulders, and slowly he sank to the floor. There had been no sound of a shot. There was no blood. I was past screaming but I heard myself in horror-laden tones exclaiming over and over again, 'You ... you ... you ...' The man was looking at the revolver in his hand and as I rushed to where Dad was lying he turned towards Don, saying, 'Look, I didn't even touch it.'

'That was a bloody mad thing to do.'

Even with my mind in the state it was, the fear in Don Dowling's tone got through to me.

'I tell you, I haven't fired it. Let's get out of here.'

Dad's mouth was hanging open, his face looked pale and soft, and I thought that he must be dead. In the agonized second during which I raised my eyes from Dad's face to that of the man, I was aware of a number of things. Constance was slumped within Don's hold, she had fainted, and outside the kitchen window, in the space between him and the man there loomed a dark shadow which I took to be that of another of them. Moreover, the knowledge that Aunt Phyllis just beyond the wall must know what was going on, what her beloved son was up to, was actually as terrifying in a way as the scene before me.

Then from somewhere there flowed into my being a wave of strength, I felt it washing away the fear. Under the pretext of helping myself to rise from my knees I put my hand on the high fender and gripped the big iron poker that lay resting on its edge, and with a twist of my wrist I sent it flying high across the room in the hope that it wouldn't touch Constance. Which one of them I was trying for I wasn't quite sure, but almost instantly I knew my aim had found the man, for he yelled and grasped his shoulder as the revolver leapt out of his hand. And it was at this moment that I saw Sam. He was standing in the kitchen doorway, right behind Don, and in his hand was a great lump of wood. As it came down on Don's head there was a horrible thudding sound. For a moment after the impact Don remained stock still, then with a long groan he crumpled up, and Constance with him. As they hit the floor, the man, yelling something at Sam, spurted into life and made a dive for the revolver where it lay not a yard from Dad. At the same instance I plunged towards it and the next minute the man and I were locked together. But only for a minute, for something happened that made me bounce away from him. It was like nothing that I can describe, except perhaps that I had been slung slap bang into a brick wall. It seemed as if my face was being pushed in, and for a moment I could see nothing, nor hear anything but a great buzzing in my head. Then my vision cleared and I knew I was leaning back against the table and looking down on a shambles of bodies. But they seemed to be a great distance away, as far away as the sea is from the top of a cliff, except the man and Sam. They were close, for they were pounding each other on the mat at my feet. Then they too receded and joined the others, and the distance between us grew greater and I was borne upwards into the air, away, away from it all, and I went, I remember, with a sort of relief, yet I knew I was crying, 'God Almighty! God Almighty!'

CHAPTER NINE

I DON'T know how much time elapsed before I opened my eyes again but when I did it was to look up into Sam's face. My head ached and I felt stiff and I was unable to turn, but when I moved my eyes I was looking at David, and David brought my mind to Constance. But I could not ask where she was, I was too tired. I felt very tired, and Sam said softly, 'Go to sleep.' And I closed my eyes and went to sleep.

Again, when I opened them, it was to see Sam's face still there, but when I turned my eyes to the other side, this time I saw Constance. She smiled so tenderly at me, and leaning over me she kissed me, and her face obliterated the white glare of the hospital ward, and again I went to sleep.

That seemed to be the trouble, I was always going to sleep. People came and went, doctors and nurses, and they dressed my head and they talked to me and said such things as, 'Wouldn't you like to sit up?' But I didn't like to sit up, I closed my eyes and went to sleep. I knew that Dad was not dead, his collapse had been a heart attack; I knew that Constance was all right because I had seen her, and my fears for her were gone, for Don was where he would be unable to hurt me or her for some time at least, Sam had told me. One night as he sat by my bed he whispered to me, 'Christine, listen to me. There's nothing more to worry about. He can't do anything to you now.'

I remember forcing myself to say one word in the form of a question: 'Dead?'

'No, he's goin' along the line.'

The battle seemed over and I was resting. I wanted to go on resting for ever.

I do not remember much of the transition from the hospital to Sam's house, it meant only a change of bed. I remembered nothing much until yesterday afternoon when I heard the doctor talking, and I opened my eyes and looked across the valley to Fenwick Houses, to where it had all begun. Then I had started thinking, thinking from the very beginning, and as I thought I wondered why I was doing it, why I was troubling myself. It wasn't until I had gone over everything right to the very end that I knew there was something gnawing at me, something bothering me, something I wanted to know. One more thing. Simply, how long would Don Dowling get? Would it be long enough to make living worth while, or would it just be sufficiently long to prepare myself for the battle again? If I was certain of one thing in my muddled mind, it was that I was preparing for no more battles. The doctor was right, I had fought all the battles of which I was capable. I wasn't made for fighting battles, I was a weakling, there was no strength in me.

So when Sam returned from seeing the doctor out he was amazed to find me sitting up, my eyes wide, staring across the valley, and he said with an eagerness that somehow hurt me, 'You're better?'

I lifted my hand and touched him, and my eyes looked into his for a long, long moment, then I asked in a whisper, 'Tell me, Sam. When ... when will you know ...?' I did not finish, and Sam's lids drooped and the pressure of his fingers tightened on my hand as he said, 'It's over and done with.'

'When?' I asked.

'Three days ago.'

'Three days?'

I stared at him and felt my eyelids stretching for knowledge. He moistened his lips twice and then he said, 'I'll get you the paper if you feel fit for it.' He was looking at me again.

'I'm fit for it.'

He brought me the paper and left me alone with it, and slowly, slowly I read it, and I learned of the stuff that Sam was made of, and the strength and courage of him both amazed and frightened me, and the self-sacrificing nature of him brought the tears raining down my face, for Sam had manacled his conscience for the remainder of his life.

Through burning eyes I read over again bits of the trial. I did not read the parts dealing with Don's abnormal tendencies, I knew all about them. The part that drew me was the report

251

of Sam's evidence and Don's reaction to it. Was it poetic justice that his scream-abuse of his brother had only helped to confirm the sentence of guilty but insane, guilty of shooting to kill me and of killing his accomplice, Reginald Shawley, who fought him for possession of the gun? How convincing it read, but not one word of it was true.

I raised my eyes and looked out of the window again. There was the picture clear before me. I could see Sam struggling with the man to get hold of the gun, while Don lay senseless on the floor, and I knew now as I did then that it was not Don who had shot me, nor could he have shot his partner.

Sam's mind, waiting all the years for this chance, had no need to fumble and ask, 'What will I do?' The gun must have gone off when he was struggling with the man. It was self-defence, and he would have had nothing to fear at any trial. Moreover Don's seizure of Constance and the fact that both men had on them a quantity of stolen money, would have been enough to put Don away for some length of time. Yet always there would have been the threat of his return. So Don had been found by the police with the gun and razor to his hand and, by his side, the young girl he had tried to abduct. In this, the paper said, he had been foiled only by his brother attacking him unexpectedly from behind with a piece of wood. This at least was true.

The reading sounded fantastic, like something in the Sunday papers but which people knew for a certainty could never happen to them, not to ordinary people. But we were all ordinary people, and it had happened to us. Yet no, Don was no ordinary being, Don was an evil being, and although he would remain in prison during Her Majesty's pleasure, he would be here with us each day, treading on Sam's conscience heavier as the years went on. It was too much to bear alone. Sam must not be left to bear it alone. This knowledge told me I must live and love him and fight my private fight against the bottle. . . .

Sam never asked me how much I remembered of that night and I never told him. I owe him that. I owe Sam so much, so very much. Sam at this moment is to me as God. Let other people judge him as they will, I cannot but love him for my deliverance. Sam has played the Almighty. Let the Almighty be the sole judge of his imitator.

CATHERINE
COOKSON
COUNTRY

HER PICTORIAL MEMOIR
by CATHERINE COOKSON

Catherine Cookson was born in 1906 into the bleak
industrial heartland of Tyneside, and rose to become one of
the most successful novelists of all time.

Life on the south bank of the Tyne was hard, often cruel,
vicious and rough; and for Catherine and her unmarried
mother, doubly so.

In *Catherine Cookson Country* she returns to her homeland,
the landscape which provides the setting for her novels. And
in the company of her best-loved fictional characters she
rediscovers its human contours: the feelings, emotions and
fiercely held passions which inspired her as woman and
writer.

0 552 13126 1

CORGI BOOKS

A DINNER OF HERBS

CATHERINE COOKSON

A legacy of hatred can be a terrible force in life, over which not even an enduring love and all the fruits of material success may prevail. Catherine Cookson explores this theme in a major novel that will absorb and enthrall her readers as irresistibly as any she has written.

Roddy Greenbank was brought by his father to the remote Northumberland community of Langley in the autumn of 1807. Within hours of their arrival, however, the father had met a violent death, and the boy left with all memory gone of his past life.

Adopted and raised by old Kate Makepeace, Roddy found his closest companions in Hal Roystan and Mary Ellen Lee. These three stand at the heart of a richly eventful narrative that spans the first half of the nineteenth century, their lives lastingly intertwined by the inexorable demands of a strange and somewhat cruel destiny.

A DINNER OF HERBS is Catherine Cookson's most stunning achievement to date – a work that displays outstandingly the true storyteller's gift.

0 552 12551 2

CORGI BOOKS

BILL BAILEY

by Catherine Cookson

As a young widow left badly off, and with three children to bring up, Fiona Nelson had come to know all the problems of trying to make ends meet in this taxing day and age. So, despite the disapproval of her mother, she advertised for a lodger. The result was Bill Bailey, somewhat rough around the edges perhaps, but nobody's fool and doing very nicely with his own builder's business.

Bill often described himself as a middle-of-the-road man, valuing his freedom where personal matters were concerned, but it was not long before Fiona found herself wondering just what her world had been before he came into it. He might be outwardly an ordinary enough bloke, but he undoubtedly possessed some pretty extraordinary qualities. And those qualities could indeed prove to have a great and lasting effect on the future lives of Fiona and her young family.

Catherine Cookson's new novel is a richly entertaining tale of human relationships in the same tradition as her immensely popular *Harold* and *Hamilton* novels. Warm-hearted, humorous and dramatic, it has this internationally popular author's magic touch that makes it a joy to read and Bill Bailey himself a special pleasure to meet.

0 552 13016 8

A SELECTION OF CATHERINE COOKSON NOVELS IN CORGI

☐ 13016 8	BILL BAILEY		£2.95
☐ 12473 7	THE BLACK VELVET GOWN		£3.99
☐ 08700 9	THE BLIND MILLER		£2.95
☐ 11160 0	THE CINDER PATH		£2.95
☐ 08601 0	COLOUR BLIND		£2.99
☐ 12551 2	A DINNER OF HERBS		£3.99
☐ 09217 7	THE DWELLING PLACE		£2.95
☐ 08774 2	FANNY McBRIDE		£2.50
☐ 09318 1	FEATHERS IN THE FIRE		£2.99
☐ 08353 4	FENWICK HOUSES		£2.99
☐ 08419 0	THE FIFTEEN STREETS		£2.50
☐ 10450 7	THE GAMBLING MAN		£2.95
☐ 10916 9	THE GIRL		£2.99
☐ 08849 8	THE GLASS VIRGIN		£2.99
☐ 12789 2	HAROLD		£2.95
☐ 12608 X	GOODBYE HAMILTON		£2.99
☐ 12451 6	HAMILTON		£2.95
☐ 10267 9	THE INVISIBLE CORD		£2.95
☐ 09035 2	THE INVITATION		£2.50
☐ 08251 1	KATE HANNIGAN		£2.50
☐ 08056 X	KATIE MULHOLLAND		£3.99
☐ 08493 X	THE LONG CORRIDOR		£2.50
☐ 08444 1	MAGGIE ROWAN		£2.95
☐ 09720 9	THE MALLEN STREAK		£2.75
☐ 09896 5	THE MALLEN GIRL		£2.95
☐ 10151 6	THE MALLEN LITTER		£2.95
☐ 11350 6	THE MAN WHO CRIED		£2.99
☐ 08653 3	THE MENAGERIE		£2.50
☐ 12524 5	THE MOTH		£3.50
☐ 08980 X	THE NICE BLOKE		£2.50
☐ 09373 4	OUR KATE		£2.95
☐ 13088 5	THE PARSON'S DAUGHTER		£3.95
☐ 09596 6	PURE AS THE LILY		£2.95
☐ 08913 3	ROONEY		£2.50
☐ 08296 1	THE ROUND TOWER		£2.95
☐ 10630 5	THE TIDE OF LIFE		£3.95
☐ 11737 4	TILLY TROTTER		£2.95
☐ 11960 1	TILLY TROTTER WED		£2.95
☐ 12200 9	TILLY TROTTER WIDOWED		£2.99
☐ 08561 8	THE UNBAITED TRAP		£2.50
☐ 12368 4	THE WHIP		£3.50